Books by Elisa Braden

MIDNIGHT IN SCOTLAND SERIES

The Making of a Highlander (Book One)
The Taming of a Highlander (Book Two)
The Temptation of a Highlander (Book Three)—Coming soon!

RESCUED FROM RUIN SERIES

Ever Yours, Annabelle (Prequel)
The Madness of Viscount Atherbourne (Book One)
The Truth About Cads and Dukes (Book Two)
Desperately Seeking a Scoundrel (Book Three)
The Devil Is a Marquess (Book Four)
When a Girl Loves an Earl (Book Five)
Twelve Nights as His Mistress (Novella – Book Six)
Confessions of a Dangerous Lord (Book Seven)
Anything but a Gentleman (Book Eight)
A Marriage Made in Scandal (Book Nine)
A Kiss from a Rogue (Book Ten)

Want to know what's next? Connect with Elisa through Facebook
and Twitter, and sign up for her free email newsletter at
www.elisabraden.com, so you don't miss a single new release!

The Madness of Viscount Atherbourne

ELISA BRADEN

ISBN-13: 978-1-53-971275-6
ISBN-10: 1-5397-1275-3

Dedication

This one is for Mom and Dad:

*Because when I said I wanted to write books for a living,
you didn't so much as snicker.*

*Because Mom volunteered to be my first reader,
and Dad volunteered to pose for the cover.*

*Because you still look at each other as though happy-ever-after
is the obvious conclusion.*

Because you are my very best friends.

I thank God every day that I was born your daughter.

Prologue

꧁

June 12, 1815
London

AS THE HEAT OF HER BATH SOAKED INTO MARISSA WYATT'S
skin, a single thought drifted through her mind, the words like
acid dripping a constant stream.

He never loved me.

She should have known when he didn't respond to her
letters, four in the past two weeks, each more urgent than the
last. Her fifth and final letter she'd written not to him, but to
her brothers. It lay on the bureau next to a vase of roses she had
cut from the garden the day before. Still tightly furled buds,
nothing more than promises of later beauty, really. The weather
of late had been oddly cold, hostile for full blooms.

She glanced toward the open window where the curtain fluttered helplessly in the light breeze.

Why could he not love me?

But then, perhaps the reasons did not matter, only the truth of it. In fact, one might be forgiven for thinking none of it mattered at all. Not the day they met, when his blue eyes had seized upon hers as though charged with some strange magic. Not the heat of his mouth the first time she had let him inside. Not the squeeze of her heart when he had smiled as though he saw the same future she did.

No. It meant nothing.

The tinkling drip of liquid sounded loud in the hushed room. *Drip. Drip. Drip.*

Powdery blue sky and wispy white clouds were all she could see from where she lay in the tub. Soon, even that faded and glowed in an iridescent mist. *Such a lovely day,* she thought dreamily, a tear tickling her cheek as it slid down, down, down.

A lovely day. It made her want to fly like a sparrow out that window and into the yellow sun, let it burn away this unbearable, bottomless pain. Let it burn away her flesh until not even ashes remained. All she had to do was let go. Sighing, she allowed her eyelids to fall.

Yes. Just let go.

On the heels of her whispered thought, the gentle lap of the water grew dimmer, the roar of the wind rose up to carry her, and Marissa Wyatt spread her wings and flew.

June 18, 1815
Hampstead Heath

THE PISTOL DROPPED FROM THE DUKE OF BLACKMORE'S HAND

with a thud on the grassy ground, smoking from the shot that still echoed in his head.

This should not have happened. How had this happened?

"You—you shot him, your grace. I do believe ..." stuttered his second, Henry Thorpe, the Earl of Dunston, his dark eyes wide in the pink, pre-dawn light. They both approached the body lying in the grass a dozen or so yards away. "Harrison, I believe he may be dead."

"I only meant to wing the man," Harrison uttered hoarsely as he eyed the haphazardly splayed form of Gregory Wyatt, Viscount Atherbourne. "He moved suddenly to his left. I haven't a clue as to why."

Lord Tannenbrook, a strapping blond man with blunt features and a grim demeanor, whom Atherbourne had introduced as his second, looked up at Harrison from where he knelt next to the viscount's sprawled, bleeding form. "Indeed, he is dead," he said tightly. "A heart shot."

The words reached Harrison from a great distance. He stepped back slowly and stared at the vile pool of dark blood growing beneath Atherbourne's torso. It was nearly black. *Strange, that,* he thought distantly. *When there is so much blood all at once, it appears black instead of red.*

Harrison had never killed a man—in a duel or otherwise—before this day. This awful, bloody day. He scraped a hand over his face and shook his head to clear it. He had taken a life. He, the eighth Duke of Blackmore, was ... a murderer.

Bile rising in his throat threatened to spew forth in violent rebellion against his control. He turned instinctively from the sight of the other man's body, staggering several paces away to where brambles grew between looming trees. Great, heaving breaths filled his lungs with the smell of crushed grass and moist earth, a respite from the metallic tang of blood, the foul odor of death.

A hand gripped his shoulder. Henry's mellow voice muttered reassuringly, "Not to worry, old friend. Atherbourne challenged you, and all was conducted properly. Prosecutions for this sort of thing are rare as virgins at Madame DeChatte's. Which is to say, quite."

Harrison had always enjoyed his friend's droll sense of humor, but found nothing amusing about these circumstances. "He is—" His jaw clenched as he stared at the ground. "He *was* a viscount. You think his death will be so easily dismissed?"

"Yes, he was a viscount. And you are a duke. Privileges of rank and all that."

A hiss left his lungs and he jerked away in disgust. Henry caught his arm. While the man was smaller than Harrison, both shorter and slighter, his grip was oddly strong, urgent. "I wouldn't have thought you harbored such naiveté, Blackmore. This distasteful situation has come to a natural, albeit unexpected, conclusion. I suggest you accept what has happened and consider the cause of honor as having been satisfied."

Rarely had he heard the affable Earl of Dunston use such a forceful tone. His friend obviously feared Harrison would follow his conscience into self-destruction. But that would be reckless. And if there was one thing Harrison was not, it was reckless.

In point of fact, he was generally regarded as rather emotionless—a cold fish, and a stuffy one at that. His brother, Colin, had told him on numerous occasions his mere presence in a room lowered the temperature to below freezing. While that was something of an exaggeration, Harrison knew his personal standards of control and strict adherence to propriety could be intimidating to some. Stuffy he might be, and yes, perhaps others would see him as cold. But that was because they knew nothing of what true coldness was.

Reluctantly, he turned to where Atherbourne lay, still and lifeless. Tannenbrook stood over the man, looking bleak as the surgeon knelt next to the body, nodding in confirmation. It settled in then, the truth of what he'd done. Dunston was right. The law would probably never come for him, but a man could not kill without consequences.

He felt a wave of ice unfurl and spread through his insides.

It might take months, or even years. But one day, he thought, pivoting toward the rising sun. One day, the devil would come to claim his due.

Chapter One

"Bah! The London season has become little more than an exhibition of vapidness. One may choose to tolerate such a display, but only a halfwit enjoys it."

—THE DOWAGER MARCHIONESS OF WALLINGHAM at her weekly luncheon, a mere five days after arriving in town.

April 20, 1816
Mayfair

IF IT WERE POSSIBLE TO SWOON FROM BOREDOM, VICTORIA Lacey expected she would now be lying on the gray marble floor of Lady Gattingford's ballroom, succumbed to a fit of the vapors.

"My dear, we will have to arrange a visit at Lord Gattingford's country estate after the wedding. Capital fellow. Has a pair of hounds he assures me are the finest in all England. Well, I can tell you I simply must see that for myself."

Victoria gazed at her fiancé's handsome features—light brown hair with a bit of charming curl, sweet blue eyes with long lashes, and nice, even teeth revealed when he smiled, which was frequently. She so wished she felt something more than mild affection. *A single, solitary tingle, dash it all. Perhaps even two or three.* But no. He was comfortable. Much like a wash-worn dress, the fabric dulled in color but soft and familiar.

"Since we will be in the area, Dunston invited us to join him at Fairfield Park. His annual hunt is in November, I believe."

She murmured agreement and glanced toward the whirling dancers at the center of the room. A quadrille. The sight made her smile. The ladies in their pastel dresses, the gentlemen in their dark evening finery. Perhaps she should have accepted Sir Barnabus Malby's invitation to dance this round. He was a portly gentleman with the unfortunate tendency to emit offensive odors when moving vigorously. Still, it would have been more enjoyable than standing here discussing hounds and hunting, of all things.

"... lemonade, my dear?"

Again, she nodded absently. Over the past month as her engagement wore on, she had adopted a strategy of compliance—just nod, murmur, or in some way indicate agreement, and actual listening was (thankfully) all but unnecessary. Feeling a twinge of guilt at her unkind thoughts, she nevertheless found the Marquess of Stickley—*Timothy;* she must remember to call him Timothy—a dreadful bore. She sighed. And he was hers for a lifetime. Handsome, tedious, considerate, bland, gentle, *boring* Timothy.

He'd been her brother's favorite of all her suitors. And who could disagree with Harrison's assessment? As a man whose greatest passions in life revolved around horses, hounds, and hunting, Stickley was unlikely to spend his fortune on gambling, drink, and other nefarious pursuits. He was dependable. Much like a well-bred hound. And very nearly as stimulating.

Absently watching a young woman miss a step in the dance and turn red as a strawberry, she sighed again. First she compared him to an old, faded frock then to a dog. Truly, she was dwelling on his shortcomings in a most unbecoming fashion. *How improper for the "Flower of Blackmore,"* she thought.

She straightened her spine and watched Sir Barnabus give a shallow bow to his partner—shallow because his girth did not allow much more. Unquestionably, Stickley was a prime catch, and her reasons for agreeing to become his wife were still as valid today as they had been a month ago. One: He was young, fit, and handsome. Two: He was a marquess in his own right and heir to a relatively new but certainly respectable dukedom. Three ... oh, what was the third reason, again? She occasionally lost track after point number two.

She glanced to her right, expecting to find him there, still rambling on about visiting various country estates during hunting season. Her eyes widened when she found him absent. Now, where had he disappeared to?

"Lady Victoria, I daresay I haven't yet mentioned how lovely that color is on you! What shade is that, might I ask?" The sunny, familiar voice came from Victoria's left. "I must tell my modiste to acquire fabric in that precise shade of blue. Why, it quite matches your eyes."

The bubbly matron who had chaperoned Victoria this evening was round in nearly every aspect: her face, her figure, even her nose was a rounded pug. Shorter than Victoria by several inches—though Victoria was only of average height—Meredith Huxley, the Countess of Berne, resembled a plump, brown wren. But her generous smile and cheerful humor made her one of Victoria's favorite people.

A childhood friend of Victoria's mother, the countess had become a surrogate mama after the Duke and Duchess of

Blackmore died three years earlier. As soon as Victoria emerged from mourning, Lady Berne eagerly took up the mantle of sponsorship, escorting her to a dizzying number of functions, offering faultless direction through the London swirl. Thrilled by her success as a sponsor, Lady Berne had now turned her full attention toward finding husbands for the two oldest of her five daughters.

"You are too kind, my lady," Victoria replied warmly, clasping the woman's outstretched hands and squeezing them affectionately. "I believe the shade is called aquamarine. My new modiste, Mrs. Bowman, is most fond of it, and I quite agree."

"Mrs. Bowman, you say? Perhaps I shall pay her a visit. Now, where is that handsome gentleman you are soon to marry, hmm?"

Before Victoria had a chance to be embarrassed by the fact that she did not rightly know where her fiancé was, Annabelle Huxley, the countess's oldest daughter, approached. The perky brunette was accompanied by two spindly, identical blond girls, both wearing a shade of pink far too pale to flatter their sallow complexions. The Aldridge twins. Oh, dear. Stickley might be a less-than-stimulating companion, but she suddenly longed for his return. This husband-hunting pair was focused, relentless, and manipulative—and their quarry was related to her by blood.

All three girls offered pleasant greetings to Victoria, and without further ado, the twins launched their assault. Miss Lucinda Aldridge—the one who always wore ear bobs—struck first. "Lady Victoria, I did not notice the duke in attendance this evening."

"I am afraid he was unable to attend."

The girl's barely-there eyebrows rose in feigned surprise. "Oh? What a pity."

Her sister, Margaret, picked up the conversational spear and sallied onward. "I do hope he's not feeling poorly." The statement was phrased more as a question. One she was expected to answer.

Resigned to what had become a familiar interrogation,

Victoria replied, "No, his grace is in excellent health. With Parliament in session, his time is much in demand."

Lucinda pressed a gloved hand to her chest and professed, "Only two days ago, we saw Blackmore riding in the park, did we not, Margaret?"

An exaggerated nod of agreement was followed by "He is a most commanding rider."

"*Most* commanding."

"Difficult to imagine anything could bring him low."

"Of course, when he marries, his wife could care for him properly, should anything untoward occur."

"Every man should have a wife to care for him."

"Indeed. Especially one so handsome and distinguished."

"Deserves someone exemplary, I daresay. Why, I would even go so far as to suggest *you* might make a fine candidate, dearest Lucinda."

The girl's ear bobs flashed in the candlelight as she turned wide eyes to her sister. "Me? I was going to say the same about you."

Honestly, Victoria thought, inwardly rolling her eyes. *I have known four-year-olds with more subtlety.* A year ago, when she made her debut, it had taken weeks to realize why dozens of young misses swarmed around her. Landing the Duke of Blackmore would be a coup of enormous proportions. Eventually, she had noticed the threads of all her conversations led back to her brother. What was his favorite color? Did he prefer light or dark hair? What time of day did he prefer to ride?

At first, it had been hurtful to realize her "friends" were more interested in her brother than in her companionship. But once she accepted the truth, it became simply another fact of her life in London, albeit a tedious one. This conversation was a perfect example: The Aldridge twins wanted nothing from her other than a recommendation to her brother that he marry one of them. *Which* one apparently did not matter.

"To my knowledge, he is not seeking a wife at present," Victoria answered. "Though, you are correct in saying he deserves someone of exemplary character. Someone *genuine*." The small poke was as much as she would allow herself.

"Ooohhh, I was just saying the other day how *genuine* you are, was I not, Margaret? Utterly without guile."

"Indeed, dearest. You humbled me with such a description."

Exhausted by the display, Victoria allowed her mind to drift away from the twins and their ludicrous exchange. All around her, the crowd grew louder, a general buzz of interest moving over them in a wave. Glancing left, she noted Lady Annabelle returning after a brief absence. The girl placed a hand at her mother's elbow and whispered something close to her ear.

Lady Berne's eyebrows rose to an alarming height. "Really? He is *here*?" Her head swiveled toward the entrance, and Victoria's gaze automatically followed theirs. It seemed whoever "he" was, his presence set off ripples of wide-eyed stares and murmurs hidden behind gloved hands. Two of the dancers stopped to take in the new arrival, resulting in a moment of chaos on the dance floor.

Since the arched entrance was a few steps higher than the ballroom, anyone entering could be seen easily from everywhere in the room. Everywhere, that was, except where Victoria was standing. A stooped-shouldered gentleman, who was thin as a post and nearly as tall, blocked her view. Curious about who could possibly cause such a sensation, worried that perhaps Harrison had decided to attend after all, she moved to her right just a bit. And saw him.

Time slowed. Voices faded into shadow. Her breath stalled. He was ... beautiful. Black hair that was truly ink dark, with no hint of brown. Low brows over piercing eyes—she couldn't tell what color from this distance. A straight, refined nose, square chiseled jaw, and perfectly proportioned chin with just the barest hint of a cleft. Oh, but his mouth. It was surely the most sensuous creation ever devised. A full lower lip, the upper thinner and finely drawn, and the whole wearing a faint sardonic smile that tilted one corner upward ever so slightly.

Her fingers itched to draw him. She had never felt such a compulsion. He looked like an angel, only darker, more brooding.

Someone nudged her arm. It was Stickley, returning to her side with a cup of lemonade. "Who is that gentleman, Victoria?" he asked, handing her the glass.

She shook her head and murmured that she did not know.

The countess turned to her with a surprised expression, but upon noticing Lord Stickley, began chatting about the unusually cold weather London was seeing. The crowd shifted and again obscured her view. She wanted to stand on her toes, crane her neck, catch another glimpse. Instead, she willed herself to remain where she was beside Stickley. It would not do to ogle a stranger.

A pair of elderly gentlemen joined their circle, and Lady Berne was pulled away by Annabelle and the Aldridge twins. Nearly ten minutes passed in which the men debated the merits of abundant rainfall, the trials of falling crop production in the north, and the need for more wool in London this year. And that was *before* Stickley started in on Lord Gattingford's hunting hounds.

Gracious, she hadn't imagined her boredom could get worse. In desperation, she allowed her thoughts to wander, and like a bee tempted by a showy bloom, her mind veered back to the mysterious gentleman. His face. His tall, broad form. Who was he? She had never seen him before. But, then, he was rather extraordinarily handsome. If he was unattached, she could imagine him wishing to avoid the voracious flock of husband huntresses and matchmaking mamas that would descend upon him at every opportunity. It was why Harrison resisted escorting her to events such as this. The day she had agreed to marry Stickley, her brother had stopped doing so altogether.

Her eyes surreptitiously sought the place where the man had been, but he was gone. Of course, she chided herself, he would not stand there posing for her, waiting for her to fetch her sketchbook. Obviously, he would be circulating now among the guests. She was surprised by her fascination. She adored painting and drawing, but the consuming need to see him, to explore his features and form in detail, went beyond all good sense.

A middle-aged woman jostled Victoria's arm, reminding her of the glass in her hand. She sighed and sipped her lemonade, cringing at the tart, watery flavor. Lady Gattingford's ballroom was a masterpiece of pale marble, her musicians as fine as any to be heard this season, but her lemonade left much to be desired. Amid the heat of such a crush, a tolerable beverage would not have gone amiss. *Why did I agree to attend this evening?*

Beside her, Stickley laughed, his white teeth gleaming in the candlelight. *Oh, yes. I am to become the new Marchioness of Stickley. Such appearances are required, of course.*

At the thought, she shifted subtly from one foot to the other, unaccountably restless. She'd had ample practice maintaining a serene mask for these types of ton fêtes, so she was confident no one knew of her rising urgency to escape. But she felt it. Oh, yes. Beneath her skin, flushed and itching. Inside her stomach, tightening with the need to get away.

Air. Her eyes scanned the room longingly, landing on the glass-paned doors at the rear of the ballroom. She desperately, *desperately* needed air.

Now deep in conversation with an elderly baron who boasted about the astounding number of pheasants waiting to be plucked at his hunting lodge, Stickley scarcely seemed to notice when Victoria quietly excused herself.

"Of course, my dear," he said, patting her hand absently and turning immediately back to the baron and his "obscenely plump" game birds. Sidling through the crowd as quickly as decorum would allow, she soon reached the doors and slipped outside into darkness.

It was shockingly frigid after the heat of the ballroom, and she had forgotten a wrap. But here at least she could feel something other than suffocating tedium, even if it was shivers caused by unseasonably cold weather. She sighed and hugged her arms to her chest, ambling toward the balustrade, seeing her breath plume out before her in the faint light cast through the glass.

She wondered, staring up at the half-moon glowing softly in a dark sky, if perhaps this was as exciting as her life would ever be. Engaged. Enjoying a season in London. Looking forward to a wedding and then to marriage and then to children and then to seasons for those children and then to grandchildren and then to old age. Her stomach cramped at the future that stretched out before her.

Not the family part. That was something she had desired ever since a vicious storm had swallowed her parents' ship, leaving Harrison and Colin and Victoria with only each other. But, in truth, her heart ached at the thought of endless days and nights with a husband who would never mean more to her than a comfortable home, a title, and the knowledge that she had done what was expected of her.

No fantasizing about some dark phantom who appeared suddenly amidst a ball. No wondering what it might be like, just once, to be kissed by such a man. Someone who made her breathless. Someone who made her want ... more.

She shook her head emphatically. Such was not for her. She was the Flower of Blackmore, after all. Her future had been written well before she'd come to London. Before she'd been born, really. Whatever she might have dreamed for her life was quite—oh, what was the word? Irrelevant. Yes, that was it.

A puff of air whooshed past the lump in her throat in a humorless laugh at the absurdity of her despair. She was being a ninny, that was all.

So Lord Stickley—*Timothy*, blast it—was not the dark and dashing hero of art and poetry. So he had never declared his love for her in a fit of passion, nor even spoken of her with the same fervent affection as he did his horse. The fact that he bored her to the point of unconsciousness actually boded well, she assured herself. He was sensible—a good man and a solid choice for marriage. That was all that mattered, surely.

"You'll catch your death out here, you know," a deep, resonant voice said quietly next to her ear. She gave an unladylike yelp and leapt to one side, spinning to face the dark form that appeared beside her. A man. Tall. Big. His face was shadowed, but he looked familiar. The arrogant tilt of the head, the square cut of the jaw. He stepped toward her into a shaft of light from the ballroom.

"You!" she squeaked. It was him. Her dark angel. What? Wait. Not hers. *The* dark angel. She did not even know his name, so how could he be her anything? Oh, but her heart recognized him. The foolish thing pounded out a frantic welcome against her breastbone.

He swept a deep, exaggerated bow. "Yes, it is I. At your service, my lady."

Chapter Two

"Virtue is its own reward.
But then, the same could be said for sin."

—THE DOWAGER MARCHIONESS OF WALLINGHAM to the Countess
of Berne upon said lady's refusal of a fourth lump of sugar.

HE WAS MOCKING HER. SHE KNEW IT, AND YET COULD SAY
nothing because she was quite ridiculously hypnotized. That
faint grin had grown into a full-scale smile. *Parliament should
declare his smile patently illegal,* she thought. *It is lethal to all
womankind.*

"I—I saw you earlier, when you entered the ballroom," she
said finally, kicking herself for the inane utterance.

"Yes, I was a bit late arriving. Caused quite a stir, I

understand. But then, the only thing the ton enjoys more than its rules is the fever created by those who break them."

His rich baritone alone was enough to weaken an aged spinster's knees. Add the subtle lift of one dark brow and the half smile gracing his sinful lips, and it was no wonder a visible shiver ran along the surface of her skin.

Without a word, he stepped closer and reached for her shoulders, chafing his gloved palms along the skin of her upper arms between the edges of her cap sleeves and the tops of her gloves. It was a shocking breach of etiquette to touch her without so much as an introduction, much less her permission.

She stood motionless for several long seconds, unable to speak. That must have been why she failed to step back and rebuke him immediately for his cheek. It could not be the fizzing excitement in her belly at having him so close, feeling the warmth of his hands on her skin, his thumbs stroking gently and causing little thrills to shoot from her arms to her spine and, most concerning, her breasts. No, surely not.

"You should have a wrap if you intend to spend much more time out here, my lady. To call this springtime would be generous, indeed."

She blinked up at him, feeling weak and slow—enthralled. Even standing this close, she could not make out the color of his eyes, only noting they were dark and glimmered in the moonlight. He was so tall, the top of her head would barely reach his collarbone.

With Lord Stickley, her forehead came even with his nose. At one time, she had thought him the ideal height, not requiring the craning of her neck to look up at him. As an added benefit, they moved quite nicely together on the dance floor, his strides more closely matching her shorter ones. However, now she was less certain about how perfectly suited she and her fiancé were on a physical level. Something about this man's height and larger, more muscular physique made her feel oddly safe.

Comparing Stickley to a stranger was not wise, she chided herself. She was engaged and now must make the best of things, rather than finding fault with her betrothed at every step. Yet, she could not help noticing he stood in this man's shadow in numerous ways.

The errant thought seemed to break the spell the stranger had cast over her. She abruptly pulled away, breathing embarrassingly fast, heart racing. "Sir, you overstep yourself. I don't even know your name."

"Call me Lucien."

She reeled back a step further, her hip bumping the balustrade. Stiffening her spine and raising her chin, she retorted, "Your familiarity is insulting. We have not been properly introduced. I could not possibly call you by your first name."

"You must call me something if we are to continue our conversation."

"Perhaps I should call you presumptuous. It seems fitting."

His slow, wicked smile seemed to speak a foreign language, one she did not understand but which caused a flush of heat to wash through her. "I have not begun to *presume*, my darling."

For a moment, she was flummoxed, her open jaw working in a fashion not unlike a fish lying onshore. She had never been spoken to in such a manner. As the daughter and then the sister of a duke, no one would dare exhibit such disrespect for her station and the simple courtesies due her. No one except this bounder, apparently.

At last, she found her voice, stumbling and ineffectual though it might be. "I—I am not your darling!"

"My goddess, then?"

"Furthermore, your suggestive tone implies a much more significant acquaintance—"

Lucien tilted his head and spoke as though she'd said nothing at all. "I have it. My angel."

"—than I would ever allow. I will have you know I am engaged to be married—"

"Although it still fails to do you justice. You are quite beautiful, you know."

"—and your behavior is entirely inappropriate ..." Her breath stuttered to a full stop as she absorbed what he had said. His tone had been so offhanded, it took a moment to sink in. "You ... you think I am beautiful?"

"Hmm. Yes, quite. Has no one ever told you?"

She shook her head and then immediately corrected herself. "Well, several of my suitors did say they found my hair attractive. And one gentleman said my eyes were like pools. Of what, I am uncertain. But I assume it was meant to be flattering."

His mouth quirked in amusement. "And your betrothed? What does he say?"

Is he standing closer than before? Victoria wondered absently. Yes, he was. His massive body nearly surrounded her now, only inches away. He gave off such heat, she no longer felt the bite of cold, damp air. Her voice grew breathless and high. "Lord Stickley? Oh, well, he is not much given to poetry or flattery."

"Has he not said that your skin glows with the purity of fresh cream?" He stroked one finger delicately along her cheek, his dark gaze holding hers rapt. "Or that your hair rivals the last glorious rays of the sun just before dusk?" His fingers sifted through the loose curls behind her ear. "Has he not even mentioned your lips, how they are as full and luscious as a ripe peach? Come, now. He must have done so at least a dozen times."

She made an inarticulate sound that was vaguely embarrassing, but she was utterly helpless to prevent it. If she could have managed to draw air into her lungs, she would have groaned. Oh, he was simply divine. Divine and devilish.

Lucien's lips hovered so near her own, she felt his breath with each word. "Surely he has kissed you, my angel. Has he not?"

"Yes," she whispered, staring at his mouth.

His head tilted. "And did it feel like this?"

This was heaven. He fitted his mouth masterfully to hers, his lips warm and firm, gliding sensually without a moment of hesitation. It was not the soft, gentle kiss of a man concerned with offending her. Nor was it the dry, obligatory peck of her fiancé. As strong arms wrapped around her waist and pressed her breasts to his hard form, she marveled at his confidence. Then all thoughts of assessing the kiss flew away like a dandelion tuft on the wind as his hot, slick tongue slipped along the seam of her lips.

Lucien pulled away for the barest moment. "Open for me, angel," he whispered, tugging at her lower lip with his finger. When she obliged, he swooped back in, this time thrusting his tongue inside her mouth and stroking along her own. She felt seared and shaken, the boldness of it shocking, unfamiliar in its intimacy.

She moaned into his mouth and clutched at his lapels. He drew her tighter against his body, his hands gripping her hips and sliding along her bottom as a flooded river of heat coursed through her. Her breasts felt heavy where they pressed flat against his chest, she ached low in her belly, and the muscles in the intimate place between her thighs clenched as though in great need of ... something.

Distantly, she noticed a hard and rather large object pressed against her midsection. But a moment later, she was distracted by one of his hands moving up over her ribcage and cupping her right breast. The most pleasurable tingles—yes, *tingles*—erupted from the center as he skimmed lightly over her breast with his palm, then returned to stroke insistently with his thumb.

Truly, she was awash in tingles of every sort, in every place she could imagine and some she tried not to think much about. She could feel herself panting, the sensations overwhelming whatever faint notion of propriety might have flitted through her head. Indeed, her mind was sluggish and spinning, every sense singing to the tune only he could play.

Abruptly, both his hand and mouth were removed from her person. But it was no reprieve.

"I must feel your skin. Now," he gritted. He took the tip of one of his gloves between his teeth and pulled his hand free, spitting the glove onto the ground and immediately running the backs of his fingers along her collarbone. Then, as she stood hanging helplessly in his embrace, not knowing what to expect, his hand turned so his fingertips traced their way along the upper slopes of her breasts. They caught on her low-cut bodice, slipped beneath the silken layers, and tugged slowly downward. Her right breast popped free, the nipple hard and flushed.

She glanced at his face, seeing the muscles tighten in his jaw and no hint of his earlier sardonic smile. Was he displeased? She couldn't decide why he suddenly looked so tense. Then his head dropped forward, his hand cupped her breast from beneath, and his mouth covered her nipple, suckling it like a babe.

What in heaven's name was he doing? This was ... this was sweet madness. She heard herself squawk, but could not bring herself to care with his fiery mouth drawing so pleasurably upon her nipple. He licked and stroked, even glided his teeth gently along the tip, causing her legs to weaken in an alarming way. She feared she might collapse, were it not for the iron-like arm wrapped tightly around her waist.

He shifted her so that his thigh wedged high between her own as he worked and laved at her nipple. At first, this seemed to soothe the infernal ache she felt deep inside. Then, like a fiendish devil, it caused an even deeper emptiness and tension. Occasionally, his thigh would brush against a hidden spot and a sharp burst of pleasure would erupt, causing her to cry out and grind herself against him. This repeated over and over, almost rhythmically, and each time, the coil inside her wound tighter.

His mouth pulled away for a moment while he tugged her other breast free and latched onto her left nipple, giving it the same treatment as the right.

She moaned and threw her head back, clutching desperately at his hair as the torturous ache between her legs rose to an unbearable height. His thigh pressed harder at that sensitive center. Without warning, the tension gave way in an explosive spiral. "Oh, my stars. Lucien!" she shouted as her body spasmed in a crescendo of echoing pleasure.

A shriek from the direction of the ballroom doors pulled her rather rudely from the heavens down to earth. "Good gracious, Lady Victoria! Have you lost your senses?"

Warm lethargy weakened her muscles, filled her head like a steam cloud. Vaguely, she knew something odd had occurred, but she was dazed, shivering in the aftermath. Lucien pulled away slightly, but still clutched her waist. Her bare breasts were suddenly cold, exposed in a way they had not been when he had covered them with his mouth and hands. Slowly blinking up at his face, she noticed he was breathing heavily, flushed and wearing a fierce frown. He shook his head like a dog casting off water after a swim.

Distantly, a thread of sanity anchored on the edge of her mind, and she realized what must have happened: They had been interrupted. She froze, seeing the same realization in Lucien's face. Simultaneously, they turned in the direction of the shrill exclamation.

And there stood Lady Gattingford, the venerable hostess of one of the finest balls of the season and a notorious gossip, staring back at her from the open door. The expression on the matron's face was astounded, appalled. Scandalized.

In that moment, as Lucien pivoted so his back blocked Lady Gattingford's view and calmly tugged Victoria's bodice up to restore her modesty, the full horror of what had just occurred— what she had *allowed* to occur—hit her with paralyzing force. She had let a man unknown to her touch and pleasure her in ways she had not even considered permitting her fiancé. This had been witnessed by none other than her hostess, who would doubtless relish notifying every member of the ton in hopes of enshrining her ball as the event of the year. The scandal would spread with the swiftness of fire through dry grass. Within a week, everyone would know. Everyone. Including Lord Stickley, who would surely cry off the engagement. And her brother, of course.

Oh, dear God. The duke would be enraged. She had shamed the entire family. Harrison placed great importance on honor and reputation. Her other brother, Colin, would be far more understanding. But then, he was hardly a stranger to less-than-dignified behavior himself.

There was no mistaking it: Her life had changed inalterably this night. And not for the better.

"Lady Gattingford," Lucien said as he turned, his tone nonchalant, even mocking. "A fine night for a stroll on the terrace, wouldn't you say?"

The tall woman's eyes narrowed on him, her mouth a flat line. "Do not imagine I hold you blameless, my lord. You are nothing less than a bounder!"

While Victoria had defined him with the same term earlier, she found herself bristling at the insult toward Lucien. They had experienced a moment of uncontrollable passion together. She suspected he had felt as swept away as she had, blind to their surroundings, and tossed amid a raging storm. There was no need to paint him as a villain.

"My dear lady," she began, "I do comprehend your dismay at what you have seen. But, please understand we were both caught up in the moment. It was simply a lapse of judgment. If— if you could see your way clear to—"

"Lapse of judgment? While that may be one acceptable description of your behavior, my lady, it in no way excuses the shameful wantonness I witnessed."

Other guests began taking notice of the intriguing and heated conversation happening on the terrace, and the two remaining sets of doors were opened. Soon, an alarming number of people—perhaps twenty—crowded around Lady Gattingford, including Lady Berne, her two daughters, the Aldridge twins, and Lord Stickley. *Oh, heaven help me,* she thought, cold dread clenching her insides. *Stickley does not deserve what is about to happen.*

Before she could say another word, Lady Gattingford regaled the crowd with a summary of her observations. Snippets of the matron's monologue repeated in Victoria's mind—*kissing, shocking, inappropriate.* As though trapped in a nightmare, Victoria froze, only able to watch and endure. The woman appeared to savor each word, her descriptions growing ever more detailed with each gasp from her audience. *Fondling, bosom, exposed.* A flush of pure shame heated beneath Victoria's skin, burning and pulsing in her face and chest. The humiliation was almost too much to bear.

Then, it got worse.

Lady Berne paled to a sickly white as her eyes darted between Victoria, Lucien, and back to Stickley. Flags of ruddy color signaled the marquess's anger and embarrassment as he glared at Victoria. When Lady Gattingford reached her triumphant crescendo, and the shocked mutterings of the crowd burst forth, he simply turned his back and walked away, charging through the doors and out of the ballroom, shouldering several gentlemen aside as he went. The din of the crowd's chatter prevented her from calling out to him, begging him to stop and listen so she could defend herself.

Not that she had a defense. She was, in fact, quite guilty.

Lady Berne, bless her, courageously approached Victoria, risking much by further associating herself with a ruined young woman. She took Victoria's icy fingers in her hands. "Are you well, Victoria?" she asked gently.

Victoria nodded, then looked down at the flagstones, no longer able to hold her friend's sympathetic gaze. She swallowed hard, bothered by the tightness in her throat. She refused to cry. She simply would not.

"He did not harm you, then? Force you?" The softly spoken words were stunning, as Victoria had not imagined anyone would reach such a conclusion.

"No. Why would you suggest ...?"

"Because, my dear, he more than any other may have reason

to wish you and your family harm."

She shook her head. "That makes little sense."

"Do you not yet know who he is, child?"

Victoria stared into Lady Berne's kind, steady brown eyes and knew she would not like this. Not at all. "Who is he?" she whispered hoarsely.

The countess took a deep breath and squeezed Victoria's hands as though to brace her for a great shock. "He is the new Viscount Atherbourne. He inherited the title after your brother, the duke, killed his brother in a duel last season."

Victoria reeled, the sounds of the crowd dimming, her head spinning with the possible implications. She had known about the duel, but Harrison had not explained why it had happened, only informing her it was a matter of honor that had been resolved, and had ended in the death of Viscount Atherbourne. He had refused to discuss it further. The incident had generated a shockwave among the aristocracy, but because it had occurred toward the end of last season, just before most families departed London for the country, the scandal had fizzled before it really began. Few of her acquaintances had brought it up after that—a testament to her brother's considerable power—and she assumed the matter had been largely forgotten.

But here stood a man who had every reason to remember, every reason to seek retribution. Could he have planned this? Was his impassioned embrace—she swallowed hard on a wave of sickness—nothing more than a cruel charade designed to ruin her? No, surely not. He must have felt the same tidal force sweeping away all reason; she could not have been alone in that. She could not have been such a fool.

She immediately sought reassurance in Lucien's gaze, shifting to look up at where he stood a few feet away, listening to her conversation. "You ...?"

The mocking smile and triumphant glint in his eyes confirmed her worst suspicions. "Yes, my darling. I am Lucien Wyatt, Viscount Atherbourne." He swept a graceful bow, his discarded glove now back in its proper place as though nothing significant had occurred. "And I must tell you, making your acquaintance has been the greatest of pleasures."

Chapter Three

"A single shot through the heart, you say?
Well, I suppose it is not entirely unexpected.
Blackmore is nothing if not a perfectionist."

—THE DOWAGER MARCHIONESS OF WALLINGHAM upon news
of Viscount Atherbourne's untimely demise.

NO ONE, BUT NO ONE, INTIMIDATED THROUGH SILENCE MORE effectively than the Duke of Blackmore. If Victoria had not been certain of it twenty minutes ago, she would be now, after sitting with her hands folded neatly in her lap, staring at the handsome blond head of her silent brother while he scratched away at some missive. For nearly half an hour.

He was formidable on the best of days. Consumed with

propriety, duty, and family honor. Strict in his adherence to—and enforcement of—societal dictates. She expected him to lecture her with his sharpest aristocratic weapon: quiet, clipped sentences that made one long for a January blizzard simply to experience warmth. However, since the moment she had entered the study and he had bluntly ordered her to sit, he hadn't so much as acknowledged her presence.

But then, what was there to say? She knew the scandal had grown to epic proportions. Belaboring that all-too-obvious fact with a scathing diatribe was unnecessary. Duke's sister or not, no self-respecting gentleman would now willingly choose her—a wanton, reckless, ruined girl—to marry. After all, her former fiancé had been thoroughly and quite publicly humiliated. His only recourse had been to cast her aside and decry her betrayal to all and sundry.

She was, not to put too fine a point on it, notorious.

While she felt shame at this knowledge, she had to admit it gave her the tiniest thrill to have overturned the assumptions of so many members of the ton. Victoria had been regarded since her debut as a paragon of quiet grace, perfect comportment, and impeccable lineage—the ideal society miss. She was not the most beautiful of women, nor the most charming, nor the most interesting, but thanks in large part to Lady Berne's efforts, Victoria had become known as "The Flower of Blackmore," applauded by the patronesses of Almack's as the example to which other debutantes should aspire. The strategy resulted in three proposals at the end of last season and two at the beginning of this, her second season. Lord Stickley's offer had come a mere fortnight after they arrived in London.

She sighed and shifted in her chair, glancing down at her hands, hearing the whisper of Harrison's pen stroking across the page. After their parents' deaths, Harrison had been driven to enshrine the family's legacy, and she became a willing participant in that effort. Being courted by and then married to the season's finest catch had been the pinnacle of the dreams both he and her parents had for her. Those dreams had been utterly dashed the moment she chose to remain on the terrace with Lucien, rather than marching back inside the ballroom at the first sign of impropriety.

Even knowing this, a part of her she seldom acknowledged was relieved she would not be marrying Lord Stickley. In truth, they had never suited. She winced inwardly. That being said, there were more preferable ways to cry off an engagement than being the center of the biggest scandal since ... well, since her brother shot the previous Viscount Atherbourne, she supposed.

Harrison began speaking without glancing up at her. "You have left yourself few options, Victoria." He dipped his pen in the inkwell and continued scratching away at the page before him. She wondered idly if he was writing a novel. Absurd, that. Her staid, traditional brother doing something so frivolous and romantic as penning fiction? The thought made a bubble of nervous laughter rise in her throat. She held her breath and pressed her lips together firmly to stifle it.

He finally ceased writing and looked up. Her amusement died before it had really begun. She'd expected his gaze to be cold, disapproving, remote. And it was. But beneath that was a deep, resigned sadness. It fairly broke her heart.

"Harrison, I ..."

"Despite the dishonor you have dealt the family, I still care for you as my sister. Although I may occasionally wish it otherwise, that shall never change. Therefore, I will offer you two choices. You may live at Blackmore Hall until I marry, at which point, you will transfer your household to our western estate at Garrison Heath. It is smaller but perfectly comfortable."

"It is a half day's ride from the nearest village."

His eyes narrowed in the first visible flash of anger he had shown throughout the scandal. She suspected a great deal of fury was being controlled beneath the surface.

"And yet, it is what I will offer you," he snapped. "If you

cannot stomach the idea, then you may feel free to choose your second option."

She took a deep, bracing breath and clenched her hands tightly in her lap, her thumb stroking her knuckles soothingly. "Which is?"

"Our Aunt Muriel is in need of a companion. You would go to live with her in Edinburgh. Whichever choice you make, you will leave London as soon as I can arrange it."

The air condensed around her, cold and sharp. She was to be banished, then. Hardly unexpected. Really, she supposed his offers were both rather generous, under the circumstances. He was sending her away, but not so far that she could not still see him and Colin occasionally.

In one case, she would be able to live as she liked, painting and sketching and managing her own household, with no one else to consider. She would be relatively independent and free of others' interference. *And lonely,* she thought. *Terribly lonely.*

In the second option, she would be companion to an elderly great-aunt she remembered fondly as eccentric but witty and fun. As she recalled, Aunt Muriel loved to travel, so at least that option might offer a chance for variety, if not true adventure. However, Victoria would have no home of her own, living instead on the whims and good graces of a woman she hadn't seen in over a decade.

But does that matter so much, since I am unlikely now to ever marry? And if I do not marry, I will have no children, presumably. It will always be just … me.

No chasing a giggling two-year-old around the garden. No shopping on Bond Street for her daughter's first season. And definitely no knee-weakening kisses with a devilishly handsome husband.

She felt a sob rise and gather in her chest. Her hands clenched into fists, her nails digging into the soft flesh of her palms. Blast it. She had cried for two days after that humiliating night. She refused to start up again. She. Would. Not.

Everything would be fine, she assured herself. Just fine. Oh, not what she had pictured her life to be, surely. But quiet and secure and restful and serene ...

A white square of fabric appeared in front of her face, its edges blurred by the tears she couldn't seem to prevent. She took the handkerchief and pressed it to her mouth, then tightly grasped Harrison's strong, capable hand where it still hovered next to her. They remained there for long minutes, he holding her hand gently and stroking her hair while tears quietly rolled down her cheeks in an unstoppable flow.

Rather than oppressive and disapproving, his silence now felt as it had when she was six years old and mourning the death of her first (and last) pet, an old tomcat she had named Salty. As Harrison had sat with her then, holding her hand just like this, his silence had fallen as a reassuring blanket around her. He was ten years older than she, but had never given her a moment's doubt about his love, had rarely treated her with anything other than steadfast affection.

A great deal of her regret over the incident at the Gattingford ball was because of the blow it dealt to her brother. For that alone, she could not forgive herself. The damage to her life would forever change his.

When a polite knock intruded into the silence, Harrison gave her hair one last stroke and pulled away to sit once again behind his desk. "Yes?"

"A gentleman is here to see you, your grace."

Seated with her back to the doors, Victoria could not see Digby's face, but she found their unflappable butler's tremulous tone rather alarming.

Harrison frowned. "Who is it?"

"Viscount Atherbourne, your grace."

White-hot fury flashed briefly in Harrison's gray-blue eyes before he blinked and they iced over. "Thank you, Digby. Please show Lord Atherbourne into the drawing room. I will join him in a moment."

Her heart stuttered, stomach twisting almost painfully as she realized what this announcement meant. He was here. In her house. The man she had been dreaming about, then cursing, then dreaming about some more for the past three-and-a-half days.

She heard the door shut behind Digby before Harrison said, "I think you should lie down for a while, Tori." His use of her childhood nickname suggested he was feeling protective; his dismissing her to her bedchamber implied he wanted her as far away from the coming confrontation as possible. She hoped he wasn't planning to shoot yet another Viscount Atherbourne, although she could appreciate the sentiment.

He rose from behind the desk and strode purposefully toward the doors. As he passed, she again grasped his hand and tugged him to a halt. "Harrison, please don't do anything rash."

He squeezed her hand, set it back in her lap, and patted it soothingly. "Not to worry. In spite of the severe nature of the provocation, I am not the reckless sort. I shall speak to the man and see what he wants. Go and rest now. Trust me to do what is best."

"STRIKING A MAN SEEMS A MOST UNPLEASANT WAY TO BEGIN A conversation, don't you agree, your grace?" Atherbourne asked wryly, wincing as he fingered his bruised jaw. Unfortunately, Harrison thought, whatever damage might have been done by his fist, it was not enough to wipe the other man's smug, arrogant grin from his face. When Harrison had entered the drawing room of Clyde-Lacey House, the horse's ass had been leaning casually with his arm braced on the back of Judith Clyde Lacey's favorite red velvet chair, the one Victoria was fond of curling up in when she worked on her embroidery. Harrison had not been able to stifle his instant, violent reaction. It was unlike him, but immeasurably satisfying.

"Perhaps. But it felt quite reasonable at the time. Now then, let us speak plainly." Harrison tugged the sleeves of his tailcoat to straighten the expertly tailored superfine. "The fact that you continue to draw breath owes more to my restraint than to your worth. Therefore, you will state why you are here without preamble or prevarication, and you will do so now. Before my patience is at an end."

Atherbourne's ever-present half-grin faded for a moment, face hardening and eyes flashing before his expression became one of calculating intent. He dropped his hand from where it pressed his jaw gingerly. "Very well. I have come with an offer."

"Does it involve you lying in a bloody heap on the floor?" Harrison inquired politely.

That infernal smile was back. "I'm afraid not, your grace."

"Then I cannot see where I would be interested."

"Oh, I believe you will be. After all, you do *care* for Lady Victoria, yes?"

Harrison ground his teeth and held his fury in check by the merest thread. How dare this blackguard even speak Victoria's name after all he had done to injure her? "You would do well to guard your tongue where my sister is concerned, Atherbourne."

The quiet statement was met with a moment's pause, a hint of wariness that seemed to dampen some of the man's arrogance. "Your sister is at the center of my offer, your grace. Therefore, I must mention her, wouldn't you say?"

"What the deuce are you talking about?"

"Lady Victoria, to put it bluntly, is ruined. The damage done by Lady Gattingford's rather dramatic recounting has only been worsened by Stickley's attempts to salvage his vanity and pride." The last point seemed to annoy Atherbourne, his nostrils flaring in a moment of anger—puzzling for a man who had intentionally brought about this very result.

"Yes, you certainly accomplished your aim," Harrison said

dryly. "Congratulations on deceiving a naive girl into trusting you and then destroying her chances at a proper match. Quite a courageous act, that."

Under normal circumstances, such a blatant accusation of cowardice and scurrilous behavior might have ended in another dawn appointment between the Duke of Blackmore and Viscount Atherbourne. However, the man seemed quite focused on his mission, ignoring the insults and, instead, tilting his head and holding Harrison's gaze with a predatory one of his own. "Whatever you may think of me or my actions, the fact remains any hope of a respectable marriage for your sister has been dashed."

"Did I not mention a lack of tolerance for preamble?"

"No peer would have her," Atherbourne continued, "and indeed, even should one be persuaded to accept her, the scandal would forever plague both her and her husband. There is, however, one exception: If she were to swiftly marry the man with whom she was caught, and the story were handled carefully, the scandal might be recast as merely a romantic intrigue, and the gossip would pass by next season. As I am that man, I propose she and I marry. Immediately."

Harrison waited in stunned silence for the too-handsome, vindictive viscount to laugh or in some way reveal his "proposal" as a cruel jest. Atherbourne's motives could not have been clearer, and were even understandable: He wanted Harrison punished for killing his brother. His seduction of Victoria was a revenge play, pure and simple. Which made today's proposal, at best, bizarre. Why on earth would he wish to rescue Victoria from social ruin, an affliction he himself had delivered?

"Just what is your angle, Atherbourne?"

"I wish to make Lady Victoria my wife. It is as simple as that."

Harrison shook his head. "Nothing is simple where you are concerned. Why should I trust you with my sister's welfare? You have proven yourself unworthy to mind my horse for an hour, let alone a member of my family for a lifetime."

"Perhaps because, while I may have administered the poison, I can also provide the antidote," he replied quietly. "Do you honestly believe she will be content to live in disgrace?" The viscount paused and glanced up at a painting perched above the fireplace. It depicted Harrison's mother as she had been just after her marriage to the seventh Duke of Blackmore. She was the very image of Victoria.

Atherbourne met Harrison's gaze and continued, "Of course, should you refuse my offer, she could never return to London, at least not for many years, nor with the status she once enjoyed. You would be forced to banish her to the country, or perhaps the Continent or America. Your family has suffered scandals before, but those were yours and your brother's. Society forgives men their failings far more readily than they do women. You know this to be true."

Harrison clasped his hands behind his back and began pacing slowly, occasionally glancing up at the blackguard across from him. He stopped, stared intently for a moment, then said, "I am well aware of the advantages such a union would offer Victoria. But what do you get out of this, Atherbourne? And do not say Victoria herself, because that is patently absurd. She is your pawn, not your queen."

The viscount's response was a slow smile and a subtle nod as though to acknowledge, if not concede, Harrison's point. "What is any gentleman seeking when he makes an offer of marriage?"

Acid burned in Harrison's stomach as his patience with the man's game grew thin. "A dowry, social connections, a mother for his children, and in rare cases, love," he snapped, each point on the list firing like a bullet at this villain who would choose to harm his sister and, indeed, his entire family. It was not to be borne. "None of which apply in this situation. You are not in need of funds. Victoria's dowry equates to less than a month's income for the Atherbourne estate. Hardly enough to consider incentive."

A full minute of silence preceded Atherbourne's reply. "I see you are keeping a close watch on things. I had no idea you'd taken an interest in the financial production rates of my family's holdings."

"One thing you will learn about me is that I leave very little to chance."

Atherbourne nodded calmly, then picked up their earlier discussion. "She is the sister of a duke. Perhaps I want her to ensure my children a greater legacy than they would otherwise enjoy."

"Perhaps. But you and I know that is not why you wish to marry *this* sister of a duke. You wish to marry her because she is *my* sister. And for that reason alone, I cannot agree to this match. Once you were wed, you could abuse her in the most grievous fashion—"

Atherbourne's eyes narrowed and grew deadly, his voice as quiet and biting as Harrison's own. "I would never lay hands upon a woman in such a way."

"I cannot take the chance. Should I allow you to marry, and should you harm her, I would be forced to kill you. And I would hate to be responsible for the death of *two* Viscount Atherbournes."

For a moment, Harrison was certain the man would charge him. Atherbourne's face hardened intensely, his tall form coiled as though poised to leap. Harrison was more than ready. He relished the thought of pummeling his enemy into a fine paste. The drawing room furniture might require some repair afterwards, but it would be well worth the expense.

The tension shattered as a crash sounded just outside the doors to the hall. Both men frowned and swiveled their heads to stare as the noise was followed by a feminine squeak and sudden silence. Then Harrison heard Digby's hushed voice. Annoyed by the interruption, he marched to the door and yanked it open. There stood Victoria, who halted her heated, whispered conversation with the butler immediately and gazed up at Harrison with sheepish eyes.

"I was just ... ah ... moving a vase from here to the table in the library. Unfortunately, it slipped and ... um ..." Her words slowed to a stop as her eyes shifted past his shoulder and landed on Atherbourne. Her mouth gaped slightly and her eyes widened.

His jaw tightened as he realized that—although it should have been impossible—this day was about to get worse.

Chapter Four

"In the art of gossip, eavesdropping is a tool most would consider both crude and amateurish. However, one does what one must."

—THE DOWAGER MARCHIONESS OF WALLINGHAM to Lady Rumstoke upon receiving her report of scandalous statements overheard at the Pennywhistle musicale.

SHE HAD THOUGHT PERHAPS SHE'D IMAGINED HIM AS MORE handsome, more wickedly sensual than he'd actually been—that in justifying her own wanton behavior, she had drawn an irresistible portrait in her mind unwarranted by reality.

She was so very, very wrong.

He was magnificent. The full light of day only enhanced his

attractiveness, as did the splendid midnight-blue tailcoat, gold embroidered waistcoat, and buff riding breeches he wore. Aside from the odd darkening along one side of his jaw, he was a vision of masculine perfection.

Having learned a bit more about his background over the past few days, Victoria now understood why Lucien was more muscular and fit than many other men of the ton, his shoulders wider, his waist narrower, and his thighs ... oh, his thighs. Ladies should never notice such things, but she could not help herself. In any event, she now recognized these physical attributes as evidence of his service as a captain in the army. According to Lady Berne, he had performed quite heroically at Waterloo, earning commendations from Wellington himself. Not that he flaunted it. Most gentlemen returning from battle wore their uniforms proudly and chose to be addressed by their military rank, as was proper. Not him. Lucien Wyatt refused to answer to his well-earned title of Captain, and at formal events where men in crimson uniforms became objects of celebration and admiration, he instead wore plain civilian black. Precisely why this was so, no one knew.

Just then, she became painfully aware of the thick silence, feeling a flush of embarrassment wash over her as both Harrison, who had not moved out of the doorway, and Lucien waited expectantly for her to explain herself. Finally, not knowing what else to do, she resorted to politeness, greeting Lucien with a curtsy and a "my lord."

At first he blinked, his eyebrows arching in surprise. But swiftly, he adopted his signature expression: mild amusement blended with sardonic sensuality. He executed a perfect bow and answered softly, "Lady Victoria."

She felt dizzy as a wave of longing swept through her body. Oh, this was not good.

He is a bounder, she reminded herself. *A scoundrel of the highest order. Or would that be lowest order?* She mentally shook her head. No matter. The point remained, he had done her irreparable harm. Deliberately and cold-bloodedly.

Stiffening her spine at the reminder, she asked in what she hoped was a stern tone, "Does your purpose in being here include a lengthy apology, Lord Atherbourne?"

"Victoria, you would do well to stay out of this," Harrison warned.

She glanced up at him and said, "I'm afraid I am already very much *in* this, Harrison." Pushing past her brother and stepping farther into the drawing room, she met Lucien's eyes again, noting that his smile had faded a fair bit. "Well?"

"No, my lady. I came with an offer—"

"Which I have declined," Harrison interrupted. "Lord Atherbourne was just leaving."

Keeping her eyes fixed on Lucien's face, Victoria reached behind her to place a staying hand on her brother's arm. "I would like to hear what the offer was," she said softly.

"It was nothing worth—" Harrison began.

"Lord Atherbourne?" she prompted, watching his expression as he moved his gaze between hers and her brother's. He wasn't smiling. In fact, he appeared far more serious than she had yet seen him.

"I came to offer marriage."

It was as though a horse had kicked her in the chest. How she wished she had been able to hear more of what was being said from where she had stood eavesdropping behind the drawing room doors. At least then the shock of his proposal would have been tempered a bit. Unfortunately, all she had heard was low, masculine mumbling. Hardly helpful in preparing her for ... well, *this*.

"You—" She gasped to catch her breath. "You wish to *marry* me? After all you've done?"

The faintest flicker of something—guilt, perhaps? mild chagrin?—passed through his eyes but was gone before she could identify it. "As I explained to your brother, it is the only way to ensure the scandal is contained and the consequences to your future are minimized."

She stared at him silently for a long while, trying to understand this beautiful, dastardly, confounding man. Altruism hadn't brought him here today—that much was clear. But what could his motivation be? And did it matter? He had put her in a rather desperate position. By definition, that meant her choices were few and undesirable.

She felt Harrison's hands on her shoulders and his tall form hovering behind her. "Victoria, I do comprehend why this might seem a convenient solution to a difficult problem," he murmured close to her ear. "But this man is dangerous. He has already shown an appalling lack of conscience where you are concerned, and I cannot allow—"

Reaching up to pat Harrison's hand where it rested on her shoulder, she nodded to indicate she understood. Quietly, she asked if she might speak with Atherbourne alone for a moment. Harrison naturally resisted quite vehemently at first, but after a few minutes of discussion, in which she pointed out it was her life and her future at stake, he conceded. "Five minutes," he bit out. "Not one second more. And the doors remain open."

She nodded, then thanked him as he strode out into the hall to speak with Digby. Crossing the room, she gestured toward a pair of chairs in front of the fire. "Shall we sit, my lord?" she said, then moved to the right chair and sank down into it, happy to give her jittery legs a rest.

As Lucien settled his muscular form into the opposite chair, she almost laughed at the contrast of such a large, overtly masculine body seated awkwardly in an ornate, Louis XV chair. Perhaps it was the gilt that did it. Stifling her wandering thoughts, she began, "Now then, why should I consider marrying you, my lord?"

He opened his mouth to speak, but she waved her hand and immediately clarified, "Aside from rather neatly resolving the scandal you used as a weapon against my brother."

He blinked and paused, clearly surprised by her bluntness. "You have preempted my most persuasive argument, Lady

Victoria." The wicked smile slowly returned. He leaned back in his seat and crossed his arms, giving her an assessing look. "Are you asking what it would be like to be my wife?"

His voice had gone low and a bit suggestive, just as it had been on Lady Gattingford's terrace. Unfortunately, knowing he was doing it deliberately to get under her skin did not prevent her shiver of pleasure. "We ... we haven't time for games, my lord."

"Who said I was playing?"

Her breathing grew faster. His eyes were so beautiful—a dark, stormy gray, lighter toward the center with black rings around the irises. She finally knew the color of his eyes. That seemed important, somehow.

Shaking her head to dispel the sudden fog of sensual awareness, she swallowed hard and said, "I am asking why marriage to you would be better than other alternatives, Lord Atherbourne. I am not without options, you know."

"Oh, yes. Your options. Banishment to the Continent or America, perhaps? An isolated life as a country spinster? Was that what you dreamed of as a girl when you imagined your future?"

"You know very well it was not," she snapped.

He sat forward, leaning toward her with his hands on his thighs, all traces of indolence gone as the full intensity of his personality came to the fore. "And what about being the Marchioness of Stickley, hmm? Did you imagine yourself the wife of a man who could not even be bothered to kiss you properly?"

"Leave Lord Stickley out of this."

"Very well. You asked what being my wife would entail. The answer is much the same as what being Stickley's wife would have entailed. Except that, as *my* wife, you will never for one moment doubt that I want you."

Shocked by his declaration, she felt herself panting, the air sawing in and out at an embarrassing rate. But she could not hear it over her pounding heart, the sound as loud in her ears as the ocean on a rocky shore. "You w-want me?" she asked faintly.

Ignoring her response, he continued, "I would never choose to spend time hunting or regaling the gents at Boodle's about my hounds when I could spend it making love to my new wife."

"Oh, that's not ... you ... making ... oh."

"Furthermore, should you marry me, you would never again be vulnerable to the kind of scandal you were caught up in several nights ago."

Her hands, moist and shaking, tightened where they rested on the arms of the chair. "I believe we've already established that this would help lessen the scandal."

He grinned. "Oh, but that is not why it would never happen again. As your husband, it would be my duty to see you so well pleasured that no other man could possibly have anything to offer you. Therefore, you would not be lured into any illicit rendezvous or stolen moments of passion. Except with me, of course."

Flustered and breathless, she rose and paced across the carpet to a spot between a settee and a low, marble-topped table. *He is a devil*, she thought. *A devil with the face of an angel. And I am a fool—worse, utterly mad—to fall prey to his intoxicating words.* Because she did not simply feel drawn to him, this conductor of her destruction. She *longed* for him, yearned for the right to trace his lips with her bare fingers, to stroke his injured cheek, to feel his tongue slide wickedly inside her mouth, the way it had before.

Turning to face him, she was startled to find him no more than a foot away. He was so tall, he fairly loomed over her, close enough to touch. *Breathe, Victoria.* Despite the inner admonition, it took her a moment to respond to his litany of contrasts between what marriage to Lord Stickley would have been and what it would mean to be Lady Atherbourne. *His* bride. "And if I *were* caught with another man, my lord?" she asked, not because she thought it a real possibility, but simply to see what he would say.

He didn't appear to like the question. Not at all. His face grew hard and shuttered, his smile fading, his lips settling into a grim line. "I think it best not to contemplate what I would do in that instance."

For a moment, her entire being paused, waiting for the answer to her next question. "Would ... would you hurt me?"

His response was immediate and emphatic: "No. Never."

She believed him. She didn't know why, but it was true. Something in his face—a flash of outrage, as if the very thought was abhorrent—gave her the answer his words could not. It appeared he did not mean to harm her, at least not physically.

"So, let me understand this correctly," she said, stepping back and retreating toward the fireplace. He was entirely too close. It was not conducive to clear thinking. "You plotted my ruination to gain vengeance against Harrison—"

"He shot my brother—"

"Yes, well, I believe we all understand your motives," she retorted sharply.

"Do you?" His voice was strange. Sad. "It was not my intention that you should suffer needlessly."

"Perhaps you should have considered that before—"

"But I was hardly alone on that terrace, my lady."

The softly spoken words jarred her terribly, not because they were false. Because they were true. This scandal was as much her fault as his. More, perhaps. She was the one who had been betrothed to another man. She was the one who had allowed foolish fantasies and romantic nonsense to weaken her. He had come to the door with devious intent, yes. But she was the one who had swung it wide.

"You believe our marriage will quiet the scandal," she said.

For the longest time, he did not reply. His eyes explored her face, his expression almost concerned. "I believe without it, your reputation will never fully recover. I do not wish that for you."

Neither did she. In truth, what he offered was a gift. She would have preferred it to come without accompanying suspicions, but it was hardly an offer she could discard easily— or perhaps at all. "I could marry another. If I waited a year ..."

He was shaking his head, giving her a dark look. He held up three fingers, wiggling each one in turn as he spoke. "Engagement. Scandalous liaison. Wedding." His arm dropped and his head tilted slightly. "Tell me, Lady Victoria. What would they say about your husband if he were not one of the first two?"

She hated him. Hated his mocking little gesture, hated the arrogant tilt, the assurance in his voice. Most of all, she hated that he was right. "Fine. Let's say I agree to marry you."

His half-smile returned. "Let's."

"Where would the wedding take place?"

Glancing around the drawing room, he said, "Why not here?"

"When?"

"As soon as it can be arranged. I shall need only a few days to acquire a special license."

A few days? Blood rushed from her head, sped on by a heart that doubled its pace. "Th-that soon?"

He was still for a moment, then walked toward her slowly. Cautiously. One finger rose to stroke her cheek. She jerked back, startled. It caught briefly on a curl at the top of her jawline, then disappeared. "You would not regret becoming my wife, Victoria," he whispered. It sounded like a vow.

She felt hunted, herded into a corner from which there was no escape. And the hunter was also the bait. Tempting. Seductive. More than that, however, she felt the walls of duty pushing her toward him. She had made a terrible mistake. One whose price must be paid. She glanced up at the portrait of her mother, serene and golden and perfect. A woman of grace, if not great beauty. A woman who had always done the proper thing. "You would be my husband." It was a whisper to herself, but he heard.

"In every way," came his hoarse confirmation.

Nodding, she clasped her hands at her waist, then dropped

her gaze to her twisting fingers. "Would we have children, Lucien?"

"Yes." His tone was softer, gentle.

Lifting her head once again, she stared for what seemed like years into his beautiful, storm-cloud eyes. In the few moments they stood gazing at one another, she imagined an entire lifetime with this man. Their wedding. The nights when he would make love to her in their bed. Children with his raven-black hair and perhaps her blue eyes. Sons who would grow tall and strong and handsome like their father. Daughters who would be doted on and spoiled. A family.

"Then that is my answer."

His eyes widened and he grew intent, seeking a confirmation in her face.

"Yes, my lord, I will marry you."

Chapter Five

*"Clever battle strategy often resembles madness.
Knowing the difference ... ah, well, the victors have
the privilege of defining that, do they not?"*

—THE DOWAGER MARCHIONESS OF WALLINGHAM upon news
of Napoleon's escape from Elba.

"IS MARRYING THE CHIT REALLY NECESSARY, LUC?" JAMES
Kilbrenner, the Earl of Tannenbrook, muttered from where he
sat slumped in a leather chair near the hearth in Lucien's library.
A glass of brandy dangled negligently from his long fingers, and
the firelight played sinister games with his craggy features.

Lucien placed the stopper back in the bottle with a clink
after pouring a glass of his own, then walked back to the

fireplace to stand with an elbow propped on the mantel. "I thought we agreed it was the only way to achieve a measure of justice."

James waved his free hand in the air as though to sweep aside Lucien's statement. "I know what we said. It's just ... she is an innocent. Seems unsporting."

Lucien frowned. He did not like James echoing his own doubts. With a plan such as this, and an enemy such as the Duke of Blackmore, doubt led to mistakes, which meant failure. He refused to fail. "She will be well cared for. As my wife, she will enjoy every comfort. It is clear she desires children. She will have that, as well. Eventually."

A look of skepticism came over his friend's face. "The original plan was to punish Blackmore, not his sister."

It was true: Lucien had not intended to involve Victoria at all. At least, not at first. "We tried. The law stops at the ducal crest, it seems. The only place Blackmore is vulnerable is his family. His brother is ... well, there is nothing we could do to Colin Lacey that he hasn't already done to himself. That leaves the sister."

James sighed and took a drink. "If only he had called you out over the Gattingford incident. You could have shot him, and the scales would have been balanced."

Shaking his head, Lucien moved to sit in the chair opposite James, sinking down into its well-worn comfort and draining the last of his brandy in a quick motion. He felt its mild sting as it slid down his throat and settled warmly in his stomach. He had never been much for drink, but right now, he was willing to try many uncharacteristic things to dampen the rage that had burned inside for the better part of a year.

Inside of a blink, his mind flashed back nearly nine months. He stood at the graves of his brother and sister on a sodden, strangely chilled August morning, wondering how it could have happened, how they could have both died within days of one another. He recalled glancing over to where his parents were buried and thinking he was cursed to survive while all those around him died. It had happened on the battlefield, and now here. The stark truth of it was an endless black pit. No air, no light, no escape.

He squeezed his eyes shut against the memories. James had been there, bullying, nudging. *What could possibly be worth living for without so much as a cousin left for kin?* Lucien had asked. It was then, perhaps in desperation, that James had offered him a torch for his darkness: vengeance.

Brought back to the present when his friend rose to stare down at the fire, Lucien picked up the thread of their conversation. "Blackmore loathes scandal. The odds of him escalating matters by calling me out were always rather slim." He sighed and ran a hand through his hair. "Besides, the scales can never be truly balanced. Taking his sister from him is the best I can do, under the circumstances."

"Yes, but haven't you already done that? The scandal means she will have to be shipped off to some distant estate or sent abroad. Let it be enough, Luc."

The fury that rose inside Lucien in that moment was as unexpected as it was uncontrollable. Like a black, sulfurous cloud, it filled him and spilled out in a volcanic explosion. In one swift move, he stood and threw his glass against the far wall, the splintering crash barely registering before he roared, "It is *not* enough!"

James jerked when he heard the glass break apart, then slowly turned to face Lucien, a look of wariness and alarm on his face.

"*Enough* will be when he remembers her as she was at seven years, all ribbons and gap-toothed smiles, and misses her as he would a severed limb. Enough will be when he reaches for a pen to write her and realizes she will never read his words. Enough will be when he understands that she is *mine*, by God, and I have taken her from him."

"You are still grieving. Think about this." James's voice grew rough with concern. He reached out to place a hand on Lucien's shoulder, but Lucien shrugged him off and stalked across the room to stand with his back turned, his hands on his hips, breathing harshly.

He despised what was inside him, a monster of hatred and pain and fury. But he could do nothing other than try to appease it. "It's what I have to do, James," he rasped.

After a moment, he felt James's hand at his back, his friend's solid presence helping him regain his composure. "I know."

"If there was another way ..."

"I know," James repeated. "It is better than leaving her to the ton's tender mercies."

Lucien nodded.

"What do you plan to tell her?"

It was a good question. "Nothing."

A single, shaggy eyebrow lifted. "And you think that will work?"

Lucien mimicked the gesture and added a small smile. "She fancies me." The look that emerged on the Earl of Tannenbrook's face sent an unexpected burst of laughter through him. "That hard to believe, eh?"

"No. But you're mad if you think you can tup a lass into forgetfulness. Might work for a night, but not forever."

Lucien crossed the room and sank into the chair James had vacated. "Not forever. Until we leave London?" He shrugged. "Eminently achievable."

James grunted and propped his hands on his hips. "You don't think you're overestimating your charms just a wee bit?"

Chuckling, he replied, "It's clear you do. But, then, your judgment is flawed. You are not a woman."

His friend snorted and shook his head. "Thank God for that. I'd be an ugly one, no doubt."

Hours later, after James had left and quiet had settled over the house that once belonged to his brother, Lucien stood at the rear window of the library, contemplating the garden his sister had loved. Modeled after the gardens at their country estate, Thornbridge, but on a smaller scale, the shapes were less orderly, more curved and natural than current fashion would dictate. Still, they were lovely with winding paths, lush plantings, and a small fountain with a stone bench at the center.

Three days. In only three days, he could claim victory. Then Blackmore's true punishment could begin. While grim satisfaction seized Lucien, knowing his goal was within sight, it did not blind him to the longer-term implications of his plan. For days now, James had been trying to help him see past the moment of triumph and point out there was a marriage after the wedding, a woman who would be a permanent part of his life, the mother of his children.

He knew it well. Could not stop thinking about it, in fact. Twinges of guilt mixed with no small measure of lust filled him each time he contemplated having Victoria all to himself for the remainder of his days. By God, when the duke had thought to deny him, Lucien had very nearly lost his head and attacked the man full on. Fortunately, Victoria had interrupted at just the right time. Her knack for falling rather neatly into his hands was one of her more endearing qualities.

At the thought, his mind veered immediately to Victoria as she had been on Lady Gattingford's terrace that night, her breasts covered by nothing more than moonlight and his mouth. He recalled her taste (milky and sweet), her smell (lightly floral; hyacinth, he thought), and the breathless moan she'd uttered when she reached her peak. He gripped the window sill, let his forehead rest against the cold glass, and gritted his teeth against a wave of longing.

His desire for her was entirely out of proportion. Despite his flowery words to her that night, she was no grand beauty. Oh, she was pretty enough in a way many young women were: golden hair, big blue-green eyes, a soft mouth, and creamy skin. Her features were even and balanced, her demeanor calm and serene. In truth, one could find nothing to fault in her appearance, but neither would many consider her a diamond of the first water.

Then what is it you find so enthralling? This girl who fades into the background has you twisted up with lust.

He had wondered more than once since first seeing Victoria at the Gattingford ball if his passion for revenge had somehow transmuted into this rather unseemly preoccupation with her. Perhaps, he thought, his hatred had begun to infect his dalliances with women. Even if that were so, however, it did not alter his plans for her.

After months of research into Blackmore's life—everything from his finances to his politics to his bloody valet—Lucien and James had found nothing more damaging than disgruntled former servants complaining about the duke's terribly exacting standards of cleanliness and thrift. Fortunately, they also discovered how deep and abiding was his connection with his sister. And so Lucien had continued investigating, but his target had become Lady Victoria Lacey. With the aid of the duke's ex-servants, Lucien was able to glean a great deal about Victoria's character. She was known as the Flower of Blackmore, her pristine reputation fiercely guarded by both Blackmore and her sponsor, Lady Berne. But, he soon learned, beneath the mannerly mask, she was a hopeless romantic. As one maid had put it, "At heart, her ladyship is as sweet and fanciful as a pot of honey."

It had presented the ideal opportunity: All he had to do was sweep her off her feet and directly into the path of scandal. From there, he reasoned, events should fall into place of their own accord—the engagement Blackmore had manufactured would be finished, the duke would be humiliated, his beloved sibling so tainted that he would have to distance himself from her permanently. Everything had gone precisely as Lucien had envisioned—better, even.

Except for one small problem: It had not been satisfying. Not even a little. He still did not entirely understand why. The idea of making her separation from her brother permanent by marrying her himself had only occurred to him a day later. Instantly, he had known it was the answer.

Now, the marriage was poised to happen, and all he could think about was her. It made no sense at all. This was not about gaining a wife, it was about punishing Blackmore. But, then, he had not anticipated Victoria.

Recalling how she had rather boldly taken the reins of his conversation with Blackmore and proceeded to interview him for the position of husband, he shook his head and felt himself smiling. It had been shocking enough to hear her consent to marry him, but after shooing him out the door, she had somehow managed to persuade Blackmore to allow it. That had been astounding.

Hell, Lucien had been prepared to seduce her into eloping to Gretna Green. But it had not been necessary. Blackmore had paid him a visit yesterday to repeatedly threaten his life if "so much as the hem of her dress is harmed in any way." They had negotiated the terms of the marriage settlement for less than a quarter of an hour, with Lucien conceding nearly every point. The marriage itself gave him full control of her, which was all that mattered. What she would be paid in allowance or how his family's secondary properties would be distributed to their children were of no importance to him.

What mattered was that she would be his. In the window's reflection, he watched his private smile turn grim, determined.

In three days, she would be his.

Chapter Six

*"Love? What rubbish. Grandchildren for your poor,
beleaguered mother. Now, there is a sound reason to marry."*

—THE DOWAGER MARCHIONESS OF WALLINGHAM to her only son,
Charles, upon his refusal to enter Almack's.

THE DRESS WAS EVEN MORE BEAUTIFUL THAN SHE HAD
imagined it, Victoria thought as she gazed at the vision before
her. It was white silk, overlaid with the sheerest muslin, rich
with tiny embroidered flowers in a vivid peacock blue and
leaves of pale spring green. On the short sleeves and just
beneath the scooped bodice, tiny pleats in the muslin formed
panels bordered by ornate silver ribbon. The overall effect was
dreamy and exquisite.

She wanted to cry.

"My dear, you are enchanting in that gown," said Lady Berne, currently seated on the sofa behind where Victoria stood gazing at herself in the full-length mirror of the Bond Street dressmaker's shop. "Mrs. Bowman is a marvel. And to have it finished so quickly! I can hardly credit it."

Victoria swallowed and gave the countess a weak smile over her shoulder. "Yes, she is extraordinary. Fortunately, I had already arranged to have the dress made last month. So, no rush was necessary."

A long pause followed this statement as Lady Berne realized the gown would have been Victoria's wedding dress for her marriage to Lord Stickley and now instead would be worn for her rather precipitate nuptials with Lord Atherbourne.

"Oh," Lady Berne finally responded. "Well, that is, indeed, fortunate."

Victoria sniffed and straightened her spine. "Yes, I thought so."

She turned as Mrs. Bowman came back into the room and knelt at her feet, pinning the hem for one final adjustment. "Mrs. Bowman, what do you recommend for my headdress? I have heard some ladies choose to wear turbans for their weddings."

The sable-haired dressmaker glanced up at her with a look of disgust. "No, no, no!" She waved a hand wildly in the air above her elegant coiffure, her light Italian accent evident even in those three short words. "You must wear flowers, my lady. The, eh, *mughetto*. Lily of the Valley. It is a dress of delicate beauty. It deserves flowers, not a turban." She spat the last word as though it were particularly repugnant.

Victoria hid a smile. Opinionated and headstrong when it came to fashion, Renata Bowman was perhaps the most talented clothier in London. However, while she was married to an English textile merchant, she was Italian rather than English—or even French. To make matters worse, she struggled greatly with showing proper deference to her titled clientele. In

Victoria's opinion, this was the sole reason Mrs. Bowman was not the ton's most sought-after modiste.

"Well, I must say I quite agree. Flowers would, indeed, be lovely, my dear," the countess interjected brightly.

"Then flowers it shall be," Victoria said with forced cheer, glancing once again at her reflection. Even to herself, her face appeared pale, her eyes pensive.

Rising beside her and examining the gown with a fierce frown, Mrs. Bowman nodded sharply. "Mm. It is good." She met Victoria's gaze in the mirror. "I have it finished for you and delivered today. The rest is ready, too. That will be sent to the duke's house as well, yes?"

"The rest?" Victoria blinked.

"Sì, your ..." The woman gestured toward Victoria's bosom and down to her knees. "... nightwear. And the day dresses and ball gowns you requested."

"Oh!" Victoria had completely forgotten the expansive trousseau she had ordered before the incident, when she had planned to marry Stickley and needed something to look forward to, even if it was a carriage load of new frocks.

Of course, her mind had been a muddled bowl of porridge since she had agreed to marry Lucien, so it was no surprise she had forgotten a shopping excursion from over six weeks ago. It seemed an entirely separate existence, the life of a young woman on the verge of a well-planned if not terribly thrilling future. Now, she felt years older. Decades, even.

"Yes, thank you," she replied finally. "The duke's house will be fine."

As the modiste ushered Victoria into the dressing area and helped her out of her wedding gown and into the walking dress she had arrived wearing, she couldn't help thinking that, as of tomorrow, Clyde-Lacey House would no longer be her home. Instead, she would be married to Viscount Atherbourne. She didn't even know where he lived.

"Is not so bad, you know." The dusky, accented voice of Mrs.

Bowman interrupted her thoughts. The modiste stood behind Victoria, fastening the buttons at the back of her pale pink, long-sleeved cambric dress and helping her into her rose sarcenet pelisse.

Victoria frowned in confusion.

"Marriage. You are afraid, yes?" Mrs. Bowman gave Victoria's skirts one last sweep to remove the wrinkles and came to stand in front of her, hands on hips and a knowing look in her intelligent brown eyes. "You should not fear. Women have much power."

Victoria glanced down at her hands where they tangled at her waist. She consciously relaxed her fingers, embarrassed to have her emotions so visible to someone who was little more than an acquaintance. Although the conversation was disconcerting, Mrs. Bowman's statement made her curious. "What power do we have? I do not even have rights to my own funds."

"You are to marry Atherbourne?"

Victoria hesitated before nodding. How did a modiste know such things?

She seemed to read Victoria's question in her face. "Ladies talk much here at Bowman's," she began cryptically. "They say he is … well, you will not find marriage as trying as you imagine."

"But you said we have power. What power?" Curiosity burned inside Victoria. She *needed* to know.

Mrs. Bowman gave her a piercing look. "You will soon discover a husband's happiness cannot be complete without his wife's happiness. If he is reminded of this at the right moment …" She snapped her fingers and waved them with an Italian flourish. "… he is yours." She held up one finger in front of Victoria's nose. "But you must not let him *know* you know you have the power. That is the key."

Victoria frowned. This was distinctly unhelpful. And confusing. "But how shall I know when is the right time?"

Mrs. Bowman pursed her lips and arched a brow,

considering Victoria with an elevated tilt of her head. "You will know."

Dash it all, the woman was full of mysterious information, and yet offered nothing. It made her want to stamp her foot in vexation.

"Lady Victoria, perhaps we should be off," Lady Berne said from the other side of the dressing room curtain. "We have much to arrange before tomorrow."

Victoria quickly tied the ribbon of her bonnet, stepped past the curtain, and smiled into the countess's round face. "Yes, let's be off."

As they strolled south along Bond toward Bruton Street and Berkeley Square, Victoria considered what the modiste had said and wondered if it could be true. The idea that a wife might have influence and power of her own within the confines of marriage had not occurred to her, but then, that wasn't too surprising. She had been raised in a proper household, her parents content with one another but rarely openly affectionate. Her mother had died when Victoria was but seventeen, and before that had never spoken of what a relationship with a man entailed, much less shared such valuable secrets as how to wield actual power over her husband.

When she had agreed to marry Lucien, standing in the drawing room gazing into his eyes, Victoria had known it was the only decision she could have made, for Harrison's sake and for her own future. But ever since, she had felt adrift on a sea of uncertainty. Would he be kind to her? Did he wish to use her—again—as leverage against Harrison? She did not know how he might do so without her cooperation, but she could hardly rule it out. Would he seek to further humiliate her? Swallowing hard, she acknowledged that it was her greatest fear. As her husband, he would hold absolute domain over her person, her assets, her life. If so inclined, he could torment her in numerous ways, both public and private. Harrison had made that very argument when she had told him of her decision. Now, however, with little more than an offhanded comment, Mrs. Bowman had given her a glimmer of hope. If she could, in fact, retain some power within the marriage, at least she would not be helpless.

"What do you think, dear?"

Victoria absently glanced at Lady Berne. "Hmm?" The countess smiled, and Victoria knew she had been caught woolgathering. "I beg your pardon, my lady. It seems my thoughts refuse to settle today."

The dear woman hooked her arm through Victoria's and patted her hand understandingly. "It's to be expected. Tomorrow is your wedding day, after all. So many changes all at once. It is exhilarating, and yet I daresay I remember feeling much trepidation myself before I wed Lord Berne." She smiled fondly, her eyes clouding with nostalgia. "He was terribly handsome, you know. Could have chosen any of a dozen beauties that season. But he landed on me, and that was that."

Victoria smiled, momentarily caught up in the countess's happy recollection. "What drew you together?"

"It was the horrid punch at the Duchess of Harrington's summer ball."

Victoria laughed. "Indeed?"

The lady's warm brown eyes sparkled merrily, and she leaned closer as though imparting a delicious bit of gossip. "Oh, yes. The duchess was a vain, haughty woman whose wig was always rather precariously set upon her head. I have no notion as to why. One would have thought she would take greater care, but ..." She shrugged. "In any event, Sir Albon Throckmorton— a more addlepated gollumpus I've never met—was having a heated exchange with a potted plant which had imposed upon his posterior. He collided with the duchess, and her wig did not survive the tussle."

Giggling and shaking her head at the absurd image, Victoria asked, "It fell off?"

"Directly into the punch bowl."

"How embarrassing for her."

Lady Berne grinned wickedly. "Mortifying, yes. But, as I stood very near the refreshment table, the incident proved providential. Lord Stanton Huxley, the dashing first son of the Earl of Berne, was just behind me, intending to fetch a cup of that wretched punch, presumably. When the wig landed in the bowl, he quickly pulled me to safety."

Victoria grinned and nodded. "Lord Berne is a true gentleman."

"Oh, I suspect it wasn't so much that he was trying to rescue me as that he wished to ensure I remained between himself and the splash. But that was neither here nor there. I said something about how the good Lord had answered my prayer in smiting both her grace's dignity and her dreadful punch in one fell swoop. I believe I referenced the miracle of Moses and the Red Sea."

"You made him laugh," Victoria said fondly.

"So loudly we began attracting attention. I was forced to dance with him just to get him to quiet down."

Several minutes of companionable silence fell between them, filled only with the din of the street—clacking carriage wheels, clopping horses' hooves, the shouts of coachmen, and the buzz of shoppers—as Lady Berne seemed lost in reminiscence and Victoria contemplated what tomorrow would bring. Quietly, she leaned toward the older woman and asked, "Is that the secret, then, to a good marriage?"

The countess's surprise was evident in her raised eyebrows. "What, dear? Humor?"

Victoria nodded.

She frowned gently and pursed her lips as though trying to puzzle through the answer. "Well, I suppose it plays a role." She nodded to confirm. "It certainly makes the thorny patches easier to bear. But I must say marriage is not so simple as one secret ingredient."

"No, of course not," Victoria murmured. "I was just wondering ..." Her voice trailed off as she debated how to ferret out the information she wished to know without invading the countess's privacy or the bounds of propriety. Deciding simply to ask the question directly, she glanced around the bustling street to be certain no one was near enough to overhear. "I have heard there are ways a wife might wield power within her marriage. Is this true?"

Clearly startled by the question, Lady Berne stiffened and slowed her stride, stopping to face Victoria for a moment before realizing they were apt to draw attention if they remained halted. Grasping Victoria's elbow again and resuming their strolling pace, the countess murmured, "My dear, did your mother never explain ... er ... matters beyond the wedding?"

Victoria shook her head, a flush heating her cheeks.

"Oh, my." The countess cleared her throat and opened her mouth to say something, then appeared to reconsider.

"You needn't answer, my lady. It was an impertinent question, and I should not have asked."

"No, no." Lady Berne squeezed her arm reassuringly. "I was simply collecting my thoughts." She chuckled. "I have not yet had this little talk with my daughters, so didn't realize ..." She waved her hand in dismissal. "No matter. A young woman should have some idea what to expect before she is married. I daresay, your dear mother was probably waiting until you'd made a match, much as I have been waiting with my own girls. I am certain she would wish for me to inform you of your wifely duties."

Victoria could feel the blood burning her face and wondered if the air around her fair shimmered with the heat. "Duties?" she squeaked.

"Yes, dear. Your husband will expect you to lie with him in the marriage bed. You must do so in order to have children, of course."

"Of course," she replied hoarsely.

"Most men desire children. Oh, that reminds me, you must maintain quiet, my dear."

"Qu-quiet?"

"Well, not absolute silence, naturally, but I can think of no gentleman who would prefer a great deal of caterwauling and carrying on rather than a state of blessed peace and quiet."

Cringing at the memory of how she had "carried on" during her embrace with Lucien on the Gattingford terrace, Victoria tried to imagine being still and quiet while Lucien touched and kissed her as he had that night. She was determined to be a good wife, but in light of this new information, it might prove an even greater challenge than she had anticipated.

"If you manage his house well, provide him with children, and do all in your power to bring him comfort and ease, you should do splendidly as his viscountess." Lady Berne beamed at Victoria. "There. Now do you feel better?"

Victoria pasted a smile on her face and nodded, eager for the excruciating conversation to end. "Thank you for your gracious advice. You have been most kind."

The countess nodded and they continued into Berkeley Square. The neat, orderly row of town houses was a familiar comfort. Just as they arrived at Clyde-Lacey House, a grand brick structure spanning double the width of the other houses, Lady Berne tugged Victoria to a stop. "Oh! My dear girl, I almost forgot the most important thing."

Inwardly, Victoria winced, hoping this nugget of wisdom would prove less embarrassing than the rest. "Yes?"

"As soon as you are able, discover what his favorite dish and his least favorite are. When you are well pleased with him, ensure the meal he loves most is served at least once a week."

Blinking in surprise, Victoria absorbed the advice and nodded. Then she asked, "And I should learn his least favorite dish so the cook may avoid serving it?"

"Oh, no dear. You should learn it so you may serve it whenever he displeases you." She squeezed Victoria's hand as they climbed the front steps. "For his sake, I do hope that occasion is a rarity."

Chapter Seven

"While I agree men fancy a good meal, Meredith, I daresay the stomach is not the most direct route to a man's heart. That organ lies a good bit lower."

—THE DOWAGER MARCHIONESS OF WALLINGHAM to the Countess of Berne upon learning of said lady's supper menu.

LUCIEN'S WEDDING DAY BEGAN WITH A CRACK OF THUNDER and a torrent of rain, the deluge washing the London streets and battering the windows of Blackmore's drawing room throughout the small, quiet ceremony.

Even now, amidst the clink and chatter of the wedding breakfast, it had not let up, a backdrop of constant whooshing punctuated by the occasional ominous rumble. With fewer than a dozen guests in attendance, the voices of Victoria's family and friends failed to drown out the sounds of the storm.

A hard hand thumped Lucien between the shoulders just as he was about to take a bite of spinach and ham torte. "Well, old friend, it appears no one else is prepared to congratulate you, so allow me to be the first," Lord Tannenbrook said evenly.

Lucien coughed on a wave of wry laughter and shook his head at his sole ally, who was seated on his right at the long dining table. "I expect you may be the only," he murmured, glancing around at those who conveyed their disapproval of him quite effectively through barren politeness. "But it matters little. What's done cannot be undone, regardless of how the duke or anyone else may feel about it."

James took a bite of toast and nodded his agreement.

Since his arrival at Clyde-Lacey House, the atmosphere had been chilly. Far from unexpected, but uncomfortable nonetheless. The duke had barely spoken to him. Colin Lacey had arrived drunk and worked at getting drunker as the morning wore on. Lord and Lady Berne had greeted him with tight reserve, even while embracing and coddling Victoria as though they were hens and she their lone chick. Clearly sensing the tension in the room, the priest had scowled and asked Victoria repeatedly if she was certain she did not wish to reconsider. All in all, he felt fortunate she had not planned a larger affair.

Lucien's eyes slid past James to the head of the table where his pale, subdued bride sat in quiet conversation with the Earl of Berne. He hadn't previously thought her beautiful, but in spite of her withdrawn demeanor today, she was strikingly lovely. Her gown, a diaphanous confection of white, silver, blue, and green, made her eyes and skin fairly glow. Her golden tresses had been swept artfully upon her head, dappled with tiny white flowers and green leaves. A few stray curls played about her face and touched the strand of pearls around her delicate white neck. He imagined unfastening the necklace and tracing his tongue along its path. Then lower, he thought as his eyes settled on her sweet, lushly rounded breasts, and lower still.

A hard, sudden thrust of desire surged through his body, tightening his groin and quickening his breath. Like a bolt of lightning, it was swift and frighteningly powerful. *Bloody hell.* The last thing he needed was a distraction of this magnitude. Forcing his attention away from Victoria, he collided with James's knowing gaze.

Damn. Apparently, his lust was obvious, at least from Tannenbrook's perspective. His fixation on bedding his new wife, while understandable in different circumstances, was unseemly and unwise here in enemy territory. He could only hope others at the table hadn't noticed him staring at her like a desperate youth mooning over a buxom milkmaid.

"I say, Atherbourne, p'rhaps we should bring these festivities to a close. You're looking rather eager to move on to a more private celebration, what?" The slurred voice of Colin Lacey, overloud and followed by a drunken snicker, arrived from directly across the table. "Or, here's a thought. Why not just take her out on the terrace? Seemzh you like that sort of thing."

Silence fell hard over the table, broken only by the protest of wind and rain against the dining room windows, as the group wrestled with the discomfort of the inappropriate outburst. Seated on Lacey's left, Lord Berne, a distinguished-looking man of roughly fifty years with thinning pewter hair and a jovial demeanor, coughed into his napkin. To Lacey's right, the earl's second oldest daughter, a plump, painfully shy girl with dull brown hair, a round pug nose, and large eyes now wide behind her spectacles, sat with her mouth agape.

The man between them took no notice of the tumult he had caused, grinning blearily at Lucien and chuckling. His pale blond hair, a shade lighter than his sister's, was cut a bit long on top, where it curled in charming disarray. His features were finely drawn and boyishly handsome, bordering on feminine, but years of dissolution had made his blue eyes dull, his skin pale, and his expression distastefully cynical.

"Colin," Blackmore rebuked frostily from the foot of the table. "That is quite enough."

His eyes resting briefly on his bride's wild flush, Lucien felt irritation itch along his spine. *Bloody whelp.* It was one thing for Lacey to make an ass of himself, or even to try to embarrass Lucien. It was another to humiliate his sister on her wedding day.

"For once, your grace, you and I agree," Lucien remarked with a cold smile. "That is, indeed, quite enough."

With that, he rose from the table and strode to Victoria's side, shocking the others into quiet gasps, then silence. His bride refused to look at him, her hands tightly folded in her lap, her shoulders stiff and head bowed. He held out his hand before her.

"Shall we take our leave, my dear?" he asked quietly, knowing she would have little choice but to comply without seeming churlish.

"But, my lord," Lady Berne protested, "we haven't yet had cake! Certainly you will want your bride to taste her own wedding cake before—"

"You must forgive me, my lady," he interrupted, glancing around the table and meeting the eyes of those who, he knew, fervently wished him to Hades. "The morning has grown ... cold. I wouldn't want my bride to take a chill."

A crack of thunder chose that moment to sound outside. He felt a delicate hand slip into his own and turned to help Victoria to her feet. She paused briefly and met his gaze with a solemn one of her own, then turned to the guests as the gentlemen rose from their seats.

Her voice tight and quiet, she said, "I thank you all for coming today. Lord Atherbourne and I shall take our leave now, but please stay and enjoy the breakfast and cake. It has been my privilege to have you here to help us celebrate our"—she stopped and cleared her throat delicately—"marriage."

Colin, listing to one side as he struggled to remain on his feet, squawked a protest and said, "Aw, Tori, come now. I bloody well know Harrison's got the sense of humor of a mossy boulder, but I didn't think you'd take offense. It was all in good fun."

Victoria's hand tightened where it rested in Lucien's, and her quiet dignity seemed to tremble like a leaf in a storm. *Good God. Is she going to weep?* The thought sent a surge of anger through him. And perhaps a small dose of panic.

"Colin, please," she said, her voice rippling with restrained emotion. "Don't."

That was it. While Lucien's hatred for the duke ran bone-deep, he now had good reason to dislike both of Victoria's brothers. If he could find a way to shut Lacey's mouth with his fist, and do so without making everything worse, he would leap across the table without a moment's hesitation.

Instead, he urged Victoria forward, eager to spirit her away with all speed. At the dining room entrance, he turned back to the guests and bowed mockingly. "Your grace. My lords. Ladies. It has been a pleasure, as always."

Minutes later, the ever-efficient servants of Clyde-Lacey House had wrapped their mistress in a hooded cape of silver velvet and ensured his carriage was brought round to the front. Holding an umbrella above both of them, Lucien lightly curled his arm around Victoria's small waist and led her through the downpour into the plush confines of his coach. Immediately settling onto the bench seat, she smoothed her skirts and turned her head to stare out the opposite window.

He handed the umbrella to his footman and climbed in beside her, making sure his shoulder brushed hers, his thigh mere inches away. She was a graceful thing, her movements efficient and smooth. If he had not been watching her closely, he would not have perceived her nervousness. But he had been watching. Wanting. Since the moment he arrived and saw her in her wedding gown.

"You have not asked where we are going. Aren't you curious about your new home?" In point of fact, she had not said much of anything to him that morning. A brief, polite greeting, then her vows. Little else.

Reacting to his voice, her head turned slightly in his direction. Her hood hid all but a hint of her profile from him. He could see the slope of her dainty nose, the curve of her full lips. "Does it matter? We shall be there soon enough."

A frown tugged at his brows. He disliked her listless tone, her muted light. The Victoria he had encountered on the Gattingford terrace and again the day he had proposed did not hesitate to meet his eyes, to engage him in a lively debate, to interrogate him or castigate him or bloody well tempt him beyond all reason. The more he thought on it, the more he hated whatever had caused her to go quiet and resigned. "Wait until you see the dungeon," he whispered next to her ear.

His blatant provocation worked. Instantly, her head swiveled to face him, her eyes wide and shocked. He laughed and winked. She blushed. "Is there a moat as well, my lord?"

As parries went, it was reasonably tart and clever. But he had not finished teasing the real Victoria out of her shell. "If the rain keeps on like this," he said, gesturing to the unending sheet of water beyond the window, "then I daresay it grows more likely by the minute." That drew a small smile. He felt inexplicable satisfaction at the sight.

Just then, the coach took a sharp turn, causing Victoria to sway toward him. Her gloved hand reached out instinctively to brace itself.

On his thigh.

He nearly groaned aloud. Dear God, this was torturous. He glanced down past the top of her hood to where her bosom would have been visible if not for that infernal velvet shroud.

"... apologies, my lord." She sounded flustered. Good. So was he.

Her hand disappeared as she struggled to scoot away, but his arm about her waist locked her to his side. "Worry not, sweet. Life is filled with unexpected turns. It is a husband's privilege to serve as ballast." He wasn't entirely sure what he had just said.

Blood was pounding through his body louder than a great, towering drum played by a mythical giant. It was most distracting.

She wriggled against him, gaining nearly half an inch of space, but also managing to forge the iron inside his trousers into steel. This time, he did groan aloud. She stilled. "Are you ailing, my lord?" He breathed through the ache. Perhaps additional space was best. Loosening his arm, he allowed their bodies to separate and moved a small distance away. Giving her a strained smile, he joked, "If you're hoping for imminent widowhood, I fear you will be disappointed. Mine is a highly ... robust constitution."

She blinked up at him, a tiny frown above the bridge of her nose. "I do not wish for your death."

"Well," he said, unable to keep the laughter out of his voice. "That is a relief."

At last catching on to his teasing, she dropped her eyes, biting her lower lip as a grin emerged. "Perhaps I should."

"Nonsense. Trust your instincts, I always say. Murdering one's spouse is a messy business. Could tie up the estate for years." She giggled, the sound light and sweet. It was the first time he had heard her laugh, he realized. Now that he had, he wanted more. "Much better to spend a decade or two forcing me to pay exorbitant sums to the modiste and milliner."

Laughing harder, she shook her head and gave him a mischievous look from beneath her lashes. "Sound advice, my lord. But you should be far more concerned about my canvas supplier and colorist."

"Enjoy painting that much, do you?" He already knew it was true. Blackmore's former servants had been both chatty and eager to share their affectionate observations about their mistress. It had made his task easier, to say the least. But she didn't need to know that.

She sighed and relaxed further into the seat, leaning toward him. "It is wondrous. One of my favorite things, actually."

The heat he had felt burning through him earlier had eased, and now became a gentle, glowing warmth emanating from his midsection. It was almost ... comforting. "You shall require a studio, then."

Suddenly looking a bit shy, as though he were a stranger offering her a confectionary treat, she demurred, "Oh, I couldn't possibly ask ..."

"You didn't. I offered. Besides, Wyatt House is not lacking for rooms, as you will soon see. Take whichever one strikes your fancy." She eyed him for a long moment as though weighing his sincerity. He leaned forward to bring his face level with hers. "You want a studio, don't you?"

"Yes," she murmured, glancing at his mouth. "I do. Want ..."

He waited, watching her eyes dilate, her breathing quicken. "A place to paint," he finished for her.

She nodded, appearing a bit off balance, then gathered her composure. "I shall—" She cleared her throat. "I shall survey the house and give you a list of possibilities."

"No need. As I said, you may have any room you like."

"It is a most generous offer, my lord. Thank you."

He waved dismissively. "Wyatt House will be your home. You are my wife now, after all."

"Yes." Her voice grew quiet, and she turned to stare out at the buildings of Oxford Street. She looked forlorn. Lost. "I am your wife now."

Chapter Eight

"An excellent servant is always present, yet rarely seen or heard. Much like a specter who happens to enjoy cleaning."

—THE DOWAGER MARCHIONESS OF WALLINGHAM to her butler.

ENTERING LUCIEN'S BRICK TOWN HOUSE IN PORTMAN SQUARE a half-hour after leaving Clyde-Lacey House, Victoria marveled that one's life could change so radically within a matter of weeks that it was nigh impossible to remember oneself from *before*. Before the mistake. Before the scandal. Before the transformation from duke's sister to marquess's fiancée to viscount's wife.

Glancing down at her left hand, where a filigreed band of gold nestled a flower-shaped cluster of diamonds and aquamarine stones, her belly flipped and clenched with a peculiar pain. She was his wife. He was—she swallowed hard— her husband. He now had certain ... rights.

Breathing deeply and reaching for calm, she instead focused on her surroundings. The entrance hall alone was opulently beautiful, with sky-blue walls, a pale gray marble floor, and a stunningly grand, curved double staircase rising in the center like two great arms reaching out in an embrace. She was struck by how much light filled the space, despite the gloom of the storm outside. Drawn forward to solve the mystery, she gaped four floors up at a magnificent glass dome ceiling.

"Simply incredible," she murmured.

Truly, she'd had no idea Atherbourne's pockets were so deep. His town residence was one of the largest houses—a mansion, really—in a quietly elegant square filled with narrow townhouses. Located in the district of Marylebone, just north of Mayfair, it was an address slightly less fashionable, though no less luxurious, than Clyde-Lacey House.

"Seems a trifle ostentatious, does it not?" Lucien's smooth voice observed wryly mere inches behind her.

She jerked in surprise and spun to face him. "No!" she squeaked. Good heavens, her voice was high and a bit loud. Cringing, she tried again. "I—I mean, no, my lord. Actually, I find it quite beautiful. You have a lovely home."

The familiar half-grin curved his wicked mouth, and light flashed in his dark eyes. Dressed in a formal black coat with a silver silk waistcoat and charcoal trousers, Lucien resembled the dark angel she had previously labeled him. The stark white cravat merely emphasized it. Gracious, he was a handsome man. And with him standing so close, she was having trouble keeping her thoughts together.

"It's your home as well, now, my dear. So perhaps you should say, '*We* have a lovely home.'"

Unsettled by the notion, she turned to stare at a set of closed double doors just off the foyer. The parlor or morning room, perhaps? "Yes, well. I suppose that is true. Though it hardly feels that way."

The butler, a stooped, wizened man of terribly advanced years who shuffled slowly and spoke loudly, returned to announce, "My lord, the servants are ready to be presented to Lady Atherbourne. They are in the dining room."

Lucien winced as the man's overloud voice echoed in the open space. "Very good, Billings."

Billings, who had taken their gloves and her cloak when they first arrived, nodded his snowy-white head and shuffled toward the second set of doors off the entrance hall.

"Shall we, Lady Atherbourne?" Lucien presented her with his arm, and together they entered a sumptuous room dominated by an enormously long mahogany table, which was flanked on either side by a dizzying number of chairs—easily two dozen in all. The vermilion damask on the walls was relieved by the soft white of the wainscoting and ornate moldings. A white marble fireplace along the wall opposite the entrance was topped by a lovely green landscape. The painting was English, but with the soft, dreamy quality of the French style. A Turner, she thought.

In front of the tall bank of windows at one end of the room stood a long line of servants. Billings and a sturdy, ruddy-faced woman who must be the housekeeper, judging from her dress, stood nearest the entrance. Billings cleared his throat. "My lady," he croaked. "May I present to you the housekeeper, Mrs. Garner."

The woman beamed warmly, revealing a wide gap between her two front teeth, and dipped a curtsy, her ring of keys jangling against her waist. "Welcome to Wyatt House, my lady. Whatever ye need, don't hesitate to call on Mrs. Garner. We're all jes' over the moon about Lord Atherbourne gettin' himself married up proper. Why, jes' the other day, I was sayin' to Cook, ye won't find a happier housekeeper in London than Mrs. Garner, I says."

Momentarily flummoxed by the effusive greeting, after a few seconds, Victoria answered with a quiet but sincere, "Thank you for your kind welcome, Mrs. Garner." To which the housekeeper responded like an excited pup, her smile growing wider and her keys once again clinking as she curtsied several more times.

The responses of the remaining staff, though less loquacious, were equally warm and courteous. Rattled by memories of the disastrous wedding breakfast, as well as the stresses of moving into a new home and—oh, *dear heaven*—thoughts of the night to come, Victoria knew she was unlikely to recall many of the staff's names. Certainly, she would remember Mrs. Garner—the woman repeated her own name enough times to assure that. Perhaps she would ask the housekeeper to make a list of the servants and their roles in the household, she thought absently.

Simply coping with the devil's own scandal and arranging a rushed wedding had occupied all of Victoria's attention of late, so she'd had little time to consider the task now before her: Becoming the Viscountess Atherbourne meant fully managing the households of her husband's various properties. While she knew herself to be more than capable, having done the same for the Blackmore properties since her mother's death, it was bound to take time and effort before she felt like the mistress, rather than a stranger, in her new home.

As the last of the footmen bowed and acknowledged Victoria with a final "my lady," she felt the large, strong hand of her husband take her elbow.

Not one but *several* tingles emanated from where his palm gently cupped her arm, causing her to shiver. How silly that she had once wished for such a thing. To be so affected by a casual touch was most disconcerting, especially considering a layer of fabric separated his skin from hers.

As though hearing her thoughts and wanting to tease her, Lucien leaned close to her ear, his clean, spicy scent surrounding her, and murmured, "Dismiss them, and I shall show you to our chambers."

Her stomach swooped and curled like a bird on a sudden gust of wind. She felt her skin heat with a wretched flush and her mouth grow dry. "But it is barely past noon, my lord," she whispered, refusing to look at either him or the servants.

He was silent for several seconds, his head remaining bent intimately close to hers. She could almost feel him willing her to do as he had demanded. Then his fingers flexed slightly where they held her arm. He straightened to his full imposing height, but did not release her.

"Billings!" he boomed loudly, causing Victoria to jerk and glare up at him. *Really,* she thought. Presumably, he raised his voice so the ancient butler could hear him across the long expanse of the room, but the least he could do was warn her.

"Yes, my lord?"

"Were Lady Atherbourne's belongings delivered this morning?"

"Yes, my lord. All of the trunks were unloaded, and her ladyship's effects have been unpacked and placed in her chambers."

Lucien turned his commanding gaze on the housekeeper. "Mrs. Garner, Lady Atherbourne and I will take luncheon and dinner in our rooms. You may leave the trays outside the door. We are not to be disturbed until morning, is that understood?"

Victoria's eyes whipped back and forth between Mrs. Garner's raised brows and Lucien's hard-edged profile. Surely he did not just say what she thought he said. He could not have simply ... *announced* such a thing.

"In fact," he continued, "deliver a bath to our chamber no earlier than ten tomorrow morning, and delay breakfast until half past."

She felt embarrassment wash over her, buzzing like angry bees in her ears and rushing through her veins, both hot and cold at the same time. Several gasps and what was clearly a smothered giggle could be heard from the line of maids and footmen.

How dare he shame her like this? In front of the entire staff, no less. Did he think the servants would believe they were *playing chess* until half past tomorrow morning? Of course not.

The implication was obvious, and their reactions suggested they had received the message. It was impossible to miss. He had bloody well *shouted* it across the room.

After Colin's drunken display that morning, it was positively the last straw. She wanted to hit him right in his ridiculously handsome face.

"Ah—Aye, my lord," Mrs. Garner replied.

He nodded briskly. "Excellent. You all may resume your usual duties."

The entire line bobbed and bowed before exiting. The moment the last of them left the room, Victoria jerked her arm from Lucien's grasp. In a low, fierce voice, she hissed, "You, my lord, are despicable."

He turned toward her slowly, even nonchalantly, and arched one brow. "But you knew that already, my sweet."

"I have never been treated so in all my life—"

"Yes, and what a long life it has been. Twenty years, is it? Give yourself time, darling."

"—and I will not be shamed in such a way again. Especially before servants. Dear heavens, have you any idea how quickly the gossip will spread—"

"Had it been up to you, our wedding night might have waited until Michaelmas—"

"I am trying to *repair* the damage the scandal has done, not set a new fire ablaze with servants bandying it about that their mistress abides being treated as little more than a common tr—"

Her tirade ended abruptly in a yelp as, without warning, Lucien stooped, slid his arms beneath her thighs and back, and scooped her up as easily as he would a sack of flour. The motion was so smooth and seamless, before her mind could process what had happened, her face was a dizzying two inches from his, her arms clasped tightly about his strong, muscular neck as he strode from the dining room back into the entrance hall.

"Lucien!" she squawked when she could breathe again. "What in heaven's name ...?"

She hadn't been carried since she was a child. It was the oddest sensation of lightness and vulnerability, which grew worse as he began to climb the stairs.

"As I was saying," he stated casually, "now that we've dismissed the servants, I will show you to our chambers."

"This is outrageous. Put me down at once."

"No."

Vexed beyond all good sense, she slapped his shoulder, likely hurting only her hand. "You cannot simply refuse to release me."

"I believe I just did."

"I shall scream."

He grinned sardonically and continued down a long corridor. "But my dear, what *will* the servants say?"

"You are mad, sir."

Lucien stopped in front of the last door on the left, jostling her a bit as he turned the knob and shouldered his way inside. Momentarily speechless at the grandeur of the chamber, she only dimly registered Lucien gently setting her on her feet. In a country manor, this would be considered a generously sized room; in a London residence, it was positively gargantuan. Spanning nearly half the width of the house, it was quite luxuriously appointed in shades of rich cream and light apple green, delightfully accented with touches of washed crimson in the leaf-patterned draperies and canopied bed coverings. A gilt-framed mirror topped the large fireplace, currently lit with a low fire. The dark mahogany bed dominated the center of the back wall, and a row of tall windows spread like wings of light to each side. Fresh, bright, and elegant, it would have made her envious if this were not now her house, as well.

"Do you like it?" he asked, shockingly close to her ear.

Her heart flipped and pounded with awareness. She nodded, too breathless to speak.

"Let me show you the rest."

And with that, he escorted her through the remainder of the suite—the adjacent dressing room, separate bathing chamber with a long, luxurious tub standing at the ready, and a sitting room that was a mirror image of the bedchamber. Similar in decor and layout to the first room they had entered, the room appeared to have been designed originally as a bedchamber for the mistress of the household, with one glaring omission.

"My lord, is there not another bed?"

Wearing an indefinable, intense expression, he slipped his hand around her elbow and replied, "We have need of only one. More seems a waste, does it not?"

She blinked several times. "But ... well ... yes. I mean, no." As he guided her back into the bedchamber, she let out an exasperated sigh and tried again. "What I mean to say is, it is customary for a lady to have her own chambers, separate from her husband's."

"Mmm. True enough." He moved closer to her, so close she felt the warmth of his body surround her and brush her skin. "But, then, we are not the usual sort of pairing, are we?"

"Aren't we?"

Sliding his arms around her waist and drawing her into his hard chest, his smoke-dark eyes lit with amused sensuality. In a voice low with seduction, he said, "You are the bold, scandalous woman who refused to settle for a conventional marriage to a conventional man."

Resting her hands on his lapels, she felt her skin tingle in a blush and dropped her eyes to the topaz pin gracing his snowy cravat. It flashed a golden wink. "And you, my lord? What are you?"

"The man who saw you, wanted you, and refused to accept that any other might ever possess you."

Her eyes flew back to his, her legs strangely weak, her heart pounding. Could he mean such passionate words? Was it possible he truly—?

"At least," he said with a cynical grin, "that is what society will believe by season's end."

A chill whistled through her and she stiffened against him.

The reminder that this was all merely a game to him was unwelcome, but necessary. Honestly, she must stop believing his nonsense. Such fanciful notions only led to disappointment.

He must have felt her withdrawal and read it as skepticism, because he attempted to reassure her of his strategy. "You may doubt me, my sweet, but believe me when I say the ton loves nothing better than a scandal which becomes a triumphant tale of requited love worthy of Drury Lane. You will see—by the time we are finished, you shall be the envy of those who once dared condemn you."

She narrowed her eyes at him. "I still fail to see what all this has to do with having or not having separate sleeping chambers."

He shrugged. "It has nothing to do with it."

Shaking her head, she blinked in surprise. "Then why ...?"

He simply stared at her for a moment. When he spoke again, his voice was dark and faintly raspy. "You are my wife. We will share one bed so I may have you whenever I desire."

"But, Lucien, I—"

"Victoria."

"Yes?"

"Be quiet so I may kiss you."

She paused, stared at his gorgeous mouth, and sighed, "Oh. Very well then."

Chapter Nine

"Never trust a man whose beauty is greater or fortune less than your own. For some, this will result in distrust of the entire male population. Even so, consider it sound advice."

—THE DOWAGER MARCHIONESS OF WALLINGHAM to Jane and Annabelle Huxley upon news of Beau Brummell's precipitous departure from London to avoid debtor's prison.

HE BEGAN NOT WITH HER LIPS, BUT WITH HER NECK. SLIDING his mouth gently along her skin from just beneath her ear down to her mother's pearl necklace, his hot breath caused shivers to course through her body. He surrounded her, his size and heat and spicy scent making her head spin.

Breathlessly awaiting his next move, her belly tightened and she bit her lower lip. "Lucien?"

"Hmm?"

Her heart leapt as his tongue slid beneath the pearls and his lips nibbled their way to her other ear. She moaned as tingles of pleasure shimmied beneath her skin, tightening her nipples.

"I don't think I can be quiet."

He didn't answer, instead suckling at a bit of flesh where her neck met her shoulder and stroking his hands along her backside, pressing her hips into his hard thighs so that her lower belly cradled the hard ridge there.

"I mean," she continued, reaching for her next breath, his mouth and touch filling her veins with hot, rich wine. "I will *try* not to carry on so that you can enjoy a peaceful interlude, but ... *oh!*" She jerked and shivered in pleasure as his palm cupped her breast and stroked her budded nipple through the fabric of her bodice. "Truly, my lord, when you touch me, I lose the ability to concentrate, and the sounds escape without my permission."

"Victoria."

"Yes?"

"What are you on about?"

She blinked and paused, panting as he plucked pins from her hair. "Oh. Well, Lady Berne was most helpful in offering advice on my wifely duties."

He removed the stems of lily of the valley, dropped them to the floor, and unwound long skeins of golden curls from their perch upon her head. His eyes glittered and burned with what appeared to be fascination. For long moments, he simply stared without blinking.

Really, she thought. *It is just hair.*

"Your wifely duties."

"Mmm. Yes. The countess said I must l-lie with you if I wanted children. And that I must try to keep qu-quiet because husbands tend to prefer it."

He frowned. "Utter nonsense," he muttered.

"My lord?"

His eyes glowed with impatient fire, his mouth firming into a straight line. "I have no idea what Lady Berne told you. It is possible you misunderstood or that she is a bloody simplet—" He stopped, shaking his head. "Suffice it to say I do not prefer silence while I make love to you. Quite the contrary."

At this, the knots in her stomach loosened, and she felt more relaxed than she had at any time in the last two days. She sighed in relief and smiled brilliantly up at him. "Truly? Oh, that is wonderful, Lucien."

He blinked several times, swallowed visibly, and the muscles along his jaw worked as though trying to control a reaction. After a few moments, he stroked a hand along the side of her head, lifted one long curl away from her shoulder and rubbed it sensually between his fingers.

"Should you have questions about your wifely duties, you must come to *me*, do you understand? No one else."

"Of course, I—"

Suddenly, he grasped her shoulders and spun her around to face away from him. Then she felt him brush her hair aside and begin unfastening the buttons at the back of her dress. Given that he was a man, had been a soldier, and came from a noble family, she was a bit shocked at how quickly and deftly he accomplished his task. Truly, he was more adept than her former lady's maid, Delphine, a young, haughty French girl who had left the duke's employ after the scandal broke. Victoria had been forced to make do with two of the upstairs maids at Clyde-Lacey House, a fact that reminded her of the pressing need to find a new lady's maid.

Although, considering Lucien's apparent skills in this area, perhaps it is not so pressing, she thought wryly. Within moments, he had finished with the buttons and unlaced her stays. She clutched the bodice to her chest as it slumped on her body. He then spun her back around to face him.

"Now, then. Your duties are as follows."

He had unfastened his tailcoat and waistcoat, and was

shrugging out of both of them, a raven wing of hair dropping rakishly along his forehead.

"First, you will submit to your husband."

He was so handsome, she was simply lost for several seconds. She longed to trace his mouth with her fingers, brush that black lock from his forehead, and trail her lips along his straight brows where they lowered over glittering eyes. "S-submit?"

"Yes. That means you will let me touch you and kiss you and make love to you whenever I desire."

He swiftly unraveled his cravat from around his neck in a few deft turns and tossed it on the chair where he had thrown his outer garments. He reached up behind his head and pulled his white linen shirt off in a quick motion, adding it to the pile.

Her eyes widened, lips parting on a sigh. His broad, naked chest was ... oh, Lord. So beautiful. A masterful creation of hard, defined muscle, tightened into ridges along a flat belly, and dressed with a black triangle of crisp, curling hair. While clothed, Lucien was a large, imposing figure of a man, his shoulders wider and his arms thicker than most other gentlemen. Nude, he was even more magnificent, the strength and force of his body clearly needing no padding.

As she struggled not to swoon on a tide of longing for those arms to once again embrace her, he continued to lecture in a low rumble. "Second, you will *not* temper your responses whatsoever. When I give you pleasure, I want to hear it. If I cannot make you scream, I am not much of a husband."

Those arms reached toward her, and, thinking he meant to embrace her, she eagerly stepped forward, nearly stumbling. But, instead, he merely grasped her wrists and pulled her hands away from where they clutched her bodice, causing her dress to fall from her breasts and further down her arms. With swift efficiency, he stripped her of her gown, corset, chemise, and petticoat.

She was naked in the suddenly cold room, but for her stockings and garters. He left those in place, his eyes burning her skin from feet to throat, pausing for long moments at the juncture of her thighs and on her flushed, hardened nipples.

In the watery white light shining through the windows, she feared he would notice every flaw. The mole on her hip. The odd dimples on her knees. The extra flesh on her thighs and buttocks that no amount of walking or riding seemed to diminish.

Wondering at his sudden silence, she shifted uncomfortably and tried to cover what she could with her long hair and her hands. His eyes, blazing with a ferocity that sent a tingle of alarm down her spine, shot up to meet hers. Without a word, he grasped her wrists to pull her arms away from her body in a repeat of his earlier action, but this time he pulled her forward until her breasts were crushed against his chest, his arms closing tightly around her bare back. The pleasure of so much heat and pressure and texture against her skin, but especially her breasts, was indescribable.

"Thirdly, do not hide yourself from me," he growled next to her ear, the vibrations rumbling from his chest into hers so she felt it in her bones—indeed, down to her woman's core, which was meltingly hot, pulsing with need. "I like to look upon your body."

Since his head was conveniently bowed beside her own, she turned her cheek to stroke against his, unable to resist feeling the faint rasp of his whiskers and breathing in the scent of what must be his shaving soap. It was crisp and green and spicy, like evergreen and cloves. Curious how his skin would taste, she settled her lips on his neck and darted her tongue out to stroke him softly, briefly.

Just as she suspected. Salt and spice. But there was something more there, just beneath. A dark, dusky undertone that reminded her of his mouth. She could only conclude it was simply the taste of Lucien.

"Angel," he groaned as though in pain. "This isn't going to last very long if you continue ..."

She did it again, this time suckling a bit as he had done to her.

A strong hand grasped the back of her neck, pulling her away so his mouth could meet and invade hers. His tongue slid inside, pulsing in and out, pushing against hers. His arm tightened around her waist and lifted her off her feet. Within seconds, the world tilted as she went from vertical to horizontal in a dizzying rush. The soft linens of the featherbed cushioned her back while the hard weight of her husband crushed her front.

His mouth left hers and immediately fastened upon a ripe, hardened nipple. Digging her heels into the bed and grasping either side of his neck, she moaned, "Lucien! Oh, that is divine."

He suckled strongly, the pressure increasing her sensitivity and centering her existence on that one small bit of flesh. Then his hand squeezed her other breast, stroked the other nipple, and her world split between the two sources of pleasure.

Maneuvering her legs to either side of his hips, she ground her core against his rock-hard staff, still contained within strained trousers.

Oh, yes. That felt nice. Better than nice. Spectacular.

His mouth, now nibbling and gently biting her other nipple, left her for a moment to smile wickedly and say, "So glad you approve, love."

Wait. Had she said that aloud?

His mouth returned to its task, but soon he trailed open, tongue-dancing kisses along her belly, sliding his bulk downward while grasping her waist and forcing her further up along the bed. With nimble fingers, he unfastened her garters and peeled her stockings slowly from her legs, tossing the scraps of silk aside and stroking her inner thighs with a delicate touch. As she lost her grip on his head, she reached for the coverlet on either side of her body, gripping the cloth in an effort to release the tension that coiled inside her.

"Lucien," she panted. "What—what are you ... *doing?*" The last word came out as squeal when a warm finger slid down the slick folds between her splayed thighs, finding the small, powerful nub from which intense, spiraling pleasure emanated. The finger continued downward, slipping into her channel and stroking gently where no one had ever touched her before. Not even Victoria, herself.

"You are so tight, angel. So wet," he grunted, his thumb circling the small nub at the top of her sex, even as his finger slid in and out below in a maddeningly even pace. It was so good, so beautifully satisfying. And, yet, not *enough*. She longed for more, but didn't know how to ask for it. All she could do was moan his name pleadingly over and over.

He kissed the inside of her leg, just above the knee, and muttered, "Yes, now. I was going to ... but damn, Victoria, I can wait no longer."

With that, his marvelously talented hand was removed, and he stood up beside the bed, his face tight and serious, his eyes hooded.

Oh, God. Was he leaving her? "No!" she shouted hoarsely. "Lucien, please, if I've done something wrong—"

"Shh, love," he rasped. "All is well." He sat on the edge of the bed long enough to remove his boots, then stood again to make quick work of his trousers. She got little more than a brief glance at something large, darkly flushed, and extending rather alarmingly upward from his body before he came over her again, and all that marvelous weight and pressure and heat surrounded her.

His mouth returned to hers a passionate marauder, crushing her lips and thrusting his tongue inside. She wrapped her arms tightly around his neck, rubbed her breasts eagerly against his chest, and gleefully welcomed his return.

He groaned, moving a hand to her breast, then down to clasp her leg and pull it wider to accommodate his hips. She could feel the hot, smooth skin of his strange, hard appendage sliding through the folds of her sex. Panic flared briefly as she considered that he might be intending to do with *that* what he had done with his finger earlier.

No. Surely not. It would never fit.

He pulled his mouth away, panting like a bellows. Giving her nipple one last stroke, and using that arm to prop himself up on one elbow above her, he grasped himself in the other hand and placed the hot, blunt, rounded tip at her entrance.

"Lucien?"

His face flushed, eyes glazed with lust, he pressed forward.

At first, it was simply strange—a too-large object stretching her flesh, trying to burrow inside her. While his finger had felt good, had even satisfied her infernal restlessness to some degree, this soon became uncomfortable. Then, as he pressed further, rather burningly painful.

She moaned and squirmed, panicky at the invasion. Her hands pressed against his shoulders instinctively, trying to push him off.

"Calm yourself, Victoria. We just have to get through this first ... bit." His words were strained, gritted out in a way that made her think this might be just as uncomfortable for him as it was for her. "Then it will be good. I promise."

She paused, concern seeping into her mind as she considered the shimmering tension in his muscles, in his face. He appeared to be in the grips of significant agony. Reaching up to stroke his cheek, she asked softly, "Are you all right?"

Eyes flaring, he stared at her incredulously. "Me? I should be asking you that."

She winced as he continued to prod her. "Oh. Well, it's just that you look so strained, and I thought it might be painful for you, as well."

He dropped his head and shook with surprised laughter. "No. Not in the way you mean." He repositioned himself so one hand could stroke her gently, rhythmically just above where they were joined. "I want to be all the way inside you so badly, it is killing me. But if I move too quickly, I might hurt you more than necessary."

She huffed and wriggled against the bed. "It hurts a lot, husband. How much would you consider 'necessary'?"

He was silent for a moment, then answered, "We haven't yet breached your maidenhead. It will be painful for a time, then it will get better."

That was all the warning she had before he thrust forward and the aching pressure and burning stretch was joined by the sharp, knifing pain of something tearing inside her. She screamed and arched against him, but he would not let up, pressing forward, inch by long inch, sinking deep inside her.

"There," he gasped. "It's done. Now for the good part."

She sobbed out a laugh at the absurd statement and slapped his shoulder in outrage. "It *hurts*, Lucien."

"I know, love," he whispered. He brushed his mouth gently above her ear, then tenderly across her lips. "Bear with me."

Then he began to move, slowly at first. When he started the steady, patient thrusting, she simply endured. The pain was not quite as bad as it had been when he first breached her, but he was so large, the pressure on her internal muscles and the flesh at her opening was a fiery ache that made the earlier pleasure seem like a fanciful fever dream.

Soon, however, as he nibbled her neck and his thumb stroked in tiny circles around that secret little nubbin, her passage grew slick with new arousal, smoothing his way as he stroked in and out.

In and out.

In and out.

Her nipples, hard again and eager to be stroked, were sweetly pleasured as well, since his chest with its crisp hair chafed them with every thrust of his hips. She kissed his neck and moaned as he quickened his motions. Before long, the pace was rather bruising, his hips slamming against hers as the coiling tension rose inside her. Her body paradoxically loved every bit of it—the burning friction, the slap of his flesh against hers, the grip of his hands, one beneath her neck and the other at her hip as he held her at his mercy.

When the pleasure transformed from a tightening spiral into

a giant, rapidly filling bubble, she dug her heels into Lucien's buttocks and her nails into his back, sobbing, "Please, Lucien. Oh, please. I can't take it."

It seemed to spur him to a lustful frenzy, a deep growl emanating from his chest. "You will. Take all of me. Now." He thrust his manhood even deeper inside her, all the way to the root, tightening his grip on her neck and hip so she couldn't possibly resist.

Her body responded to his ferocity by bursting into flames. She screamed his name as the starburst of unbelievable pleasure exploded, seizing her muscles and rippling over her skin in wave after wave of ecstatic shivers. Her woman's core seized around him in a fierce grip, spasming and milking him where he continued the deep, unrelenting thrusts.

Within four strokes, he gave a loud shout of "Christ. Victoria!" before every muscle in his body grew stone-hard, and she felt a gush of warmth surge deep inside, filling her as he groaned in climactic pleasure.

Minutes later, as he lay atop her, his manhood still inside her, now softer, and yet not entirely soft, his lips played with hers, and one of his hands stroked her hair gently, almost soothingly. Limp with lethargic bliss, she felt like a cat who had just eaten a bowl full of cream and lazed in a patch of warm sunlight. But her husband did not want to let her nap.

"Lucien?" she murmured.

"Hmm?"

"Aren't we finished yet?"

He smiled against her mouth and grew harder, larger inside her. "Oh, no, my angel," he said, shaking his head in a gently chiding way as her eyes widened and she gasped. "We're just getting started."

Chapter Ten

*"If you value either your position or your life,
pray do not speak to me before breakfast."*

—THE DOWAGER MARCHIONESS OF WALLINGHAM to her
newest lady's maid, the fifth in as many months.

THE DISTINCT SCENT OF KIPPERS WAFTING FROM THE
sideboard mere feet from where he sat alone in the morning
room was perhaps the only sour note in an otherwise glorious
day. Even the mild fishy odor was not enough to dampen his
appetite.

For food or anything else.

Lucien grinned at the thought, recalling his inexhaustible ardor
of the previous day. And evening. And throughout the night.

But, really, what red-blooded male could blame him? Victoria was ... He paused to consider, taking a sip of coffee and popping a warm piece of buttered roll into his mouth.

Extraordinary. Yes, that was it. She was an innocent in many ways, starting with her virginity, or rather, former virginity. But it was more than that. The way she had admired his house upon arriving, her wide-eyed appreciation of elements he took for granted—a splendid staircase or a painting that, for him, had long since become background—demonstrated how she viewed her surroundings with fresh eyes, unjaded by her wealth and privileged upbringing. She loved and honored beauty in all its forms, but with, it seemed to him, a pure heart rather than avarice.

Her public behavior, notwithstanding her vulnerability to his sexual advances, was beyond reproach. She treated him with far more graciousness than he deserved, was kind and courteous to servants, and within society comported herself with exemplary decorum.

On the other hand—and he fervently thanked the Maker for this—she was also an enchantingly sensual, passionate creature, her body lush and highly responsive, her need to touch and be touched obvious in her reactions to him.

The memory of those reactions slithered like a curl of intoxicating vapor from his head directly down to his cock, stirring him to a hardness baffling in its intensity, given the activities of the previous twenty hours and the fact that Victoria was not presently in the room. Honestly, his body's obsessive preoccupation with bedding her was a trifle concerning. He had never reacted so to another woman. And there had been many other women.

Gregory had long teased him about his "supernatural luck" when it came to attracting the fairer sex. In truth, gaining access to a wide variety of females had always been easy. When he was young, country maids in the village near Thornbridge had sighed over his face and form, readily encouraging his randy proclivities. Later, as a member of the cavalry, women swooned over the uniform and flocked around his regiment from Spain to Brussels and back to England.

He *liked* women, loved sex, and since the age of fourteen, had made a grand effort to be exceptionally skilled at wooing the first and performing the second. However, this did not explain his ever-present need for Victoria. Even for him, it was just this side of unseemly to be so fixated on one female.

Especially his wife.

"My lord, is something amiss?" Billings bellowed as he entered the room with a fresh pot of tea.

Lucien winced and cleared his throat. "Why do you ask, Billings?" he inquired, his voice raised to reach the man's mostly deaf ears.

"You appear most displeased with the marmalade. Shall I remove it for you, my lord?"

Confused, and thinking perhaps the ancient butler had finally achieved full senility, Lucien glanced around to determine what the deuce the man was talking about. When he spotted the silver dish of marmalade directly in front of him, he realized he'd been scowling at it while pondering his lust for Victoria.

"No, the marmalade is fine. Perhaps you might remove the kippers, however. When did we begin serving those vile things, anyway?"

"Cook wondered if perhaps Lady Atherbourne might care for them, my lord. I believe she wished to give her ladyship the opportunity to partake."

"Well, I cannot abide them. Take the dish away, if you please."

Billings nodded and moved to do so, but his "Very well, my lord" was interrupted by the arrival of Victoria, who paused in the doorway to get her bearings. Lucien immediately rose to his feet.

Standing, as she was, in a shaft of light from the windows, she fairly glowed in her white morning gown. The softly curling hair that had given him such fierce pleasure when wrapped around her body like so much silk, was once again coiled high on the back of her dainty head. It shone like a halo.

Having obviously not heard her entrance, Billings turned while holding the dish of kippers and let out a loud, startled, "My lady!" Quickly regaining his composure, the butler bowed deeply and croaked, "Good morning, Lady Atherbourne. I do hope you find breakfast to your liking."

Victoria beamed at the white-haired Billings as though he were a handsome beau delivering a bouquet, rather than an aged butler bearing a platter of dead fish. "Good morning to you as well, Billings," she said brightly, her voice elevated so he could hear her, but not so loud as to be shouting. "It looks positively lovely. I am certain I will adore it."

The old man blinked several times as though dazzled by her brilliance, then the wrinkles in his face formed what appeared to be an answering smile. He nodded and shuffled out of the room.

She turned her smile on Lucien, and he felt a bit dazzled, himself. She curtsied prettily and greeted him with a twinkle. "My lord husband. 'Tis a fine morning, is it not?"

It took him several seconds to answer, and when he did, his voice was gruff, even to his own ear. "Wife," he greeted her simply. In truth, the single word was all he could manage.

When had he decided she wasn't beautiful, precisely? It had been the conclusion of a fool.

He eyed her backside as she bent slightly over the sideboard while filling her plate. It was softly, generously rounded, her hips a luscious curve flaring out from a trim waist.

A bloody blind, addlepated fool.

"I was not aware you didn't care for kippers, my lord," she said, turning around and seating herself at the table.

As her bottom came to rest on the seat, she winced and her shoulders tightened in discomfort before she relaxed, her face again smoothing into pleasant serenity. It was but a brief flinch, her reactions subtle. Most people would never have noticed.

But, then, he was watching her quite closely. Much as a cat's gaze follows a plump, juicy mouse. The feelings that flooded him in that moment were so inappropriate, so powerfully dark, he reeled under the weight of them. He sat and tore his eyes away from her by force of will.

She was sore. It was obvious to him. He should feel guilt. Husbandly concern.

He did not.

Instead, what he felt was a deep, thrumming possessiveness. *She is mine*, his body insisted. *I must have her again.* This was not mere lust—that old, familiar friend. Lust was pleasurable, even playful. An itch that was rollicking good fun to scratch. *This* was something else altogether.

"Husband?" the object of his thoughts queried.

"Yes," he said, his voice rasping past a suddenly constricted throat.

"Is it fish you don't like? Or kippers in particular?"

He cleared his throat. "Fish."

"Not even cod or haddock? There are some delicious preparations for both that the cook at Clyde-Lacey House is fond of making. He is French, you know. They are so delicate, they don't even taste like fish—"

"Victoria," he snapped chillingly. "If I want to eat something that does not taste like fish, I have only to eat that which is not, in fact, fish. Wouldn't you say?"

All traces of her earlier smile were gone, as though a cloud had covered the sun. She swallowed hard and dropped her eyes to her plate. "Oh. Well, yes, I suppose that is true."

A cold shaft of remorse knifed through him. *I am a wretched husband*, was all he could think. First, he lured her into a ruinous scandal, then virtually forced her into marriage. As if that were not enough, on their wedding night, he showed his virginal bride all the patience and restraint of Viking marauders upon an unguarded monastery.

Adding insult to injury was perhaps not an ideal way to

begin their first morning together.

"I was sick on it," he said in a milder tone. "As a child. I haven't been able to stomach it ever since. Even the smell is offensive to me."

The vivid blue-green of her eyes rose and held his for several seconds before a small, gentle smile lifted the corners of her mouth. She nodded understandingly. "My brother Colin had a similar experience with cherries. Although, I must say, a bit too much brandy may have had something to do with it."

He grinned at her and chuckled.

Her lashes lowered as she took a delicate bite of ham. Her plump lips slid over the tines of the fork, and his smile faded. As she sipped her tea, a sheen of liquid remained behind on those lips. They were lush. Inviting. Wet.

Good God, this was like a sickness. Did other men feel such ... absorption with their wives? Such barbaric impulses? He had never heard of such a thing. Now and then, there would be talk of some poor chap becoming excessively attached to a mistress, but never a wife.

"My lord, I was thinking that since we did not have a terribly ..." She paused to search for the right word. "... *conventional* courtship, we may need to do some catching up, as it were."

"How do you mean?"

She poked at a baked egg as though testing its texture. "For example, I now know you do not care for fish. But what would you say is the dish you like best?"

"Trifle. Simply delicious." He raised a brow. "Anything else you're curious about?"

She swallowed a bite, seemingly surprised by his willingness to answer.

Damn, he should not have snapped at her earlier. It set a bad precedent, made her hesitant when he wanted her receptive. Eager.

"Do you have a house in the country?" she asked tentatively.

"Of course. Several, in fact. Thornbridge Park is the primary estate. It's in Derbyshire."

"Is that where you grew up?"

He nodded, taking a sip of coffee. "You'll quite like it, I think." For several minutes, he described the estate, with its graceful green hills, surrounding patches of woodlands, the brook winding through the center of the property, and Thornbridge Hall, which had been rebuilt and expanded by his grandfather forty years earlier.

Her eyes took on a dreamy quality, and she sighed. "It sounds ... oh, just lovely, Lucien. I cannot wait to see it."

There she was—the glowing angel from earlier this morning. Her face was once again luminous with happiness. And Victoria's happiness was pure aphrodisiac to Lucien: intoxicating, arousing, and addictive. He pictured all the ways he could cause her to remain in such a state for extended periods of time. Most of them involved his tongue.

She shifted and another flash of discomfort briefly shadowed her brow.

An idea, wicked and delicious, formed in his mind. A way to make her very happy and perhaps a bit more comfortable. If he could control himself, that was.

Of course I can, he scoffed. *I am no longer an adolescent youth, at the mercy of every prurient impulse. I will simply indulge in a little play, but stop before it goes too far.*

"My lord, my lady. I trust everything is satisfactory?" Billings bellowed, abruptly intruding on Lucien's thoughts.

"Oh, yes, indeed," Victoria replied. "Please tell Cook breakfast was delightful. I am particularly fond of the rolls."

"Pardon me, my lady. I do believe those are irises."

She appeared puzzled, glancing around in confusion. Upon spying the silver vase of flowers on the sideboard, her brow cleared. "Yes, you are right, of course. How silly of me."

"Billings," Lucien shouted.

"Yes, my lord?"

"You may leave us now. Please close the doors on your way out. And make sure we are not disturbed."

"Yes, my lord."

As the doors closed behind Billings and the footman who had been assigned to breakfast duty, Lucien eyed his wife across the expanse of the table. The distance was a mere six feet, so he could easily watch as Victoria's eyes darted to the doors and back to him.

"Lucien. Was that strictly necess—"

"Come here, Victoria."

Her eyes widened and her lips remained open in a small "O." She did not move, however.

"Victoria, you are my wife, are you not?"

"Well, yes, I—"

"And did you not just yesterday promise to obey me?"

"Oh. Um. About that, I suppose it is true in the strictest sense—"

His stare turned predatory. "Then, when I say 'come here,' I expect you will do so."

She narrowed her eyes at him, her lips tightening. Finally, she huffed out a "very well." Tossing her napkin on her plate, she rose to her feet and flounced over to stand before him. He turned his chair to the side so his knees brushed against her skirt.

"May I ask why you so urgently require my proximity, my lord?"

"Certainly," he said softly, his hands now circling her waist and tugging her between his legs. He grinned wickedly. "But it is better if I show you."

He stared at her bosom, rising and falling in an increased rhythm as she sensed what he was about. By God, she had magnificent breasts—round and full and tipped by sweet little rosebud nipples that now poked pleadingly at the white muslin of her bodice.

"Lucien?"

He ran his hands over her buttocks soothingly, calming her as he would a nervous mare.

"I don't think I can ..." she began in a whisper.

"Shh. I know, angel." His hands worked their way beneath her skirts. One trailed up between her legs to stroke her inner thigh while the other gently massaged the taut muscles of her backside. Using his middle finger to brush her damp curls, he then explored further to find her soft folds already slick with desire. His thumb found and delicately circled her swollen clitoris. When his exploring finger stroked her tight opening, she jumped and tried to pull away.

"No, love. Stay with me. You are sore here, are you not?"

Her eyes tightly shut and a fierce frown on her face, she bit her lower lip and nodded emphatically.

"And do you know why?"

She hesitated before nodding again, this time less assuredly.

"It is because I was deep inside you so many times I lost count, stretching this secret place over and over. I could not help myself, Victoria. I could not stop."

He had intended the words as seduction, but they were nothing more than the raw, unvarnished truth. The effect they had on her was instant and galvanizing. She squirmed against his thumb, grasped at his shoulders and leaned into him, whimpering in desire.

"Now, what is a husband to do after he has been such a brute?" he rasped, nuzzling her breast with his cheek. "It is his duty to soothe his bride, to ease her."

Leaving his hand in its warm nest between her thighs, he removed the other from beneath her skirts to push all the dishes from his side of the table. The clinking and rattling of china, crystal, and silver being shoved aside startled open her glorious, sea-blue eyes. He wrapped his arm about her waist and lifted her bottom onto the edge of the table, pressing her to lie back.

She panted and looked at him uncertainly but did not resist.

He quickly slid her skirts over her knees and up her thighs to rest above her waist, then grasped her legs and spread them wide, falling to his knees to worship at her altar. And the masterpiece that was her feminine core deserved to receive his tribute, he thought. Golden curls served more as a frame than a mask for dark pink folds, ripe and juicy-sweet. At the center, her hard little bud, swollen and straining after the dance of his thumb, begged to be caressed.

He lightly ran two fingers from her clitoris to where she parted at the entrance of her channel, flushed an angry red and weeping for him. Barely pausing to spread her lips for his kiss, he stroked his tongue over that hard little bud, and immediately trailed down to where she was so tender, repeating the journey several times.

She moaned his name and clutched at his hair, writhing against the hard surface of the table. Lapping at her delicately, he bathed and soothed her with his tongue, letting his fingers lightly squeeze and tug at her sweet bud. As a reward for his efforts, he inhaled her scent—wildflowers and a storm at sea— and consumed her honeyed nectar until he was drunk on it. The finest ambrosia, it was.

As he felt her climax draw closer, he thrust his tongue deep inside the tightly clenching little mouth, giving her needy sheath what it demanded—a firm presence to cling to. She exploded and rippled around his tongue, arching up against his mouth and hands while yanking at his hair.

And she screamed. She screamed *his* name. No one else's.

No other man would ever see her like this, eyes hooded, expression dreamy and replete, skin misted and blushing. No other would ever taste her the way he had. The way he could whenever he desired. Which would be often.

It was almost as good as coming himself.

Suddenly, the ragingly hard cock he had managed to ignore while tending to Victoria decided to make its demands known. Vociferously.

He groaned as he rose between her legs, bracing his fists next to her hips and dropping his head as he leaned over her. Teeth clenched against the need to take her fully, he drew shuddering breaths and tried to think of terribly *un*arousing things. Like the Prime Minister. Or coal dust. Anything, for the love of God.

A small, gentle hand stroked his forearm. "Lucien, you can ... I mean, I want you to ..."

He laughed humorlessly and shook his head. "No, angel. You are too tender. I must give you a day or two to recuperate."

In a swift, unexpected motion, Victoria shifted and pushed herself up to sit before him, her eyes meeting his, her hands cupping either side of his neck, and her knees straddling his hips.

"But, I *want* you to be fulfilled, as well. It is not enough for me to experience such pleasure alone. You must be with me." She kissed him passionately, tenderly, stroking his cheeks with her thumbs.

Breathing heavily and feeling the blood pulsing in his cock, he wrapped his arms tightly around his wife and let himself savor her kiss, her soft lips, her slick tongue.

She broke away and drew his forehead down to touch hers. "Is there not some way I can do for you what you have done for me?"

He stared into her eyes, telling himself she deserved so much better than someone like him. She deserved to be cosseted and pampered, handled gently and treated with reverence. Not reduced to servicing his uncontrollable lust.

But right then, the darkness beckoned, proving irresistible.

He nodded, swallowed hard, and took her hands in his. "I'll show you," he whispered.

And then he did.

Chapter Eleven

"Just when you begin to think a man worthy of admiration, he suffers a moment of candor, and your misapprehension is corrected at once."

—THE DOWAGER MARCHIONESS OF WALLINGHAM upon overhearing the Prince Regent's marital advice to the Duke of Wellington.

"TRIFLE, MY LADY?" MRS. GARNER EXCLAIMED. "TWICE A WEEK, you say?"

Victoria nodded, still perusing the list of servants the good-natured housekeeper had provided a week ago. A few of them would travel to Thornbridge Park with her and Lucien when the season ended, but she was still debating over the precise number. Since she was not familiar with Lucien's country estate, she could only make an educated guess. Her new lady's maid, Emily, was a delight and would certainly be among them.

She tapped a finger against her lips absently. Oh, bother. Did Thornbridge already have a full contingent of footmen? Perhaps she should leave most of them here.

"Cook is known to say she's better with savory than sweet. Jes' yesterday, she says, 'Mrs. Garner, now, ye knows I'm a mite better with ham than honey cakes.' Tha's true enough, my lady. But if ye wants trifle, twice a week no less, Mrs. Garner will make certain-sure it gets served."

Victoria turned to the housekeeper with a wide smile. "Of course you will, Mrs. Garner. No doubt you can persuade Cook to create trifle that will cause Lady Reedham's new French cook to weep with envy."

The ruddy-faced woman stood taller with each word, her gap-toothed smile beaming with pride. "Consider it done, my lady."

Victoria nodded. "Now," she said, folding her list and slipping it inside her sleeve. She glanced around the sitting room, her eyes landing on the trunk near the window. "Let's discuss my painting studio."

The ruffled edge of Mrs. Garner's white cap fluttered as she bobbed her head. "Ye mentioned ye might need furniture moved about, so I told Geoffrey and Donald to be prepared."

"Excellent. I will need a room with the best possible light."

"Aye, my lady. The yellow room on the second floor is quite nice—"

"Oh, but I was thinking the one at the front of the house."

Mrs. Garner's face froze, her expression bordering on horror. "The—the blue room, my lady?"

"Yes. I noticed it is already cleared of furniture. And the windows face south, which allows much better light throughout the day. London has little enough as it is." Noting that the normally animated servant had gone pale and terribly still, Victoria asked, "What is it, Mrs. Garner?"

The woman shuddered as though a ghost had passed

through her. "P-perhaps ye should speak wif Lord Atherbourne first, my lady."

Victoria blinked in puzzlement. "He has given me leave to choose any room in the house."

"He—he did? *Any* room?"

"Is there a problem with the blue room?"

"Ah, no, my lady. It's been cleaned, top to bottom."

Baffled by the housekeeper's bizarre reaction, Victoria gave the woman a confused smile. "Of course it has. The whole of Wyatt House is pristine."

"I jes' meant ..." She swallowed visibly and took a deep breath. "Pay no mind to silly old Mrs. Garner, my lady. If it's the blue room ye be wantin' for yer studio, tha's the one ye shall have. Geoffrey and Donald will move yer easel and supplies within the hour."

A thrill of anticipation ran through her at the thought of having a brush in her hand again. Standing before a fresh canvas was like being washed clean, the world newly born. At Clyde-Lacey House, she had set up her studio in a guest bedchamber, but the eastern light had meant fewer hours to paint. While in London, social demands did not allow much time for solitude, but ah, those few stolen hours when she was alone with her art. To savor a swirling stroke of crimson or bold slash of ochre, to witness the vision only she could see, now pouring through her mind, down her arm, out her fingers, and onto cloth. Becoming *real*. It was almost mystical, a conjuring of powerful sorcery.

"... empty the chamber pots three times a day instead of four. Well, I can tell ye right now, Mrs. Garner will not tolerate such laziness." Focusing on the housekeeper's voice, Victoria realized she hadn't a clue what the woman was talking about.

"So, now Agnes is back in the kitchen helpin' Cook."

Ah, yes. Agnes, the troublesome chambermaid. Victoria recalled Mrs. Garner mentioning her yesterday. Mrs. Garner was fond of informing Victoria about every detail of household happenings. Very, very fond.

"Mrs. Garner, have we a spare table somewhere in the house? I would like one for my studio. A simple work table should suffice."

"Yes, my lady. Saw one in the attic jes' last week. The maids and I—"

"Excellent! What a marvelous memory you have. Please ask Donald and Geoffrey to place it beneath the windows furthest from the fireplace. Also, I should have more supplies later this week, as I will be visiting my former home and believe there are some items I left there."

Mrs. Garner went silent. Her keys jangled as she folded her hands at her waist, tense and uncomfortable. How odd, Victoria thought. Perhaps she wasn't feeling well.

"My lady," Billings bellowed from the open doorway.

Victoria smiled and called out, "Yes, Billings, please come in."

He shuffled forward bearing a silver tray upon which lay a paltry stack of papers. Thanks to the scandal, invitations and correspondence had been quite sparse.

"Your correspondence, my lady." Billings bowed and held out the tray.

Victoria quickly thumbed through the stack. Three envelopes, none of them from her brother. She frowned. "Billings, is this all the correspondence? Did we not receive anything from the Duke of Blackmore?"

Billings did not answer, instead standing solemnly, his mouth pursed as though in deep thought. Or tasting something bitter that should not have been. Victoria wondered if perhaps he had fallen asleep or simply hadn't heard her.

She tried again, louder this time. "Billings?"

"Yes, my lady?"

"Have we received any letters from the Duke of Blackmore? Is this"—she held up the stack—"all that has come?"

He was silent again for a few seconds, then replied, "That is all the correspondence for my lady today."

Victoria slumped a bit and sighed deeply. She looked down at the stack in her hands. Was Harrison angry with her? True, she had disgraced herself and, by extension, the duke. But she had thought marrying Lucien and working to restore her reputation largely resolved the matter. Harrison did not often demonstrate warmer emotions, but Victoria had never doubted his affection. Surely, he must forgive her. *But, then, why has he not at least written? It has been ten days since the wedding. And I have written him twice.*

She looked up at Billings and Mrs. Garner, who both still stood before her, shifting uncomfortably. "Thank you, Billings. Mrs. Garner. You may be about your duties."

Once they departed, Victoria distracted herself from thoughts of a possible rift with Harrison by opening her correspondence. The first letter was from Great Aunt Muriel, congratulating her on her marriage; the second was a rather staggering bill from Mrs. Bowman. *Oh, my,* she thought, eyes flaring at the number on the final page. *Perhaps I should have exercised greater restraint.* Until now, Lucien had been a kind and indulgent husband, but that did not mean his goodwill was endless. In truth, Victoria could not be certain how he might react. She had married him. They shared a bed. But try as she might, she could not say that she knew him. *Well, biblically speaking, you know him spectacularly well.* A faint smile touched her lips and a small shiver climbed her spine. However, if asked to predict his behavior or to understand his decisions, she found herself quite at a loss.

She bit her lip and set the bill aside. *Better not to think of it now.* Besides, the third letter most interested Victoria. It came from Lady Berne, inviting Victoria and Lucien to dinner next week with the intent to "discuss a stratagem whereby matters might be restored to their proper order."

Relief flooded her; the countess intended to help with the scandal. Lady Berne was a godsend, constant and generous where others would unquestionably abandon her. Having such a well-respected matron on her side would make her reentry into society significantly easier.

Warm lips caressed the nape of her neck.

"Lucien!" she yelped. "You startled me." Indeed, her heart hammered away at her breastbone. Or perhaps that was the effect of his tongue stroking along the side of her neck.

"Sorry, love. Too tempting, you know."

His voice, low and smooth, echoed down her back, becoming warm tendrils of need that wrapped around her womb. His strong arms curled around her shoulders from behind, and he whispered in her ear, "What are you reading?"

"Hmm?"

He chuckled sensually and kissed the shell of her ear. "The note you are holding. What is it?"

She glanced down, surprised to find the invitation still clutched in her hand. "Oh! Lady Berne would like us to join her and Lord Berne for dinner on Tuesday next."

He froze, slowly withdrawing his arms and straightening behind her. She turned sideways in the chair to glance up at him. His face was dark and taciturn, his posture stiff. "For what purpose?"

His tone sent a chill over her skin. She blinked up at him. "I believe she wishes to help with the scandal."

Stepping back, Lucien crossed his arms over his chest. "Who else will be there?"

Victoria shrugged. "She did not say. Is it important?" He did not reply, his gaze moving through her without stopping. *A strange reaction, indeed.* "Lucien?"

His smile returned, but this time it felt detached, as though she were a casual acquaintance, not the woman he had made love to less than four hours earlier. "Only insofar as those present can be trusted."

Frowning, she stood and set the letter upon her desk, then pivoted to face her husband—who now felt very much a stranger. Cold settled over her like a cloak. "Lady Berne has been a true friend to me," she said softly. "I believe she feels responsible for my current predicament and wishes to rectify the situation. I have every reason to trust her."

"Do you?"

"Yes," she replied, her temper beginning to rise. "She has always had my best interests in mind."

"Your best interests. Stickley, for example."

The mention of the man she had betrayed—especially coming from the cause of that betrayal—sent resentment and shame knifing through her. "I will not discuss Stickley with you. Pray, do not speak of him again."

Lucien lowered his chin and gave her a burning glare. "My point is that Lady Berne—and others who should have known better—steered you toward a man as ill-suited for you as a boar for a goose."

"Others ...?" She frowned, then realized to whom he was referring. "You mean Harrison." Stiffening in outrage, she retorted, "Frankly, my lord, the only one who has demonstrated ill intentions toward me is you."

If his expression was anything to judge by, Lucien was most displeased with her candor. "Careful, my darling," he said. "You do still require my cooperation to regain your place in society, yes?"

A ripple of shock rolled through her at the implication. "Are you threatening to withdraw it?"

"Depends."

"Upon?"

He smiled at her, not one of his oh-so-charming, devil-may-care smiles. This one had menace in it. "How well you comport yourself as my wife."

Backing up until she felt the edge of the desk behind her hips, she shook her head. "What does that mean?"

He moved closer, now mere inches away. Betraying shivers of remembered pleasure rippled over her skin. "A good wife would understand that I want nothing to do with the man who shot my brother."

Her eyes had dropped to his lips while he was speaking, but then quickly flew up to meet his flat gaze. "I do understand. Still, you cannot think to avoid him forever."

"Can't I?"

Surely he could not mean ... "Lucien," she said, her voice hoarse with disbelief. "He is my brother. And a duke."

"And a murderer."

She swallowed hard against the accusation. She did not know what the duel had been about, but she did know Gregory Wyatt had been the one to issue the challenge. "That is deeply unfair."

"I owe him nothing, least of all fairness."

Searching his face for signs of the man he had been only that morning, she found only deadly determination, hard bitterness, and old rage. Inside, a part of her that had begun to hope, perhaps even to love, shriveled and bled. But years of being the Duchess of Blackmore's daughter occasionally came in handy, and she quickly composed herself. "Fine. You do not wish to see Harrison. But surely you do not intend to prevent me from doing so."

He leaned forward until his eyes were level with hers, bracing his hands on the desk behind her, enclosing her until she could see nothing but him. "That is where you are mistaken, my dear. You are my wife, an extension of me. He is my enemy, and you will have nothing to do with him."

He could not mean it. "You cannot mean it," she rasped.

"I assure you, I am most sincere."

"But I must visit Clyde-Lacey House to retrieve my supplies—"

His face hardened further, the muscle in his jaw flexing. "No contact, Victoria, do you understand? None."

"But—"

"Not letters. Not visits. Not chance encounters. Nothing."

She stared at him, this stranger she had married. The man who had given her unspeakable pleasure for the past ten days. *You should have known,* she told herself bitterly. *Such indulgences have only ever led to disaster. You must learn to control your desires, Victoria. Otherwise, they will control you.* The admonition was a familiar one, though it had been years since she'd heard her father's voice in her head. It reminded her of Harrison. Chin rising, eyes narrowing, she declared, "I will not abide by such an absurd demand."

His head tilted in a most predatory way. "Then I fear you shall suffer the ravages of the gossips on your own."

"You honestly mean to allow your wife to continue being the subject of such a scandal? No gentleman would do so."

He gave her a single nod, the gesture slow and faintly mocking. "Now you're catching on."

The threat was real enough to feel like a sword piercing her stomach. The very purpose of marrying Lucien had been to restore her reputation. If he refused to cooperate, it would all have been for nothing. Oh, he was a skilled seducer. And, yes, perhaps she had begun to indulge in daydreams of making this marriage into something more than a convenience. But he obviously did not share her foolish sentiment. A husband who wanted a real marriage would not threaten to abandon his wife.

Victoria lowered her eyes and forced herself to think logically, as Harrison often encouraged. Admittedly, her options were limited. One: She could defy him, which meant any benefit gained from the marriage would be largely moot, and she'd be right back to where she had begun—disgraced and hopeless. Or, two: She could comply, gain his cooperation for however long it took, and then see about Harrison later.

"You are despicable," she muttered.

He grinned. "So you have said." He ran a finger down her cheek, which she promptly batted away. She could not bear for him to touch her.

"I will do as you ask in regard to Harrison."

"Splendid."

She shoved hard at his shoulder. He did not budge. "For now," she said emphatically. "Assuming you are of use to me."

His hand fell over his heart, his voice low. "I live to be used by you, my darling."

Ignoring the innuendo, Victoria pushed away from the desk and sidled past him to pace the room briskly. The distance helped clear her mind, but it did nothing to ease the coldness inside her. "We'll begin with Lady Berne's dinner. I shall expect your *full* cooperation, my lord."

"So long as you heed my wishes, I will aid you with your little project."

Straightening her shoulders, Victoria faced him and nodded, clasping her fingers at her waist. "It is good we understand one another." And it was. She would not be fooled again.

Something of her thoughts must have shown on her face, because he paused, searching her with his eyes, then slowly moved forward until he stood less than a foot away. "We needn't be so at odds, love. There are many pleasures yet to be explored between us," he said softly, sounding too much like the man she had begun to fall in ...

No. That way lay disaster.

"Your position is entirely clear, my lord husband." The starch of dignity gave her voice an icy snap that more resembled Harrison's than her own. "Now allow me to explain mine. Whatever pleasures we may have once enjoyed are at an end. If it would not stoke damaging gossip among the servants, I would move into the guest chamber this very day. And you would *never* touch me again."

Slowly, his eyes dropped to her bosom and made a leisurely return to her face. "You are angry now, but you will change your mind."

Breathing around a gnawing ache at the center of her chest, Victoria wondered if she would ever be able to look at him and not want him so badly it made her fingers curl. Right now, she longed for that time to come as soon as possible, for she very much feared if it did not, he might prove correct.

"We shall see, my lord. We shall see."

Chapter Twelve

"A scandal is like a wolf that has been too long without a meal.
You must first feed it something other than yourself.
Only then do you stand a chance of taming it."

—THE DOWAGER MARCHIONESS OF WALLINGHAM to Lady Berne
upon learning the unfortunate consequences of failing in one's
chaperone duties.

THE BRISK CLACK OF HARRISON'S HESSIANS ON THE STEPS OF
the Berne townhouse echoed along a relatively quiet stretch of
Grosvenor Street. The afternoon was unusually crisp, the skies
cloudless, the air promising warmth but not yet delivering. He'd
thought perhaps the short walk from Berkeley Square would help
clear his mind, ease the worry that plagued him. But as he raised

his arm to knock on the oak door, his thoughts stubbornly circled the same point: He had failed her. His baby sister.

He paused, staring at his gloved fist where it hovered just shy of grasping the brass knocker, but seeing only her tight, pale features as she left his home with that conniving blackguard. Now her husband.

"Bloody hell," he muttered. He had been outmaneuvered—he, the Duke of Blackmore, a man so powerful, the Prince Regent once privately expressed envy for his influence. Atherbourne had gained more than the upper hand. The bastard had Harrison's sister. God only knew what would come of that union, but he found it difficult to imagine anything good. Now, he was left to wonder, left to watch over her from a distance, to try to help repair what Atherbourne had broken. Because of him. Because of what *he* had done.

The door swung inward, startling Harrison out of his thoughts. He dropped his arm and gave Berne's butler a blank stare. The middle-aged servant must have taken his look for disapproval, because he instantly bowed. "My deepest apologies, your grace. I did not hear your arrival." He stepped back and waved Harrison inside, accepting the hat Harrison automatically handed him. "I shall alert Lord and Lady Berne straight away. Would you care to wait in the drawing room?"

Harrison gave a brief nod, barely glancing at the servant. "That will be fine."

The butler escorted him upstairs to the small but elegant drawing room with its blue silk walls, oak floors, and tall windows. He departed, saying something about tea. Still distracted by his earlier thoughts, Harrison wandered toward the window in the far right corner of the room. With a single finger, he knuckled aside the gold striped draperies and glanced out at the street below. A high-perch phaeton rumbled past, the tow-headed buck at the reins recklessly pushing a pair of roans too fast. Harrison frowned. The man—or, to be more precise, boy—was tempting fate mightily. Did today's youths not understand how irresponsible their behavior was? How it endangered others? And for what? A moment of exhilaration, of emotion. Shameful.

He shook his head and clasped his hands behind his back. Colin was the same, perhaps worse. He dove headlong into the brandy bottle, never thinking how his careless, foolhardy behavior might embarrass those who shared his name, his bloodline. Never wondering if it was right to subject others to his drunken idiocy.

Harrison's inability to comprehend Colin's lack of control had proven a barrier to correcting his behavior. He had tried everything—limiting his allowance, sending him abroad, scolding, cajoling, threatening. Nothing had worked. The drinking had only grown worse, especially in the past year. Victoria had suggested cutting Colin off completely. And for his gentle, softhearted sister to even hint at such a thing, Harrison knew the situation had become critical. But he could not bring himself to do it. Colin and Victoria were his responsibility, and despite the fact that he appeared to be failing them both rather miserably, he would not abandon them. Ever.

A high-pitched squeal followed by the staccato thud of racing footsteps was muffled by the closed doors, but it drew his attention nonetheless. Loud peals of feminine laughter— *young* feminine laughter—reached his ears, generating an instant reaction. That of annoyance. He scowled at the doors, then reached into his waistcoat pocket to retrieve his watch. One fifteen. What the bloody hell was keeping Lord and Lady Berne?

"Genie, I swear to you," another voice sounded through the doors, this one slightly deeper, though still feminine, and obviously vexed. "If you damage that book in any way, I will cut every hair ribbon you own into tiny, unrecognizable bits."

"Oh, Mr. Darcy! You are my heeeerooooo. How could I not fall madly in looooove!" He could not be certain, but he suspected what followed the girlish, singsong voice was the sound of either smacking or exaggerated kissing noises. Either way, it ended in a shriek, as though the one who had produced the noise had been abruptly set upon.

"Give it back, you wretched brat. Do not force me to threaten your bonnets."

Another shriek, a hard thud, more rapid footsteps, then the doors to the drawing room flew open. A dark-haired girl who could not be above twelve careened into the room, clutching a small brown book to her flat yellow bodice. She was immediately followed by a taller—though, by no means tall—considerably more buxom girl of perhaps eighteen or nineteen. This girl was also dark-haired, but was plump, bespectacled, and narrow-eyed with determination. She looked familiar, but it took him a moment to recognize her. She was one of the daughters who had attended Victoria's wedding. Was it Joan? Anne? He couldn't recall. That day had passed in a haze of red for him.

The younger girl rounded one of the sofas set in the middle of the room, placing it between her and the older girl. "I shall burn it, see if I don't!" she pronounced, dramatically extending the book toward the fireplace. Which happened to be at least ten feet away.

The spectacled one narrowed her eyes and lowered her voice. "I shall burn *you*, see if I don't."

"Ha!" came the immediate reply. "You cannot even lift Katie any longer. How do you expect to throw me in the fireplace?"

Small, feminine hands landed on rounded hips. "Well, Genie, you have me there," Joan/Anne/Whoever replied sarcastically. "I suppose I shall have to bring the fire to you."

Genie's expression grew mutinous. "You wouldn't."

"Wouldn't I?"

"Sisters should not threaten to burn one another."

"Sisters should not make it necessary by pilfering one another's possessions. Now give it back before I am forced to do something drastic."

Genie pouted in a way that made him think she had practiced the expression in front of a mirror countless times. "I was only having a bit of fun. You are forever *reading*, Jane. It is so *boring*."

The briefest shadow flashed over the spectacled one's face. Jane. Now he remembered. Her name was Jane. His brows lowered and his jaw tightened. Heedless children, both of them. They threw hurtful words at one another, flailing wildly about without a thought to the damage they could do. Neither had stopped long enough to notice him standing in the corner of the room.

He cleared his throat. Loudly.

Two pairs of dark eyes swung his direction, flared comically wide, flew back to one another, then back to him. Genie's mouth gaped. Jane's face and throat flushed a mottled, unbecoming red.

"My ... your ... y-your grace," Jane managed, stumbling on an awkward curtsy.

"He's a duke?!" Genie hissed. Before her sister could reply, the girl shoved the book into Jane's hands and ran pell-mell out of the room. Jane pressed the brown leather volume to her ample bosom, and Harrison's eyes followed it automatically, watching the rapid rise and fall of her chest. His frown deepened.

"What book is so precious, I wonder, that it draws threats of burning one's sibling?" He watched as her flush deepened and spread. Her mouth remained open as though she wanted to speak but could not.

"Nothing to say for yourself, then?" Even to his own ears, his voice sounded harsh. Cold. Before his vexation could get the better of him, he turned his back on her to gaze once again out the window. Minutes passed in silence. After a while, he glanced behind him to where she had stood, but she was gone. A pang of conscience struck. Perhaps he had not handled that well. He'd been angry with Colin and Atherbourne and, yes, even Victoria for their reckless behavior. Perhaps his reaction to what was likely routine sisterly squabbling had been a touch severe.

Lady Berne entered through the open door, her short, round frame bustling forward in a rolling, harried rush. Lord Berne, lean and distinguished, followed more sedately, a bemused smile on his face. Harrison acknowledged them both with a nod and a brief bow.

"Your grace, I am so sorry to have kept you waiting," the countess began. "I'm afraid there was a bit of an ... incident with the supper menu." She held her hand up as though to stop him from interrupting. "No need to panic, however. The crisis has been averted. Lord Berne will have his pheasant, and domestic tranquility may resume uninterrupted." This last bit she said with a wry grin and a twinkle.

He blinked, feeling as though he had missed something. First, the earl's daughters chased one another through the halls like a couple of harridans, screeching and threatening all manner of bodily harm, then the countess admitted she was late to an appointment with him—a duke, no less—because she had not properly managed arrangements for the evening meal. Honestly, he'd had no idea the Berne household was in such disarray. After a long, uncomfortable silence, Lord Berne intervened. "Well," the older gentleman said in his usual affable tone. "Perhaps we should sit."

By the time they all took their seats and tea had been delivered, offered, and declined, the tension along the back of Harrison's neck had crawled up inside his skull, gnawing its way forward in a vague, pounding ache.

"Now then," Lady Berne began, a few strands of silver-laced brown hair peeking from beneath her ruffled cap. "I must first apologize, your grace. As a chaperone, it was my duty to ensure Victoria came to no harm while under my care. I failed her, and I failed you." The matron stopped, apparently overcome by emotion. She pressed her lips together, her eyes welling with a sheen of tears. Reaching inside the cuff of her gown, she pulled out a handkerchief and held it to her nose.

He opened his mouth to speak, but she halted him by raising her palm and choking out, "No, no. Do not so hastily offer forgiveness."

Lowering his brows, he felt the headache tighten and intensify. He had not been about to offer forgiveness. She was right. Her lack of vigilance was, in part, to blame for the disaster at the Gattingford ball. Before he could say as much, however, Lord Berne reached over and stroked his wife's arm soothingly. "There, there, dearest. You cannot blame yourself. Atherbourne knew what he was about before he ever entered the ballroom. It's likely if you had thwarted him there, he would have merely found another opportunity."

"I should have warned the poor girl. She did not even know who he was," Lady Berne murmured, then sniffed and met Harrison's eyes. "Your mother was one of my dearest friends. I will do all in my power to restore Victoria's good standing. It is what she would have wanted."

Feeling as though his muscles had been shot full of mortar, Harrison could do little more than nod. Lord Berne squeezed the countess's hand gently, and gave Harrison a small smile. "We may have an idea about that, actually."

His eyes shifted back and forth between the earl and countess. "Yes?"

Lady Berne nodded, the lace on her cap bobbing as she scooted forward to perch on the edge of the sofa. "I am bosom friends with a certain marchioness," she whispered loudly.

He blinked. "Is that so?"

She wrinkled her short, rounded nose and grinned secretively. "I may be owed a small favor." Ignoring what must be his puzzled expression—for he could not fathom what the blazes she was talking about—she rushed on, waving her handkerchief dismissively, then tucking it back inside her sleeve. "Unfortunately, even that may not be enough. The scandal is positively ghastly. Do you know what they are saying about your poor, dear sister?"

His frown became a scowl, his headache now a vise wielded by the devil himself. "No. Tell me."

She cleared her throat delicately. "It is simply dreadful, your grace. But you must know the truth. Both last season and this, Victoria was heralded as a premier example of virtue and grace. While that made her quite successful in attaining honorable suitors, it also engendered a great deal of envy among other debutantes and, more to the point, among their mothers. Her fall from such a high pedestal, I fear, has invited viciousness on a scale I have seldom witnessed."

"What, precisely, are they saying?" he asked softly.

Lady Berne glanced at her husband, who nodded and patted her wrist, encouraging her to continue. "The mildest of the accusations is that she is a hypocrite and a fraud. Others speculate she was Atherbourne's mistress all along, and that the two of them planned to continue their liaison after her marriage to Stickley. The worst rumors suggest a conspiracy to do away with Stickley after he inherited, leaving Victoria a widowed duchess."

"These rumors, are they widespread?" Harrison asked, his jaw tight, his stomach churning. He'd known it was bad. Lord Dunston and even Dunston's sister, Mary, had warned him that the ton was gleefully digging its claws into the juicy carcass Atherbourne had served up. But he hadn't realized just how far it had gone.

"I am afraid so," Lady Berne replied. "It is much worse than I anticipated. Victoria's marriage to Atherbourne has helped a bit, but Lord Stickley continues to accuse her of wanton faithlessness. He refuses to deny that she may have been carrying on an affair during their engagement. No, the scandal is still burning bright, I fear."

Damn Atherbourne to hell. Harrison had half a mind to make his sister a widow just as soon as he could locate a new dueling pistol. He had sold his pair shortly after shooting the previous Lord Atherbourne. "I will take care of Stickley," Harrison said, his tone flat.

Lord Berne sat forward. "With all respect, Harrison, I think in this case, you may be better off staying clear of the fray."

Every instinct rose up with the need to shout his refusal at the older man, but before he could take a breath, Berne continued, "I know you want to protect Victoria. That is only right. But solving this particular malady requires a specialist."

"Specialist?" he asked, still unsure about this vague plan they kept referring to.

Lady Berne nodded emphatically. "In matters of gossip and rumor, her authority is unmatched. Victoria will be in excellent hands."

Harrison met Lord Berne's sympathetic eyes, wishing like hell he did not have to place his sister's welfare in the care of these well-meaning but somewhat exasperating people. However, Lord Berne was correct in saying Harrison was not the best person to combat the scandal. Because of his feud with Atherbourne, his direct involvement would serve only to inspire the viscount's resistance. As much as he despised the man—now his brother-in-law—Harrison knew they could not possibly succeed without Atherbourne's cooperation. It was the only reason he had agreed to Victoria's marriage, the only reason he hadn't bloody well killed the blackguard outright.

Besides, the women of the ton were the ones driving this scandal. In their jealousy, they were eager to tear Victoria apart. The best person to reverse the damage was probably a female, one who knew how to navigate the gossip circles, one who might even have sufficient power to change perceptions. As he generally tried to remain far removed from such circles, he hadn't a clue who such a figure might be.

His consternation must have shown in his expression, because Lady Berne smiled reassuringly and said, "Not to worry, your grace. If anyone is capable of dousing this fire, it is Lady Wallingham."

Good God, he thought. *Wallingham?* It was like using a hammer to catch a butterfly. That woman was both a termagant and a tyrant. She was powerful, yes, but also blunt, tactless, and at times outrageous. Such a solution was fraught with risk, which was unacceptable.

"Lady Berne," Harrison said, his voice deliberately patient. "I am most appreciative of your efforts on my sister's behalf. However, I fear involving Lady Wallingham will do more harm than good. I must ask that you allow me to handle the matter."

Lord Berne began to speak, probably to offer reassurances, but the countess suddenly stood, appearing agitated. It forced Harrison to his feet, where he remained, stiff and wary, as she came around the low table to stand directly in front of him. At not even five feet tall, Lady Berne was well over a foot shorter than he, and it was most marked when she stood next to him. He was reminded of a scene from one of his favorite boyhood stories, *Gulliver's Travels*. As she gazed up at his face, the awkwardness of the moment grew, causing him to want to fidget like the boy who had devoured that book in one day.

She reached out slowly and took his hands in her own. Startled at the gesture, he could only stand, speechless, as she squeezed his gloved fingers. Other than the occasional impulsive hug from Victoria or clap on the shoulder from Dunston, no one touched him without his permission. Ever. And while his parents had been close with the earl and countess, he was not, though he valued the connection to such a well-respected family.

"Ah, my lady," he began gently, wondering how to extricate himself without giving offense.

She did not waver, her large brown eyes filled with some indefinable emotion. He would almost describe the look as maternal, but that was ridiculous. He was the Duke of Blackmore, not some poor weakling in need of mothering.

"Dear boy," she said softly, almost sighing the words. "You are so like your father."

It was hardly the first time he had heard the sentiment. Such comparisons were inevitable—and only partially accurate. Harrison was considered by many to be cold through and through, as his father had been. But he had never managed more than a fair imitation of it.

"Allow me to pose a question," she continued, seemingly unfazed by his rigid posture. "Do you wish Victoria to be happy?"

He frowned, wondering if the woman was bloody daft. "Of course."

She smiled, squeezed his fingers one last time, then stepped back as though satisfied with his answer. "Good. Then you will permit me and Lady Wallingham to proceed."

Opening his mouth to refute her claim, he was halted when she pressed on, her voice harder, more emphatic. "Otherwise, your grace, there is very little chance of her recovering her standing within society. The scandal may eventually fade in its significance, but frankly, without Lady Wallingham, it will never completely disappear."

Reluctantly, he mulled her statement over in his mind. It was a risky plan. The old woman was unpredictable. Furthermore, she lived by her own set of rules, which did not include reverence for anyone else's authority. However, perhaps *because* of her formidable nature, when she chose, Lady Wallingham could wield an astounding degree of influence. Although it pained him to place his sister's welfare in the hands of someone so volatile, he had to admit Lady Berne was likely correct—it was the best option available if they wanted to reverse the damage, rather than simply weather the storm.

Bloody hell. He felt like a bull that had been neatly herded into a stall. It was becoming an all-too-familiar sensation. "Very well," he said after a long silence. "You may solicit Lady Wallingham's assistance."

Lady Berne gave him a delighted grin and clapped her hands excitedly. "Splendid!"

"However," he said repressively, "You will alert me should any problems arise. Immediately and without hesitation. If Lady Wallingham becomes more of a hindrance than a help, I shall take action, and she will not enjoy the consequences. Feel free to advise her so."

Lady Berne waved her hand as though unconcerned. "You

worry needlessly. When she puts her mind to a task, Lady Wallingham is positively a force of nature."

That, he thought grimly, *is precisely why I should worry.*

Chapter Thirteen

"Have a care, my dear. Others may dabble. I wage war."

—THE DOWAGER MARCHIONESS OF WALLINGHAM to the Duchess
of Rutland upon her grace's stated desire to host a competing
weekly luncheon.

"DO YOU THINK SHE WILL AGREE TO HELP US?" VICTORIA ASKED
nervously a week later.

Seated beside her in the carriage, Lucien replied, "Probably.
Lady Wallingham may be a dragon, but her influence allows her
many eccentricities. I imagine she will help, if only to amuse
herself for the remainder of the season."

Victoria nodded and bit her lip. She prayed he was right.
Soliciting Lady Wallingham's assistance in resolving the

surprisingly severe scandal had been a stroke of genius on the part of Lady Berne, who was friends with the "dragon," as Lucien accurately described her. Lady Wallingham was a rarely seen yet inexplicably powerful figure within the ton. She arrived in London each season approximately a month later than most other women of her age and station, preferring the country for its "blessed absence of cacophony and suffocating stench."

When she finally came to town, it was with a great deal of fanfare. Society matrons clamored for invitations to the dowager marchioness's weekly luncheons, in which only the finest gossip was shared, discussed, and given final declarative judgment by Lady Wallingham herself.

Her commentary was often tart, occasionally cutting, and always incisive. By the mere lift of an eyebrow, she could set a presumptuous matron in her place or revoke a debutante's good standing. Certainly, if anyone had the influence necessary to recast a virulent scandal into a romantic triumph, it was Lady Wallingham. The only question in Victoria's mind was, would soliciting a dragon's help gain them a powerful ally or the fire of the lady's scorn?

As they arrived at the Earl of Berne's white stone townhouse, Victoria's stomach tightened in dread. She unconsciously reached for Lucien's hand where it rested on the seat between them, her gloved fingers brushing lightly over his before she realized what she was doing and jerked her hand back.

But he noticed. How could he not? It was the first time she had touched him in even the most casual way in seven days. After ordering her to avoid all contact with Harrison, then threatening to throw her to the proverbial wolves if she did not, Lucien had dared to act as though nothing had changed. But to her, everything had changed. He was using her to punish her brother. Again. It was plain to see, now that the initial fog of lust had dispersed. *Then why can you not simply accept the truth and cease this infernal wanting?*

In her weaker moments, before she could stop herself, she

would lean toward him for a kiss or reach out to caress his jaw. Fortunately, thus far, she had been able to regain her senses before he noticed her lapses. Until now. Seeking reassurance, her hand had moved of its own accord to brush his, and this time, she would not escape so easily. His hand chased after hers and found it in her lap. The small contact sent alarming tingles up her arm.

"Victoria," he whispered.

She looked down at where their hands entwined, his so much larger than hers. Her whole body was suffused with the grinding ache of need. Perhaps more than her body. One would have thought his callousness toward her would have made her immune to the dangerous desire that filled her at his nearness. At the very least, she had supposed withdrawing from him—refusing to allow him to encroach upon her half of the bed at night, speaking to him only when necessary, ensuring they were seldom alone together—would dim the attraction between them.

But no. Quite the opposite, actually. She *craved* him.

Most compulsively.

Shaking her head, she gathered her strength and pulled her hand from his. It made her feel tight, empty. "In the presence of others, you may play the part of the devoted husband, but in private, we both know I do not desire your attentions, my lord." Her voice sounded positively frosty.

Lucien was in no mood to heed the warning. His hand—the same one that had cradled hers moments earlier—rose to clasp the nape of her neck and turn her head from where it focused out the window to face him and his descending mouth.

She squeaked in surprise at the hard kiss, his sleek tongue invading and demanding her compliance. She pushed at him weakly, but if she was honest, it was little more than a token gesture. The rapturous pleasure that filled her whenever he kissed her was simply too much to resist. He grasped her hands and repositioned them around his neck, then snaked his arm about her waist, pulling her snugly against him. She moaned into his mouth, her breasts swelling against her stays, her gloved fingers digging into his nape.

A dark growl came from deep within his chest, the rumble sending a sharp thrill through her entire body. It felt like it had been years, not days, since he had last touched her. She was a desert and he a wild rainstorm. It wasn't until she felt his hand bunching her skirt at her knee that sanity began to worm its annoying way back into her consciousness.

Just as she was preparing to break away from the kiss—for surely that was what she intended at the earliest opportunity— the carriage door opened and they both froze. The footman cleared his throat, staring straight ahead. Blushing furiously, Victoria jerked away from her husband, who looked disheveled and hungry, his breathing fast. Swallowing hard against a suddenly dry mouth, she cleared her throat and scooted to exit the carriage, with Lucien following her after an oddly long interval. The cool evening air eased the heat in her cheeks as they both paused to gather themselves. Seconds later, Lucien offered his arm to escort her inside, their kiss left behind in the confines of the carriage. *As it should be,* she thought, sending a prayer of thanks heavenward for the footman's execrable—er, *excellent*—timing.

Victoria had visited the Berne townhouse on several occasions, and it always struck her as a place of warmth, comfort, and familiarity. Much of the house was clad in medium-toned, golden oak, from the floors to the staircase to the paneled walls in the entrance hall, parlor, and library. More than that, it was a house redolent with the laughter, affection, and bustling energy of family. She had long wondered whether having sisters would have given Clyde-Lacey House and Blackmore Hall more of the same feeling. Harrison was not known for an effusive nature, after all.

She stole a glance at Lucien as they climbed the stairs to the drawing room. *Blast.* He was even more handsome to her now than he had been before their marriage, his dark blue tailcoat perfectly tailored and fitted tightly over wide, muscular shoulders. She sighed, feeling the embers of her earlier arousal glow hot low in her belly.

"I see now what you meant, Meredith," an old woman's voice trilled. "He's as handsome as Lucifer himself. Had he but winked at *me*, I would have dragged *him* out to the terrace, no doubt."

The declaration from the front of the drawing room was unmistakably that of Lady Wallingham. The woman's arch manner and trumpeting voice had always disconcerted Victoria. It was odd coming from such a diminutive person.

The Dowager Marchioness of Wallingham was a towering figure in society, but in form, she was several inches shorter than Victoria, her thin face and triangular nose giving her the appearance of a fragile bird. This evening, she wore a dark purple velvet gown and a plumed turban. The lavender feather bobbing to one side of her white coiffure added to the avian resemblance.

"Oh, dear," Lady Berne muttered. She bustled forward to make the formal introductions.

Lucien's bow over Lady Wallingham's hand was impeccable, but his smile was mischievous. "I daresay an assignation between us would have set the patronesses of Almack's on their ears, would it not, my lady?"

The dowager marchioness arched a single white brow and pursed her thin lips. "Atherbourne, I am too old and not nearly fluff-brained enough to fall prey to your flimflammery." Her chin rose slightly and a glint of humor entered her jewel-green eyes. "Besides, a shallow curtsy is enough to send those clucking hens running for their smelling salts, so that is no great measure."

She turned her dagger-sharp gaze to Victoria. Several seconds ticked by while Lady Wallingham seemingly assessed Victoria's very soul. Or, at least, it felt so.

"Your mother was a saint of propriety, girl. I find it difficult to imagine the duchess behaving in such a fashion."

Lady Berne turned surprised eyes to Lady Wallingham. "But

you always said the Duchess of Blackmore should wear brighter colors so one did not mistake her for a piece of furniture, did you not?"

Lady Wallingham sniffed. "I did not say I found her interesting, Meredith. Merely that she would not have been caught up in such a scandal. Which is true."

"I understand, my lady," Victoria said quietly, a flush of shame washing over her.

"And?" Lady Wallingham queried imperiously.

Victoria blinked. "My lady?"

The dowager marchioness huffed and shook her head. "Gracious, child, you will be eaten alive if you do not show some spine. How am I to help you if you cower at the merest challenge?"

"Oh, er. You—You wish to help me, then?" Victoria's heart thumped with hope.

Lady Wallingham turned to meet Lady Berne's eyes, her lavender plume bobbing slowly. "You did not mention she was dim."

Lady Berne shook her head and cast her eyes heavenward as though seeking patience. "That is because she is not, Dorothea. Perhaps we should go in to dinner. You are always more reasonable after a meal."

An hour later, it was clear Lady Wallingham did, indeed, wish to help Victoria restore her reputation, and she intended to command the effort herself. While they dined, the dowager marchioness, from her honored position at Lord Berne's right, handed out marching orders like a battlefield general.

Her first directive was for her son, the Marquess of Wallingham. A quiet, scholarly gentleman of perhaps forty years, he had been widowed young shortly after gaining his title. From all Victoria heard, he had so adored his wife that even now, fifteen years after her death, he behaved as though in perpetual mourning.

"Charles, seeing as you *refuse* to remarry," Lady Wallingham declared, "your usefulness in hosting a ball or any other amusement is minimal. But you can certainly silence Stickley. Offer to sell the man one of your horses if he will retreat to his country estate."

Lord Wallingham, owner of one of the finest stables in England, almost never parted with his prized horseflesh. Victoria recalled Harrison's unsuccessful efforts to purchase a new hunter from the marquess, and his rare frustration at the man's "infernal stubbornness." Nevertheless, in this instance, Lady Wallingham's son nodded complacently, much accustomed to his mother's authoritarian ways.

"Tannenbrook," she barked next, causing Lucien's giant, blunt-featured friend to straighten in his seat and lower his brows. "Everyone will expect you to be in Atherbourne's confidence. Put it about that he is besotted."

"Put it about, my lady?" Tannenbrook asked calmly.

Lady Wallingham waved her fork in the air like a scepter. "At the clubs and such. Use your colossal head for more than hammering stone, boy. Must I think of everything?"

Eyes narrowing, Tannenbrook stared intently at her for several moments. Victoria watched as the earl, who had always seemed as solid and stoic as a great mountain, took on a dangerous, volatile air. Lady Wallingham sniffed and raised one brow, holding his gaze unflinchingly. As though reaching a decision, Tannenbrook mockingly inclined his head in her direction.

"Excellent. That takes care of the male portion of our problem. Always the simplest to resolve, I daresay."

With that, Lady Wallingham proceeded to charge every person at the table—Lord and Lady Berne, Lucien and Victoria, even Annabelle and Jane Huxley—with specific instructions and tasks. Of everyone present, only one dared to object, and it was the most unlikely of the lot.

"My lady," Jane began, her rounded cheeks coloring a blotchy red. "I—I should warn you ..."

"Eh? Speak up, girl. I cannot abide mealy-mouthed mumbling. And at my age, I should not have to."

Jane cleared her throat. "What I mean to say is I will do whatever I can to help, b-but you've asked that I spread the story amongst my friends, and ..." Her voice trailed off as she glanced around the table, clearly embarrassed.

"I see you have the gist of it. What is the problem?"

Annabelle, seated next to her sister, placed her hand briefly over Jane's and said, "It might be best if I handle this part of the plan, my lady. I am friends with not only Lord Aldridge's twin daughters, but also Miss Matilda Bentley."

Lady Wallingham's eyebrows rose at the mention of three of the season's busiest young gossips. She eyed Jane's bowed head piercingly for a few seconds, then said, "Fine. I don't care who does the gossiping, I simply want it done. Jane!" Her voice was a loud crack in the room, startling the girl's head up, eyes wide behind her spectacles.

"Lady Atherbourne will need allies surrounding her. If your only useful purpose is to be present and visible at her side, then that is what you will do."

"Yes, my lady," the young woman said hoarsely.

"And if I should see a book in your hand at one of these functions, Lady Jane Huxley, you will have nowhere to hide from me. Understood?"

Jane nodded, clearly regretting she had drawn such attention.

Although Victoria considered Lady Berne a good friend, and she was fond of Lord Berne, she had never spent much time with their daughters. Her impression of Annabelle was that she was bubbly, popular, and good-humored. While Victoria liked the girl—her personality being similar to Lady Berne's—they tended to gravitate toward different circles, and so remained little more than acquaintances. Jane was quite the opposite of her sister: painfully shy, quiet, and unassuming. On that basis alone, Victoria had not formed much of a connection with her, either. It was hard to become friends with someone who did not speak.

However, Victoria's estimation of the young woman's character rose several notches this evening—standing up to the dragon was brave for anyone to attempt, but especially for meek little Jane Huxley.

"Lady Atherbourne," the dragon said, drawing Victoria's attention, "I do believe we have a plan. If everyone executes their roles properly, before season's end, the scandal shall disappear like a foul odor exiting an open window."

Victoria smiled at Lady Wallingham and thanked her sincerely for her generosity.

"No need to thank me, girl," she said, turning a rather pointed gaze to meet Lucien's. "Gifts will suffice. Send them to the Park Lane house."

Lucien half-grinned and chuckled. He acknowledged the request—although, command was perhaps a more apt description—with a dip of his head.

Later, as they entered the carriage to return home, Lucien's big, warm body settled next to Victoria, leaving her no space and no time to draw a proper breath. His arm slid behind her shoulders and pulled her against his hard frame. "Now, where were we?" he whispered, his wicked tongue taking a turn around the shell of her ear, causing shivers to run across her skin and settle in her breasts.

"Lucien," Victoria protested weakly.

"Mmm?" He nuzzled her neck, his lips playing havoc with her good sense.

"Surely you do not expect ..."

"Oh, but I do," he rasped, his hands finding their way inside her bodice.

You must not give in, Victoria. You must resist him. He has done nothing but betray you, use you. She knew it was the voice of reason, a voice she should heed. But it had been so long since she had felt this way. Hours, at least.

His thumb stroked her nipple, his fingers squeezing gently. Victoria moaned and met his mouth with her own. The man was a sorcerer, beguiling her senses with repeated strokes of his tongue and little nips at her lower lip. Minutes later, he had his trousers unfastened and she straddled his hips, poised above him, dripping wet and ready to take him inside.

"This does not mean what you think it means, Lucien." Breathing so heavily she could barely get the words out, she nevertheless knew she must be clear about who was in control.

He groaned, then panted, "Of course not."

She hovered over him, her thumb tracing his beautiful mouth. "I want you now. But it is just this once."

"Whatever you prefer, angel." His fingers curled and squeezed her backside. "All I ask is that you proceed with haste."

Slowly, she lowered her hips and felt his thick, hard cock slide into her. They gasped simultaneously, the friction and heat and fit of him inside her feeling like a fire burning in a hearth: welcome, relieving, and right. The thought was vaguely alarming. No. This could not be so perfect. She could not bear to be offered heaven and have it torn away, made impossible by his hatred for her family, by his willingness to use her. Not again.

Hiding her face in the crook of his shoulder, she paused, savoring the stretch of her body around his. She breathed once, twice, then schooled her features before straightening away from him, laying her hands flat against his chest. "Do not assume this will happen again," she said, her voice hoarse but resolute. "Or that you are forgiven."

Lucien's hands rose to her waist and tightened. His chest heaved with each labored breath; the muscles on either side of his jaw flexed. Flashing eyes met hers in the darkness of the carriage. All hints of his earlier teasing fled.

"You are my wife. Nothing will change that," he growled. His fingers bit into her hips as he gave a sudden, deep thrust, forcing a gasp of pleasure from her throat. Stroking deep and hard into her core, he demanded, "Say it."

Surprised by his sudden anger, her body still ecstatically welcomed each relentless thrust. The roughness of his movements only heightened her pleasure.

"Damn it, Victoria," he gritted. "Say it!"

Her mind fogged by exquisite sexual excitement, it took a few moments to decide what he so desperately needed to hear, longer to grant it. But, in the end, the words were pulled from her, a truth that scared her senseless.

"I am your wife," she panted.

"Yes," he hissed.

"And nothing will change that."

Her words sent them both tumbling over the precipice into a release that seized every muscle in her body, spinning her out to the edge of the ether and back again.

Afterward, her head lolling on his shoulder, she pressed against his neck, breathing in starch and spice and sex, delectable and achingly familiar. Steeled arms held her as though fearful she might escape. To where, she could not imagine. They were in his carriage, headed to his townhouse. For all that she might pretend to hold the higher ground in their battle, the truth was she was very much at his mercy. The thought did not sit well with her.

"Victoria," he began softly.

She shook her head, slowly withdrawing from him, untangling herself from his embrace, letting him slide out of her as she rose up and pushed away to sit on the opposite bench. *Why does it feel as if I am leaving a part of myself behind?*

"Look at me," he demanded.

She squeezed her eyes closed, the sticky wetness between her thighs a reminder of her weakness. "This was a mistake," she murmured, more to herself than to him.

"No." His voice had gone raw. "The mistake was letting you keep us apart for the past week. We are married. There is no reason we should not enjoy each other–"

"Oh? Have you decided to change your mind about Harrison, then?"

Even in the dark, she could see his glower.

"I thought as much."

A long, assessing pause came from his side of the carriage.

"How long do you suppose it will be until that sweet little body of yours once again demands what is rightfully yours? Another seven days, perhaps?"

That very question had burned inside her from the moment she had allowed her hand to drift instinctively toward his. It was terrifying to contemplate how desperately she wanted him. Enough to sacrifice her pride, to risk the disaster that would surely follow. "We had an agreement. What just happened doesn't change anything."

"I never agreed not to touch you, wife. In fact, it is well within my rights to do so."

The breath she had just managed to catch flew from her at his statement. "You ... you would force your attentions ..."

"Bloody hell, Victoria." He sounded genuinely vexed. "Of course not."

Well, that is a relief. I think.

She could scarcely see more than an outline of his large form, but it was enough to note how he slowly lounged back into the seat, one ankle propped on his knee—an arrogant pose if ever there was one. "I will not have to. As evidenced by tonight's ... adventures."

His presumptuousness irritated her. "Did you enjoy yourself, my lord husband?"

He sat upright, suddenly quite alert. "Oh, yes, angel. Being inside you is pure splendor."

She leaned forward, allowing the upper swells of her bosom to catch the dim light coming through the window. "Then might I suggest you hold the memory close, for it shall be the only splendorous thing keeping you company in the long, lonely weeks ahead."

Chapter Fourteen

"Ah, the gentleman's club. A fine and venerable institution. Quite useful for removing irritants from a lady's presence for several glorious hours each day."

—The Dowager Marchioness of Wallingham to her son, Lord Wallingham, after he reluctantly shared information found in White's betting book.

"I bloody well despise the clubs," Tannenbrook muttered as he and Lucien sat in the coffee room at White's.

Lucien raised a brow and took a sip of rich brew as he set his copy of *The Times* on the table. "Best not let any other members hear you say such a thing. Considered blasphemy, you know."

James grunted and wrapped his too-large hand around a too-small cup.

"Besides," Lucien continued, "your efforts here and at Brooks's are a smashing success."

His friend glared at him from beneath heavy brows. "The old woman has me gossiping like a schoolroom chit. It's a bloody disaster."

"Alvanley stopped by the table before you arrived."

Tannenbrook's brow smoothed. "And what did the prince of dandies have to say?"

Lucien took another sip and sent him an amused look over the rim. "He expressed disappointment."

James wore his usual deadpan expression, waiting patiently for elaboration.

Setting his cup on the table, Lucien obliged. "He implied behaving like a swain devoted to one's fair Juliet is certain to end in premature death, the only question being whether it will be by poison, stabbing, or plummeting from a balcony."

James snorted.

"It seems, Lord Tannenbrook, you have a gift."

His friend's face tightened in a grimace of disgust as he sat back in his chair and folded his massive arms.

Lucien grinned. "In any event, the current arbiter of all things fashionable among gentlemen of the *beau monde* believes I am a calf-eyed fool distastefully enamored of his wife. Impressive after a mere five days."

Clearly uncomfortable being praised for his adept manipulation of the rumor mill, James shrugged off the compliment and changed the subject. "Stickley left London."

"When?" Lucien demanded.

"Yesterday. Wallingham bought his absence with a yearling, or so I heard."

Lucien sat back, satisfaction surging through him. The pompous worm had carried his outrage at Victoria to disgraceful lows, mewling to all who would listen about her betrayal. He deserved a sound thrashing, but disappearing to the country would have to do.

Loud guffaws came from the hall, probably some young lord deep in his cups too early in the day. Moments later, Lucien's conclusions were confirmed when Colin Lacey stumbled into the room. He was followed by Lord Chatham, tall, lean, dark-haired, and almost certainly drunk, though he hid the fact remarkably well. A third man, bleary-eyed and decidedly less jocular, shook his head and headed for the stairs.

Must have lost a fair bit at the tables, Lucien thought, noting the trio had come from the direction of the card room.

Spying Lucien and Tannenbrook sitting near the window, the two men approached. Lacey's bow was sloppy, his greeting slurred. Lord Chatham's bow, by contrast, was the picture of elegance, executed to perfection.

"I sssay, Atherbourne," Lacey said, "where've you been hiding Tori? Haven't seen her sh-since the wedding."

Annoyed at the question, Lucien answered, "Such a thing might be of consequence if you could recall one way or the other, Lacey. As it is, I am surprised you remember even having a sister."

Before the younger man could answer, Chatham clapped his companion on the shoulder and advised drolly, "Not to worry. I'm sure your sister is in good hands with Lord Atherbourne. Most *exceptional* hands, if Mrs. Knightley is to be believed."

Colin Lacey, too drunk to understand Chatham's quip, much less respond to it, listed to his right and caught himself on the back of an empty chair.

Lucien met Chatham's flat turquoise gaze with a sharp one of his own. So Benedict Chatham, the current Viscount Chatham and future Marquess of Rutherford, was servicing the widow Knightley. Exhausting work, that.

Lucien arched a brow. "Long night, eh, Chatham?" he asked softly.

The man's cynical smirk faded to dead nothingness.

Warning apparently received—good. The subject of Mrs. Knightley was not one Lucien wished to have bandied about, and if rumors of her relationship with Chatham were true, then the dissolute lord almost certainly would share the sentiment. He did have to wonder how his own amorous past had come to be a topic of conversation between the two, and why Chatham was choosing to bring it up now.

He had been two years behind Lucien at Eton, and they had been fast friends early on—games of cricket, chasing petticoats, pranks on the older boys. Chatham was astoundingly clever, had a devilish sense of humor, and, even at fourteen, had taught the older boys a thing or two about wooing the fairer sex. Women utterly craved him, even thin and pale with the ravages of drink, as he was now.

Their friendship had waned as Chatham had begun his descent into disgrace and debauchery, but Lucien had always wished the man well. Given his jab about Lucien's prior bed sport with the depraved and tireless Mrs. Knightley, however, perhaps the feeling was not mutual.

Frowning, he glanced from Chatham to Lacey and back again, a connection clicking in the back of his mind. Chatham had always had a talent for influence. Other males—older, younger, it mattered little—loved to follow and emulate him. It seemed Colin Lacey was no exception.

Lucien turned to Victoria's poor excuse for a brother. "Lacey, I suggest you return home before you do the furniture here serious damage."

"You sh-sound juss like Harrison."

A dark, curling rage seeped into his bones, working its way outward from a frighteningly familiar place. Lucien did not like being compared to Blackmore. Not for any reason. They were nothing alike, and even the implication fired the hatred he kept banked, yet never dormant. Finally noticing the dangerous glint in Lucien's eye, Lacey wisely backed up a step. Chatham interjected coldly, "Perhaps we will take our leave, then. My lords."

As they left the room, Lacey protested drunkenly that he thought they were to have coffee, to which Chatham replied he'd suddenly developed a taste for something stronger.

"Never liked the shape of the spoons here, anyway."

Startled by James's quietly amused statement, Lucien glanced at his friend, who casually gestured to Lucien's hand. It lay fisted on the table, having bent a silver spoon in half. Immediately, he felt sick inside, opening his hand wide and letting the bit of metal thunk onto the linen-covered wood. Damn it. He hadn't had one of his episodes in weeks. Not since his wedding.

"He was drunk. And a bloody imbecile besides. You shouldn't pay him any mind."

Lucien nodded. James always made sense. After an episode, it helped a great deal to hear sound reason and calm patience. He breathed slowly, allowing the residual anger to flow out of him. It was a trick he had learned after deciding to leave Thornbridge and pursue justice. Picture the dark, endless well of poison running like a river out of his veins, out of his body, just like the air expelled from his lungs. Sometimes, like today, it worked.

When he met James's eyes, he was even able to smile. "It is fortunate I do not plan to spend much time in his company."

A short while later, Lucien and Tannenbrook entered the billiard room and began a quick game. James, who had been silent since they left the coffee room, asked quietly, "How is your wife, Luc?"

His muscles tightened and something squeezed hard in his chest. He glanced at James over his shoulder, wondering how he should answer. *She is beautiful. She is mine. She is much more than I thought she would be. Better than I deserve.*

He leaned forward to take his shot. "She is well."

James nodded. "She hasn't tried to see Blackmore?"

He watched as James calmly potted Lucien's cue ball and left him double-baulked. Bloody hell. Tannenbrook had a killer instinct when it came to billiards.

"Victoria understands my wishes."

Surprise lifted James's brows. "And she has agreed?"

Clearing his throat, Lucien replied, "For the time being." He glanced over at his friend. "Your skepticism is unwarranted. I've taken precautions. Once the scandal settles, we will leave for Thornbridge, and the matter should be easily managed."

"You still plan to keep her from him, then. For the rest of her life."

The base of Lucien's cue thumped against the floor. "That was the general idea, yes. If you have a better way to deprive Blackmore of the only thing he holds dear, short of outright killing her, I am eager to hear it."

James held his palm out in surrender. "No, I understand. I have always understood. Just ..."

Lucien scowled and snapped, "What?"

"Tread carefully, Luc. Sometimes getting what you want most is the worst thing that can happen."

Lucien considered his longtime friend for several seconds, wondering at the man's haunted expression. James Kilbrenner was three inches taller and about three stone heavier than Lucien—a strapping hulk with a face like a granite cliff. Seeing him exhibit any emotion that could not be explained by a bad meal, an obnoxious companion, or a stubborn mount was rare, indeed. That was just James. Seemingly rather uncomplicated and slow to boil. Of course, Lucien knew there was much more to him than that, but it did not often rise to the surface.

"Duly noted." He moved forward to take his next shot, and continued casually, "On the other hand, getting what you want can be immensely satisfying." With that, he banked off the cushion to pot the red and sent James a triumphant grin.

The Earl of Tannenbrook uttered a foul curse under his breath.

"Not to worry," Lucien said affably as he clapped his friend on the shoulder. "A wise player is never truly out of the game."

Tannenbrook's serious green eyes met Lucien's. "The game has to end sometime."

"Yes," he replied. "It ends when I win."

Arriving home two hours later, Lucien handed his horse over to Connell, the coachman and head groom. Connell's red hair and freckles gave him the look of a schoolboy, though he was, in fact, old enough to have married one of the upstairs maids and fathered three small children. Still, he was young for a position of such responsibility, but his gift with horses had earned first Gregory's, then Lucien's respect. Hugo, Lucien's gelding, was both oversized and vigorous, requiring daily runs to keep him calm. But in Connell's capable hands, the horse melted and all but simpered for affection. Today, the young man wore an apprehensive expression, eyes wide and face tight. He paused in taking the reins as though he wished to speak.

"What is it, Connell?" Lucien asked impatiently.

"It's 'er ladyship, m'lord. She's—she's taken up residence in the stable."

Lucien blinked. "Pardon?"

The groom nodded vigorously and pointed toward the two-story brick structure behind him. "I advised 'er ladyship it's no fit place for—"

"And what did she say?" Lucien queried grimly, now stalking toward the stable.

"She laughed, m'lord."

He stopped and stared back at Connell, who stopped as well, Hugo trailing after him like a giant lapdog. "Laughed?"

Connell nodded and rubbed the horse's nose absently. "Said that was nonsense and I could be on my way, as she 'ad work to do." The man's eyes were round as coins, his alarm clearly rising at the notion of the lady of the house desiring to enter his domain, much less sullying her hands with *work*.

Lucien shared his dismay, but for slightly different reasons. She did not belong there, that much was certain. Further, he did not want her getting strange ideas about taking one of his horses out for a ride, perhaps to her former home. If he was to ensure she adhered to his command, he needed to control her movements while they were in London, and he couldn't do that if she took it into her head to defy him. Fortunately, thus far, Victoria had proven to be a stickler for propriety—a product of Blackmore's influence, no doubt—and never ventured out without her maid or another companion. She nearly always took the carriage into Mayfair, as one had to cross the crushing bustle of Oxford Street to reach it, and such was not a quick, carefree jaunt on foot. But it was not impossible that she would suddenly take a notion to stretch her proverbial wings, he well knew. She was a spirited one, his wife, beneath the dutiful surface.

"Take Hugo for a short walk. I shall speak with Lady Atherbourne."

"Aye, m'lord." Connell tipped his cap and led the horse away.

As Lucien entered the dim, dusty confines of the mews, he paused a moment to let his eyes adjust. Along one side, a row of stalls held six horses, placidly munching hay and snuffling and snorting to draw his attention. The last few stalls were empty. One belonged to Hugo. The others remained to be filled, as he had intended to leave London much earlier than this, and hadn't thought it necessary. Of course, he also hadn't anticipated taking a wife quite so suddenly. It was still a bit of an adjustment.

Wandering forward, he was now able to see into the depths of the malodorous space. Just past a row of saddles and tack, near the entrance to the coach house, a rounded swath of flower-dappled muslin bobbed and wriggled behind a wooden post.

"Here, now, my love," a sweet, feminine voice cooed. "Don't you wish me to stroke you? I promise you'll enjoy it."

Everything in his body halted—his heart, his breath, his feet. All came to a standstill as he realized what he was staring at, whom he was hearing speak those provocative words. Victoria. She was bent over, peering behind a crate. Her lush, rounded bottom gave another wiggle as she extended an arm toward her quarry.

"You are a shy one, aren't you? Just let me touch your little head. I shall be gentle as a whisper. If you're good, perhaps I will kiss it. Would you like that?"

He couldn't help it—he groaned loudly, his body going from watchful to intensely aroused inside half a second. *Bloody hell. I am demented with lust.* Her delectable backside twitched fetchingly as she twisted around, trying to get a look at him over her shoulder. "Who is—?" She jerked upright, reeling backward. "Ow! That hurt, you little devil!"

She staggered back, off balance and shaking one hand madly as though she'd been burned. Before she could knock into the stall gate that splayed awkwardly into the aisle, he hurried forward and caught her around the waist. Her buttocks met his hardened staff with a momentous *whump*, causing him to groan again, this time in considerable discomfort. His back hit the wooden post between two stalls.

"Oh! For the love of heaven," she squawked, tugging out of his suddenly limp arms and spinning to face him. Flushed and disheveled, she braced her hands on her hips and blew a puff of air upward to usher a wayward curl out of her eye. "Lucien?"

He grunted. Actual speech was not possible at the moment.

"What are you doing in here?"

Several deep breaths seemed to help the waves of pain recede, at least enough for him to form words. "I could ask you the same, wife. This is hardly an appropriate place for the Flower of Blackmore to wile away the hours."

She flinched as though he had insulted her, then replied with quiet dignity, "Perhaps. But as you well know, that moniker has not carried the same meaning in a great while."

"Since you met me, you mean." The bitterness in his voice surprised even him. He was tired of her resentment, tired of not being able to touch her.

"If you expect me to deny your part in my ruination, you shall be disappointed."

He sighed. "The constant reminders are—"

"It was not my intent to argue, Lucien," she said calmly. "I would simply like to complete my task and be on my way." Sweeping both hands down her skirt in a dusting motion, she soon winced and cradled her right hand in her left.

"Are you injured?" he asked, his own pain all but forgotten.

She shook her head and muttered, "It's nothing." But he straightened away from the post and grasped her wrist gently. A trio of bloody scratches marred the fleshy pad at the base of her thumb. "Really. It's only a scratch."

"What happened?"

Cheeks pinkening a bit, she sent him a sheepish look from beneath her lashes. "I made unwelcome advances and was given a decidedly harsh set-down." She wrinkled her nose. "My fault entirely. The little devil is obviously quite particular about his suitors."

Confused for a moment, he sidestepped her to look behind the crates. There, curled up on a bed of hay, was an orange striped kitten. It glanced up at him with alert, golden eyes. And hissed. He scowled and turned back to Victoria. "The damned thing is feral. What were you thinking?"

Her hands returned to her hips and she gave an exasperated shrug. "I want to sketch him, but he is determined to remain hidden. It is most vexing."

Curls of blond hair that normally were perfectly disciplined had escaped her pins, causing her coiffure to slump a bit to one side. A small streak of dirt marred her chin. And her dress looked as though she had gone tromping through a stable. Which, in fact, she had. He coughed to disguise a chuckle.

"Are you laughing at me?"

Stiffening his lips, he mumbled, "No. Not at all."

He watched her own lips tremble, one corner quirking helplessly into a grin. She shook her head. "I suppose I deserve it." She brushed again at her dusty skirts. "I daresay I look a fright. Little wonder he rejected me."

Moving close to her, he cupped her jaw and stroked his thumb across the small streak on her chin. "Even when you look a fright, you are still the loveliest woman I have ever seen."

Eyes softening, lips parting, for a moment it looked as though Victoria might melt into his touch. Desire, fierce and insistent, snaked through him. But just as he moved to wrap an arm around her waist, her hands grasped his wrists and pushed him away. "Do not start with me, Lucien."

"Start what?" he asked innocently.

Her chin tilted up, her mouth tightening into a disapproving pucker. "I have neither the patience nor the time for your nonsense. I must finish my sketch this afternoon while I still have sufficient light. It is a gift for Lady Berne. She adores cats, but cannot have one because they make Lord Berne sneeze most terribly."

Running a hand through his hair, he sighed. "How long will this process take?"

She tapped a finger against her lips. "It depends."

"Upon?"

"How cooperative my subject is. It took me fifteen minutes to get close enough to be scratched." She gave her hand a resentful glare. "Sketching is the easy part."

Without another word, he stripped out of his tailcoat and grabbed a nearby bucket, then purposefully approached the cat's hiding place.

"What are you ...?"

He signaled Victoria to be quiet with a finger to his lips. Slowly, carefully he placed the bucket to the left of the crates, blocking the kitten's escape route. Then, he stretched his coat like a net along the right side and reached down to roust the little bugger out of his nest. Hissing and spewing, the kitten clawed mercilessly at Lucien's hand, his orange fur standing on end, his tiny body writhing in protest. Nonetheless, Lucien was able to get the animal's scruff between his thumb and fingers and hold it aloft long enough to retrieve his coat. He wrapped the kitten tightly inside, drawing the sleeves around the small bundle, so only its head poked out.

"A magnificent feat, my lord," his wife said, her voice redolent with laughter. "Truly, one would suppose you had trekked the wilds of Africa hunting mighty beasts." She was teasing him, but he could see she was pleased he had secured the tiny creature who had given her such trouble. His heart gave a peculiar flip.

"It is astonishing what a husband is capable of when given proper motivation." His words drew her eyes back to his. Blue-green and luminous, they caught and held him in an unrelenting grip, suspended breathlessly inside a strange, frozen moment. A swirling sensation, rather like falling backward into water, swelled inside him. It was confusing, disorienting, exhilarating. It made him want to pick her up and carry her off to their bed. It made him want to drop to his knees and beg her forgiveness. It made him want to shout triumphantly that she was his forever.

Good lord, he thought, not for the first time. *What is this thing?* It was like a foreign invader—a dangerous concoction of gratitude, guilt, and obsession, all centered on this one small woman. He had experienced stirrings of it before their marriage. But it only appeared to be growing worse.

She petted the furry head of the kitten he held for her, her fingers stroking gently, rhythmically.

Yes. Much, much worse.

"Thank you," she said, her reluctance evident in her tone. "Now, if you will hold him steady—perhaps over here by the door." She pointed to the entrance to the courtyard, which remained open. With her trademark efficiency, Victoria gathered her sketchbook from the top of another set of crates, picked up the bucket he had used earlier, and led him to the area she had indicated, just inside the door where daylight streamed in. She overturned the bucket and seated herself as though on a royal throne, pulling a pencil out of her sleeve and leafing through pages until she found a blank sheet.

"Do you need to see the rest of him?" he asked, watching her pencil fly over the page with quick, decisive strokes.

"Not just yet. The face is always the most difficult part for me." Her eyes met his briefly, then slid to his mouth, a mysterious expression stealing over her gentle features. "Well. Perhaps not always. But for this piece, I am determined to give Lady Berne something she will treasure. It must be right."

The kitten yowled plaintively. He rubbed a finger over its head to soothe it. "So, are you quite fond of animals, then?"

"Mmm. Not particularly."

"What about horses? Many artists love to paint them. Or so I've heard."

Her hand slowed, the pencil lifting for a moment. "Horses have their uses, I suppose."

Lifting a brow at the tension in her voice, he replied, "Useful. Yes. You don't enjoy riding?"

The sketching began again, her movements now almost ferocious. If she was not careful, she would tear the paper. "I don't."

"Why?"

Sighing loudly, she blew upward again, as she had done earlier, to drive her hair out of her eyes. He could see frustration wrinkling her brow. "If you must know, I was thrown once. I was quite small, and the accident broke my leg. Being confined to bed for months afterward was rather unpleasant. There is only one horse I will consent to ride, and that is my mare, Bitsy. She remained at Blackmore Hall this season, as she was due to foal."

His heart twisted at the thought of Victoria in pain. She was a light, delicate woman. He found picturing her as a little girl, her leg broken and bent at an odd angle as she screamed in agony, difficult to bear.

"So, you see, I will not be taking one of your horses for a jaunt to Clyde-Lacey House. You may rest easy on that score, husband." Her acerbic tone aside, he couldn't help feeling some relief. Keeping her away from the duke while in London was not strictly necessary—he could have simply allowed events to play out and begun the bastard's punishment after the end of the season—but he had decided early on that a more immediate dose of revenge was required, one he could witness personally. It sent Blackmore an unmistakable message: Victoria belonged to Lucien now. *He* controlled where she went, who she saw, what she did. She was at his mercy, and there was nothing *his grace* could do about it.

Now, if only he could persuade his wife of the same thing, all would be well. He had a plan for that, actually. Well, not a plan, precisely. More of an idea. Oh, very well, a recurring fantasy involving his mouth and Victoria's eager surrender.

"He is purring."

Blinking in confusion, he looked down, realizing she referred to the orange tabby. The creature was, indeed, emitting a quiet purr.

"I think he likes you," she said. The light shifted over her face and, for a moment, lit her up in a glorious nimbus. The little furrow of concentration between her brows. The mischievous half-grin that tilted her lips. The golden glint in her disheveled curls. She stole his breath.

"Hmph," he grunted, since anything more eloquent was beyond him. "Are you finished yet?"

"Patience, my lord. It is a virtue."

"Never been fond of virtue. Frightfully boring."

Her hand paused over the paper and her wide eyes met his as though he had said something profound. "Perhaps you are right." Having seemingly come to some sort of conclusion, she dropped her gaze again to her sketch, slowly running her pencil back over the kitten's whiskers. "But the alternative is worse." A strange sadness shadowed her face, as though she had lost something precious.

Women, he thought in bafflement. *Confounding creatures, all.*

"There! That should do for his face." Over the next ten minutes, Lucien unwrapped the kitten a bit at a time, first one leg, then two. Victoria sketched each part as it was revealed, filling in details such as the stripes and claws. Soon, the entire body was free of his coat, but the kitten was still purring. Finally, she finished the sketch and held it up for him to see.

"It is excellent. A perfect likeness."

"Do you suppose Lady Berne will like it?" she asked anxiously.

"Of course," he murmured, hurrying to place the kitten back in its nest behind the crate and shaking out his coat. Blast. The lightweight green wool was covered in orange fur. He draped it over his arm. "Now, I believe we were discussing virtue, or the joys of a lack thereof." Turning to give her a wicked smile, he was dismayed to see Connell returning with Hugo. The groom drew up behind Victoria, who was lost in thought, absently tracing her finger over a page of her sketchbook.

Later, the incident would seem almost predictable. Hugo entered behind Connell, the chestnut Thoroughbred a gigantic presence coming alongside Victoria. Suddenly, the horse whinnied, sidestepped, bumped hard into Victoria's shoulder, knocking her off balance. She yelped, jerked, and shrank into a tight curl against the wall.

"Connell!" Lucien barked, running toward the melee. "Get him under control."

"Aye, m'lord." The groom tugged at the harness, making a tick-tick-tick sound as he tried to calm the massive hunter. Eventually, he managed to persuade the prancing Hugo to place all fours on the ground and walk steadily to his stall.

"Victoria?" Lucien asked quietly, stroking her shoulders, her back, her hair. She clutched her sketchbook to her chest, her arms wrapped about herself. She was trembling and would not look at him. But he was thankful she allowed him to draw her close. "Are you well?"

She nodded. But he didn't believe it. He enfolded her in his arms, holding her tightly and feeling her shudder roll through him as though it were his own. "It's so silly," she said in a tiny voice. "Most horses do not frighten me at all. He startled me."

"Shh, love. Everything is fine. You are safe." At first, as her shaking subsided, he thought to release her. But then she leaned into him as though she still needed his strength to hold her up.

"I should not have gone riding that day," she whispered, laying her ear against his chest. "Papa warned me never to ride his hunters. But I was bored. I had only ridden ponies and the oldest, slowest gelding in Blackmore's stable. Balthazar was magnificent, a great, shining black beast. I knew that together, we could fly." She nuzzled her face further into his chest, the memory clearly painful.

"And did you, angel?" His voice came out oddly strangled.

She nodded. "It was wonderful. I had never dreamed of going that fast. Then, he was no longer beneath me. Just like that. Later, I discovered he had stepped in a hole and his leg simply ... cracked. That is why he disappeared. I kept going and landed badly. We both broke our legs, can you imagine?" Her laugh sounded dry and forced, trailing off into a long silence. "Papa had to shoot Balthazar. He was quite furious. I was fortunate he did not consider the same remedy for me."

Lucien simply held her and stroked her back, wondering about a father who showed more concern for his horse than his daughter.

She sighed and stirred, slowly stiffening and drawing away as she recovered from her fright. "You must think me the veriest ninnyhammer—"

"I do not." Sliding his palms around to her back to prevent her escape, he held her in place. Where she belonged. "You were just a girl."

"Papa said that seven was old enough to know better. And

he was right. I should have known."

He shook his head in disbelief. Seven. Truly, he was beginning to see where Harrison Lacey's stone-hearted nature stemmed from.

"Ahem. M'lord, 'ugo's been returned to 'is stall," Connell said from behind him. "If I may, sir, I would like to 'umbly apologize to 'er ladyship."

He turned to glare at the red-faced groom. "Then do so."

Connell nodded and removed his cap before facing Victoria. "M'lady, I beg yer forgiveness. I did not see ye there as we came in—"

"Nonsense," she replied, her chin tilting up at a proud angle.

"N-nonsense, m'lady?"

"You shall not apologize, as it was not your fault in the slightest."

Connell blinked, his hands wringing his cap into a tight roll. "It weren't?"

Lucien stared at his wife, who looked every inch the viscountess, albeit a rumpled one. "It wasn't?" he asked dubiously.

"Certainly not. The horse jostled me unexpectedly, and I was startled. It is not your fault or the horse's, but mine." She gave them both a brave smile. "No harm done."

Simultaneously, Lucien and Connell protested, but she held up a hand for silence. "I'll hear no more about it." One arm clutching her sketchbook, she turned pertly on her heel and walked away from him, her hips swaying in a way he was beginning to suspect was designed to torture him.

Bloody hell, he thought, his groin clenching and hardening into an all-too-familiar ache. *If this is an illness, then there is only one cure: I must seduce my wife.* He watched her sweet, rounded backside taunting him from across the courtyard. For his sanity's sake, he must have her again. And soon.

Chapter Fifteen

"I can no more abide a rambling servant than I can a squeaking carriage wheel. Both are intolerable and must be either silenced or replaced. I prefer 'replaced.'"

—The Dowager Marchioness of Wallingham to her newest new lady's maid, the sixth in as many months.

The following morning, the invitation to Lady Wallingham's luncheon arrived. Nervousness quivered in Victoria's belly, echoing up through her fingers and causing the paper she held to tremble. She had never attended one of the dragon's luncheons, had only heard about them from Lady Berne. This would be her gauntlet, a test of her courage. By all accounts, the luncheons were both subtle and brutal, a gaggle of pinch-faced matrons passing judgment on everything from one's choice of slippers to one's choice of husband. It made the presentation at Almack's seem like a warm embrace by comparison. *But it is necessary, and so I shall do what must be done.* She took a bracing breath.

Lucien entered her sitting room as though he owned it, which she supposed he did. Still, he had been acting increasingly presumptuous of late, ignoring her formal demeanor, deliberately brushing against her at every opportunity, saying provocative things she only half-understood. It was most disconcerting. He behaved for all the world as though they'd simply had a minor tiff, and it was only a matter of time before she came to her senses and let him back into her bed.

"Another invitation, my darling? It seems our efforts are beginning to bear fruit."

"Mmm. Lady Wallingham would like me to join her for luncheon on Thursday. And please stop calling me your darling. You know very well I do not like it."

Ignoring her demand, he sauntered casually to her chair and studied the note over her shoulder. "So, is this the luncheon in which other women attempt to throw daggers at you, and you attempt to evade them?"

"I believe so."

Lucien paused, his eyes glittering, then narrowing. "You should not put yourself through this, Victoria."

She stood and busied her hands with straightening the papers on her desk. "It will be fine. Besides, this is only the first step. After the luncheon, we should begin receiving more invitations, which will allow us to reestablish ourselves within society."

Suddenly, she felt the heat and strength of his body surround her from behind, his arms circling her waist. His chin settled gently atop her head. "I shall go with you."

Frozen in place, she soaked in his nearness like a rose deprived of sunlight for too long. Why could he not keep his distance? He seemed determined to break down her will to resist, not with kisses and seduction, but with warmth, wit, and husbandly concern. The first she might be able to defend against, but nothing weakened her like Lucien's strength and care.

Straightening away from his body, she braced herself against the onslaught. "You were not invited, my lord. It is a luncheon for ladies only."

"Then I will wear a dress."

She couldn't help it. The unexpected rejoinder caused her to snort with laughter.

Seizing the opening, his voice rose to a falsetto. "My dears, where *do* you find your bonnets? I daresay mine are sadly last season."

Consumed by helpless giggles at the image of Lucien Wyatt in a woman's gown, taking tea and simpering over fashion with the ton's most notorious gossips, Victoria had tears rolling down her cheeks before she managed to regain her composure. By that time, Lucien's hands were sliding over her hips, drawing her back into his embrace, where his arms banded across the front of her shoulders and waist, and he rocked them slowly side to side. It was like dancing.

She wiped her cheeks, sighed, and shook her head. In these kinds of moments, more than anything, she mourned what she had lost. A husband who might love her. A family of her own.

A fantasy, you mean. And how can you lose something you never really had?

The thought was sobering. "Release me," she said quietly.

He stilled their swaying motion, but kept his arms locked across her front. "Must we be enemies, Victoria?" he whispered, his lips unnervingly close to her ear.

"We are what you have made us."

"I am not the one who denies us the pleasure of the marriage bed. I am not the one who pulls away when offered comfort or affection."

Her eyes squeezed shut, honesty forcing her answer. "No."

She felt his sigh at her back. "He killed my brother, Victoria. Is it not natural that I would want nothing to do with him?"

"Lucien—"

"You are angry. Understandably. But *you* are not my enemy, love." His voice was low, persuasive. Her heart ached for him, for what he had been through. Dear God, how was she supposed to resist this man? "Can we not find a way to at least be friends?" She couldn't be sure, but she thought she felt his lips brush her temple. "We live in the same house, after all."

Perhaps if he had pushed for more than friendship, had demanded to reclaim his rights as her husband, she could have continued to deny him. But she needed someone. She had never felt lonelier in her life, cut off from her brothers, isolated from most of polite society. At least Lucien offered the comforts of companionship. And he was right: Like it or not, they were married, and that would not change. Maintaining the wall of hostility between them had already proven exhausting. Perhaps if they could establish a kind of truce, it would ease her desire for him, make lying next to him every night more bearable.

"Very well."

Wrapped around her as he was, she could feel tension harden every muscle in his body. "You agree?"

Her hands settled on his thick forearms. "I agree that we needn't be enemies." Sliding her fingers to grip his wrists, she gently pried them apart, stepped out of his embrace, and turned to face him. "Are you ..." She bit her lip and continued. "Are you sincere in offering friendship, my lord?"

His expression unreadable, Lucien moved closer but did not touch her. "I am."

"And this is not a ruse to ...?"

His half-grin finished the thought for her, even before he replied, "A ruse, no. But if you expect me to stop wanting you, to give up hope of being inside you again, I fear you ask the impossible." The bald statement and the flash of lust in his dark eyes sent gooseflesh over her skin. Her tongue darted out to moisten her lips. His gaze followed, his nostrils flaring on a deep breath.

"I do not wish to fight with you, Lucien." Her voice, while thready, was strengthened by raw honesty. "Perhaps we might put our differences aside—"

His full-scale grin spoke of triumph.

"—for the sake of peace between us. However, I have not changed my mind about ... certain ... intimacies." She cleared her throat as his grin receded, although it did not disappear entirely. "So long as you understand this, I see no reason we shouldn't behave ... cordially toward one another."

His grin returned, this time with a devilish glint that made her slightly uneasy. He bowed formally and winked. "It is my honor to begin a new, *cordial* path with you, Lady Atherbourne." He offered his hand. She stared at it for a long moment before giving him her own. "May our friendship prove most gratifying for us both."

THE HEAVY CLEAVER LANDED WITH A LOUD THUNK, EMBEDDING itself into the dense wood of the butcher block. Cook wiped her hands on her apron and scowled at Mrs. Garner. "I've half a mind to take a wooden spoon to his backside, I do."

Mrs. Garner shook her head in disgust. "She don't deserve none of this, tha' much is certain. Never known a sweeter soul. Whatever her brother might'a done."

"Hmmph."

"A real shame, it is."

Agnes entered with a basket of onions. She was a haughty one, with her pretty face and buxom figure. But Mrs. Garner knew working the kitchen would humble her in no time, the lazybones. "What's a shame?" the girl asked, setting the basket on the floor.

"Just never you mind," Cook barked in her gravelly voice. "Fetch me a bundle of mint from the garden, and be quick about it."

Agnes huffed resentfully, but did as she was told. Cook cast a glare at the girl's flouncing exit, then turned back to Mrs. Garner. "Regular Jezebel, that one. You sure you want to keep her about?"

Mrs. Garner scoffed. "She couldn't tempt his lordship *before* he married. Think ye she could do it now?"

Cook laughed roughly. "Not likely. Only one woman's got that boy's breeches on a string, and that's his wife." She lifted the lamb shank from the board and skewered it on the spit. "Never thought I'd see it, either. After the sad business with Master Gregory and all."

Shuddering, Mrs. Garner felt a chill run over her flesh. "She chose the blue room fer her paintin'. I tell ye now, I'll not go in there. Gives me the shivers jes' thinkin' about it."

Connell entered, arguing quietly with his wife, Georgina. "It's wha' 'is lordship wants, Georgie. Think ye I should thank Lord Atherbourne for making me 'is coachman by disobeying 'im?" He dumped an armful of split wood next to the fireplace.

Georgina, a slight, flaxen-haired chambermaid—one of Mrs. Garner's best—took on a challenging posture as he turned back, brushing his hands down the front of his coat. She swatted his arm, sending dust pluming up from the cloth. "After you let Hugo knock the poor lady sideways, she could have demanded you be sacked, Connell O'Malley. If anyone should be thanked, it should be her."

The coachman looked distinctly uncomfortable. "Now, don't go gettin' in a dither. It's not good fer the babe."

Georgina cast a skittish glance over her shoulder at Mrs. Garner, probably wondering if the housekeeper overheard. She needn't have worried. Mrs. Garner knew everything that went on in Wyatt House, including that her best chambermaid was expecting her fourth child. The truth was, the lass should have been sent home after the first one. But she begged to be allowed to continue her work, said that her mother was happy to care for the wee ones while she and Connell saved up for a house of their own.

Their situation was unusual, but that was true of many of the servants working for Lord Atherbourne. Billings was mostly deaf and well past the age when he should have been shuffled off to retirement. Connell, an Irishman who'd grown up in Whitechapel, was too young to be considered for any position other than a lowly groom. Cook had spent a spell in Newgate after a nasty disagreement with her not-so-dearly-departed husband. And then there was Mrs. Garner, herself. Try as she might, she could not manage the decorum demanded of most housekeepers in the finer households of London. She talked too much, had the wrong accent, and as a former employer once said, exhibited "an abundance of energy which is taxing to witness."

Lucien Wyatt, and his brother before him, did not care a whit for appearances. They had kept Billings on because the dear old man loved being a butler, and despite his deficient hearing and painfully slow gait, he was one of the best she had ever seen—efficient, proper, discreet, and a firm but fair manager of the male servants. Similarly, Connell and Cook had been elevated to their positions upon demonstrating excellence in their tasks. Very few employers took any interest whatever in their servants' lives. Most would prefer to hire new, rather than rewarding their staff with greater responsibility and increased wages. But both Wyatt boys were a different breed. They were reasonable in their demands, generous, and loyal, which had, in turn, earned the undying loyalty of Mrs. Garner and the others.

That sentiment was being challenged, however, with Lord Atherbourne's latest mandate. When he had first introduced his new viscountess, none of them had known what to expect. They had all heard tales of new mistresses turning into monsters after the honeymoon. But they soon discovered *their* new mistress was as sweet as a sugar cone, listening to Mrs. Garner blather on, patiently repeating herself so Billings could hear, and insisting Connell's mistake with Hugo be forgotten. In a thousand tiny ways, she had shown herself to be rather extraordinarily kind. Mrs. Garner could not fathom how Lord Atherbourne could gaze into those big, blue-green eyes and see the man he hated, rather than the wife he should love. Why, just this afternoon, she had longed to hug the young woman, herself. But even Mrs. Garner knew some overtures were beyond the pale.

Agnes sauntered back into the kitchen, placed the requested herbs on the work table, and planted her hands on her hips. Cook glanced at the maid over her shoulder. "Mint's taking an awfully long time these days."

Unfazed, her chin rose. "Some bloke came by the mews gate. Curious one, he was."

Mrs. Garner frowned. "What 'ave I told ye about flirtin' with all and sundry—"

She snorted. "Wouldn't flirt with that one. Ragged as a dog's forgotten bone. He was asking about her ladyship."

Lady Atherbourne's new lady's maid, Emily, spoke from behind Mrs. Garner. "Dark-haired, bit like a wolfhound about the face?"

Mrs. Garner turned to stare at the young, blond girl, who had worked as one of the upstairs maids before being reassigned by the new viscountess. "Ye seen this gentleman, Em?" she asked. It was one thing for saucy, disobedient Agnes to engage a stranger in conversation while working, but Emily was a good girl.

Nodding, Emily answered, "Aye. Week before last, at Covent Garden. Claimed he worked for her brother."

"And he ain't no gentleman, you ask me," Agnes muttered.

Alarm rang a peal down Mrs. Garner's spine. "Ye didn't tell 'im nothing, did ye?" The two maids looked at each other, then back at Mrs. Garner sheepishly. It told the housekeeper all she needed to know.

"Seemed harmless enough, Mrs. Garner," Emily said

abashedly. "All he said was her brother, the duke, wanted to know she was well."

Coming back through the doorway with another armload of wood, Connell stopped mid-stride. "You talkin' about the runner?" he asked.

They all blinked at the coachman. "Runner?" three of them said in unison.

He dumped his burden on the previous pile and dusted his hands. "Aye. One o' them Bow Street blokes. Me cousin Davey works in 'is grace's stables. 'E said the duke 'ired the runner straight away after the weddin'."

Well, well. It seemed the duke was determined to look after his sister, even from a distance. *And she deserves looking after,* thought Mrs. Garner. Shaking her head and planting her hands on her hips in a posture the others knew meant business, she announced, "I've heard enough. It's time to get back to yer tasks, not stand about gossiping." She gave them all a stern glare. "If I hear ye all are talkin' to tha' Bow Street fellow, tellin' him of his lordship's private doings, ye can be certain-sure ye'll be missin' a day's wages fer that week, as ye'll not be workin' on Saturday. Now, off with ye."

They all scampered out of the kitchen, leaving her and Cook alone. Wiping her hands on a cloth before bending over the fancy new range Master Lucien had ordered installed, Cook said wryly, "Don't want to tell you your job, Gertie, but giving them an extra day off ain't much of a deterrent. More like incentive."

Starting toward the doorway leading to the dining room, Mrs. Garner sniffed. "Can I help it if they flap their jaws? No. All I can tell 'em is what happens when ye do—ye don't work Saturday, and her ladyship might end up reunited with her brother." She returned Cook's sly grin with a small one of her own. "The rest is up to them."

Chapter Sixteen

"We are frequently referred to as the gentler sex.
Foolish notion. Women are far more vicious than men.
We are simply better at disguising it."

—THE DOWAGER MARCHIONESS OF WALLINGHAM to the Countess
of Berne after a particularly spiteful Thursday luncheon.

WITH ITS WALLS OF PALE CANARY SILK, ORNATE SETTEES AND chairs upholstered in pink florals and burgundy stripes, and assorted portraits of female ancestors on every wall, Lady Wallingham's parlor was an ode to femininity.

How appropriate, then, that it was currently occupied by no fewer than seven women, Victoria included, sipping tea from delicate china cups and chatting about the latest *on-dits*. Lady

Wallingham sat near the fireplace, holding court. The regal tilt of her head as she listened to Lady Berne's account of a recent musicale gave her the look of a swan surrounded by ducks.

Annabelle Huxley chimed in, describing the horrid orange dress one performer had worn. The other ladies tittered and joined in with their own observations. Baroness Colchester, a pinch-faced brunette with gray at her temples and wrinkles around her mouth, suggested the girl's intent had been to distract from her lackluster skills at the pianoforte. Next to her, the tall, bony Viscountess Rumstoke—who rather eerily resembled a horse—huffed and wished aloud that such a distraction had been possible, as she had not experienced such agony since the Pennywhistle cousins debuted. A collective shudder ran through Lady Berne, Lady Wallingham, Lady Colchester, and Lady Rumstoke.

That must have been quite a debut, Victoria thought.

"Must have been some debut."

The murmured comment from beside her did not immediately register, first because it had been barely above a whisper, and second because it closely echoed her own thoughts. When she glanced at the normally silent Jane Huxley, however, it was to discover a glint of humor quirking the young woman's lips and dancing behind her spectacles.

Victoria cleared her throat and leaned closer to say quietly, "I was just thinking the same thing."

Wide, dark eyes flew to her own, and flags of red bloomed on Jane's round cheeks as though embarrassed to have been caught expressing a thought.

Victoria smiled at her mischievously and nodded in Lady Wallingham's direction. "How long do you think she will wait to declare all musicales a torturous waste of time?"

From across the room, Lady Wallingham said archly, "Musicales are, at best, tedious and, at worst, abject misery. I shall never attend another."

Jane and Victoria blinked at one another and stifled their laughter behind their hands. Tension left Jane's shoulders, and she looked at Victoria curiously. "Do you know Lady Wallingham well, then?"

Victoria took a sip of tea and shook her head. "I have only seen her on three occasions. Four, including today."

Jane tilted her head as she examined the dowager marchioness. "I have often wondered whether she was born with such boldness or if life has made her so," she said, her tone almost wistful.

"Likely some combination of the two, I would imagine."

The plump young woman sighed, nodded, and sipped her tea, wrinkling her short, rounded nose at the flavor.

"The tea is excellent, is it not?" Victoria said, more to keep a conversation going than because of any special fondness for it.

"Oh! Yes, I suppose so. Um, what I mean—I am ... Oh, bother!"

Victoria smiled encouragingly. "Not to your taste?"

"I—I prefer coffee, actually. I take it with cream and a bit of sugar. It is my favorite thing. Well, except for chocolate. And books, of course." The last bit came out breathless, as though Jane had been holding the confession inside through force of will.

"What is your favorite book?"

One of Jane's dark eyebrows lifted. "Rather like choosing a favorite shade of blue, my lady. Each is beautiful in its own way."

Victoria nodded. "As a painter, that sounds perfectly sensible to me. But you still haven't said what your favorite is."

Gleaming with fierce intelligence, Jane's eyes reflected her quick cataloging and discarding of titles as she considered her answer. "Understand you are forcing an artificial construct upon that which cannot possibly be measured."

Victoria smiled. "Of course."

Pride and Prejudice." The young woman whispered it, a slight flush lighting her cheeks.

"I have heard of it, but have not read it yet. Is it wonderful, then?"

Victoria was surprised at how Jane came alive in that moment, animatedly describing the romance of Miss Elizabeth Bennet and Mr. Darcy. Jane was positively rapturous over the surly Mr. Darcy in particular, explaining that he was woefully misunderstood.

"You see, *pride* in his position within society was in many ways to be expected, but he shows admirable strength of character in setting aside those presumptions and following the dictates of his heart—devotion to his Elizabeth."

"You describe it so beautifully, Lady Jane. I shall purchase the book myself as soon as I can arrange it." Victoria wrinkled her nose. "I would do so after the luncheon today, but I must return home directly, as we are to attend the theatre this evening."

Her companion glanced right and left, then stared hard at Lady Wallingham, who was harrumphing over the "abominable" refreshments offered at Almack's. Jane then reached surreptitiously behind her and withdrew a slim, brown book. It was creased and careworn, the leather lighter at the edges from being handled and read frequently.

She slipped it to Victoria, placing it on the cushion between them. "Take mine," she whispered.

Victoria immediately shook her head. "I couldn't possibly ..."

"I have several other copies stashed about the house. Besides, it is only the first volume of three. Take it. Please. If you like it, I can lend you the rest."

Tucking the book beneath the fold of her skirt, Victoria clasped Jane's hand in her own, squeezing warmly. "Thank you, Lady Jane."

She squeezed in return. "Just Jane will do. And you are most welcome. I hope you enjoy it as much as I have, though I am not sure it is possible."

Victoria chuckled at the young woman's wry tone. "And you must call me Victoria."

"With pleasure. Victoria."

They chatted amiably for several minutes before Lady Colchester interrupted with a shrill, "Lady Atherbourne must certainly know."

The room fell silent as Victoria focused on the woman. "I beg your pardon, Lady Colchester. What must I know?"

"Why, whether dampening one's skirts is common practice among the demimonde," she sneered.

Victoria should have been prepared for the insulting comment. She had walked into the Wallingham parlor expecting just such an attack on her moral character. However, coming amidst her pleasant conversation with Jane, the verbal slap momentarily stunned her. As she reeled from the impact, the silence stretched and sagged under its own weight.

Finally, although her heart pounded and a cold flush of discomfort washed through her, she managed to reply calmly, "I am sure I do not know, for I do not associate with anyone in the demimonde."

A haughty lift of the woman's brows signaled she would not be so easily put off. "That is surprising, as I have heard Lord Atherbourne favors such women. Most recently, a certain Mrs. Knightley, if I am not mistaken."

The gasps upon hearing the name Knightley spoken in polite company suggested the woman must be quite notorious, even if Victoria had never heard of her.

"And, of course, there are the circumstances surrounding your ... *marriage*. Forgive me if I have drawn a conclusion that, while obvious to those with higher standards of conduct, is perhaps too presumptuous." Disdain fairly drizzled from Lady Colchester's thin, downturned lips like the blood of prey on the muzzle of a wolf.

Anger tightening the muscles around her spine, Victoria sat straighter and raised her chin as the daughter of a duke was wont to do. "I daresay you know very little about Lord Atherbourne and nothing at all about my marriage, Lady Colchester."

"I know what occurred at the Gattingford ball, as I heard it from Lady Gattingford herself. Such an incident has a way of illuminating one's character quite well, wouldn't you say?"

Victoria had long hated the viciousness of the nobility, the sharp knives one must either avoid or parry at every turn. Until Lucien, her defenses had consisted of an impeccable reputation and avoidance of cruel harpies like Lady Colchester. But, as she was now learning, when the enemy changed tactics, one must consider alternative weaponry.

Shaking her head and clicking her tongue against her teeth, she said, "'Tis a shame true love is such a rarity in most society marriages. Particularly of the, shall we say, *older* generation."

Both Lady Colchester and Lady Rumstoke stiffened at the dig. "True love?" Lady Rumstoke scoffed, looking down her alarmingly long nose at Victoria. "Is that what you call it?"

Victoria's smile was deliberately secretive and knowing. "Indeed. Oh, I suppose Lord Atherbourne and I could have chosen differently. We could, even now, be trapped in unions with no real affection, and certainly no passion." She met Lady Rumstoke's eyes directly. "Dry. Cold. Lifeless." She shifted to Lady Colchester. "*Barren* marriages."

The woman flinched, her nostrils flaring and eyes narrowing ominously.

"Thankfully, we have found happiness in one another that is, well ..." She dropped her eyes modestly, picturing Lucien as he'd been the night of the Berne dinner. Inside the carriage. Between her legs. "... astonishing." This last word she uttered breathlessly, with a blush.

Their reaction was everything she could have hoped. Both women sputtered wordlessly, swallowed hard, and looked nothing short of bitterly envious.

Before either could continue her attack, Lady Wallingford stepped in. "True love is delightful when it results in so fine a match as yours, Lady Atherbourne. While I cannot recommend high-flown sentiment for every young miss, I must say it has proven its worth in this instance. Besides, Lady Gattingford is prone to exaggeration. Why, if she were to spy a kitten on her doorstep, she would declare it a lion simply to weave a spectacular tale."

Lady Berne, watching the exchange with wide eyes, blinked as though suddenly realizing she was to participate. "Yes! Did she not several seasons ago insist she had grown not only lemons but also pineapple in her orangery? To be sure, she could not even grow oranges there, as the glass was to be replaced that year."

As the four matrons continued their discussion of Lady Gattingford's rather flexible definition of truth and moved on to decry Lord Gattingford's appalling taste in waistcoats, Jane nudged Victoria and leaned closer to murmur, "You handled them superbly. I am in awe."

Victoria gave her a brittle smile, still shaking inside from the confrontation. "Thank you for saying so. I hated every minute of it, but it was necessary." She dropped her gaze to her hands where they twisted in her lap. "How I wish it were not."

Jane was quiet for a moment, then said, *"Strange fits of passion I have known ..."*

Victoria turned a startled look upon the young woman's serene countenance. Had she missed something? A sudden turn in the conversation? Victoria freely admitted she tended to get lost in her own thoughts at times.

"And I will dare to tell, but in the lover's ear alone, what once to me befell." Jane noticed Victoria's confused frown and clarified, "Wordsworth."

Victoria simply looked at her blankly.

"No? Well, no matter. Suffice it to say you cannot explain love or passion to those who are bereft of both and, consequently, more sour than Lady Gattingford's lemons."

Shaking her head and chuckling, Victoria whispered, "That sour, eh?"

Jane grinned mischievously, revealing a pair of dimples. "Seems to defy the laws of nature, but yes. Have you tasted her lemonade?"

Victoria rolled her eyes and puckered her lips in a dramatic representation of a "sour" face. This set both of them to giggling. When the laughter trailed off, she turned to the spectacled young woman beside her and gave her a grateful smile. "I do believe we could become great friends, Jane."

Jane grinned back, her eyes sparkling prettily in her plain face. "I do believe you are right, Victoria."

Chapter Seventeen

"Heavens, boy, who attends the theater to watch a play?
The real entertainment is not found on the stage.
Everyone knows that."

—The Dowager Marchioness of Wallingham to her son,
Charles, upon his inquiry about a recently attended production
of *King Lear*.

While the luncheon had gone much according to plan,
later that evening, Victoria's spirits were troubled once more.
All because of Lucien.

Quite simply, the man confounded her. For the last several
days, he had been all she could have hoped for in a husband—
amusing, solicitous, protective. She kept him company in his

study while he finished correspondence with his solicitor. He made her laugh with his tales of boyhood pranks and a furious maid wielding a large laundry paddle. They dined together, strolled in the park together, conversed quietly together—it was the kind of comfortable companionship she'd sorely missed since being cut off from Harrison. Of course, her feelings toward Lucien were the furthest thing from sisterly, but still, the last few days had been surprisingly ... nice.

Then, he spoiled it.

Seated beside him in a box at the Drury Lane Theatre Royal, Victoria studiously ignored her husband and focused on the riveting performance of Edmund Kean as Richard the Third. The famed actor was brilliant, pacing the stage with vigor and delivering Shakespeare's words with a subtlety few had ever achieved.

But she scarcely noticed. All she could think of was Lucien's irritating, intractable, overbearing, *unreasonable* behavior.

"Are you going to be vexed with me all night?" he inquired, his tone nonchalant.

The lummox. He would do well not to speak at all.

Without looking his way, she held her palm up to signal her desire for silence.

He sighed loudly. "I can see you are determined to be unreasonable."

Immediately, her hackles were reignited into a veritable blaze. Wide, furious eyes met his. "I am unreasonable. *I* am unreasonable?"

With a half-grin and an arrogant nod, he replied, "It is good you understand."

"If anyone is *unreasonable*, my lord, it is you," she spat in a fierce whisper, glancing around to be sure their argument was not overheard.

Across the theater, Harrison sat in a box with Lord Dunston and Dunston's sister, Mary. She could not tell whether he had spied her with Lucien yet, as he had not looked their way. A lump formed in the middle of her chest, sadness surrounded by a hard shell of anger. It was one thing to avoid her brother sight unseen, another to see him in person and be prevented from speaking with him.

"It is entirely *expected* that I would wish to visit Harrison's box—"

"Equally so that I would not," he said grimly.

She shook her head in exasperation. "Then, why should I not go alone?"

His eyes glittered, his face hard and unsmiling. "You know the answer to that. Besides, even if, by some magical spell, you convinced me to change my mind, I would not allow my wife to wander about a darkened theater without escort."

"Then *escort* me, for the love of heaven. Why must you be so difficult?"

He stared at her for a long time in the dim light. For a moment, she thought perhaps he was reconsidering, but he said nothing more, instead turning back to watch the play. She released a hiss of frustration and shifted angrily in her chair.

Their argument—a repeat of one they'd had upon arriving—ended with silence, thick and suffocating, which only fueled her anger and drained whatever drops of enjoyment she might have had from the outing.

The night had begun with such promise, too. She'd surprised Lucien with her new evening gown of sea-green silk, designed with a low, square neckline and elbow-length sleeves. Knowing how it brought out the green hue in her eyes and hugged the swells of her breasts, she had fought helplessly against shivers of anticipation as she had imagined his reaction. And he had loved it, his dark eyes flashing and flaring as he watched her descend the stairs. Unable to look away from her bodice for a long while, his jaw had flexed visibly before he finally offered his arm.

Fortunately, he had not pressed his advantage on the way to the theater, behaving with perfect propriety, and their journey had been most pleasant. But, upon arriving and seeing her oldest brother sitting opposite them, an aching sense of homesickness had overwhelmed her. So strong was the emotion, in fact, that she made up her mind to approach Harrison, whether Lucien liked it or not. And their argument had ensued. Now, she battled tears of both indignation and heartache. She *missed* Harrison. Until her marriage, he had been her guardian, her friend, the one who loved her without question.

She did not know if Lucien cared a whit for her. He had never said so. She was reasonably certain he wanted her, and perhaps enjoyed her company on occasion. But, was he concerned that she was unhappy? Clearly not. At least, not more than he hated her brother. She could understand his resentment, really she could. Harrison had shot someone Lucien held dear. It was natural to want to avoid such a person. But did he believe she would agree to this forever? The very idea was laughable.

She sniffed and swiped at a tear with her gloved hand.

On the stage below, Kean's Richard knelt before Lady Anne, inviting her to stab him with his own sword rather than continue to rage at him, declaring her beauty the reason for his murderous impulses. *Clever man, appealing to her mercy and her vanity in the same breath.*

Lucien was every bit as clever, she thought, wooing and charming her into compliance. Was she, Victoria, similarly being played for a fool? In the darkness, she slid her gaze sideways and studied Lucien's profile: Gentle lips that had sent her to heights of pleasure she hadn't imagined possible. Strong, sculpted jaw that reflected his determination and stubbornness. Dark eyes, which could fill with storms of passion, light with twinkling humor, or soften with a lazy smile. Try as she might, she could not simply dismiss him as a villain and toss him aside.

He had offered friendship, and she had accepted, hoping that, in time, she might convince him to set aside his hatred, his need to punish Harrison. Obviously, at present, he had no such intentions. His stubbornness made her want to hit him. Scream at him, too. Force him to admit he was wrong. Her anger still burned in her stomach, her fists clenching in her lap.

But he simply sat there, stone silent. *That* was infuriating.

She glanced again at the blond head of her brother, just visible in the faint glow from the stage, now tilted slightly to hear what Mary Thorpe whispered to him. Harrison nodded, then he straightened and stilled, seeming to peer directly ahead at the box opposite his.

Her box, or at least, the one she was currently sitting in. *Oh, God.* Did he see her? Would he want to speak with her? If he made the journey across the theater to visit her, then Lucien could not prevent it from happening. It was the perfect solution, if only he would—

Harrison's face angled back toward the stage, giving no sign of recognition or acknowledgement of her presence. Not so much a wave or even a nod. Victoria's heart fell. Either the duke did not see her—unlikely, considering she could see him and there was nothing wrong with his eyesight—or he was deliberately ignoring her. Whichever the case, it was difficult to swallow.

This is patently absurd, she thought, shaking off her despair. *I should stop being a ninny and simply rise and go to his box. What can Lucien do, after all? Refuse to accompany me to a few ton functions? Well, yes, but perhaps he could be persuaded to relent if it was only this once. What else can he do to stop me—toss me over his shoulder?* Remembering he had done almost that very thing on their wedding day, she bit her lip and glanced sideways. He was still watching the action on the stage below.

Before she could think better of it, her decision was made. Breathing deeply, she stood and moved swiftly—or as swiftly as her skirts would allow—toward the darkened rear of the box. A hard hand circled her upper arm almost immediately, jerking her off balance and turning her to face her husband. Correction—her imposing, obviously angry husband.

She swallowed hard, her mouth going dry.

"Where do you think you're going?" he asked quietly, his voice silky and menacing in a way she had never heard.

She shrugged, though she felt anything but casual. "Am I not allowed to visit the privy either, my lord?"

"Victoria, I told you I do not want you going about this place unescorted. Now, either sit back down or I shall assume you are bored and take you home."

"You are being ridiculous!" she hissed. "Let go of me." She jerked at her arm, but to no effect. His grip, while not painful, was quite firm.

He pulled her close and turned until her back faced the wall. Stepping forward so that she could not help but retreat, he loomed over her, his mouth inches from her own. They were far enough from the lights of the stage that it was difficult to see, and certainly others would not be able to see them in the shadows. As she bumped against the wall, his white cravat and the flash reflecting in his eyes filled her vision amidst the darkness.

A nervous flutter in her belly grew and caused her breath to quicken as his chest brushed the very tips of her breasts. She drew in his scent, spicy and familiar and delicious. His hot breath washed over her face, making her want to sink her nails into the skin of his neck and pull him down into her kiss.

"Apparently Mr. Kean could not hold your interest, my darling," he uttered hoarsely. "Perhaps I can do better." The hand that had held her arm now dropped to her waist, slid around her hip to the small of her back, then lowered to caress her backside.

"Lucien," she sighed, her muscles meltingly weak. "You agreed ..."

"It appears this is a night for breaking agreements, wife." With one hand, he forced her hips to cradle the rigid erection between his legs. With the other, he clasped her neck and tilted her head back for a hard kiss, his tongue sleek and searching, sliding against her own.

Her arms circled his neck, seemingly of their own volition, and her fingers threaded through his hair, digging into his scalp and pressing his lips harder against hers. She ate at his mouth, hungrier for him than she had ever been. Volatile and riotous, the excitement inside her combusted with lust and anger and yearning.

Bending his knees and pressing upward against her with his hips, he forced her legs to spread for him, forced her onto her toes for him, held her pinned between his heat and the unyielding wall. He ground the hard length of his cock against the very center of her, sending curling waves of delight spinning from her core to every part of her body. She groaned into his mouth.

Cool air wafted across the backs of her thighs. Before she could protest, the hand that had inched up her dress once again stroked her buttocks, but this time there was nothing between his flesh and hers. His fingers trailed down the crease, now splayed open for him, and found her wet and ready for him. Two sank deep inside her womanly core, the path slick and easy with her arousal.

She whimpered, her head falling back on her neck, exposing her throat to his feasting mouth. Two fingers, then a third stroked and pumped inside her, stretching her with the slightest pinch of pain—just enough to keep her excitement at a fever pitch.

"You will come for me now, love." The guttural statement rumbled in his chest, murmured next to her ear, resounded in her core. "Then we will leave here, and I will take you fully in the carriage. Would you like that?"

She licked her lips, tasting him there, the scent of her own desire and his spice blending into an intoxicant. She nodded frantically, her peak approaching in a rush as his words played in her mind. Seizing around his fingers as they slid and pressed, stroked and pleasured, her climax suddenly cascaded like water over a fall, then crashed in paroxysms of radiant pleasure.

He took her soft moans into his own mouth, the sounds

masked by the soaring strains of the orchestra and the dramatic oratory of those on the stage below. All the while, as her body slowly returned to earth, he held his fingers firmly inside her, allowing her time to complete the journey. She tore her mouth away from his and slumped against him, her cheek lying on his fine woolen lapel. His chest heaved as he struggled for breath, jostling her slightly.

He removed his hand and let her skirts drop back into place. Inside, she felt molten—hot and liquid, yet still somehow needy. Empty. She could barely stand as his hips drew away from hers, requiring that she support herself on her own legs. She wanted to tell him such a thing was impossible, as her legs were now the consistency of softened butter, but she was having difficulty speaking.

His big body, still rigid with tension, shifted, and as though he had read her mind, he scooped her into his arms. She began to protest, murmuring that others would see.

"Not to worry. Hold on to me, Victoria."

She obeyed, wrapping her arms tightly about his neck and hiding her face in the comfortable notch between his neck and shoulder. The scent of starch and spice filled her nose. It was the scent of her husband, who carried her as though she weighed nothing, who thrilled her and fulfilled her until she could think of nothing else, indeed could not think at all.

Swiftly, he descended the stairs to the lobby, pausing now and then to assure concerned passersby that his wife was not feeling well, and he was taking her home. Within minutes, he was setting her on the padded seat of their carriage and climbing in beside her. Immediately, he tried to take her onto his lap, but she refused, brushing his arms aside.

His darkly muttered "Victoria ..." trailed into a groan as she unbuttoned and lowered the fall on his breeches, releasing his fully aroused cock.

Peeling the gloves from her arms, she stroked him several times with a firm grip, just the way he had taught her. The heat and satiny texture of his member fascinated her, the veined flesh hard and thick, an instrument of ultimate pleasure. Her head lowered as a bead of moisture rose to the tip.

Ah, yes. She loved this part.

Her tongue delicately flicked at him, taking his essence into her mouth. His hips writhed, and he growled low in his throat, his hands gripping the cushion.

"Stop," he gritted.

She smiled up at him, savoring the stark desire on his face. Her lips played with him, then she suckled lightly on the tip, curling her tongue around the domed head like the veriest treat.

His hands gripped her arms and hauled her onto his lap. Before she could say a word, or even have time for the world to stop spinning, she was on her back, her skirts flung up around her waist, his cock stretching her sheath.

He shoved inside her forcefully, filling her completely. They groaned together, the sense of rightness almost unbearable. *This* was where he belonged, deep inside her where she could surround him and caress him and ease him.

This was where *she* belonged, wrapped in his arms, his mouth capturing hers, his body invading hers, his heart pounding against hers in synchronized rhythm. He filled her emptiness, and she welcomed him, consumed him in her heat.

To Victoria, their connection was so profound, she wanted to weep. Her chest tightened, and she sobbed against his neck. It was as though, with each thrust, her emotions were forced to the surface until they lay bare and exposed.

Thrust. The ache of longing.

Thrust. The burn of frustration.

Thrust. The sweetness of adoration.

Thrust. The spiraling of desire.

Taking his head between her palms, she positioned him so she could stare intently into his eyes. He resisted at first, but she gently stroked his cheeks with shaking hands and waited.

It was dark inside the carriage, but muted, broken light did shine through the curtains, playfully shifting amidst the shadows. It was enough to see what was in his eyes, in his face.

Desperate, desperate need.

For her.

She had never seen the like. But she had felt it. Oh, yes. It was the twin of her own yearning. For him.

And it set her on fire.

Sobbing his name, she arched and squeezed her eyes shut, clenching her teeth as her body surrendered everything. She wrapped her legs around his furiously hammering hips, locked her arms around his neck, and held him tightly as the world exploded in a shattering burst. The muscles of her sheath seized and gripped him almost painfully as her release hit.

Lucien's mouth covered her scream as he slammed into her and came in a violent frenzy. Low, animalistic growls rumbled from his chest as his seed shot deep inside her core. The spasms lasted seemingly forever, rippling pleasure echoing through them both for long minutes. Eventually, their breathing slowed, but he remained atop her, his head beside hers, her thighs straddling his hips.

"This is how it should be, angel," he rasped next to her ear. "You can see that now, can't you?"

For a moment, she considered agreeing, for the same thought had occurred to her only moments earlier. *No. How many times must you be hurt before you understand, Victoria? How many ways must you be shown the truth? You've known since you were seven. Such joy carries a price you cannot afford to pay.*

She stroked his hair and gently kissed his jaw, the faint bristle of his whiskers chafing the tender skin of her lips. "I wish it were that simple," she said softly.

He stiffened and raised up to look into her eyes. His were serious, searching. Then he dropped his gaze, a lock of dark hair falling over his forehead as he nodded. "So do I," he whispered, almost soundlessly, as though saying it aloud might make it true.

Chapter Eighteen

"The nightmare is over? Foolish boy. One does not exile such darkness. It must be extinguished beyond repair."

—THE DOWAGER MARCHIONESS OF WALLINGHAM to the Duke of Wellington one year before the Battle of Waterloo.

IN THE BEGINNING, IT WAS ALWAYS THE SAME—A WARM FIRE crackled in the hush of the library at Thornbridge. Lucien was small, seated on the floor looking up at his father, who was reading. Black hair much like his own gleamed amidst a bright shaft of sunlight. A long, bold nose created a shadow on Papa's cheek. Gregory had inherited that nose, and Lucien knew he hated it, even though Mama called it "distinguished." But she was not here and neither was Gregory. It was just him and Papa.

A frown wrinkled his brow, a bubble of anxiety swelling in his chest like a black cloud on the horizon. How could Papa be here? He was dead, long ago taken by a ravaging fever. Lucien recalled watching him struggle through his last, rattling breath. Presently, Papa gave him a smile, setting his book aside and crouching in front of Lucien.

"I am here. Of course I am here," he said, grasping Lucien's small hands in his own.

The anxious tightening in his chest did not dissipate. The sound of footsteps behind him made him turn. There was Gregory, who looked all of fifteen. He was followed by a giggling, black-haired toddler. Marissa.

"Gregory, did you know Papa has returned?" Lucien asked, a wave of relief surging through him. If Gregory could see him, perhaps this was real. But Lucien's brother shook his head and gave him a whack on the arm.

"Another jest, Luc? Papa's dead. You know that."

Lucien swung back to where his father had been only moments before. Gone. He was gone. The light grew dimmer, grayer. The carpet disappeared, the wood-paneled walls replaced by trees and a curtain of rain.

Laughter sounded behind him. He now stood on a rise overlooking the brook that cut through the center of their land. In the distance, he could see the sprawling stone mass of Thornbridge. Strangely, his mother's voice sounded faintly in his ears. "Take care of them, Lucien. They are all you have now."

Rain soaked his shirt, the cloth clinging to his skin, squeezing him. Drowning him. Choking him like a noose. "I know, Mama. I tried." Water poured down his face; he wiped his eyes over and over, trying to see. At last, he was able to make out her small form. She was so far away, he could not see her features, but she was there. She had died giving birth to Marissa, he knew. But his heart leapt upon seeing her again. Stumbling forward, he drew closer, but for each step he took, she receded. Rain drummed against his skin, chilling him. Light faded and hid behind iron clouds. Wind battered the leaves of the willow trees.

His mother became a shadow, and he could not stop the cry of grief that tore from his chest. She was gone, too. Why must they all leave him?

"You never take anything seriously, Luc." It was Gregory, now a full-grown man seated on his bay, which snuffled and munched the grass beside Lucien.

"I do now. I wish you were still with me, brother." His voice was thready, squeezed tight by the need to wail. To cry and scream like a small babe.

The distinctive sound of girlish giggles came from his left. He turned to see Marissa, probably no older than six or seven, spinning beside the brook. She wore a white dress, her long, black hair loosely tied with a blue ribbon. She beamed and twirled, her arms thrown wide as she danced to music only she could hear. A bright red poppy was clenched in one of her hands, the bloom seeming bigger than she was.

"Look, Luc!" she shouted in delight. "The rain has stopped."

"Be careful, Mary Sophia," he shouted back. He'd always used her full name when he wanted her attention. "You don't want to fall in the water and drown, do you?"

She glanced up at him, her expression transforming from joy to sorrow in a blink. "But you're here to save me. Don't you wish me to be happy?"

"Of course, little one," he said, instantly regretting his warning, which had been much too dire. She was just a girl. She should be able to play and dance without fear of dying. But they had already lost Mama and Papa.

The rain began again, falling softly at first. He felt it, cold and damp. Soon, it wrapped around him in a wet cloud. The wind picked up, creaking the branches of the trees. A sudden gust rocked him from front to back. Clenching his eyes closed, he waited for it to pass. When he opened them again, Marissa was farther away, about fifty feet downstream. She was no longer dancing. Instead, she walked slowly, somberly, the wilted red poppy sagging in her loose fist.

She was too close to the edge. The need to warn her burned in his throat. He shouted her name. Again. And again. She didn't respond.

Gregory's horse crowded against Lucien's shoulder, pushing him off balance. "She can't hear you, little brother. You're too far away."

A peal of thunder boomed overhead. The horse shied nervously, knocking Lucien sideways with its enormous bulk. Lucien slipped, his feet going out from beneath him in the grasping muck. He landed painfully on his side, then watched in horror as the horse reared above him, one of its terrified eyes visible as it folded its neck to the side. Falling. It was falling. Onto him.

Horrifying pain like nothing he'd ever experienced ripped through his legs as a thousand pounds of horseflesh landed, crushing him. Pinning him. He writhed, screamed. The world went dark. Thunder cracked louder and louder. Men were shouting, wailing. Dying all around him.

He waited for it to end. Prayed for it to end.

Then, suddenly, it did.

"Wake up, Luc."

It was his brother's voice. The voice he'd heard countless times in the early dawn, telling him he'd better get up if he wanted to catch any fish. He opened his eyes. He was lying on the bare wooden floor of an empty bedroom at Wyatt House. It was quiet, but for the ticking of his mother's ormolu clock.

"Are we going fishing?" Lucien asked, relief flooding through him at the thought that it had all been a nightmare. A terrible, awe-inspiring dream. Gregory was not dead. Marissa was not in danger. It was a day like any other. Except that he was lying on the floor. That part was unusual.

He stared up at the white paneled ceiling, studying the ornate moldings along one edge where it met the blue walls of the room. It was blessedly quiet. No booming thunder. No rushing wind. No screaming horses or cries of agony. The ticking clock only served to make the silence thicker. A chill ran through him. Afraid to glance around, knowing he would find the room empty, he focused intently on a shell-shaped plaster flourish, then closed his eyes.

"It is time for me to leave, Lucien." It was *her* voice, sweet and sad.

Tears leaked from his eyes, trailing down along his temples. "No," he whispered. "Please don't go."

Finally, although dread weighted his muscles and made his movements stiff, he opened his eyes and looked at her. She was older now, but still wearing white. The red poppy was sodden, dripping crimson on the floor. "I must. It hurts too much to stay," she replied, her eyes both sorrowful and empty, her skin as white as her dress.

"No," he said again, repeating the word over and over. As though that would make a difference. As though it would change what happened. But it never did. Even as he said it, he knew. It never did.

VICTORIA WASN'T CERTAIN WHAT AWAKENED HER. IT COULD have been Lucien's arm brushing her shoulder. Or the shifting of the mattress as he tensed and rolled onto his back. But she suspected it was the whimper. Such an unusual sound coming from her strong, commanding husband. The quiet cry sent ice trilling across her flesh.

"Lucien," she queried softly, turning onto her side so she might see him better in the early light. Propping herself on one elbow, she shifted beneath the blankets and slowly reached out to stroke his bare shoulder with her fingertips. Damp. His skin was soaked with sweat.

He writhed and turned his head away as though in terrible pain. "No," he moaned. "No." His breathing quickened and every muscle tensed. Victoria's chest squeezed around her heart. She stroked his arm where it lay, seemingly pinned to his side. His muscles were hard as stone. Pulling back the blankets, she saw that his entire torso fairly vibrated with tension.

What on earth? she thought, concern gripping her hard. Victoria debated the wisdom of waking him. Being awakened in the midst of a nightmare could be disorienting and embarrassing, especially if he knew she had seen him in such a vulnerable state. On the other hand, she could not bear to see anyone suffer so, even if it was inside a dream. Abruptly, he sighed, and as though a dam had broken, air surged out of him. His forehead smoothed, and within minutes, his muscles fully relaxed.

She murmured nonsensical reassurances, continuing to stroke his shoulder. Hours earlier, they had arrived home after making love in the carriage, both quiet and pensive. As he had slipped into bed beside her, she had fully expected to feel his arms slide around her waist, to have to explain why, after letting him seduce her in a darkened theater, she would once again deny him in their own bed. But he hadn't touched her, had only sighed and drifted off to sleep, his breaths deep and long.

She was not so fortunate. As she'd lain next to him in the dark, she could not deceive herself: He was a constant temptation, the finest nine-course supper imaginable offered to a starving woman. Friendship had not eased her desire; but then, neither had holding him at arm's length. *So, what would you like to do now, Victoria?* The answer came swiftly: To be his wife in all ways. But that was far too costly. Wasn't it? The confusion had kept her awake well into the night. Finally, sleep had come, only to be interrupted by the troubled man beside her.

Slowly, she lowered her head back down onto her pillow, but remained watchful, listening for any change. It came minutes later with a whisper she almost missed. Immediately, she sat up, staring closely at his face. His mouth was open, working as though he were speaking, but no sound was coming out. It looked as though he was saying "no" over and over and over. The soundless plea amidst such stillness chilled her to the bone. It spoke of pain so deep, it could not be healed. Instinctively, she scooted closer to him, grabbing his arm and wrapping it around her, then hugging his side with her body. She lay her cheek against his chest, stroked his belly, and spoke his name gently. Again, and again, and again.

She repeated it a dozen times before she sensed him awaken. She knew because that airless whisper stopped. But he did not move, instead lying in perfect stillness.

"Husband?" she murmured. "Are you all right?"

When he didn't answer, she lifted herself up to sit beside him and searched his face with worried eyes. His arm dropped onto the bed as though he had no strength. He was pale, but perhaps that was the watery gray light coming through the windows.

"Lucien, you were having a nightmare." Carefully, she reached out and stroked his cheek, needing the contact probably more than he needed her touch. "It's over now. Please tell me you're all right."

Several moments passed, several beats of her sluggish heart, before his dark, troubled eyes met hers. They were unreadable, but gleamed in the weak light. He turned away for a breath, then turned back but refused to meet her gaze, instead reaching up to stroke the small of her back through her night rail.

"I am fine. You should go back to sleep."

She shook her head. "Your dream, it must have been terrible."

He pulled away, throwing back the covers and sitting up on the edge of the bed. She watched as his strong, bare back slumped and his head hung forward for a moment before he stood and made his way toward the dressing room. He did not answer her question. He did not say another word. He simply dressed in riding clothes, came back to the bed to lay a gentle kiss on her forehead, then left her alone, wondering what had just happened.

Chapter Nineteen

*"A woman has needs, Charles. Unfortunately for you,
the greatest ones are the most expensive."*

—The Dowager Marchioness of Wallingham to her son,
Lord Wallingham, upon being confronted with the bill from a day of
extravagance at Mrs. Bell's shop on Upper King Street.

"Take a look at this one." Victoria shoved another
fashion plate beneath Jane's nose and watched her new friend
roll her eyes. "Come now, the waistline is perfect. It's a bit lower
than most current styles, but I think for your shape—"

"You mean the shape of a giant strawberry?" came the wry
response. "Please. Unless the cloth magically turns a sphere into
a cylinder, this dress would prove no more flattering than every

other gown in my wardrobe."

Victoria sniffed. "Rubbish. You are not a sphere. You are simply generously endowed with ample curves."

Jane turned to face Victoria, who sat beside her on a settee in Mrs. Bowman's shop. She removed her spectacles and promptly offered them up. "Here," she said. "I fear you may need these more than I do."

Chuckling at her friend's antics, Victoria shook her head and resumed examining sketches of gowns and accessories.

"You really do enjoy this, don't you?" Jane asked.

Victoria glanced up, seeing genuine puzzlement on the young woman's face. "It appeals to my love of beauty," she answered. "Fashion is color, shape, and texture. It is an enhancement of one's form." She shrugged. "In some ways, it is like painting."

On the opposite side of the room, Mrs. Bowman strode through with wide sweeps of her arms, rattling off instructions in accented English, and leading two assistants behind her like puppies. Abruptly, she stopped mid-sentence, her eyes locking on Jane. Victoria looked over at her friend, who sat frozen in place. Mrs. Bowman walked toward them, a slight frown settling between her dark brows.

"*Spaventoso*," the elegant woman muttered, her gaze fixed on Jane's gown. Victoria could not be certain, as she knew only a smattering of Italian, but she thought the modiste's comment was something along the lines of "appalling." Mrs. Bowman reached forward and plucked at Jane's pale yellow sleeve, which puffed out from her shoulders, then sagged rather sadly. "Hmmph," the modiste grunted. "Who dresses you?"

Jane's head jerked back a bit. "I—I beg your pardon?"

Victoria decided to intervene before Jane's distaste for this outing grew any worse. "Mrs. Bowman, allow me to introduce Lady Jane Huxley, the daughter of Lord and Lady Berne. Lady Jane, this is Mrs. Bowman."

Jane rose to her feet, her face flushing slightly. She greeted the modiste, who still examined her with a clinical, disapproving eye.

"I thought perhaps a new gown or two might be just the thing—" Victoria began, only to be interrupted by a long string of rapid-fire Italian. "Ah, pardon?"

Looking impatient, Mrs. Bowman turned to snap her fingers at a mousy assistant. "Take her to the back. We must measure first."

"Oh, but I thought we were just going to look at fashion plates," Jane protested weakly, her voice fading as Mrs. Bowman grasped her elbow and propelled her toward the curtained doorway to the dressing area.

A half hour later, Jane emerged through the same curtain, her face a study in misery, her hair slightly mussed, her yellow gown wrinkled on one side. She looked as though she had been caught up in a violent whirlwind.

"Oh, dear," Victoria said, smothering an inappropriate urge to laugh. "Was it terrible, then?"

Jane picked up her shawl from where she had left it on the settee, sniffed, and pushed her glasses further up on her little round nose. "That depends on one's perspective," she replied matter-of-factly. "Do you enjoy torture by a thousand tiny pins and abject humiliation whilst unclothed?"

Victoria shook her head.

"Then yes. I believe 'terrible' would be accurate."

Despite Jane's resistance and numerous protests, over the next hour Mrs. Bowman and her two assistants drew up an order for a dizzying number of gowns, many in darker, more dramatic colors than were typical for a girl in her first or second season. The modiste commanded the effort like a conductor of a grand symphony, her hands waving theatrically, Italian phrases intermingling with English. In the end, the eight-page order was presented to Jane, who took one glance and blanched to approximately the color of chalk. Eyes wide as saucers, Jane shook her head, first slowly, then adamantly. "Absolutely not."

"Oh, but Jane, you must at least consider the bronze gown—" Victoria protested, only to be stopped by her friend's flat stare.

"There is perhaps a month left in the season," Jane said. "This kind of extravagance cannot be justified, even for one's debut. And I am well beyond that."

It was true. Jane was in her second season, and had yet to acquire a single suitor, much less a proposal. At nineteen, she had time left before she was considered on the shelf, but Victoria had hoped a new wardrobe might revitalize her friend's prospects and boost her confidence. As it was, Jane was the quintessential wallflower—quiet, colorless, and invisible. And with her refusal of Mrs. Bowman's efforts, that appeared unlikely to change.

"Bah!" Mrs. Bowman scoffed. "You English. Cold as fish and just as miserly." The modiste snatched the pages from Jane's hand and gave her an imperious glare. "Come back when you tire of looking like a dumpling." She turned on her heel and stalked away, her assistants following like two obsequious shadows.

Nonplussed, Jane looked at Victoria, who shrugged apologetically. "Well," the spectacled young woman said briskly. "I don't know about you, but the mention of dumplings has stirred my appetite. Shall we adjourn for luncheon?"

Grinning at her friend's good humor, Victoria agreed and looped her arm through Jane's. As they stood outside the shop waiting for the Berne carriage to pull up, Victoria's neck prickled. It was the oddest sensation, almost as though someone was staring at her without her knowing. She glanced around at the crowded walkways along Bond Street, but did not see anything unusual. It was most peculiar. She had experienced the feeling on two other occasions recently, but had not been able to pin down its source. Turning her head to scan the crowds again, she looked from left to right, only to freeze as she spotted a familiar face.

Mary Thorpe, sister of the Earl of Dunston, walked out of a

neighboring shop and ambled toward them, her petite frame and cinnamon-colored hair instantly recognizable among the crowd of blond misses who accompanied her. While Victoria was not especially close with Mary, they were the same age, and their brothers were good friends. She got on rather well with the girl, who had always been perfectly amiable. Victoria had even considered her a possible match for Harrison, if he would only turn his attention to finding a wife.

Preparing to greet the girl, whom she had not seen in weeks, Victoria stood a bit straighter and pivoted in the group's direction. Several of the blonds met her eyes, instantly stiffened, then whispered to one another. Mary's eyes remained focused straight ahead, her mouth flat, as the group neared. Then, just before they would have passed Victoria and Jane, the girls halted, crossed to the opposite side of Bond Street, and continued north for a short distance before crossing the street again to resume their original course.

Her stomach cramped. She felt the sickness of embarrassment wash over her, prickling heat settling in her cheeks. What Mary and her friends had just done was as close to the cut direct as one could get without an outright confrontation. Such deliberate avoidance—as though merely breathing the same air as Victoria would somehow taint them— was a clear signal that the scandal raged on, a poison that could not be drained.

"I saw a pigeon do that once," Jane's dry voice interjected. "Turns out the poor thing had bashed its head and knocked itself silly only moments before. It's to be expected, I suppose, when one's brain is not quite up to snuff."

Victoria struggled for a smile, swallowing hard. Jane squeezed her arm reassuringly. It was then that it struck her how risky their association was for Jane's reputation. If their plan failed, being seen with the object of such notoriety could taint the girl and permanently damage her chances at a match.

"Jane, I ..." Victoria began, but was interrupted when the

coach emerged onto the street from the alley and pulled up in front of them.

"Ah, finally!" Jane sighed, waiting for the footman to open the door. She climbed inside, quickly scooting to make room for Victoria. As Victoria settled onto the seat, Jane reached over and patted her hand. "On our next outing, I shall take you shopping for books. There is this place on Piccadilly you will love. Well, I believe you will, but then I am hardly impartial—"

"Jane," Victoria interrupted, hating this moment. "I am so grateful to have your friendship, but ..." Tears—blasted, unruly tears—sprang into her eyes, choked off her well-intentioned words. She had so few true friends. Most of her female acquaintances were more like Mary Thorpe, polite and pleasant but superficial. In the past two weeks, Jane had become more dear to her than all of them combined, her steady nature and self-effacing humor a balm to Victoria's spirit. While Lucien and Victoria had settled into a kind of cautious cordiality, they had not resumed their previous friendship, nor had he made any overtures of the amorous variety. It was most disappointing—er, refreshing. *Yes*, refreshing *to be all but ignored by one's husband*.

She took a bracing breath and continued. "Until it happened to me, I never thought much about the people involved in scandals. I felt sorry for them, I suppose. That they had erred so badly. But this is ... it is painful, Jane." She glanced up from her gloved hands to meet Jane's warm brown eyes. "To be constantly reminded of your humiliation. To be scorned by everyone around you. I don't think I could bear it—"

"Nonsense," Jane replied firmly. "If I can bear Mrs. Bowman's poking and prodding with her mighty pins, you can endure this. It will get better, you'll see. Lady Wallingham has said it, and therefore it is so."

This brought a brief smile to Victoria's face. "I was going to say I don't think I could bear it if you suffered in any way because of me. Already this scandal has burdened my brother, the duke, dreadfully."

Jane went oddly quiet, her expression shuttered. "You still have not heard from him?"

Victoria shook her head. "Lucien has forbidden me to contact him, but there is nothing preventing Harrison from writing or visiting me."

"Perhaps Lord Atherbourne has warned him away."

"That may be so. But my brother is hardly one to concede to such a demand. No, after what happened at the theater, I fear Harrison is angry with me. Disappointed, certainly. Concerned about being further linked to such a scandal." She watched Jane's lips pucker in staunch disapproval. "It is no small matter, Jane. You could easily be tainted, as well. Perhaps we should not be seen together until matters are more ... settled."

One dark brow rose above the rim of her round spectacles. "You are presuming my *many* suitors will abandon me, and I will be left to wallow in isolation on the fringes of London's ballrooms. Unheralded. Unnoticed. Un-danced-with. Oh, the horror."

"Jane ..." she whispered, finally chuckling and shaking her head.

"Besides," Jane said, her tone migrating from sarcasm to determination. "I will not allow a gaggle of narrow-minded know-nothings to dictate with whom I may associate. Really. As though they are so perfect. Adorra Spencer has teeth larger than my slippers. And don't get me started on Lady Phillipa Martin-Mace." Jane huffed in disgust at two of the four blonds who had crossed Bond Street to avoid Victoria. "Saw her kick a dog once. Poor thing. I pity the man who marries her. He'll be black and blue, mark my words."

The carriage rocked to a stop outside the Berne residence. Before the footman opened the door, Victoria took Jane's small hand in her own and squeezed affectionately. "I don't know what I have done to deserve such a dear friend, but I am ever so grateful," she said quietly. "If you should decide it prudent to keep your distance, I will think no less of you."

"Well, I would," Jane retorted. "Come now, let's have luncheon. I find a good meal does much to calm one's nerves."

They stepped out of the carriage onto the walkway in front of the Berne townhouse, and again, Victoria felt that strange tingle along the back of her neck. It was a small, localized shiver at the top of her spine, the sensation of hairs rising away from her skin. Immediately, she spun around in a circle, her eyes searching the quiet street.

There! It was a man, dark-haired, wearing a greatcoat and a tall hat pulled low over his brow. The brim made it difficult to see his face, but his clothes looked somewhat worn and rumpled. Something about his demeanor, his shuffling stride, suggested he did not belong on this street, among these houses. He stared at her a moment, then looked away, strolling casually in the opposite direction to disappear down a set of stairs into the area below one of the houses.

Must be a servant or a deliveryman. She shook her head, wondering if perhaps her imagination was getting the better of her.

"Victoria, are you coming?" Jane called from the doorway.

She plastered on a smile and ascended the steps to link arms with her friend as they walked inside. "So, let's discuss this bookshop you would have me visit."

Chapter Twenty

"I have said it before, and I shall say it again: Intelligent men are dangerous men. It is good there are so few of them."

—THE DOWAGER MARCHIONESS OF WALLINGHAM to Lady Berne after meeting privately with the Prime Minister.

THE RUNNER SLOUCHED IN THE SEAT ACROSS THE DESK FROM Harrison, his expression wary and haggard, his dark clothes rumpled.

"Atherbourne is also preventing her receiving my letters, then?" Harrison asked softly.

"Near as I can tell, your grace. The servants don't like it much, but what can they do?"

Harrison nodded, his thoughts churning. He had known

Atherbourne had *something* planned. All considered, it was better than he had feared. According to the Bow Street runner he paid to keep an eye on Victoria, his sister had not been harmed since her marriage, aside from being commanded to keep her distance from Harrison. After he'd spotted her at the theater, he had asked the runner to make further inquiries, thinking perhaps her refusal to see him or answer his letters stemmed from Atherbourne's interference. He'd been right.

The runner shifted and cleared his throat. Harrison raised a brow. "Eager to depart, Drayton?"

Pinned under Harrison's gaze, the other man squirmed. "N-no, sir. Er—your grace. It's just that it's been three days since I've seen a bed—"

"Are you saying you'd prefer I hire someone else for this task?"

That perked the scruffy creature up directly. "Not at all. I'll do the job, for certain, your grace."

Harrison stared at the man wordlessly for a full minute. He had always found silence useful. Others often attempted to fill it, which tended to benefit him. "Excellent. I shall expect another report in three days' time." With that, Harrison dismissed the man from his mind. Drayton, accustomed by now to the duke's manner, departed with a brief bow. Harrison heard the door click as he turned his attention to the most recent figures from Blackmore Hall's household accounts. It appeared the cook Victoria had hired last fall was rather profligate with the spices. He'd have to put a stop to that.

Victoria.

His hand tightened on the paper, causing the numbers to wrinkle and fold in on themselves. She had always been a romantic sort, soft as thistledown beneath a composed surface. Her practical decision to marry Stickley had misled him into forgetting that fact. But somehow Atherbourne had seen it, exploited it. *Damn him to hell.*

Harrison spent most of his time lately trying to keep Colin from complete destruction, and the rest dealing with the vast assortment of problems and decisions related to running the Blackmore properties. Victoria had managed the households, and when she married, those tasks fell to him. He did not have time for a brother-in-law with a grudge and a devious agenda.

Glaring at the crumpled paper in his fist, he forced his fingers to relax, then smoothed the page with his palm. This was precisely the reaction the blackguard wanted, he thought. He refused to give Atherbourne the satisfaction of missing her, of resenting the severed connection to his sister. Besides, if he thought too much about her absence, a peculiar ache settled in his chest. It was most unpleasant.

No, rather than dwelling on these things, he would keep a watchful eye on her and await his opportunity to set things right. At some point, Atherbourne would assume he had triumphed, assume Victoria would allow herself to be cut off from her family permanently.

A subtle grin tugged at the corner of Harrison's mouth.

Such assumptions were foolish, indeed.

DAPPLED SUNLIGHT WOVE A DAZZLING SPELL AS VICTORIA strolled on her husband's arm. Hyde Park was not as lovely as the lands around Blackmore Hall, but it had its own kind of beauty—green, open, and orderly amidst the stone, brick, and grime of London. She suspected she would always prefer the country, but walking in the park was a treat, especially on a rare sunny day.

It would be a shame to ruin such a peaceful interlude, but something must be done. In the weeks since the confrontation at the theater, Lucien had withdrawn from her, behaving for all the world as if she were a houseguest—he was polite, even gentlemanly. Most unsettling.

Then there were the nightmares. While he was careful not to touch her, he continued to sleep beside her. Three times now, she had awakened to find him frozen inside a dark hell. Nothing she did seemed to help, and he ignored her attempts to soothe him, often disappearing from their bed well before dawn. She knew precious little about the secrets that weighed on Lucien's mind, and the last thing she wanted to do was cause him pain, but patiently waiting for him to broach the subject had proved fruitless.

Why, just yesterday he had returned from riding with Lord Tannenbrook, robust and flushed, smelling of brisk morning air as he passed her in the hall outside her studio.

"It is early to be so filled with vigor, my lord husband," she had teased, wanting to see the grin that was so much a part of him.

For the first time in too long, he obliged, his eyes twinkling as they dropped to her bodice. "Remarkable what a little fresh air can do for a man."

As was customary when he was like this, she went hot and weak, sighing and leaning back against the door. Only, the door was not there. It brushed her back then disappeared behind her. She stumbled awkwardly into her studio, and he leapt forward to catch her, his chin grazing her forehead. Laughing, she braced her hands on his arms and steadied them both, saying, "I forgot I unlatched it earlier."

Feeling him tense unexpectedly, she'd wondered if perhaps he had hurt himself. But that made no sense; he was as strong as a Thoroughbred—hardly prone to turned ankles and such. Her laughter had tapered and died as she got a look at his face. He paled to stark white, his eyes vacant as they stared fixedly over her shoulder.

"What is it, Lucien?" she had asked, twisting around to look about the room, wondering what had him so riveted. All seemed in order. Unable to find any obvious cause, she turned back to her husband, who remained frozen just inside the doorway, the muscles in his face rigid.

For long minutes, he had simply stared at the walls of the room. She spoke his name several times, but he did not seem to hear. His eyes brushed over her face without recognition, then returned to a spot on the wooden floor just in front of the fireplace. Ice bloomed beneath her skin as she watched him. This man was a stranger. Not her Lucien.

It had so terrified her that she immediately grasped his hands and yanked as hard as she could. "Lucien!" she shouted. "Answer me." She mimicked the voice her soft-spoken mother had used when particularly vexed with Colin's antics—firm and authoritative. It appeared to work, as his face snapped back toward her, and something sparked in his turbulent eyes. "You must tell me what is wrong."

A full-body shudder had run through him, similar to the trembling she had witnessed during his nightmares. Was this simply grief? she wondered. Had the loss of his brother damaged his mind such that these episodes of—what? Shock? Despair?—came on like a sudden squall, random and disquieting? She did not know. All she knew was that he hid a great deal from her.

"What is it?" she'd demanded again.

He had stiffened and pulled away from her, stepping slowly back toward the door. Her hands remained outstretched, colder as he retreated. "It's nothing," he whispered, then shook his head briskly, his hair falling down over his forehead. He pulled in a stuttering breath like a man who had nearly drowned. Clearing his throat, he repeated without meeting her eyes, "Nothing at all." And then, like they followed a script only he had read, but which must be repeated each time she drew too close to the source of his pain, he backed away and left her alone. Later, he would return to normal, acting as though the incident had never happened.

Brought back to the present when a bird swooped in front of them, she released the memory with a deep sigh.

"That was rather wistful. What are you thinking about?"

Plastering a smile on her face, she looked up at Lucien where he walked beside her and shook her head. "Nothing, particularly. Just that I prefer the country."

His gaze brushed over her. "We're to depart for Thornbridge at the end of June, but we can leave sooner if you like. I have no special love for town, myself."

A part of her longed to say yes, to leave as soon as possible. To forget London existed. He assumed she would travel with him to his country estate after the season was over, continue living together as husband and wife. She, on the other hand, was sure of nothing. "I wish we could," she said softly.

"Why can't we?"

"You know why. We must dance the dance society demands. The more we are seen this season, the less the scandal will matter next year and the year after."

He was quiet for a long time, seemingly content with her answer. They had passed several groups of acquaintances earlier, when they first entered the park, but now they were alone on this stretch of pathway. As they arrived at a bench beside a pair of tall linden trees, Lucien gestured toward it. "Shall we?"

She nodded and sat, gazing across the green expanse of lawn toward the water of the Serpentine. "Do you miss it?" she asked, feeling the light breeze play across her cheek, the heat of his body next to her on the bench. "Thornbridge, I mean."

Sensing his hesitation, she glanced up at his face. He was frowning. "It is beautiful. You will love it, I suspect."

She smiled gently. "So you've said." Folded in her lap, her hands refused to be still, her fingers clasping and loosening, fidgeting and twisting.

Why is this so difficult? she wondered. *Just ask him.*

"Does it remind you of—of your brother?"

As expected, the mere mention of Gregory caused Lucien to stiffen. He did not look at her, but stared straight ahead. "Most things do. Wyatt House was his, as well."

She waited for him to continue, but he didn't. "That must

pain you, to live in the same places, to be called by the same title." Hesitating only a moment, she laid one hand on his arm. He looked hard at where she touched him, saying nothing. The furrow between his brows might be sadness or irritation—she could not be certain.

But she was determined to have this conversation, and so forged ahead. "When my parents ... when they died, I pictured them everywhere. I even thought I saw Mama once in the morning room at Blackmore Hall. I turned and realized it was merely a shadow." Her voice grew wispy. Remembering was difficult, and she knew it was worse—more recent and raw—for Lucien. "You were close to Gregory, were you not?"

He appeared captivated by the sight of her hand resting on his forearm. "As close as brothers ever are, I suppose. I was away a good deal."

"With the cavalry."

"Yes."

Silence fell between them. His reluctance to discuss his past, his brother's death, was palpable, a force pressing her to retreat. She would not. She refused to give in. "But you miss him."

Slowly, his eyes rose to meet hers. Terrible, hollow pain filled the charcoal depths. "Yes," he rasped. "I miss him."

Sliding her hand down his arm to clasp his fingers, she squeezed tightly and leaned into him, placing her face inches from his. "That is as it should be. When such a connection has been severed, it is as though a part of yourself is gone."

His throat worked visibly, and his gaze dropped to where her hands now grasped his, holding him in place. Sensing she was reaching beyond a barrier that had been between them since the beginning, she continued, "Don't you suppose I would feel much the same?"

Tension suffused his body. "Victoria ..."

"I am your wife, Lucien. He was your brother. And, yes, it is true Harrison was involved in his death—"

"I do not wish to discuss this."

"—but can you not see how your insistence on keeping me from *my* brother—"

He extricated his hands from hers and stood abruptly. "I said I do not wish to discuss it. We should return home."

She stood as well, vexation with his stubbornness causing her to stamp her foot and glare up at him. "What if I am with child? Have you considered that?"

His eyes widened to an alarming degree, dropping to her belly and flying back to her face. "You aren't ...?"

She crossed her arms, gratified to finally have a reaction from the great lummox. "The babe would be part Lacey, would he not?"

Lucien appeared both appalled and thunderstruck, as though she had taken a trout by the tail and struck him across the face with it. He grasped her shoulders. "Are you with child, Victoria?"

"No. I do not believe so." She watched him slump then turn wary. "I was simply pointing out that you are bound to Harrison through me. And through any children we would have together."

He snorted, seemingly regaining his equilibrium. "Perhaps you are not aware, my dear, but certain activities are necessary to beget children."

"Are you saying you would like to resume ... said activities?"

Brows arched, he crossed his arms over his chest, mimicking her own posture. "Are you?"

Suddenly uncomfortable with the public setting, Victoria glanced around the park, mollified that no one was near enough to overhear. "You were right. We should make our way home. The hour grows late."

Lucien grinned wickedly and bent his head down to hover near hers. "So eager, love. Not to worry. I am ever at your disposal."

Blushing, she lightly slapped his arm and set off along the path. "I meant we shall be late for the Rutherford affair."

An amused "hmm" from beside her was the only response she received. They strolled in silence for long minutes until they reached the more populated area of the park, where she felt his hand slip into hers and wrap it securely in the crook of his arm. Startled, she shot him a questioning look. He answered with a subtle nod toward the small crowd of matrons gathered near the park's entrance.

Oh, yes. We are supposed to be in love, she thought, a small sigh of disappointment escaping. *Odd how one forgets such things.*

As they approached the group, the ladies eyed them and whispered behind their hands. One of them—Lord Underwood's widow, if Victoria was not mistaken—wore a disapproving expression and an ugly gray pelisse buttoned up to her pointed chin. It was rather surprising to see Lady Underwood puckering more than usual, but such had been the reaction of many ladies since the scandal.

Lucien slowed as though he intended to stop for a chat. Victoria tugged at his arm. "Let us continue on, husband," she murmured.

Raising a brow, he glanced between her and Lady Underwood, who now tilted her nose in the air and deliberately turned her back to them. A tic appeared along his jaw. Beneath her fingers, his muscles turned hard as stone. "Not just yet." Propelling them forward, his strides became purposeful.

Victoria whispered, "What are you about?" Truly, the look in his eyes was worrisome.

He grinned. It did nothing to comfort her.

"Lucien?" she hissed.

He did not answer. By then, they were a few feet from the women, most of whom were chatting with one another, pretending not to see them. "Ladies!" he said jovially. "A fine afternoon, is it not?"

Two of them—a younger woman in a blue gown and a lady with a cheerfully wrinkled countenance and a sparkle in her eyes—turned to greet them, but the rest of the group acted as though they hadn't heard him. "Lord Atherbourne, isn't it?" the older one queried. Victoria did not recognize her but immediately wanted to sketch her; even the woman's wrinkles appeared to be smiling.

He bowed. "Lady Darnham, it has been too long."

The younger woman, who stared at Lucien in a most disconcerting way stood mute and wide-eyed. Lady Darnham introduced her as her granddaughter, Miss Clarissa Meadows. In turn, Lucien introduced Victoria. Lady Underwood's back remained a gray woolen wall behind the two women, although the three others in the group stood sideways, casting glances at Victoria, apparently undecided whether greeting her constituted a breach of moral cleanliness.

"And who are your companions?" her husband asked innocently. Inside, Victoria cringed. Oh, dear. This was not going to end well.

Lady Darnham introduced the others. The sideways ladies actually managed to turn three-quarters toward Victoria, nodding as they were named. It was a good sign, she supposed. At least they acknowledged her presence. Lady Underwood, however, was not so easily swayed. When she finally pivoted to face them, her cold black eyes stared over Victoria's shoulder, her silence a firm condemnation.

Lucien squinted and tapped his chin. "Underwood, Underwood. Ah, yes. I remember now. I met your husband on several occasions. Fine fellow. Never knew anyone with a better nose for good brandy and a favorable game of hazard."

The ladies shifted nervously. Victoria hoped her suddenly rapid blinking was the only outward sign of alarm. *Lucien, please don't do this,* she thought. But he failed to receive her frantic unspoken message. God help her, he charged forth like a warring knight armed with razor-sharp innuendo.

"His appreciation for the pleasures of life was nigh unparalleled, in my estimation. Now, some would say he appreciated himself into an early grave, but not I. Those rumors are nothing but conjecture."

Red-faced and narrow-eyed, Lady Underwood spat, "You are a vile liar, sir."

"Liar? Oh, no, I assure you I don't believe a word of it. What kind of shriveled, dishonorable wretch would I be if I credited every sensational accusation that made the rounds?" He gave a mocking chuckle. "A sad excuse for a gentleman, I daresay. And a painfully dull one, at that."

"Lucien," Victoria muttered beneath her breath. *Make him stop, Lord. Please.*

Lady Darnham cleared her throat, but before she could intervene with some polite redirection, Lady Underwood turned on her heel and stalked away, a stiff, gray figure striding alone down the path toward Park Lane.

"Well," Lucien said cheerfully, giving them all a broad, dashing smile. "I do hope you enjoy the rare bit of blue sky we are graced with today, ladies." He sent Victoria a glance of smoldering adoration. "Of course, when I am with Lady Atherbourne, the splendors of fine weather fade into insignificance. For her beauty outshines even the sun on a cloudless day."

Victoria thought she heard Miss Clarissa Meadows sigh with longing. But perhaps that was herself. After they bid their farewells, and she managed to recover from the wave of heat and melting weakness, she muttered to Lucien, "Was that really necessary?"

His smile had faded, his expression now hard and resolute. "No one turns their back on you without paying the price."

Oh, dear, she thought, gripping his arm a bit tighter. *There goes that weakness again.* It was difficult to say which was worse: Watching him pretend to be in love with her or wanting more than anything for it to be true.

Chapter Twenty-One

"Jealousy can be tiresome but useful.
And, occasionally, humorous."

—THE DOWAGER MARCHIONESS OF WALLINGHAM to
Lady Colchester, upon her complaint that Lady Reedham
had attempted to lure away her new French cook.

I REALLY SHOULD STOP STARING AT MY WIFE, LUCIEN THOUGHT.
No fewer than four gentlemen had approached him since he and
Victoria arrived at Lady Rutherford's rout. Each had felt it
necessary to mention the rumors of his infatuation, one citing
tales of Lucien whisking her out of the theater, another teasing
him about being "tangled in a woman's skirts," and two others
noting his reluctance to take his eyes off of her as she crossed

the Rutherford ballroom to chat with Jane Huxley.

True, this had been part of the plan to restore her reputation, he reminded himself. As it happened, he found it rather easy to play the part of a besotted suitor. He had not even tried very hard. *Perhaps not at all,* he thought with a frown.

But it would not do to become a laughingstock.

Look at her, though, a voice whispered inside his head. *Is she not exquisite? The way she lights up when she laughs, the way her hips sway when she walks, the way her eyes soften and melt for me alone.*

A man would have to be daft *not* to be enthralled with such a creature.

Tonight, she wore a gown the color of a sunset—bright, blushing pink with a hint of orange in a sheer, shimmering overlay. Decorated with ruffles and rosettes at the hem, he supposed it was not terribly different than what other ladies wore. But the vibrant color, the way the dress seemed to move and cling to this curve or that, and—most of all—the woman inside it, drew his eye with hypnotic intensity.

The thump of a cane striking the floor next to him jerked his attention away. "Lord Rutherford," he said, greeting the old man with a polite bow. "I was given to understand you would not be attending this evening's revelry."

At nearly seventy years, the Marquess of Rutherford was almost entirely bald, save the long, pointed set of whiskers flanking his cheeks. It was a startling contrast to his much younger, remarkably beautiful wife, who stood ten paces away flirting with a buck fresh from the schoolroom. In her prime, Lady Rutherford had been compared to a goddess, and indeed, her blond perfection was rather Venus-like, even now that she was nearing fifty. Her morals also mirrored those of the Roman goddess of love, as she was legendary for her many liaisons. Her desire for stimulation was tinged with desperation, and when her beauty had begun to fade, she had turned to hosting salacious events attended by the most virulent gossips and scandalous figures within the aristocracy. All for the titillation of stirring the pot, as it were.

Lord Rutherford was said to despise the entertainments his wife enjoyed hosting. But, then, he was said to despise his wife, as well. The man now harrumphed and leaned on his cane, squinting at the crowd, a look of disgust on his wrinkled, age-spotted countenance. "Distasteful things must occasionally be tolerated, Atherbourne. For a proper cause, you understand."

Lucien murmured a noncommittal reply and let his eyes settle where they most wanted to be: on Victoria. She was laughing at something Lady Berne was saying, her gently curved chin tilting upward. Jane Huxley touched her arm and pointed toward a set of doors on the opposite side of the room, just past where he stood. She glanced toward them and collided with his gaze. Even from this distance, he could see her breath quicken, her lips parting, her lashes fluttering. One of her hands settled over her midsection as though trying to contain herself.

He knew the feeling.

"I say, Atherbourne, did your brother, by chance, mention his desire to purchase one of my properties in Sussex?" The crackling voice of Lord Rutherford forced Lucien's attention back to the old man.

Lucien shook his head, partially to clear it and partially to answer Rutherford. The man's eyes—a deep turquoise that was faded and milky with age—still reflected wily intelligence.

"Superior wooded parkland. Excellent for hunting." Droning on for several minutes about the sixteenth-century house and its grounds, Rutherford managed to hold Lucien's interest, but only because he was curious why the marquess was so intent on selling.

In need of funds? Lucien wondered.

"... your brother had all but taken possession of the place before he—" The old man stopped mid-sentence, his eyes narrowing on someone standing near the tall statue of Poseidon positioned between two columns at one end of the room. Lucien followed his gaze and spotted Benedict Chatham, one lean arm propped on Poseidon's knee, looking decidedly bored and a bit more rumpled than usual.

Rutherford immediately excused himself and made his way toward his son.

Trouble there, Lucien thought, crossing his arms and leaning back against the wall. As before, his gaze soon gravitated back to where he'd last seen Victoria—like a billiard ball following a rut.

She wasn't there. He searched the crowd, finding Jane Huxley sitting along one wall, staring down at her hands. Next, he saw Lady Berne and Annabelle Huxley talking animatedly with a group of young ladies. No Victoria.

He straightened away from the wall and scanned the ballroom. Where the hell was she?

Out of the corner of his eye, a flash of pink silk whipped by amid twirling dancers. She was ... dancing? Yes, he realized as her golden head dipped and rose again in the movements of a lively reel.

Frowning fiercely, he sidestepped a group of young lords guffawing over a recent mishap with a phaeton, and quickly made his way to the edge of the dance floor.

So, it was Malby, he thought. She was partnered with Sir Barnabus Malby, a fat, smelly little toad who, even now, panted after her lasciviously. Of course, it could just be that the weighty man was out of breath as he tried to keep up with the steps of the energetic dance.

Grinding his back teeth, Lucien felt rage uncoil in his gut. No, the toad's bulging eyes were glued to her breasts, which jiggled delightfully as she moved and bobbed in time with the music.

What the bloody hell was she doing dancing with Malby? With anyone, really? She was *married*. To him. If he were not certain it would earn him her utmost outrage, he would toss her over his shoulder and haul her immediately to Wyatt House. Or, better yet, to Thornbridge. Just he and Victoria, alone at his country estate. Yes, that would be ideal.

But, first, he would choke Sir Barnabus Malby until the toad's eyes bulged for a very different reason. Lucien's fists clenched and his nostrils flared in anticipation.

Victoria pivoted, and he could see her face again. She was smiling brightly, clearly having a great deal of fun. Good God, he was fantasizing about killing a man simply for dancing with his wife. Taking a deep breath to regain a sense of calm, he slowly, deliberately loosened his fingers. The black anger receded as he watched the delight on her lovely face.

Patience, he thought. *Time enough to kill the toad later.* First, he must reclaim what was his. And no one else's.

CURTSYING PRETTILY TO SIR BARNABUS AT THE CONCLUSION of the reel, Victoria thanked him for the dance. The man was breathing heavily from exertion, his somewhat protruding eyes widening alarmingly as they darted past her shoulder.

"Sir Barnabus, is something ami—"

"Appears you could use a rest, Malby." The low, gritted statement came from behind her. She swung around to see Lucien, tall and imposing, glaring at the shorter, considerably more portly gentleman. "Breathing is a precious thing. Perhaps you will remember that next time you contemplate ogling another man's wife."

Shocked at his bizarre reaction, Victoria cried, "Lucien! What on earth ...?"

Sir Barnabus pressed a handkerchief to his dampened forehead and stammered, "I—I say, Atherbourne—"

Lucien moved around Victoria to stand less than a foot from Sir Barnabus. His aggressive posture conveyed an unmistakable threat. Sir Barnabus paled and stumbled back, mumbling, "Positively stifling in here. Perhaps I will take my leave."

The man disappeared into the crowd, and Victoria tugged Lucien's sleeve to gain his attention. "Don't you think you're carrying the possessive husband charade a bit far, my lord?" she asked in a hushed voice.

"A woman dances with a man for only two reasons, Victoria. She is seeking a husband or she is seeking to make one jealous." His expression was an odd blend of indignation, self-satisfaction, and typical, Lucien-like arrogance.

"That, as you well know, is utter nonsense. I can name at least one more reason a woman might accept a gentleman's invitation to dance."

He arched one brow in inquiry.

Victoria stepped close to him. "She enjoys dancing."

His mouth quirked in a wry smile. "Perhaps. But she should choose her partners more wisely."

"Perhaps better partners should offer," she replied pertly.

As the first strains of a waltz began, Lucien responded wordlessly by stepping back, bowing elegantly, and holding out his hand for hers. Victoria hesitated only a moment before she grinned, slid her fingers into his, and dipped a curtsy. He swept her into his arms and moved them gracefully into the steps of the dance, his body breathlessly close, his face within kissing distance.

The size and heat of him engulfed her as they spun and swayed. It was the first time they had danced together, so she should have been surprised by the flawless way he moved. But she was not. This was the Lucien she knew—his confidence, his strength as he guided her, almost as though he were carrying her in his arms. Indeed, it felt like floating. The intoxicating joy of dancing with her husband filled her veins like champagne, making her long to laugh aloud and brush his beautiful lips with her own. Knowing such a thing was impossible caused a bittersweet wave to sweep through her. But as he met and held her gaze, the room around them disappeared until they moved alone together. When the final notes of the waltz faded, she sighed and murmured, "That was lovely, Lucien."

Before he could answer, they both spied Jane waving frantically from beside the refreshment table. The young woman's expression, typically either shuttered or placid, was now animated by urgency.

"I do believe you are being summoned," Lucien remarked dryly.

After excusing herself, she quickly crossed the room to where Jane stood. "What is it?" she asked in hushed tones.

Jane swallowed, grasped Victoria's hands, and pulled her to a quiet corner where they both sat on an empty chaise. "I—I heard them talking. About you. And ... and Lord Atherbourne."

Victoria frowned. "Who was discussing us?"

"Lady Colchester told Lady Rutherford that you and Lord Atherbourne should never have been invited, that it would only bring further shame upon the Rutherford name."

"And Lady Rutherford's response?"

Jane glanced nervously about, then tucked her chin down and whispered, "She said that was the point precisely. She invited you *because* of the scandal."

Relieved, Victoria inhaled deeply and huffed out a mild chuckle. "Oh, Jane. You had me worried." She patted her friend's hand soothingly. "We knew that was the reason for the invitation."

Victoria's smile soon turned into a puzzled frown as Jane shook her head frantically and said, "That is not—not the terrible part. I mean, it is awful, but ..."

Seeing the deep concern and turmoil in her dark eyes, Victoria swallowed. "Tell me."

Jane's teeth worried at her lower lip, her eyes drifting away from Victoria's. "Per—perhaps I shouldn't."

"Jane." Victoria's firm tone caused her friend's gaze to snap back to meet her own. "Tell me."

Flushing, Jane answered with a question. "What do you know of Mrs. Knightley?"

Chapter Twenty-Two

"A lie is most effective when it is planted in the soil of truth."

—THE DOWAGER MARCHIONESS OF WALLINGHAM to Lady Berne
upon news of Lord Tannenbrook's hidden talent
for spreading gossip.

"THE RUMORS ARE TRUE, I SEE."

At the sarcastic comment, Lucien turned away from watching Victoria across the ballroom where she huddled in intense conversation with Jane Huxley.

He raised a brow. "Chatham. What rumors are those, precisely?"

Thin and pale, the jaded lord leaned negligently against a white column, his cravat rumpled, his arms crossed over his chest. He glanced at Lucien. "When Alvanley suggested you got yourself leg-shackled out of some misguided infatuation with Blackmore's sister, I thought him rather amusingly gullible. The Lucien Wyatt I knew was no woman's fool. It seems I was mistaken." Chatham's lips quirked. "Rare. But it does happen."

"You know nothing about me."

"Ah. So, Malby owes you money, perhaps? A much better reason to nearly come to blows with the man than his fondness for your wife's breasts. Lovely as they are."

Lucien's earlier anger, tight and coarse and dark, returned in a rush. He moved closer to Chatham, using his larger, heavier frame to intimidate. While similar in height, the man's body was lean to the point of frailty after years of dissolution. He was near enough that the fumes of whatever he'd been drinking wafted to Lucien's nose. Whisky, perhaps.

"Mention any part of my wife again, and I will put you out of your misery."

At the gritted threat, Chatham's expression went blank, his bloodshot eyes flat and cold. "Many have tried, Atherbourne. I should warn you, I am strangely hard to kill. Besides, I have no interest in your wife or her parts. I do, however, find it fascinating that both seem to be the object of your fervent ... *regard,* shall we say."

Lucien eyed Viscount Chatham narrowly. With his unfathomable intelligence and charisma, he could have been the darling of the ton. Instead, the younger lord was consumed by old hatreds, self-destructive habits, and a profound lack of shame. In large measure, Lucien was more saddened than offended at so much wasted potential.

But the fact that Chatham took any sort of interest in Victoria, enough to discuss her with Lucien in a provocative fashion, gave him pause. Then there was the man's friendship with Colin Lacey. How much of Lacey's drunken carelessness was due to Chatham's influence? At one time, the viscount had been Lucien's friend, too, and remnants of that old bond still remained. But he did not want Benedict Chatham anywhere near Victoria or her brother, not in his present state.

Lucien sighed deeply and ran a hand over his mouth, then crossed his arms. Eyeing Chatham, he spoke in a low voice. "There are better options than the ones you've chosen, old friend."

Surprise, then resentment, then coldness flashed swiftly over the other man's face. "Oh? Perhaps I could run off to the glories of war. Ravaging the French in exchange for medals sounds like a jolly good time. Unfortunately, being my father's only living heir does have its downside. Wait! I know. I could ruin my enemy's sister, then trap her into marriage to punish him in perpetuity." His face fell mockingly. "But, then, I have no particular enemy. And I would not wish to be accused of rank imitation."

Lucien's head snapped back. *How does he know? It's bloody well impossible.* But even as he thought it, he knew better. Chatham was not simply clever, he was dangerous. Capable of ferreting out secrets from the unlikeliest of sources, he should have been working in the clandestine services. Instead, he used his talents to manipulate and stir trouble.

"Have a care," Lucien warned silkily. "One who swings his sword incautiously is most likely to cut only himself."

Chatham opened his mouth to respond, then slid his gaze past Lucien's shoulder. He raised a brow and grinned slowly. Lucien turned to see what had captured the viscount's attention. Victoria, white and shaken, made a beeline to where they stood near the room's entrance.

He kept his expression carefully blank as he watched her approach, wondering what she and Jane had been discussing that had disturbed her so. He offered her his arm. She did not take it.

Instead, her lips firm and flat, she aimed a frown at Chatham, seeming to notice him for the first time. He sketched an elegant bow, his turquoise eyes glittering. "Lady Atherbourne. We have not yet been introduced."

Much to Lucien's dismay, Victoria responded by extending

one gloved hand, which Chatham quickly grasped in his own. There was nothing inappropriate in the exchange, nothing he should object to. But his gut tightened and his jaw flexed as a now-familiar dark resistance rose inside him. Lucien did not want a man like this touching his wife, not even through two layers of gloves.

Deciding the quickest way to end the contact and find out what was bothering Victoria—for surely *something* had badly rattled her—was to finish the introduction and get her alone, he said, "Benedict Chatham, Viscount Chatham. My wife, Lady Atherbourne."

Chatham bowed again over her hand and smiled appreciatively. Instantly, it transformed the man from a wastrel into a dashing gentleman wreathed in magnetic charm. *Uncanny, really. And disturbing to watch.* "What a pleasure to meet the woman who has stolen Lucien's heart, my lady. I can certainly see what has him so … enchanted."

Lucien's eyes narrowed. The snake may have slithered out of one skin and into another, but he was still a snake.

Victoria returned his smile, appearing dazzled by the blackguard. "A pleasure to meet you, as well, my lord. Are you a friend of my husband's?"

Lucien's emphatic "No" was drowned out by Chatham's reply. "We were at Eton together. I am afraid after school, our paths diverged." He glanced at Lucien, his eyes mocking. "We have only recently become reacquainted."

Intent on ending the exchange with all possible speed, Lucien kept his eyes on Chatham's face as he addressed Victoria. "Lord Chatham was just about to search out his mother when you arrived, my dear. Most fortuitous for us." He wrapped his arm around Victoria's waist and pulled her into his body. She stiffened but did not resist. "Chatham, perhaps you will give Lady Rutherford our thanks for the invitation. Unfortunately, we must depart early, as Lady Atherbourne is suffering a headache." He sensed the surprised swivel of Victoria's head.

Bowing again to Victoria, Chatham answered dryly, "Of course. I do hope you are feeling better soon, my lady." He gave Lucien a knowing grin. "Atherbourne."

An hour later, Lucien and Victoria arrived at Wyatt House in tense silence. After several attempts to persuade his wife to tell him what had disturbed her, Lucien was ready to thrash someone. Preferably Chatham or Malby.

Once inside the entrance hall, Victoria draped her long wrap over her arm and immediately climbed the stairs, saying not a word to him. Sighing, Lucien pinched the bridge of his nose between thumb and forefinger. It seemed the headache that had been his excuse for leaving was now real and throbbing behind his eyes.

In the carriage ride home, he had demanded to know what was wrong, but her answer had been a persistent and infuriating, "Nothing is wrong. I am simply tired." Which was rubbish. After their dance together, Victoria had been aglow with transparent joy. Jane Huxley had told his wife *something,* and it had upset her deeply.

His fists curled. *What could it have been, damn it all?*

He glanced up the staircase. Only one person knew the answer, and she was freezing him out. He hated it. He much preferred her anger. For several minutes, he debated following her up to their chamber and insisting she confess what Jane had shared.

Skull pounding and frustration eating at his insides, he headed instead for the library, where he poured himself a brandy and sank into the chair near the fireplace, propping his feet on the hearth. By the time he poured his second glass, much of his earlier anger had uncoiled, and his headache had loosened its grip.

Marriage was proving much more complicated than he had anticipated. No, he thought. Marriage to *Victoria* was more complicated. His feelings for her were ...

He took a large gulp of brandy, feeling it warm his throat. ... unexpected.

"Are you going to sit there drinking yourself into a stupor, then?"

Lucien shot to his feet so quickly, the world wavered and spun for several seconds before righting itself. When it did, he was greeted by the sight of his wife standing inside the door, wearing only a thin, white night rail, her long curls swept over one shoulder. She looked like an angel, the firelight flickering and caressing her curves.

Then, he met her gaze. *An avenging angel, perhaps,* he revised. She was angry, her body held stiffly, eyes hard and accusing.

Bloody hell.

"It would take far more than this," he gestured with his glass, "to achieve a stupor."

Her eyes narrowed and she took two steps closer. "I will not have a drunkard for a husband."

"Victoria—"

"Neither will I tolerate being played for a fool."

He froze. She now stood no more than three feet from him, her chin tilted pugnaciously, her body fairly bristling with outrage. It was worrisome. And inconveniently arousing.

Setting his glass on the small table next to the chair, he took a cautious step toward her. Instantly, her hand flew up to stop him, hovering inches from his chest. Her eyes blazed up at him. He seemed to have a rare talent for making her angry, but even he had never seen her this furious.

He shook his head. "You are not making sense."

"Who is Mrs. Knightley?"

He blinked rapidly, disoriented by her question. "Mrs.—?"

"*Knightley,*" she spat.

Frowning, he frantically searched his mind for what to tell her. None of the responses seemed the slightest bit appropriate for his wife's ears.

Impatient with his hesitation, Victoria continued, "Shall I tell you, *husband?* Seeing that you appear at a loss for words at the moment. Mrs. Knightley is your mistress. And has been for the past four months."

Reeling in disbelief, his breath flew from his body. His lungs heaved three times before recovering enough to speak. "Who told you such a thing?"

"Why should that matter?"

His jaw cracked. "Oh, it matters."

Her chin rose and a militant gleam shone in her eyes. His wife might be nine parts angel and one part Valkyrie, but that one part had a will of fire-forged steel. "All you need to know," she gritted out, "is that your plan to further humiliate me by flaunting this glorified trollop before all of society is doomed to failure." She poked him in the chest to emphasize her words. "I will not." *Poke.* "Be shamed." *Poke.* "By you." *Poke.*

"Victoria—"

"*Ever* again, do you understand?"

"Victoria."

"You have no idea how miserable I can make you. I will not hesitate to do so if I should hear even a whisper of that whore's name—"

He grabbed her wrist and bellowed, "Victoria!"

She yanked at her arm. "Do *not* touch me."

"Mrs. Knightley is not my mistress."

With a disbelieving snort, Victoria used her free hand to shove at his chest.

"I am telling you the truth."

Flustered from her useless struggling, she stilled, her eyes gleaming with unshed tears, her throat working on a hard swallow. His heart twisted at the sight. She shook her head, then tilted it sarcastically. "I suppose Lady Rutherford invented a fanciful tale to tell Lady Colchester. For what purpose would she lie?"

Lady Rutherford, eh? It seemed Chatham had found a way to cause mischief after all. Spreading false rumors through his mother was the least the man was capable of. Lucien would have to find a way to deal with him. But for now, all that mattered was repairing the damage with Victoria. Seeing her distraught was unbearable.

"I don't know. She enjoys stirring controversy, so perhaps

that is it. Regardless, you must believe me when I say I have no mistress. I have not looked at another woman since the night I met you, much less taken one to my bed."

She scoffed and pushed at him. "You must think me an idiot—"

He clutched her by the shoulders, shaking her gently. "I swear on my brother's grave, Victoria."

Silenced by his declaration, her mouth fell open and her eyes widened, swimming with a sudden welling of fresh tears. "You—" she whispered.

His own voice was ragged. "I swear you are the only woman I have touched since that night. Good God, angel, I am consumed with wanting you. There is nothing left for anyone else."

She searched his face, a tear trailing its way down to her delicate jaw. He rubbed it with his thumb, stroked her cheek with the backs of his fingers. *So soft,* he thought. His wife was as soft as a rosebud. And just as easily bruised.

"Lucien, I ..." She shook her head and swallowed.

He drew her into his arms, wrapping her tightly against him. Her head settled against his chest, right over his heart. As it should be.

"Perhaps I should not have believed them so willingly. It's just that I ..."

With a finger beneath her chin, he tilted her head up so he could see her eyes. "What, love?"

"We have not ... well, you know ... for many days."

He grunted his agreement. "Feels like an eternity."

Her gaze dropped to his chin, then his chest, hiding from him. "I do not like the idea of you having a mistress, Lucien."

His mouth quirked. "So I gathered." In truth, her fury gladdened his heart. Perhaps she would come around sooner than he had hoped. He ran a hand down the silken fall of curls draped over her shoulder, sliding down over her breast. As his palm stroked across her beaded nipple, he heard her breath catch and quicken. Gently clasping her wrist, he drew her hand to the front of his breeches, letting her feel the hardness he was helpless to prevent. "You have nothing to fear in that regard," he rasped, the familiar weakness invading his muscles at her touch. All muscles except one, it would seem. "I crave only you, angel."

Her beautiful eyes lifted to meet his. What he saw there made *his* breath catch. Desire. And determination. Her hand fell away. "I have never wanted anything as I want you," she confessed in a whisper. "So much it frightens me."

Hope surged through his body with such force, he feared his heart might explode. "It is the same for me—"

"But how am I to trust you, Lucien?" The question seemed to be dragged from her very soul, rasped past a tight throat. "You have used me to wage a battle against Harrison. You do so even now."

For a moment, he simply absorbed the impact of being confronted with the truth. "I am doing what I must. Harming you was never my goal. You have to know that."

"And yet, that is the result." Her voice was small and quiet. It should not have sliced him open like a blade. But it did.

For a moment, the pain of it made him reconsider. Could he find another way to punish Blackmore? A way that did not involve Victoria? Could she simply be ... his? His wife. His angel. The mother of his children.

There is no other way. You have already considered other strategies. No, if Blackmore is to answer for his crimes at all, you must follow through. Or else accept failure.

For now, she needs me at her side. In time, she will understand. She has to.

Fists clenching helplessly at his sides, he watched as she moved to the library entrance, then turned slowly, sadly to face him, her hand braced on the open door's edge. "What we desire most always comes at a price, Lucien. What you must decide is whether it is worth it. I must do the same." With those simple, devastating words, the door gently closed.

And she was gone.

Chapter Twenty-Three

"Violence seldom resolves problems without spawning new ones. But men are inordinately fond of it, and I find that an endless source of amusement."

—THE DOWAGER MARCHIONESS OF WALLINGHAM to her nephew after a particularly bad day at Gentleman Jackson's.

BEHIND AN INNOCUOUS RED DOOR OF A QUIET BRICK BUILDING in an obscure square off of St. James, Lucien stood admiring one of London's most sumptuous hells. Rather than the hushed, understated luxury of White's or Brooks's, this place was a masterpiece of ostentation: gilt-framed mirrors, chandeliers dripping with crystal, silk-lined walls of deep jade, and wherever possible, candles whose light reflected off ornate surfaces to dazzling effect. In the center of the foyer stood a life-sized statue of the goddess Fortuna—she was holding a cornucopia overflowing with gold coins, a smiling siren luring men to their doom.

To the left was the dining room where, rumor had it, a French chef named Gaspard could serve a divine version of any meal a man could imagine—and some he couldn't. In front of him, the grand staircase rose to the upper floor, where gaming rooms were packed to the rafters with the dissolute, the unlucky, and the tragically optimistic. The proprietor of Reaver's wouldn't have it any other way.

"My lord, may I take your hat?" The quiet, dark-skinned majordomo asked. Though the man spoke flawless English and was dressed formally in a black tailcoat and trousers, gold waistcoat, and white cravat, his exotic features bespoke perhaps Turkish or Indian origins.

"No," Lucien replied. "I don't plan to stay long. I am meeting with an old friend."

The man bowed his head. "Very good, my lord. Right this way."

He had begun his search hours earlier with a visit to the Marquess of Rutherford. The old man, while intent on discussing the proposed purchase of his "damned fine" hunting property, assured Lucien he hadn't a clue where Viscount Chatham might be, as "my son and I do not frequent the same establishments, nor do we discuss such things." From the Rutherford townhouse, Lucien had ridden to St. James, where he combed every room at every reputable club. Still nothing.

Only then did he move on to the less respectable establishments. Reaver's was the third he had entered, and easily the most exclusive of the lot. It was not well known outside of elite circles because few could afford the stakes. Thousands of pounds were won and lost each day on a single turn of a card or roll of dice. Not for the faint of heart or light of pocket.

Presently, the majordomo led him up the stairs to the primary gaming room. He swept open the doors and gestured

Lucien through into a bustling scene. The room was opulently furnished, three large chandeliers casting brilliant light upward onto a frescoed barrel ceiling and downward along richly paneled walls. While the corridor had been quiet, this room was filled with dozens of gentlemen, their voices scrambling over each other in a boisterous din. Excited murmurs vied with sudden, triumphant shouts as the men crowded around green baize tables to watch their fortunes turn and tumble.

Scanning the crowd methodically, Lucien's gaze snagged on a lean, elegant hand playing idly with a stack of chips at the faro table. The man himself was not visible, hidden behind a pudgy, balding mass wearing too small a coat. But Lucien would recognize the gesture anywhere.

"Chatham," he muttered under his breath, a wave of heated anger warring with satisfaction at having finally found his quarry. He rounded a set of chairs to approach the viscount from behind. Reclining indolently in his seat, Chatham appeared at ease, but as Lucien drew alongside, he could see subtle signs of strain around his mouth and eyes.

"Still charging headlong for disaster, I see."

Chatham's fingers paused, hovered. It was the only acknowledgement of Lucien's presence. The dealer called the final turn.

Lucien continued in a low, bored voice. "If you wished me to end you, you had only to say so."

A fresh pile of chips was shoved toward Chatham as the bets were settled. He pushed away from the table and stood to face Lucien. "Am I to guess what you're nattering on about?"

Stepping closer, Lucien tilted his head and gave a slow smile. "Perhaps you should ask your mother. Or your benefactress."

Chatham's dark brows drew together over turquoise eyes, their contrast with his paper-white complexion somewhat startling. "Look, Atherbourne, if your intent is to provoke me into a duel or something equally tedious, you've got the wrong chap. I am rarely awake at dawn, and if it happens that I am, the last place I would be is forty paces from you." He grinned. "You are pretty, but not that pretty."

Someone cleared his throat pointedly. An older gentleman, tall and whiskered, nodded at Chatham's vacated seat. "Beg pardon. Are you to play another round?"

Signaling to a club employee, who promptly exchanged chips for pounds, Chatham pocketed his take and clapped the man's shoulder. "Have at it, Sir Giles."

Lucien trailed Chatham as the viscount blithely turned and began weaving through the crowd to the doorway. As they exited into the corridor, Lucien gripped Chatham's sharp-boned shoulder and shoved. Hard. It caused the other man to spin sideways until they faced one another.

For a moment, black fire blazed from inside turquoise eyes, and Chatham's lean frame took on a fighter's posture—aggressive, provoked. A heartbeat later, the starch left as though it had never been, his expression resuming its customary devil-may-care cynicism.

Interesting, Lucien thought. For all his vices and hedonism, Benedict Chatham was always in command of himself. Always. This reaction was yet another sign that the future Marquess of Rutherford was wearing at the seams. *So much the better.*

"You have gone too far this time, Chatham. I do not know what demon has hold of you, but you will soon learn the depth of your error."

Chatham shrugged. "So call me out."

Lucien stood silent, gauging the lord's expression.

"No?" The other man smiled slowly, but his eyes were empty. Cold. He gestured toward the stairs. "Then might I suggest the venison. Monsieur Gaspard serves it with an otherworldly truffle sauce." His eyes flared with mocking drama. "Positively transporting."

Lucien eyed the man in disgust. "What the bloody hell happened to you, Ben? I know it's been a few years—"

"Try ten."

"—but you've crawled so deep inside the bottle that every shred of dignity is lost. Good God, man, I don't even recognize you."

Chatham sneered. "Then we are alike in that regard, are we not? You have crawled so deep inside your wife's ... charms that I am surprised you do not wear her as a hat."

Rage thundered through him, exploding in his chest at the insolent vulgarity coming out of Chatham's mouth. Even as he spoke the last word, Lucien's fist rammed into his jaw with a satisfying crack. The sheer force of the facer caused the viscount to reel back, thudding against the far wall. It was far from enough for Lucien's liking.

Unfortunately, the commotion drew attention from a pair of outsized bruisers positioned just inside the doors of the gaming room, clearly employees of the club. "No fighting, milords," the taller one said, his accent purely east Londoner. "Reaver's rules. Iffen ye wants a brawl, take it elsewhere."

Lucien's gaze remained locked on Chatham, who continued to stare back at him with deadly calm. "That can be arranged," he said softly. "Gentleman Jackson's. If you would care to reclaim what remains of your manhood."

Chatham snorted. "Haven't had any complaints in that regard. Besides which, I have no intention of wasting yet more of my time with you." With that, he shoved himself away from the wall and headed for the stairs.

Following closely on his heels, Lucien gave the bastard a verbal jab he hoped would penetrate the fog of drunkenness keeping the old Benedict Chatham imprisoned, provided that man still existed, which was questionable. "Yes, I'm sure Mrs. Knightley would not bother to complain about you. Likely she would have cut you off long ago if she were not getting her money's worth."

Chatham flinched visibly and halted three steps short of the marble floor. Lucien thought he had him then, but the man shook his head, loosened his suddenly tight fists, and continued on as though he did not want to tear Lucien limb from limb. Fortunately, it was obvious he did, and it would only take a bit more prodding to send him over the edge.

The majordomo reappeared as if by magic, holding out Chatham's hat and walking stick. "Shaw. You have impeccable timing, my good man," Chatham said with false joviality, taking the items from the dark-skinned servant. "Have my horse brought 'round, would you?"

"Mine as well," Lucien murmured.

Shaw bowed and replied, "Right away, my lords."

Apparently determined to ignore Lucien's presence, Chatham wasted no time in crossing to the door and stepping out onto the cobblestones. But Lucien did not give up so easily. "I suppose one could understand your wretched lies about me," he mused, keeping pace. "Considering the disgrace of your 'arrangement' with Mrs. Knightley, you would have to find some way of deflecting attention away from yourself."

The other man said nothing, but his hand twisted on the knob of his walking stick. It tapped against the cobblestones in an uneven rhythm. Tap. Tap-tap. Tap-ta-tap.

"However," Lucien said softly, drawing closer to Chatham's side so he could not possibly ignore him. "When it is my *wife* who bears the consequences of such brazenly false rumors, I'm afraid I must answer with some forcefulness."

Finally, Chatham raised a brow and looked at Lucien. "Pardon me, was Mrs. Knightley not your mistress?" The sarcasm made Lucien want to choke the bastard. "Oh, but I would have sworn she was. She does have rather startling fondness for your ... let me see. Ah, yes, 'vigor,' I believe she called it. Difficult to gain such appreciation for goods one hasn't yet sampled."

His eyes narrowed on the man, who nonchalantly donned his hat and gave it a tap with his cane. Damn it, he needed to shut Chatham up for good, and that meant reminding the insolent wastrel of the secrets Chatham, himself, did not want revealed. Lucien drew within inches, his voice going low. "She was my mistress. *Was*. But at least I was never her whore."

The attack he had been waiting for came with sudden, bruising force. Chatham's cane sailed into his gut with a sickening *whump*, bending him in half for a moment as he struggled to breathe. But the heir to the Marquess of Rutherford didn't stop there. He followed Lucien's stumbling trail, slamming his fist into his ribs with first his right, then his left. Blast, the man's reflexes were quick for someone constantly in his cups.

It did not last long. Chatham was frayed, thin, and weakened, his mind faster than most men, but slowed and dulled from its customary sharpness by too much drink and too little dignity. Lucien backed away and studied his adversary, slowly circling, letting the grinding pain of the blows to his midsection absorb and echo until it became background. Chatham's eyes were a turquoise blaze, his jaw reddened by Lucien's earlier hit. He clearly wanted to fight. But he was breathing heavily, his shoulders slumping, his cane rattling to the ground. *Pathetic.*

"You bloody hypocrite," Chatham spat, his full hatred of Lucien twisting his features. "The *wife* you claim to defend married you because you groped her before the entire ton and ruined her chances at a better match. Do not preach to me of honor. You have none."

Lucien stopped, watching as pieces of his old friend—albeit warped by bitterness and dissolution—reassembled in front of him. No more cold disaffection. No more casual sarcasm. Just pure, wild fury.

"It doesn't matter, does it?" Chatham raved. "Lucien Wyatt always gets what he wants. Ballocks. I could toss you into a pile of horse shit, and you'd come out with the fucking crown jewels." He threw his arms wide, shaking his head up at the gray sky in wonderment. "It's a bloody miracle!"

Glaring, Lucien tightened his jaw, saying nothing. Clearly,

the man had built up a great many resentments, which wouldn't matter if not for one thing: He knew of Lucien's true motives for marrying Victoria. Lucien did not know how Chatham had divined such information, but he had. And with the younger lord eager to stir trouble, how long would it be before the entire ton learned the truth? How long before Victoria was made a laughingstock again, the object of pity and scorn? Because of him. He could not allow it. Such a result might have once seemed acceptable. But no longer—not when he could do something about it.

"Then, by all means, Chatham," he said darkly. "Let us settle our differences. Tomorrow. Gentleman Jackson's."

"To what end?"

Lucien smiled. "A mutual understanding. Between gentlemen."

Chatham crossed his arms, appearing skeptical. "A wager."

"Aye," he replied softly. "For the victor, a guarantee of silence. He need never fear certain, shall we say, *unfortunate* information will be shared by his opponent."

"And the loser?"

"Shall take his chances."

Lucien knew it was a gamble, this offer. While he could easily defeat Chatham in his current weakened state, trusting the man to keep his word after the fact was more than a risk—many would believe it foolhardy. Tannenbrook had said that very thing when Lucien had posed the idea. But James did not know Chatham the way Lucien did. The thin, pale shell known as the future Marquess of Rutherford was a sham, a carefully constructed lie born of misery and self-inflicted wounds. He should know—he'd been lost himself, once. The real man, the one Lucien remembered, was a bit wild, but fundamentally decent. If a thread of that man remained, and Lucien could reach him, then the agreement would hold. He hoped.

"Well," Chatham said after a long pause. "Never let it be said I passed up an opportunity to beat you senseless. Gentleman Jackson's it is."

Lucien nodded, hearing the clop of hooves as their horses were led out of the mews behind the club. For a moment, seeing Chatham's sardonic expression, he doubted the wisdom of this plan. Perhaps he was wrong, and the viscount really was too far gone. But, then, Chatham dropped his gaze briefly, and when it returned, his eyes were serious. It was like looking at a ghost, seeing the Ben he remembered for the first time in a decade. "You should do whatever it takes to keep her, you know. Not that I care. But she seems a good sort."

Swallowing hard at the unexpected statement from an even more unexpected source, Lucien turned away from his old friend. Not because the lad from the stables approached with his horse. Not even because Chatham was wrong. The problem was he was right. But it was far too late.

Chapter Twenty-Four

"A little off the chin, if you please. Devotion to detail is laudable, but I see no reason to frighten future generations."

—THE DOWAGER MARCHIONESS OF WALLINGHAM to Sir Thomas
Lawrence upon viewing her son's commissioned portrait
for the first time.

IT WAS ENTIRELY UNACCEPTABLE.

Hands on hips, Victoria stepped back from the canvas and glared at the washed-out, translucent blue of Lucien's waistcoat. Blast it, she *needed* her ultramarine pigment from the case that was still stored at Clyde-Lacey House. It was terribly expensive, prepared for her by a famed colorist who also served Sir Thomas Lawrence; otherwise, she would simply purchase more.

I may have to anyway, she thought, *if things continue as they have been.* Harrison still had not answered the letters she'd sent just after the wedding, one of which requested her supplies be delivered to Wyatt House. And it appeared Lucien was determined to follow through on his bid for revenge, even though his expression had been tormented when she had all but begged him to reconsider. *Do you care for me at all?* she wondered, gazing at the storm-cloud eyes she had painted with careful, adoring strokes. *Do you? For, I love you with everything inside me. It seems you might feel the same, but you won't say it. And part of you still hides from me.*

She sighed. Those shadowy unknowns had made their way into the painting. They were there in the slight furrow of his brow, the flash of light in his eyes.

So many questions.

One thing, however, had become clear in the week since the Rutherford rout. Within the ton, their marriage was now regarded as a true love match, the object of admiration if not outright envy by all but the highest sticklers. Invitations had poured in at an ever-increasing rate. Furthermore, the vicious rumors regarding an association between Lucien and Mrs. Knightley had been neatly quashed by Lady Wallingham at one of her recent luncheons.

It was good to have a dragon on one's side, she supposed. Just yesterday, a note from Lady Wallingham had suggested Lady Gattingford was considering hosting an end-of-season ball and inviting Victoria and Lucien. It seemed the project of neutralizing the scandal before most of the ton left London was a rousing success.

Soon, the scandal would no longer pose a threat, and Lucien would have nothing left to hold over her. Perhaps then her choices would prove easier. *Is that really what's stopping you?* a voice whispered in her mind.

Bothersome voice. Go away.

You are allowing him to manage you the way he would a servant.

I can wait until after we have left London and the scandal is behind us.

You are afraid to lose him. But if you allow this to go on much longer, you will lose your brother. And perhaps yourself.

Standing motionless, she stared yet saw nothing, only heard the ring of truth in the words streaming through her head. Suddenly, her acquiescence to his demand seemed less like the sensible, safe path and more like cowardice. She had given Lucien his way, and it was destroying what little chance they had of making their marriage more than the devil's bargain it had been at the beginning.

She eyed the unfinished portrait. *At the very least, you must have your paints. This simply will not do.*

He deserved better.

And so did she.

Removing her apron and folding it neatly, she placed it on the table behind her, then carefully draped a cloth over the unfinished canvas.

"Time enough for you later," she murmured to the portrait. "Once I retrieve my ultramarine."

After donning a lilac-hued, velvet spencer and matching bonnet, she hurried downstairs and found Billings tidying the sideboard in the morning room. Watery light shone through the windows, reflecting off the butler's white head.

"Billings," she said loudly from the doorway.

He turned. "Yes, my lady?"

"Could you please have the carriage brought 'round?"

"Certainly, my lady. Might I inquire as to your destination?"

Tugging on a pair of gray kid gloves, she answered, "Berkeley Square. I must retrieve some painting supplies from Clyde-Lacey House."

Silence followed her response. She glanced up at Billings' stooped form, surprised to see him frozen in place, much like a stag staring down a hunter. *Well,* she thought upon examining his wrinkled countenance, *perhaps more akin to a hedgehog sighted by an owl.* He appeared to be frightened into stillness, his brows lowered in consternation.

"Billings?"

He met her gaze.

"The carriage?"

He pressed his lips together briefly as though wishing to say something, but he remained motionless next to the sideboard.

Victoria did not relish reprimanding servants. She much preferred guiding them through praise and high expectation. But every now and then, Billings used his poor hearing as an excuse to ignore her, often when she asked after correspondence from her brothers or when she desired to use the carriage. She suspected Lucien had something to do with it, but the servants of Wyatt House never spoke a word against their employer.

She approached Billings, coming within two feet of him so she could be heard without shouting. She would not wish any of the other servants to witness her set-down of the butler. He needed to command respect in the household to maintain his authority.

But, honestly, enough was enough. It was well past time she wielded some authority of her own.

"Billings, I must say, it is extraordinary that you carry on your work in so competent a fashion, given these moments when you clearly have a great deal of trouble *hearing* me."

The man's spine stiffened and he grimaced. "Madam, I ..."

"I *said,*" she continued crisply, "I would like you to have the carriage brought 'round to the front, as I will be visiting my brother's home today. Please do so now."

Several seconds of uncomfortable silence followed this pointed command, before he reluctantly replied, "My lady, if it were in my power to comply with your request, I would do so immediately. However, I cannot. I apologize most sincerely."

She shook her head and frowned, the beginnings of anger stirring to life. "This is preposterous. Of course it is within your power. Simply tell the coachman I have need of the carriage. What is so impossible about that?"

Billings winced at her snappish tone and cleared his throat. "Perhaps if my lady were to choose another destination ...?"

"Why should that make any difference?"

Silence. While the man's face remained stony, his eyes were filled with apology and something else. Something that looked very much like pity.

Anger bloomed full-force as her suspicions were confirmed. Lucien had ordered the servants to prevent her visiting Harrison. As she recalled the distinct lack of correspondence since her wedding day, the scope of his possible machinations grew, along with the fire of her temper. Had Harrison written, only to have his letters intercepted? Had *her* letters been intercepted?

The answer came almost immediately, making her feel like the veriest dupe. *Of course. Lucien would not leave such things to chance.* Fury filled her like a hot, poisonous cloud, firing her skin from the inside out.

"Billings, I asked you a question," she said distinctly.

His gaze was sympathetic as he reluctantly answered, "I have been ordered not to comply with any request to visit Clyde-Lacey House."

"By my husband?" She knew the answer, but she wanted to hear him say it.

He swallowed. "I am not at liberty to say."

Well, she thought bitterly, perhaps Billings could not say, but his reaction was all the confirmation she needed. No matter, she decided quickly. If her arrogant, insufferable husband thought he could dictate where she went and when, he had a thing or two to learn about his obedient, loving wife. And his lessons would begin right now.

"Did Lord Atherbourne forbid my visiting my modiste?" she asked tightly.

"No, my lady."

She nodded and gave the butler a forced smile. "Then have the carriage brought 'round. I have a sudden desire to do some shopping."

Chapter Twenty-Five

*"Do not wrap your poor choices in gold thread and ruffles,
and then expect me to offer praise. I may be old,
but I am not blind."*

—The Dowager Marchioness of Wallingham to her modiste,
upon being shown a dreadfully over-embellished pelisse.

A tall, redheaded woman in a dark-green riding habit
bumped Victoria's shoulder as she strode through the narrow
entrance of Bowman's on Bond Street. The woman apologized
for the collision, but Victoria hurried past her with little more
than a nod.

She glanced around the small front room of the shop, seeing
several ladies seated around a table, cooing over fashion plates.

One of Mrs. Bowman's assistants, a harried girl with flyaway blond hair escaping a chignon, brushed aside the blue curtain separating the dressing area. She carried several bolts of fabric.

Halfway to her destination, Victoria intercepted her to ask for Mrs. Bowman.

"She be in back, milady." The girl's lowly London accent was even thicker than Mrs. Garner's, her eyes wide and startled. "Shall I fetch 'er for ye?"

Victoria nodded. "If you would."

"Straight away." The girl bobbed a curtsy and placed her colorful burden on a table near the front window before smiling uncertainly at Victoria and retreating once again behind the curtain.

Minutes later, Mrs. Bowman made an entrance worthy of a Drury Lane actress, sweeping aside the drapery and rushing forward to greet Victoria.

"Ah, Lady Atherbourne. An unexpected pleasure. Lovely to see you again." The modiste's dark eyes fell and rose along Victoria's frame, one brow lifted in critical contemplation. She waved casually at the simple, embroidered white gown beneath the fitted spencer Victoria wore. "You are here to, eh, enhance your selection of walking gowns, yes?" A long, elegant finger lifted the curved collar of lilac velvet, letting it flop back into place. "A new spencer, perhaps?"

"A new ...?" Victoria frowned slightly, then shook her head at the dressmaker's implication. She rather liked the design of the spencer, but Mrs. Bowman had never cared for the color, and had sewn the garment only under protest. "No, actually, I am not here to purchase anything." She reached for the woman's hands, clasping them pleadingly. "Mrs. Bowman, I must ask you for a favor."

Typically rather unflappable, the Italian modiste seemed genuinely surprised by Victoria's overture, lapsing into her native language. "*Qual è il problema, signora?*"

"Do you have another entrance I might use?" Victoria stood on her tiptoes to peer over the modiste's shoulder toward the rear of the shop. "Perhaps in the back," she whispered.

Mrs. Bowman squinted at Victoria and tilted her head as though seeking the answer to a confounding question. The woman blinked, her frown cleared, and she nodded. Tugging Victoria's hands, she muttered, "Come."

She led her through the curtain, past the dressing area where two of her assistants knelt, pinning the hem of a wide-eyed matron, and finally, into a tiny room cluttered with bolts of fabric, books of fashion plates, and a desk piled high with papers. Mrs. Bowman picked up a large ledger from a wooden chair and slid it onto a shelf, waving to indicate Victoria should sit, then seating herself in a red-cushioned chair before the desk.

The modiste brushed her hand absently along the side of her neat coiffure, folded her hands together, and leaned across the desk to stare shrewdly at Victoria. "You are good customer, Lady Atherbourne. But this request, it is ... unusual, yes?"

"Oh, well, yes, I suppose it is. Normally, I would never ask such a thing. But I am afraid extraordinary circumstances demand an unusual response."

"Hmm. And what are these extraordinary circumstances?"

Victoria blinked, pausing to decide how much to tell the woman. And what, precisely, to say. "I need to visit my brother's residence."

"The duke, yes? Berkeley Square."

"Yes."

"Why do you not simply drive there in your carriage?" Mrs. Bowman waved a hand in the direction of the street, where the Atherbourne carriage was parked, awaiting her return.

"That is a bit complicated."

The woman nodded knowingly, uttering another "Hmm," and waving to signal Victoria should elaborate.

Victoria sighed. "The coachman will not drive me there."

"But he will drive you here."

"Yes."

"You could hire a hack."

"I suppose I could," she replied reluctantly, "if reaching my destination were the sole purpose of today's outing."

Mrs. Bowman again nodded, then sat quietly staring at Victoria for a full minute. It made her want to squirm in her seat. But if she could not persuade the modiste to allow her use of an alternate entrance, she would be forced to abandon her plan. And that was intolerable.

Finally, the woman's fingertips tapped firmly on the desk, and she nodded. "Your husband, he is ... kind to you?"

She thought for a moment, then answered honestly. "Yes."

"You love him?"

Victoria glanced down at her hands. The gray kid gloves had been a gift from Harrison. And her husband had arranged to separate her from him. Her family. Her brother.

"That is not the question," she said softly, meeting the modiste's dark, understanding gaze. "The question is, does he love me?" She swallowed against a sudden tightness in her throat, her chest squeezing around an aching heart.

Mrs. Bowman smiled in the mysterious way she often did before saying something cryptic. "Men can be ... how do you say? Goat-headed, no?"

Victoria frowned. "I believe you mean pigheaded."

She waved dismissively. "Bah. Pig, goat. It is all the same. Do not mistake stupidity for coldness, *cara mia*. All men are stupid sometimes. This does not mean they do not love." The dark-haired woman stood and took Victoria's elbow. "Come. There is a door you may use." With that, she guided her through a short series of corridors, then opened a green painted door to reveal a rain-washed, narrow alley running along one side of the building. "Do not tarry, eh? And when you come next time, perhaps you will buy a new spencer."

Victoria grinned at the modiste. "Thank you, Mrs. Bowman. Perhaps I will." She descended four wooden stairs, then stepped carefully around the deeper puddles, trying hard not to breathe the putrid air. The alley was strewn with refuse of all sorts, clearly serving more as a dumping ground than a pathway between buildings. At last, she approached the opening to Bond Street, flattening herself against the edge of the building and peering around the corner. Connell stood with the footman who had accompanied them next to the Atherbourne carriage, about thirty feet away. She timed her exit carefully, waiting for a thick group of young misses and their chaperones to approach before exiting the narrow space onto the thoroughfare, weaving amongst the other pedestrians so as not to be noticed. With every step, she was sure Connell would spot her, would demand she return to the coach, would run off and alert Lucien. The thought made her heart pound and quickened her feet. She wanted Lucien to know he had been thwarted, but not just yet. Not while he could still stop her.

Fortunately, she turned onto Bruton Street without raising any alarms. She twisted her head around to be certain no one followed—and ran directly into a bony wall housed in a greatcoat much too heavy for the mild summer weather.

"Ooph!" It took her a moment to reel back and get a look at what she had collided with, which turned out to be a rather scruffy man wearing a brimmed hat that shadowed his face.

"Beg pardon, my lady. Didn't see you there," he said without meeting her eyes. Of course, he was a good deal taller than she, but it seemed he was in a hurry, as he quickly steadied her with a hand beneath her elbow, backed up, and nervously tried to sidestep her.

She spun as he passed, grabbing his sleeve. "Wait! I know you, don't I? You look familiar."

He shook his head and tugged out of her grip. "Never met you, ma'am. Must be off, now." Moving away with a shuffling gait, the rangy man appeared eager to escape. But now she knew with a certainty only a portraitist could muster—he was the one she had seen that day outside of Jane's house. The one she suspected had been following her for some time.

"I know you've been hired to watch me," she shouted. It stopped him dead, giving her a chance to catch up. "All I wish to know is who retained your services. Was it Lord Atherbourne?"

Reluctantly, he met her eyes. His were tired and red in a creased, unhandsome face. He looked as though he had not slept in weeks. "Nay, my lady."

Her chin tilted. "What is your name?"

He looked around the street in discomfort. "Drayton, ma'am."

"Who hired you, Drayton?"

He sighed and rubbed at the bridge of his nose. "Don't suppose it matters if I tell you, so long as it don't get back to Atherbourne."

She folded her arms and shot him an expectant look.

"Blackmore hired me to keep an eye on you, my lady. Make certain you'd come to no harm."

"My brother hired you?" She'd thought surely Lucien had done so to ensure that she complied with his wishes. The idea that it was Harrison instead had not occurred to her. "Why would he not simply come for a visit and see for himself?"

She murmured the question to herself, but Drayton answered, "It's my understanding he tried, my lady. A few times, in fact. Was turned away at the door."

Shock flaring through her, she watched the disheveled Mr. Drayton shift from one foot to the other as though he desperately needed to visit the privy. He glanced furtively around Bruton Street. "Are you in a rush, Mr. Drayton?"

"Be honest, ma'am, yes I am. Must be off, now." He tipped his hat to her distractedly as he backpedaled away. She watched in bewilderment as he tossed a warning over his shoulder. "Best hurry on to the square, my lady. Never know who you might encounter on the street." He turned at the corner and was gone.

Heeding his advice, and eager to find answers, she wasted no time in traversing Bruton Street into Berkeley Square. Within minutes, she was ascending the steps to Clyde-Lacey House, the familiar brick edifice and tall, symmetrical rows of windows sending a wave of comfort and longing over her in a shiver. Distracted, she nearly entered without knocking, but paused with her hand hovering over the knob. This was not her home any longer. The thought was both sad and strange. She knocked and waited, shifting her weight from one foot to the other, glancing down at her dress to ensure she hadn't muddied the hem on her ignominious journey through the alley.

The door opened. "Lady Victoria! Rather, Lady Atherbourne. What a delight it is to see you."

Victoria gave Digby, the duke's sandy-haired, starchy butler, a beaming smile. As always, the man was impeccable, without a hair out of place. Typically stiff as a north wind, he had always had a soft spot for her, his brown eyes currently sparkling with genuine pleasure. "Won't you come in, my lady?"

"Thank you, Digby." Once inside, she shocked the man with a quick hug. "I have missed you." She tugged at his lapel playfully, the way she had at ten years old. "I see you have not yet taken the Earl of Dunston up on his offer to change employers. That is good for the duke, but perhaps less than wise."

Digby gave her a rare wink and replied, "Someone must prevent the kingdom from descending into chaos. I fear that duty falls to me."

She laughed. "Is the duke here? I must speak with him."

The butler's smile softened into an apologetic expression. "I'm afraid his grace is out at the moment, my lady, and is not expected back for hours. He will be most distressed to have missed you."

Her spirits slumped at this news, disappointment deflating her like cold rain on a loaf of bread. She'd been so certain if only she could reach Clyde-Lacey House and speak to Harrison, all would be well. Her brother had a way of making everything all right again. She shook her head against the tide of welling emotion, willing her tears to back down. It would not do to weep in front of Digby.

The butler cleared his throat.

"Well, I suppose there is no point in waiting, then." She sighed, glancing around the entrance hall, absently noting the familiar green walls and black-and-white marble floor. Harrison was fond of green. So was Colin, for that matter. It was one of the few things they had in common.

She paused, a thought occurring to her. "Digby, is Colin in?"

Digby hesitated before answering, "Yes, I believe so, my lady. Perhaps you would like to wait in the parlor. Mrs. Jones will bring you some tea, while I inform his lordship of your arrival."

And, just like that, her spirits came in out of the rain. "That would be lovely, Digby. Simply lovely."

MUD SPLASHED ONTO HIS BOOTS AS LUCIEN DISMOUNTED, BUT he barely noticed. He ran his hand over Hugo's flank and patted the horse's shoulder affectionately. The gelding nodded his head and snorted softly. Lucien smiled for no particular reason and handed the reins to the stable boy.

His knuckles and ribs were a trifle sore, but all in all, his lot was far better than he would have predicted a year ago. Victoria was his. The duke had been punished. Chatham had been dealt with. Soon, they would return to Thornbridge, and he would dedicate himself to getting Victoria with child.

Anticipation ran down his spine at the thought. Yes, he would relish seeing her blossom with his babe. She would make a wonderful mother, loving and gentle. And once she had little ones to dote on, a family of her own, her determination to reunite with her brothers would fade. He was certain of it.

His step light and brisk, he entered the house, calling for Billings. The stooped butler shuffled in from the dining room. "Welcome home, my lord. How was Gentleman Jackson's?"

Lucien grinned and handed the man his hat and gloves. "Quite bracing. I met up with an old friend." Indeed, teaching Chatham a well-deserved lesson about the dangers of spreading lies had been worth the damage the other man had inflicted. Flexing his fingers to test the soreness, he glanced toward the curved staircase, wondering if Victoria was still painting as she had been when he left. "Is Lady Atherbourne in her studio?"

Billings paused, long seconds ticking by before he answered. "No, my lord."

Lucien frowned, turning slowly to face his butler. "Then where is she?" he asked softly.

Swallowing visibly, the old man straightened and answered, "I believe she is visiting her modiste."

Something in Billings's demeanor—the slight tremor in his voice, the carefully blank expression—caused dread to spread inside Lucien's chest like frost over a windowpane. "She took the carriage, then?"

"Y-yes, my lord."

"And she asked only to visit her modiste? Nowhere else?"

Billings hesitated. "Connell is quite aware of your wishes, my lord. I made certain of that before they departed. He would not drive her to Berkeley Square, even were she to order it directly."

Lucien ground his teeth, his gut tightening against a tide of anger and alarm. "So she did ask to visit Clyde-Lacey house," he said grimly.

The butler cleared his throat, but did not answer.

"Billings!" Lucien barked.

The man sighed, defeat entering his eyes. "Yes, my lord."

Bloody hell.

One week, damn it. That was all that remained of the season. One more week, and he would have whisked her off to Thornbridge. But he should have known she would not give up easily, would not simply let it go.

Well, my darling, he thought grimly, all but running to retrieve his horse. *That is something we have in common.*

Because now that she was his, letting go was the last thing he would ever do.

Chapter Twenty-Six

*"Drunkards are useful only as opponents for whist.
Otherwise, they are no better than vermin which have
infested one's residence. And they should be dealt with
in much the same manner."*

—THE DOWAGER MARCHIONESS OF WALLINGHAM to her nephew
upon discovering his association with Viscount Chatham.

COLIN GROANED AND WRITHED IN THE GREEN VELVET CHAIR,
the heels of his hands pressed into his temples, his hair clutched
between his fingers as he attempted to escape Victoria's
interrogation. Eyes squeezed shut against the gray light from the
windows, he whined, "Must you shout, Tori? My head is killing me."

Victoria loomed over her brother, hands on hips. "*Drink* is killing you. And if you do not answer my question, I will gladly hasten the process."

One blue eye popped open and peered up at her. "What was the question?"

Exasperation burst from her lungs in a loud hiss. "How many times has Harrison tried to see me at Wyatt House?"

He sighed, slumping even further into the chair, his thumb and finger pinching at the bridge of his nose. "Not sure. Five or six."

Five or six times. It was worse than she had thought. More than letters. More than avoiding him at the theater.

He had been turned away from Wyatt House—*her* house, by God—five or six times.

Victoria stood up straight, turned on her heel, and paced to the other end of the room. Picturing Harrison's proud face, imagining how he must have felt, thinking she was deliberately cutting him from her life, she wanted to cry. To scream. It swelled around her heart like a roiling cloud.

Striding back to stand before Colin, she shoved hard at one of his shoulders. "Did *you?*" she demanded fiercely.

He winced. "For Christ's sake, Tori. Did I what?"

"Did you try to see me?"

He shook his head. "I asked after you, though."

She gripped each side of his face, forcing his squinting gaze up to her own. "When?"

He grasped her wrists and pulled her hands away, unsteadily rising to his feet and pushing her gently to one side. The action freed him from her grip, but agony must have followed, for he moaned pitifully and dropped his head into his hands.

"Perhaps we could discuss this another time," he muttered.

She crossed her arms and glared at the wretched drunkard who had once been her charming brother. "Colin, the moments when you are sober are few and far between. There *is* no other time. Now, answer me."

He shot her a resentful look, but she was far beyond caring. Stumbling toward a settee on the opposite side of the room, he said, "Chatham and I saw Atherbourne at White's a few weeks ago." He sat with an inelegant thump, his trembling hands reaching for a cup of tea from a tray Digby had earlier placed on the low table. "I asked after you."

"What did he say?"

Colin took a careful sip then glanced at her over the rim. "He didn't. Just tossed some insults at Chatham and me." His grin looked more like a grimace, but it was edged with satisfaction. "Chatham repaid him, though. Always does. Bloody clever like that."

Her hands twisted at her waist, and she swallowed a lump of hurt. "You've asked after me once in all the weeks since the wedding. He didn't answer, and so you just ... gave up?"

China clinked as he set his cup on the table and leaned forward to brace his elbows on his knees. His expression was as serious as she had ever seen it. "He is your husband, Tori. He was not about to let me or Harrison see you. Ever."

"You could not have known—"

"He said as much."

She frowned. "I thought he didn't answer."

Colin scraped a hand over his face, then dropped his head to stare at the floor. "It was later. He and Tannenbrook were playing billiards. Chatham and I overheard them discussing his plans for you."

"You eavesdropped on them. Perhaps you misunderstood."

Eyes that were the same blue-green as her own rose to search her face. They were sad, regretful. "Atherbourne said he only married you to take you away from Harrison. His aim was to 'deprive Blackmore of the only thing he holds dear.' It was his plan all along, Tori. I'm sorry."

A part of her had already known. That voice she wished to silence whispered it over and over. She'd chosen to ignore it, to believe Lucien's plan was one of opportunity, rather than design. Why it mattered, she wasn't certain. But it did. Oh, how it did. She slowly backed away from Colin. The air grew thin, the light ashy. Eyes frantically darting about, she sought a different answer, one that would allow her to breathe.

You never meant anything to him.

No, he cares for me, I know he does.

He used you, and he will toss you aside as soon as his revenge grows cold.

No, please. Not that.

"... not going to swoon, are you?"

Colin's voice drew her attention to her brother's concerned frown. Shaking her head, Victoria gripped the back of a nearby chair and sucked in a stuttering breath. It brought the room back into focus, but did nothing to staunch the frantic internal quarrel.

"I don't understand it," she whispered achingly. "What would cause him to go to such lengths?"

The silk of the settee rustled as Colin shifted restlessly, then shrugged with studied casualness. "Must still be vexed about losing his brother."

"Did you know Gregory Wyatt?"

Tossing back the last of his tea in a swift motion, Colin nodded and set the cup on the table with a clink. "Met him a few times. Nice chap. Shame about the duel."

She moved around the chair, plopping gracelessly into the seat. "What—what was it all about, do you know?"

Colin's eyes glinted sharply, narrowing on her. "Atherbourne didn't tell you?"

She shook her head. "He refuses to discuss his brother at all."

Dropping his gaze from hers, Colin rose unsteadily to his feet and paced to the windows, staring out at the square, his arms folded over his chest. "Atherbourne—the last one, that is—accused Harrison of dishonorable behavior."

She glared at the back of her brother's tousled blond head. "Thank you, Colin," she said tartly. "I had deduced that much.

What, precisely, was his accusation?"

"It is not for a lady's ears."

Victoria snorted disbelievingly. "You expect me to believe Harrison—our brother, the Duke of Blackmore—was accused of something so dastardly, you cannot even speak of it in my presence? What poppycock. He is far from perfect—"

This time, it was Colin who released a snort.

"As I was saying, Harrison is not without his faults, but he is, above all things, honorable. Besides which, he is a duke with considerable influence. For a peer to call him out, there must have been a dreadful misunderstanding."

Colin's voice was thin and rather muffled, but she heard him reply, "Atherbourne did not appear to think so."

Her patience teetering, Victoria threw up her hands and cried, "What in heaven's name could be a matter of honor so dire that a man died over it?"

"That is an excellent question."

The words whipped across the room from the parlor entrance. Victoria stood, spun, and gasped, her hand splaying across her midsection in a protective gesture.

"Lucien," she whispered breathlessly.

He looked ... explosive. Dark fury fired his eyes, flexed his jaw, bristled through his taut form as he advanced menacingly into the room.

"Shall I answer, my darling?"

She shook her head. "I—I don't ..."

His eyes refused to leave hers, burning through her weak protest. He stopped directly in front of her, his size and nearness overwhelming. "The most *honorable* Duke of Blackmore seduced my sister then left her to suffer the consequences alone. She was seventeen."

Pain. So much pain shone in his eyes, it made her throat tighten on the longing to soothe him, her arms aching to hold him. What he was saying made little sense, but there was no denying he believed it to be true.

"She could not bear it. The humiliation," he rasped. "He took her innocence. And she took her life."

Again, Victoria whispered her husband's name, reaching for him. He reeled back several steps as though she had tried to cut him.

"That is your paragon of virtue and honor, Victoria. He caused my sister's death. Then he shot Gregory without so much as wrinkling his cravat." Lucien stopped as though out of breath. A muscle beside his mouth twitched with emotion. "Within a fortnight, I lost all the family I had left. And your brother is responsible."

Chapter Twenty-Seven

"Were we ever such fools when we were that age, Meredith?
I think not. Perhaps it is something in the water."

—The Dowager Marchioness of Wallingham to Lady Berne
upon spying a young lord falling into the Serpentine.

For a full minute, Victoria struggled to breathe, to absorb Lucien's accusation. It couldn't be true. It was, quite simply, impossible. The Harrison she knew was strong, intelligent, principled. He was also one of the most controlled people she had ever met, especially when it came to women.

As the Duke of Blackmore, her brother represented the ultimate catch—handsome, wealthy, and titled. She had watched him over the past two seasons, fending off one boldly flirtatious debutante after another, eluding and deflecting their advances like a wily cat escaping capture.

The idea that he would involve himself with a seventeen-year-old girl at all, much less ruin and then abandon her, was so far out of character it was patently absurd.

But Lucien, who still stood broodingly several feet away, clearly believed it, as had his brother, Gregory. For Victoria, it was confusing, exasperating. She knew almost nothing about the circumstances surrounding the duel, as Harrison had never deigned to discuss it with her. She had not even been aware Lucien *had* a sister, for heaven's sake. Given the unfortunate manner of the girl's death, it was somewhat understandable—one did not even whisper of such things in good families. But how could Victoria be expected to unravel such a tangle when it was shrouded in the secrecy of shame and infernal male pride?

Taking a deep breath, Victoria eyed her husband, steeling herself against the urge to simply accept his version of events and wrap him in her arms. Unquestionably, her foolish heart felt it belonged to him, wanting to forgive him for its deep wounds, yearning to heal his.

"I can see you believe Harrison to be responsible for your sister's death—" she began hoarsely.

"Because it is the truth," he interrupted, his voice low and dark.

Victoria gritted her teeth and sighed. "Honestly, Lucien, I did not even know you had a sister. Do you not think you could have explained the situation a bit more fully? I am your *wife*, after all."

Brows lowered in a scowl, he took two long steps toward her, causing her skin to prickle and her heart to thud once. Twice.

"About that," he said silkily. "The wishes of your *husband* were perfectly obvious, my dear. How is it that you are here?"

Righteous anger bloomed from deep within her, outrage returning in a fiery surge. "You dare to ask me that? I am here to see my brothers. And thank goodness I came, or I would not have suspected Harrison had been turned away from *my home* five or six times!" By the last word, her voice had risen to a full-on bellow.

Fuming and fixated on her dark-haired devil of a husband, she only dimly noticed Colin edging toward the parlor doorway. As he passed Lucien, he murmured, "Best take cover, Atherbourne. Last time I saw her like this, I nearly lost a toe."

Without removing her eyes from Lucien's glowering face, she pointed toward the entrance and spoke one word to her brother. "Leave."

Brows raised and eyes wide, Colin held both palms out in surrender and backed out of the room. "Leaving," he said.

By contrast, Lucien was not intimidated by the threat of her unusually intense anger. Beyond mere vexation, she was incensed that he could treat her so callously, profoundly hurt that he did not care for her enough to alter his strategy.

He either did not realize or was not bothered by the depth of her feelings. He propped his hands on his hips and tilted his head almost casually. "Perhaps the promise to obey me should have been removed from our marriage ceremony. It is clear you never intended to keep it."

She sucked in a breath, disbelief flooding through her. "You—you insufferable—"

"I give you credit for cleverness—"

"—scurrilous, despicable—"

"—but it is time you returned to where you belong."

"—pompous, controlling ass."

Unwisely, he smirked. "Now, now, my dear. Language."

That. Was. It.

She screeched straight through her boiling point and, before she could stop herself, she charged him, her straightened arms shoving hard at his chest. If she had not been so blinded by fury, she might have laughed at his wide-eyed gape.

Much like a stone wall, Lucien was typically unmovable. But

taking him by surprise, her physical attack was a shocking success, causing him to stumble backward. As she swung wildly, pummeling his thick arms and chest, their feet tangled. Lucien lost his balance, then his footing.

With a loud thump, he dropped hard onto his backside, taking Victoria to the floor atop him where she soon directed her blows to his face. He managed to grasp one of her arms, but her right fist sailed straight into his left eye. Shards of pain shot through her knuckles as they glanced off his brow bone.

Simultaneous cries of "Ow!" echoed in the room. Victoria scrambled to stand, hampered by her skirts, yanking at the fabric where it was trapped beneath his boot. Meanwhile, Lucien cupped his injured eye, uttering a foul curse.

Her hand throbbed, and she felt like an idiot for losing her temper so abominably, but she had to admit to a twinge of satisfaction at finally bringing her husband to his knees. Or, rather, his backside. At last gaining her freedom, she stood over him, breathing heavily, watching him scramble to his feet, one hand still over his eye. He lowered the hand. And the remorse began. His poor eye was red and rapidly swelling, especially near the brow line.

Backing up a few paces, she absently rubbed her knuckles. She hadn't meant to *hurt* him. Not really.

"Good God, Victoria," he said incredulously. "Where did you learn to hit like that?"

She tightened her lips and raised her chin. "I grew up with two brothers. Not that it matters to you." Brushing briskly at her skirts, she continued bitterly, "If you had your way, I would never see them again. What did you think I would do, hmm? You claim Harrison robbed you of your only family. Did you expect me to sacrifice mine without a fight?"

He tentatively pressed the skin at the corner of his eye, wincing and clenching his jaw. "Considering you are my wife, I expected you would accede to my wishes."

"Rubbish. You knew better, or you would not have enlisted

the servants to aid in your deception. Tell me, how many letters from Harrison were intercepted by Billings?"

Lucien sent her a dark look from beneath lowered brows.

"I thought as much," she said tartly.

He shook his head, suddenly appearing tired. "I do not wish to discuss this here."

"I can only surmise you place a dear value on the punishment for Harrison's sins—"

"Victoria."

"—but surely you considered the consequences for me. Your w-wife." She heard the strain, the heartache in her own voice, causing it to go thready and high. "Did you want to punish me, as well, Lucien? Losing your brother must have been agonizing. Did you ever think I might experience similar misery upon losing mine? Is that what you wanted? Or was it simply a wound you were willing to inflict, so long as you could have your revenge?"

"Victoria, stop," he growled.

She couldn't. She wouldn't. She needed to know.

"Do I matter to you in the slightest, husband?" she whispered.

He hissed and moved swiftly toward her, grasping her upper arms before she could take her next breath. It hurt—not physically, for while his grip was firm, it was also gentle. But, oh, how it hurt to be touched by him, to feel her breasts press against him, to be surrounded again by his heat and spice. As though sliced and bleeding inside, her heart writhed and became sluggish. Her head grew light, her body weak.

He gave her a small shake. "Stop this. You are upsetting yourself needlessly."

She braced her palms on his gray woolen lapels and leaned closer to him. Her forehead slowly fell into the cushion of his cravat. Her eyes squeezed closed, forcing tears down her face in a warm trickle.

When she spoke, her voice was raw, muffled. "Please just tell me, Lucien. Do I matter to you?"

A long pause was followed by his deep baritone rumbling above her head, beneath her fingers. "He must pay for what he's done."

The simple statement was all the answer she needed. Darkness yawned before her, clawed viciously at her, whispering and then murmuring and then shouting that he did not love her at all. He never had.

She had been his weapon. Nothing more.

Stupid, stupid girl.

His hands stroked up and down her arms in a soothing motion, much as a parent would gentle a child. A cold shiver ran through her, and she pushed away from him. He let her go, his expression strangely closed, vaguely desperate. His arms remained stretched outward for several seconds as though he did not know what to do with them. They dropped to his sides.

That was how Harrison found them a moment later, standing in his parlor staring at one another. Utterly lost.

"Tori? What the devil is going on here?"

She and Lucien swung around to watch her oldest brother stride into the room. He swept off his hat and handed it to Digby, who followed him like a shadow then retreated without a word.

Seeing him again, so tall and solid, his handsome features so familiar, caused Victoria to rush toward him instinctively. His eyes widened before he frowned and enfolded her in a tight embrace. Tears coursed silently down her cheeks, and she whispered his name.

Harrison's arms hardened and his entire body stiffened. When he spoke, his voice was quietly ominous. "Atherbourne, I warned you what would happen if she was harmed."

Alarmed by his threatening tone, Victoria shook her head and wiped her face. She pulled away enough to gaze up at Harrison. His jaw was tight, his face stony as he glared over her head at Lucien.

"I am all right, Harrison. Simply happy to see you." Her

weak, wobbly smile did nothing to erase the furrow of concern from his brow.

"You are a fine one to speak of harming a woman, Blackmore," Lucien remarked coldly.

She could almost feel Harrison bristling at the implication. He set her gently to one side and approached Lucien. "Your accusations are as baseless as your brother's. If you continue, you may reach the same end. Right now, making my sister a widow is rather tempting."

"Spare me your denials. And your threats, *your grace*," Lucien spat. "Both have grown tiresome."

Harrison's head tilted in a predatory way Victoria had seen before, albeit rarely, in her dignified sibling. He could be intimidating, but this particular look signified a rather alarming seriousness of purpose. He opened his mouth to reply, but before he could utter a word, she interrupted by blurting out the first thing that came to mind. "Harrison, did you mistreat Lucien's sister?"

Both men swiveled to stare at her. Harrison was the first to recover. "I never met the chit."

"You lie," Lucien growled.

Harrison ignored him, addressing his answer to Victoria. "The previous Lord Atherbourne accused me of grave misdeeds against her, but I have no idea how he reached such an appalling conclusion. I told him as much, but ... well, it is obvious he did not believe me." He glanced to where Lucien stood, visibly fuming. "It appears your husband is suffering under the same misapprehension. Unfortunate, that."

"A mistake, was it?" Lucien said, his voice a lash. "I suppose it was mere coincidence that Marissa was seen entering and leaving this very house on multiple occasions. Or that her letters were delivered here over the course of several months."

In an unusual show of agitation, Harrison's nostrils flared and his jaw flexed. "To my knowledge, your sister was not even out yet."

Victoria blinked. "She wasn't? Then, how could you have met her?"

Her brother's blue-gray eyes flashed with a spark of irritation. "As I said, I knew nothing of her until the day Gregory Wyatt stormed in here demanding satisfaction. Even if I had, I would not have touched her. She was little more than a child."

"A child you seduced and then discarded as you would a common doxy," Lucien snarled.

Turning toward her husband, Victoria said softly, "What if he didn't?"

Lucien's glower grew fierce, his lips flattened. "He did."

"What if you are wrong, Lucien? What if Gregory was wrong?"

His eyes narrowed. "Fine. You want to play this game? If I am wrong, explain her presence at this house. Not once, mind you, but again and again. Explain why she would have her letters delivered here if she were not corresponding with someone in this household."

"Perhaps she was visiting someone else. Writing to someone else," she suggested.

His mouth twisted in a mockery of a smile. "She left a letter for me and Gregory, did you know? Before she ... died. It was on her bureau beside a vase of flowers."

She was afraid to ask, but she had to know. Being kept in the dark had led to this ... this disaster. Although she would probably not like the answers, it was well past time that Lucien told her the truth, ugly though it might be. "What did it say?"

"That the man she loved considered her unworthy of marriage. She had been raised in the country. It was her first visit to London. Terribly unsophisticated, you know. He worried she might sully the exalted Blackmore legacy."

Victoria shook her head in confusion and glanced at her brother, who stared back with an equally puzzled expression. "She mentioned Harrison by name?"

"Blackmore, yes. Still convinced your brother is so bloody pure and righteous?"

Just then, the clack of boots on marble floors sounded from beyond the open doors of the parlor. Colin's voice, slightly slurred, could be heard in the entrance hall, echoing as he spoke a bit loudly. "Digby, old boy. The library is appallingly bereft of brandy. Be a good chap and fetch me a bottle, would you?"

Forever afterward, Victoria would wonder what made a prickle of suspicion race through her head in that exact moment. It was two puzzle pieces fitting together precisely. It was a voice whispering, "Not Harrison. Colin."

And when she once again met Harrison's eyes, she could see the same voice had spoken to him. Almost as one, they turned toward the doorway through which Colin could be seen clapping Digby on the shoulder.

Not Harrison. It was Colin.

It had been Colin all along.

Chapter Twenty-Eight

"Some secrets are better left undiscovered. Not by me, of course. But generally speaking."

—THE DOWAGER MARCHIONESS OF WALLINGHAM to her son, Lord Wallingham, upon learning of his remarkable cache of French cognac.

LUCIEN WATCHED HIS WIFE TURN PALE AND WIDE-EYED. BOTH she and Blackmore were staring silently through the open door at Colin Lacey, who chuckled at something the butler had said. What the bloody hell had them so riveted? Victoria glanced back at Lucien, a stricken expression in her eyes. The dawning horror and sadness he saw emerging there caused a chill to run through him.

"What is it?" he demanded.

Her gaze dropped, briefly met Blackmore's, then returned to Lacey. Her hands twisted at her waist, a clear signal of her distress. "Please don't hurt him, Lucien."

Every muscle in his body tensed. She was begging him not to harm her brother. There was just one problem—she was referring to the wrong brother. And she appeared genuinely anxious, as though at any moment, he would discover a devilish secret about Colin Lacey and explode in rage.

A dark suspicion seeped along his mind's lower edge. Instincts honed on the battlefield drove him to contemplate the notion that his true enemy was not the one he had been targeting, but another entirely. One he had not previously considered. Part of him protested, remembering Marissa's final letter in which she mentioned Blackmore. But as he stared at Colin, her precise wording echoed in his head.

Marissa had discussed her lover's concern over the Blackmore legacy, which was more characteristic of the duke than his brother. That was why Gregory had assumed Harrison was her seducer, and Lucien had not questioned it. But she had never written or spoken the man's name.

And if it truly was Colin, rather than Blackmore ...

The very thought sickened him, his gorge rising, the room receding, Colin's laugh becoming muffled and faint. Lucien wrestled with this new possibility, wondering if he was slipping back into madness. But no. Victoria and Blackmore remained fixed, frozen in an odd tableau. It seemed they were all caught in the same sticky web, and it was up to him to untangle the mess. For his sister's sake, for all their sakes, he must learn the truth.

Within seconds, he had crossed the parlor, entered the foyer, and without slowing, drove Lacey backwards until he was pinned against a wall, his forearm braced across the younger man's throat. Lucien watched as he struggled and shoved, his face growing red.

"Did you know my sister?"

Choking and gasping, Lacey managed to wheeze, "You've gone mad, Atherbourne."

Lucien clutched fistfuls of cloth and slammed Lacey against the wall. "Answer me, damn you," he gritted. "Did you know Marissa Wyatt?"

Lacey coughed roughly, sucked in a deep breath, and muttered, "Mind the waistcoat. It's new."

The flippant response caused black rage to engulf him. His fists instantly tightened and, almost of their own volition, shoved Lacey violently upward until the man's toes barely touched the floor. "You will pray your waistcoat is the only thing torn asunder."

Distantly, he heard Victoria say his name. Face reddening alarmingly, Lacey sputtered for several seconds, then nodded. Lucien loosened his grip and allowed him to slip down onto his feet.

"You knew Marissa," Lucien barked.

Lacey coughed and eyed him balefully. "Yes. What of it?"

Stunned, Lucien gradually released him and staggered back several steps. The pale green walls seemed to shift and waver around him as he absorbed what he now knew to be true.

Marissa's seducer had not been the Duke of Blackmore. It was Lacey.

Gregory had fought a duel with an innocent man, and had died because of it. Lucien himself had attempted to punish Blackmore, who had only sought to defend himself. A part of him wanted to laugh at the absurdity, the farcical nature of such a grievous misunderstanding. Another part wanted to roar in an agony of guilt.

Lucien's eyes drifted to Victoria. She stood strangely still, white and tear-stained, her eyes awash with sadness, sympathy, and shock.

He had wounded her. His wife. The one he should have protected from all harm.

He had been wrong. So very wrong.

Blackmore, who had been silent and remote, now stood before his brother, firing questions crisply and coldly. "When did you first meet Miss Wyatt?"

Lacey ran a finger between his cravat and his throat, wincing as he tried to loosen the cloth. "Last year. Early spring, just after we arrived in London."

"Where?"

Lacey frowned mutinously and crossed his arms over his chest. "What does it matter?"

Blackmore inched forward until he stood intimidatingly close. "Because, dear brother, you have disguised the truth for long enough. Explain what happened," he snapped. "It is the least you owe Atherbourne. And me."

For a full minute, Lacey glanced at each of them, his expression shuttered. At first, Lucien was certain the man would refuse. Then his eyes met Victoria's for a long while. Shame slowly crept over his face like a shadow. All resolve seemed to leave him, and his back slid down the wall until he sat on the floor, his arms propped limply on his knees, his head bowed in defeat.

"Hyde Park. We met in Hyde Park."

His voice was subdued, almost expressionless, as he told the story of his relationship with Marissa. How she had been strolling with the sister of Lacey's friend, how he had been enchanted by her beauty, and she had been charmed and flattered by his attentions. Soon, they'd begun writing to one another, arranging secretive assignations, and sneaking her into and out of his rooms at Clyde-Lacey House.

"At first, we were both simply enjoying ourselves. Nothing serious. I liked her very much. So pretty and fey, like a woodland sprite."

Lucien ran a hand down his face then threaded it through his hair. Marissa had always been rather fairy-like, with her delicate features and enormous brown eyes framed by ink-black curls. Her smile had beamed with innocent wonder, her rare heart open and exposed. She had been so vulnerable. It was one of the things that drove him, his failure to protect her.

"But then she began talking of marriage, assuming we would be wed at the end of the season. I didn't know what to say." Lacey glanced up at Blackmore, his expression as tortured and confused as a little boy's. "I could not marry her. I was too young to marry anyone. So I lied. I told her you would never approve of the match."

"Oh, Colin," Victoria whispered.

Both of Lacey's hands gripped his head as it dropped forward again. "Her letters kept arriving," he mumbled hoarsely. "She begged to see me. Said over and over that she loved me and did not care if Harrison cut me off. I–I stopped responding. Stopped reading her letters. They had become unbearable. She wanted me to love her, and the simple truth was I did not."

Before Lucien could interject, Blackmore responded, his voice cutting like an ice-encrusted whip. "Your *feelings* for the girl were entirely irrelevant. You should have offered for her the moment your relationship moved beyond propriety."

Lacey eyed his brother resentfully. "Is that what you would have done, *your grace?*"

"Yes," Blackmore hissed. "It is the only honorable course."

Lacey snarled bitterly, "Well, I leave honor to you, brother. I was not about to toss away my remaining youth for the sake of a girl who, I daresay, would have been fine had she merely accepted our parting gracefully and waited for her first season to trap another poor sod in her leg shackles."

Nausea churned in Lucien's stomach, his throat clenching hard in an effort to contain it. "You bloody whoreson," he growled, his voice rising quickly to a roar. "Was she to bear your bastard before or after this phantom suitor offered for her?"

Lacey paled until he resembled a fish's belly, his mouth gaping wide as he stared up at Lucien. Dead silence fell over the room, the only sound the faint patter of rain outside the front door. Finally, Lacey whispered, "She was with child?"

Lucien's dark glare was the only answer he was willing to offer.

The other man looked sickened, shaking his head absently. "I never knew. If she wrote to tell me, I did not read the letter." He glanced at Blackmore, whose face had hardened in disgust. "I would have offered for her, Harrison. I swear I would have done, had I known."

Saying nothing, Blackmore simply shook his head, then turned away from his brother, his nostrils flaring in obvious revulsion. "Atherbourne, may I presume you intend to demand satisfaction?"

The remnants of Lucien's rage shouted, *Yes! I will annihilate him. He must be punished.* But the greater part of him slumped in exhaustion, wrung out and spent after everything that had been revealed. He was tired. Too bloody tired.

Without thinking, he sought Victoria. Her face was streaked with tears, her little nose reddened, her arms hugging herself for comfort. It was painful to see. *He* should be the warm, safe place for his wife. But, as their earlier argument played again through his mind, he was forced to acknowledge how profoundly he had erred.

She had trusted him. Had, for all intents and purposes, offered him her heart. And he had chosen vengeance instead. He had not intended to do so, had wanted both. Expected both.

How could she ever forgive me? he wondered.

At last, he gave Blackmore the only answer he could summon. "Right now, my intention is to leave here and return home. The rest will keep." Turning to Victoria, he asked, "Will you come with me?"

The raw agony he felt as he awaited her answer nearly brought him to his knees. Her eyes searched his face, briefly visited Blackmore and Lacey, then returned to him. She opened her mouth to speak and closed it again. Finally, she looked down at her hands and nodded silently. She moved toward the front door.

He followed helplessly, knowing it might well be the last

time she agreed to accompany him anywhere, the last time she thought of his house as her home.

Over the past two years, he had faced French cannon fire, the deaths of his sister and brother. He had taken on one of the most powerful peers in England in a bid for vengeance. He'd thought fear had been burned out of him. So foolish.

Losing Victoria was an abyss from which his soul would never return. He presently stood reeling at its edge. And nothing had ever terrified him more.

Chapter Twenty-Nine

"How dare you, sir! One may only be considered
an 'interfering busybody' if one does not possess judgment
superior to all others. Which I, of course, do."

—THE DOWAGER MARCHIONESS OF WALLINGHAM to the
Duke of Blackmore, upon being accused of overstepping
her bounds most egregiously.

FOUR DAYS LATER, WYATT HOUSE FELT LIKE A FUNERAL—MRS.
Garner's staff went about their duties as usual, but they were
slow, hushed, morose. "Haven't seen such a pall since Master
Gregory's passing, God rest his soul," the housekeeper
commented to Cook as they broke their fast.

"Eh?" Billings shouted from his end of the table in the

servants' hall. "There's to be a ball, you say? Why was I not informed?"

Mrs. Garner sighed in exasperation. "A *pall*, Billings," she bellowed. "Been quiet as a tomb 'round here of late."

The butler nodded somberly and resumed buttering his roll.

Cook leaned toward Mrs. Garner and muttered, "It's to be salmon again tonight. Her ladyship came to the kitchen to inform me herself. Looked like a cat poked with a stick, all bristles and outrage."

Mrs. Garner tsked. "Men. Did ye know he ran off to White's yesterday? She was tryin' to speak to the man, and he gets this panicked look in 'is eyes, turns tail and bolts fer the door." She sniffed. "Poor thing was left standin' there, fightin' back tears. Such a shame."

"Seems to me the boy's got the wrong end of this thing. Why does he not just tell her he regrets what he's done?"

Mrs. Garner gave the other woman a wry glance.

Cook's mouth quirked. "You're right, o' course. Some men would sooner be parted from their heads than their pride."

Taking a sip of tea, Mrs. Garner tidied the crumbs on her plate into a small pile in the center. "This is the fourth mornin' I had to clean the yellow chamber. I tell ye, such is not a sign of a marriage on the mend."

"Still sleeping apart, are they?"

The housekeeper nodded. Just then, Emily entered the room, her usual sunny smile nowhere in sight. "Beg pardon," she said, her voice muted and solemn as she took her seat.

"See?" said Mrs. Garner. "Gloomy as a rain cloud, it is. Fixin' to send Ol' Mrs. Garner to purchase a few yards of black bombazine."

Emily sent her an apologetic glance. "Her ladyship awoke early so she could see Lord Atherbourne at breakfast. When she discovered he did not intend to partake, she was gravely disappointed. She dressed for visiting and said she was headed to Clyde-Lacey House."

A trill of alarm struck along the back of Mrs. Garner's neck.

"Did she ask ye to pack 'er trunks?" Relief filled her as the girl shook her head.

"But she is most unhappy, Mrs. Garner. What shall we do if ...?"

Silence fell over the table. Emily had just asked the question none of them wished to contemplate, but all of them feared the answer to. What if Lady Atherbourne left him? Could the master survive it? Would he revert to the tormented man who had arrived in London six months ago?

Billings cleared his throat. "I find one makes the best decisions when one has all the facts at one's disposal."

Everyone blinked at the aged butler.

"Perhaps her ladyship could be assisted in that endeavor." With that, Billings calmly sipped his tea and retreated into his customary deaf bubble.

Cook nudged Mrs. Garner's arm. "He's right, you know."

Eyebrows raised, she looked askance at her friend.

"She should know the truth."

"She does," Mrs. Garner retorted. "Tha's what's got 'er so torn up."

"Not all of it."

Cook was right. Lady Atherbourne knew the bare bones of the tragedy that had struck the Atherbourne family last year, but not the depth of it. And she seemed wholly unaware of the difference her presence had wrought in Lord Atherbourne and, indeed, in Wyatt House.

"It wouldn't be proper to hear such tales from Mrs. Garner," said Mrs. Garner.

Cook strummed her fingers on the table. "No," she mused. "But from somebody of her station. Someone who knows the master, knows what happened."

Mrs. Garner blinked, her eyes widening as they met Cook's. At the same moment, they both said, "I have an idea." Then they grinned at one another.

Two hours later, Mrs. Garner waited for her ladyship to arrive home. Her key ring jingled as she shifted restlessly, her eyes peering through the front window of the parlor yet again. At last, she saw the Atherbourne carriage pull up in front of the house, Connell's ginger hair gleaming from beneath his cap.

Geoffrey, the footman, opened the door and assisted the lady down onto the cobblestones. Beautifully dressed in a dark blue spencer and lighter blue walking gown, Lady Atherbourne carried herself with dignity and grace, almost floating as she ascended the steps. But Mrs. Garner could see the strain of sadness around her eyes, the dark circles and pale complexion signs of sleepless nights. It was like looking upon a room that needed cleaning—as far as Mrs. Garner was concerned, it was her mission to see the thing set to rights. No housekeeper worth her salt would do less.

"Ah, Billings," she heard the mistress say upon entering the house and removing her bonnet. "Would you be so kind as to ask Donald to assist Geoffrey? I retrieved a trunk from my former residence, and it is quite cumbersome, I'm afraid."

"Of course, my lady," Billings said, his voice soft and gentle. He was ever so solicitous with her these days. Old, deaf, and sometimes forgetful, the butler had nevertheless fallen under her spell, the same as the rest of them.

Mrs. Garner breathed deeply and took this moment as her cue. She entered the foyer to see the mistress absently removing her gloves. Her expression was forlorn, her eyes distant. "My lady, shall I fetch ye some tea? Nothin' soothes the spirit like a nice cup or two."

Lady Atherbourne stared at her for a moment as though trying to determine who she was and what language she spoke.

"Tea, my lady?"

Finally, she smiled, but it did not reach her eyes. Those remained hollow. "That would be lovely. Thank you, Mrs. Garner. I shall be in my sitting room."

Donald entered, bowing as he passed through the foyer on his way outside. Lady Atherbourne nodded to him and moved up the stairs, her gait diffident and slow.

Frowning in concern, Mrs. Garner watched her mistress ascend, thinking what a shame it was that matters had come to this—depending on a housekeeper to mend what was broken. "Hmmph," she muttered. "Harebrained, it is. But it must be done." With that, she bustled to the kitchen, where Cook had already prepared the tea.

"How did she seem?"

Mrs. Garner shook her head. "Like one o' them ghosties what haunt the graveyards."

Cook handed her the tray. "Best get to it, then."

Five minutes later, Mrs. Garner stood before Lady Atherbourne, watching the lady pen a note to some swell or other. She tidied the tray she had placed on the long table beside the desk, pretending busy-ness until her ladyship paused in composing her correspondence. At last, the quill stopped.

"Billings asked Geoffrey and Donald to put yer trunk in the blue room, my lady. That Donald is a fine one. Not too many things 'e can't lift, one way or t'other. Yes, indeed."

The lady sighed quietly. "Thank you, Mrs. Garner."

"Oh, ye're most welcome. Why, I recall the week we hired the lad. Must've been the very same week his lordship arrived. Those were dark days, I reckon. Lord Atherbourne hadn't visited Wyatt House in some time. Staff had dwindled by half. Then, one day he shows up. I can tell ye, both Billings and Mrs. Garner had a tall order getting this place running proper. But we was happy to do it."

Mrs. Garner watched Lady Atherbourne's reactions carefully, noting a sudden perk of interest in the tilt of her head. "He arrived without notice?" the lady asked softly.

"Oh, aye. All rags and bones, lookin' like he'd ridden through death's own valley. A pitiful sight to behold, he was. Lord Tannenbrook had to help him off his horse, sad to say."

Blue-green eyes met her own, a spark of curiosity mixing with sudden sympathy in their depths. "Lord Tannenbrook came to London with my hus—with Lord Atherbourne?"

The housekeeper gave an exaggerated nod, then remembered what Cook had said: Don't appear too eager or give the information too easily, lest her ladyship become suspicious. She pointed to the tray. "Would ye like me to pour, my lady?"

Lady Atherbourne followed her gaze briefly, then shook her head, clearly impatient to learn more. "How—how long have they been friends, do you know?"

Deliberately tightening her mouth so as to appear reluctant, Mrs. Garner pursed her lips, then said, "I couldn't say, my lady." She glanced surreptitiously toward the door, then continued in a whisper, "But iffen anyone would understand the sad business from that time, it would be his lordship. Tannenbrook, I mean. Known the family fer years, if I'm not mistaken. He was there through the whole of it. No one else Lord Atherbourne's like to confide in, so they been thick as thieves these past months."

Watching her ladyship spark to life in that moment, seeing her make the connection Mrs. Garner had so artfully proffered—well, it was satisfying, to say the least. "Will there be anything else, my lady?"

Still clearly lost in thought, Lady Atherbourne shook her head. Mrs. Garner turned to leave, but stopped when her mistress suddenly reached out and clasped her hand. The contrast between a refined lady's soft, white hand and her own callused, work-worn one was stark and slightly embarrassing. "Thank you, Mrs. Garner. You are the finest of housekeepers." With that rather startling declaration, she let go and returned to her correspondence, pulling out a fresh sheet of paper with, apparently, renewed vigor.

As Mrs. Garner exited the sitting room, closing the door quietly to give her mistress plenty of time to think, she smiled to herself. Among the many duties a housekeeper must perform, first and foremost was maintaining a pristine and orderly residence. And like a filthy chamber, this particular mess was about to be cleaned up proper, or her name wasn't Mrs. Garner.

Chapter Thirty

"Yes, I suppose London is delightful, providing one prefers breathing noxious air and being surrounded by filth. And that is merely its residents."

—THE DOWAGER MARCHIONESS OF WALLINGHAM to Lady Rumstoke during a ride along Rotten Row.

LONDON'S LIGHT WAS ALWAYS SOMEWHAT WEAK, BUT TODAY it was positively dim. Fog blanketed the streets, causing late morning to feel more like dusk. Victoria sighed as she squinted at the portrait of Lucien. Despite the low light, she noted with satisfaction that his waistcoat was now a vivid, eye-catching blue, thanks to her ultramarine pigment.

In the week since the confrontation at Clyde-Lacey House,

she had visited her former home twice, once to retrieve her art supplies and once to speak with Harrison. Fortunately, Lucien had lost interest in preventing her seeing her brothers.

Unfortunately, he also had lost interest in her. After they'd arrived back at Wyatt House, she had retreated to her sitting room, needing a few hours of solitude to digest what had occurred. Lucien had not attempted to touch or speak to her. In fact, he had closed himself up in the library until well past midnight.

She had fallen asleep without him. He still had not returned to their bed.

Hugging herself against a chill, she wandered to the windows of her studio, staring vacantly at the gray. The muffled clacking of carriage wheels could be heard through the glass, but all she could see was fog. It was eerie, really; knowing something was so close, yet being unable to see it. Breathing against a faint sense of despair, she stiffened her spine. Lucien had studiously avoided her for the past week, spending most days away from the house, his nights in one of the guest chambers.

On two occasions, she had caught him on his way out, had tried to speak to him about Colin and Harrison, to discuss what should happen with their marriage. Both times, he behaved as a stranger—remote, polite, even dull—brushing her off as he would an overly aggressive fruit seller. At first, it was understandable. Then, it was vexing. Now, she was angry. If he thought he could ignore her forever, he was the greatest of fools.

Last night was the fifth evening Cook had served fish for dinner. He had said nothing, although her intent had been to solicit some sort of reaction. She swallowed against a roll of nausea. Even she was growing weary of the stuff.

A change of tactics was required, that was all. He *would* speak to her, blast it. They *would* resolve this one way or another. They must. Otherwise, she was terribly afraid their marriage would continue to deteriorate until only dust remained. Perhaps that was his intention, she thought. It was still possible he felt nothing for her, that revenge had been his sole reason for being with her, and she was no longer useful to him. After all, now that Colin had confessed his part in Marissa's death, everything had changed.

Or, had it? Lucien might, at this moment, still intend to deliver justice upon Colin. A part of her would understand if he did. What Colin had done was contemptible, and as his sister, she was both ashamed and furious with him. Not only had he badly mistreated Marissa, he had remained silent while Harrison fought a duel over the consequences of his actions.

Looking back, it was clear Colin had felt guilt over the incident. His drinking had increased dramatically during that time, and had been a curse ever since. Truly, her brother's recklessness and lack of honor had set a series of disasters in motion. And that would be difficult to forgive, even for those closest to him.

But was he the only one at fault? Marissa herself bore some responsibility, surely. Victoria tried to imagine herself in the same situation—deeply in love with a man who abandoned her. Disgraced. Unmarried. With child.

Her hand drifted to her belly.

Would she, Victoria, choose to take her own life, and that of her unborn child?

No, she decided instantly. Not in a thousand lifetimes would she willingly deliver such grief and suffering upon those who loved her, or deprive her child of the chance to be born. As heartsick as she would be if Lucien treated her in such a way, she would always choose life over death.

Marissa had made a different choice, and it had been devastating.

Her hand fisted around the cloth at her midsection. She imagined a babe growing inside her body. Lucien's child. Perhaps with his dark hair and strong features. A wave of love and longing rushed through her in a warm tingle. Steadying herself, she gritted her teeth and raised her chin. Perhaps her marriage was a sham. Perhaps he did not give a fig about her. But at some point between deciding to defy Lucien's mandate and deciding to accompany him back to Wyatt House, she had realized he was likely the only husband she would have, the only one who could give her children. He might not love her, but he had married her, and he would not escape his responsibilities so easily. He would not escape *her* so easily.

She gave a startled jerk as Billings bellowed from the doorway, "My lady, Lord Tannenbrook has arrived. Shall I show him up?"

"Please do, Billings. Thank you."

He nodded and disappeared. Victoria quickly covered the portrait and gathered her sketchbook from the work table. She ran a hand over its soft leather cover, a half smile emerging. If Lucien would not speak to her, she would do what she must.

Moments later, Lord Tannenbrook filled the doorway of her studio—quite literally. His shoulders brushed the jam on either side. The man was as big as a mountain. Dressed simply in a dark brown woolen coat, green waistcoat, and tan riding breeches, she fancied he wore the colors of one, as well. James Kilbrenner reminded her of the Scottish Highlands she had visited as a child—stalwart, intimidating, and inscrutable.

She smiled brightly in welcome, thanking him for coming.

But for the mildly awkward way he hovered in the doorway, he was as unreadable as ever. "Your note said Lucien required my help." He glanced pointedly around the room. "Is he late arriving, Lady Atherbourne?"

The flat question implied she had done something improper. Perhaps she had, inviting a man who was not her husband to meet with her privately. But, dash it all, she must have answers—answers Lucien was unwilling to provide.

There was a time when she had simply accepted the rules of society, playing the role assigned to her by birth and station and expectation. But after the scandal, she had begun to realize how arbitrary those rules sometimes were, particularly for women.

Strangely, it was her marriage to Lucien that had given her the courage to fight for what she wanted, rather than allowing others to choose her fate. And if the past few days of cold civility had served any purpose at all, it had forced her to acknowledge what she wanted most: Lucien himself.

The infuriating, manipulative, disgustingly handsome, intelligent, romantic, dashing devil.

She shook her head, annoyed at herself. She could not even sustain a good rant against the man in her own head.

Tannenbrook took her gesture as an answer to his question about whether Lucien would be joining them, and shifted as though preparing to leave. "I'm not certain I understand, then. Perhaps we should wait to discuss this until Lucien is available."

She walked toward Lucien's friend, hugging her sketchbook to her breast with one hand and gesturing toward a pair of chairs with the other. "Please, Lord Tannenbrook. Won't you sit and talk with me? I promise my intentions are exactly as my note described—to help Lucien."

Sharp green eyes met her own, studied her for several seconds. Then, slowly, Tannenbrook stepped into the room, the knock of his boot heels against the wooden floor echoing in the largely empty chamber. He came to a stop near the corner adjacent to the fireplace and stood beside one of the chairs she had indicated.

Victoria smiled gratefully and seated herself, waiting for the dark-blond giant to do the same. As he lowered into the chair, he asked, "My lady, forgive me, but are you not concerned what your husband might say should he discover we have met privately?"

She patted the cover of her sketchbook, then opened it cheerfully and pulled a pencil from the pocket of her apron. "Not a bit," she replied. "You are here so that I may sketch you. While I do so, we shall simply pass the time in conversation." Giving him a conspiratorial grin, she smoothed an empty page and immediately began long, sweeping strokes of her pencil, her eyes moving quickly between him and the emerging image.

While at first he appeared surprised, then skeptical, she glimpsed what appeared to be the faintest half-smile. Well, well. The stone-faced earl seemed agreeable, at least enough to remain in place. That was good, because she had questions that must be addressed.

"How long have you known my husband?" she began casually.

The chair creaked as he repositioned himself, the faint light from the windows doing intriguing things with the furrow on his heavy brow. "Since I inherited the title. Fourteen years or so. Tannenbrook lands border Thornbridge to the north."

"You knew his brother, Gregory, as well, I presume? And ... Marissa."

The strokes of pencil over paper whispered in the long silence before his deep, rumbling voice finally answered, "Yes."

"What were they like?"

He tilted his head subtly, considering her question. "Marissa was guileless. A bit wild, perhaps, but in the way of a bramble rose. Delicate."

"And Gregory?"

"Good."

Her brows arched in inquiry. "Good?"

Tannenbrook grunted affirmatively. "A good man. Good brother. Good friend."

She nodded, perceiving the earl's emotion surrounding Gregory's death. To most, his face would appear expressionless. But as she drew his features, she could see the nearly imperceptible changes in the cast of his eyes, the tic of muscles tugging down the corners of his mouth. The grief was there, just well hidden.

"And how would you describe Lucien?" she continued.

"That is more complicated."

Victoria struggled for a moment with the shading of Tannenbrook's temple, focusing on the sketch. He was a difficult subject to capture well, as his face changed radically depending on the light, from sinister to calm, craggy and blunt to surprisingly elegant. It was disconcerting, as though his identity changed moment by moment.

Returning to their conversation, she asked absently, "How so?"

The man's chair creaked again as he shifted. "Death has changed him a great deal."

Victoria's eyes flew to meet Tannenbrook's. "You mean the deaths of Marissa and Gregory."

"Yes. But also before that. Waterloo. Lucien was a Dragoon captain—heavy cavalry. During a charge on Napoleon's forces, his horse was shot from beneath him. He was pinned, unconscious for hours. Much of his unit was decimated. Later, he was able to rejoin the battle, and he fought as though his life meant nothing. Wellington reportedly said Lucien either possessed extraordinary courage or wished to die."

Cold settled over her skin, causing a sickening shiver. She had known he'd been a soldier, knew he'd been at Waterloo, knew he'd fought bravely. But to realize he had almost died, that many of his men had fallen around him, and he'd been unable to do anything about it ... She pressed her lips together and stared down at her hand where it lay clasping the pencil above her sketch.

She felt sadness for the men who had been lost, wounded. She wanted to weep at the guilt that must have driven Lucien to risk himself so recklessly. But, most of all, she felt grateful.

That he had survived. That she had been granted the opportunity to love him.

Tannenbrook's voice intruded once again. "I knew him before he was either a captain or a viscount, merely Lucien Wyatt. He was good, like his brother. Laughed all the time. Couldn't stop him, in fact." One side of his mouth quirked in a half-smile. "Gregory tried a few times. Said Luc would have to take life seriously at some point." The smile faded. "Then Waterloo. I think if that had been the only blow, he might have borne it. But he returned to England broken, only to discover his sister and brother were both dead. It was ..." He halted, seemingly unable to continue.

"It was too much for anyone to endure," she ventured softly.

Tannenbrook's eyes, the dark green of a forest after sundown, became echoing caverns of past pain. "Yes," he said hoarsely. "Luc was lost. The grief ate him whole."

Victoria firmed her trembling lower lip and swallowed hard against the tears that burned to be released. Now was not the time to crumble. She returned her attention to completing the sketch.

"How—" She cleared her throat. "How did he recover? Find his way back to—how should I phrase it—himself, I suppose?"

Again, the chair creaked as Tannenbrook repositioned himself. She glanced up briefly, but he did not meet her eyes.

He seemed most uncomfortable.

"My lord?"

This time, it was Tannenbrook who cleared his throat. "He did not."

"What do you mean?"

After a long hesitation, he sighed, appearing resigned. "Luc was in a very bad way."

She opened her mouth to ask for further details, but he stopped her with a stern, "It is best to leave it at that."

Sensing he was likely to be stubborn about protecting Lucien's privacy, she nodded and gestured for him to continue.

"I did what I could to help him. Spent a good deal of time at Thornbridge. Occasionally, it seemed he was improving. We would ride together. Discuss the estate. But then he would disappear again. I grew a bit desperate, I'm afraid." He turned his head to watch the wisps of fog float past the windows. "Did you know I was Gregory's second?"

She shook her head, but he didn't see. Her hand flew over the paper, shading and reshading as the light shifted over the man's face.

"Luc is my friend. I refused to lose him, too. So I suggested he consider who would gain justice for Gregory and Marissa if he was ... gone." His gaze returned to hers. "It was the only thing that seemed to revive him. I have never seen him more fired with determination."

Victoria understood. "You gave him a reason to continue on. To live. For them."

Big hands curled into fists on the arms of the chair. "For the better part of a year, this bid for revenge has been the only thing keeping him upright. I have worried a great deal. It is why I remained in London."

She stared down at her sketch, wondering if the Earl of Tannenbrook knew how transparent he was when one bothered to study his face with the eye of an artist. It was all there—strength, loyalty, compassion. Secrets.

"My estate in Derbyshire is in the midst of considerable repair. After he married you, and I saw how you were together, I thought perhaps I could return there. I made plans to leave this afternoon. Then I received your note."

Her eyes flew to his face once again. "Why would seeing us together ease your worry, my lord?"

He blinked twice, appearing puzzled. "You do not know?"

She released an exasperated sigh. "Why do you suppose I have asked you here? I have no idea how he feels."

He sat back, seeming discomfited by her outburst. "Perhaps you should speak to Lucien."

"Lord Tannenbrook, if I could obtain such information from my husband, I would have done so before today. He will not speak to me."

The earl now appeared distinctly uncomfortable, fingers flexing, one hand fussing with his cravat where it wrapped about his thick neck. His eyes darted toward the door.

"Now then," she continued firmly. "Let us address the reason for my note. Lucien wanted vengeance upon my brother, so he generated a scandal and coaxed me into marriage. He then attempted to cut me out of Harrison's life entirely, thus simultaneously humiliating the duke and depriving him of his sister. Do I have that about right?"

Tannenbrook went still, his fingers now gripping the arms of the chair. He nodded.

She smiled tightly. "Good. I have only one question. Does Lucien care for me, or was this always about revenge and nothing more?"

This was it. Better to know the truth, surely. Her palms dampened, making her grip on her sketchbook and pencil slick. His answer might change everything. Her marriage, her very life. And he was taking an awfully long time. Blood rushed loudly in her ears, her stomach clenching, her skin chilled. *It is better to know,* she repeated. *If he will simply tell me—*

Finally, he sat forward, opened his mouth to speak, closed it, then replied, "He has not said that he loves you."

Her heart tore. Blood drained away from her skin, causing a flush of ice.

I was wrong, she thought. *Knowing is much worse than not knowing. It is agony, in fact.*

"However—"

At that one word, her entire being paused. Without thinking, she reached forward and gripped the man's wrist, her pencil falling to the floor with a quiet clack. "However?"

He glanced to where her fingers attempted to circle his wrist. They could not even manage half the circumference. "However, I will say this: I have never seen Lucien happier than he has been since your marriage. Not in all the years I have known him."

The revelation sent her heart—broken only moments earlier—thumping and twirling and positively *leaping*. "Truly?" she asked breathlessly.

A grudgingly full smile transformed Tannenbrook's face. "Truly." He patted her hand where it still grasped his wrist, gently pried her fingers loose, and set it back in her lap.

She scarcely noticed.

"Rest assured, the man has been a bloody mooncalf for weeks now. I daresay if he does not care for you, not only is he daft, he should be treading the boards at Drury Lane."

The sun had burst through the clouds. Music had broken a

long and desolate silence. Rain had come to parched earth. Hope. There was hope again.

Victoria beamed at the earl, just barely restraining herself from jumping into the man's arms. "Lord Tannenbrook, this has been ... I cannot express ..." She struggled against tears. "Well, perhaps simpler is better. Thank you, my lord. You have been *most* helpful."

He bowed his head and said, "You are quite welcome, Lady Atherbourne."

She rose to see him out, and he stood, his massive form towering over her. His eyes landed on her sketchbook. "Are you finished, then?"

She looked at the leather cover then at him. "With the sketch? Yes, actually, I am."

"May I see it?"

Though she had to crane her neck to do so, she looked up into his eyes. Something there resembled the look of a shy boy. She grinned. "Of course." Quickly flipping to the page with his portrait, she handed him the open book. He took it carefully in his big hands, his face shadowed and inscrutable as he examined her work. A slight frown furrowed his forehead.

"Is—is something wrong?" She stepped closer, moving to his side so she could see the page herself. "I had trouble with your brow, but I thought I got it right in the end."

"No, nothing is wrong," he said. "It's fine. Quite the best I have ever seen, in fact."

A thrill ran through her at the unexpected praise. It was not often she heard such things from anyone apart from Harrison or Lady Berne. Rising onto her tiptoes, she gave a little bounce of happiness, beaming up at the kind and obviously discerning Lord Tannenbrook.

The chamber door slammed loudly, echoing in the room.

"Well, isn't this a cozy picture," her husband said sardonically. "My best friend and my wife."

Chapter Thirty-One

"Do not glower at me, dear boy.
I am not the one keeping secrets."

—The Dowager Marchioness of Wallingham to the
Earl of Tannenbrook during a particularly vexing discussion.

Lucien had never enjoyed killing. As a soldier, it had been necessary at times, but he took no pleasure in it. Until now. He pictured dispatching Tannenbrook with the same brutal efficiency he had employed against the French. It was ... satisfying.

Seeing Victoria standing bare inches from James, smiling up at him in radiant joy, her petite curves all but embraced by the much larger man—it was acid eating away his veins. It made his hands clench in longing for a sword, a pistol, anything to snap the connection between them.

That look belonged to Lucien. *He* was the cause of her angelic smile. *He* made her laugh and dance on her toes. No one else.

"Lucien," his wife exclaimed. A sweep of pink flared in her cheeks as she stepped back, adding several feet of space between her and James.

Better, he thought grimly. *But not nearly enough.*

"I—we ... That is, Lord Tannenbrook and I ..." Victoria stammered, her voice a bit higher than usual. Something in his expression brought her explanation to a halt.

Looking annoyed, James placed the book he was holding on the chair behind him and moved toward Lucien, his shoulders squared as though preparing for a bout at Gentleman Jackson's. "Don't be a damned fool, man," his friend warned. "She asked to sketch my portrait. The door was open."

Lucien's lips flattened. "You sat for her. Nothing more?"

Tilting his head slightly, James sniffed. "Bit of conversation."

"Conversation." Lucien's tone was deadly.

"Perhaps I should take my leave."

"Perhaps you should have left long ago," Lucien retorted.

James nodded, a dry half smile emerging on his face. His steps rang loudly in the room as he slowly approached Lucien standing in front of the closed door. As he passed, he paused, clapping a large hand heavily onto Lucien's shoulder.

"Have a care, my friend," James murmured so only Lucien could hear. "You would be wise to recognize the jewel that rests in your palm, even if the reason you possess it is less than noble."

With a final bruising pat, James exited, the door closing with a quiet click.

Eyes fixed on Victoria, Lucien watched as she puttered about the room, first to her work table, then to her easel, then back to the table. Reaching behind her back, she untied and removed the paint-smudged apron, revealing a pale pink, long-sleeved gown of simple muslin.

His eyes dropped to her breasts, full and lush. They were modestly covered, but he could not help wondering if James had noticed them. *How could he do otherwise?* Lucien thought, his stomach tightening. *She is exquisitely made.*

He missed her skin. Her sweet floral smell. The feel of her lips on his body. The wave of peace as he lay his head over her heart, his cheek cushioned by her pleasure-flushed breasts.

He nearly groaned at the memory.

She capped a glass bottle of blue pigment and placed it carefully in a wooden case. Tendrils of hair escaped the simple coil at the back of her head, falling along the frame of her jaw.

He felt his own jaw clench. *What did you expect her to do?* he asked himself bitterly. *How was she to feel, knowing you schemed to keep her from her family, that you used her for your own purposes—and only repented when you discovered you had targeted the wrong brother?*

Angry. She should feel angry. And she had made it plain that she did.

He felt a wave of sickness. She had served fish every night since the confrontation at Clyde-Lacey House. First, she had fled to her sitting room without a word. Then she had fallen asleep without him. Then she had communicated her displeasure through the dinner menu.

Perceiving she desired a bit of distance, he had retreated. They slept apart, spent most of each day apart, essentially lived apart. They barely spoke. Outside of the dark months after Waterloo, it had been the worst week of his life.

"You are quite fortunate, you know," she said quietly, swishing a paintbrush in a small cup of solvent. "Lord Tannenbrook is a most devoted friend."

Lucien folded his arms across his chest, irritation making him bristle. "What does that mean?"

She wiped the brush clean with a cloth, then laid it neatly next to a row of others. "Simply that he appears to have been an anchor for you amidst great storms."

As her eyes met his, blue-green and unflinching, he realized she was sincere. Her honest assessment of James was that he had been a stalwart friend to Lucien. And that was true. But how would she know? "You've been meeting with him regularly, have you?" he asked softly.

She rolled her eyes. "Of course not. Today was the first time." Her expression grew sad, sympathetic. "He explained what happened last year."

Dread, thick and paralyzing, flooded through him. How much had James told her?

"Suffering so much loss all at once," she said, her voice gentle. "I cannot bear to imagine how you endured it."

The air fled his body, leaving his lungs to struggle and burn. She knew. Oh, dear God. She knew about the darkness. The madness. *No. No, no, no, no.* It was his greatest shame, his inability to escape from the black pit. If she knew ...

"I understand better now, Lucien. You believed Harrison was responsible. Vengeance became your purpose. But now you must surely see this path can only end in further destruction. For you. For me. Is that what Gregory or Marissa would have wanted, do you suppose?"

Unable to hold her gaze, he drifted toward the windows, staring out at the swirling gray fog. He braced his hands on the sill. "It was not what anyone wanted," he confessed hoarsely. "Including me." His head fell forward, bowing under the strain of remembering. "At the time, it was the only thing that would permit me to sleep."

Her silence was filled with understanding. Regret. The rustle of her dress as she moved about the room was the only sound he heard for a long while. When she finally spoke, she was but a few feet behind him. Closer than she had been in days. He thought perhaps he caught a hint of her scent. Hyacinth. So sweet.

"The Gattingford ball is this evening. Do you still intend to accompany me?" Her voice, previously soft with empathy, had returned to its normal, quiet cadence.

Thank God. The last thing he wanted was for Victoria to witness him collapsing in grief or exploding in a fit of anger. He could not bear her pity. Better she should hate him.

But was that true? If she hated him, she might leave him. Nothing could be worse than that.

"Lucien?"

His fingers curled into the painted wood of the sill. His chest felt tight, the ache around his heart intensifying.

Answer her, you bloody fool.

He felt her approach, felt tingles of awareness run down his spine, curl around his hips and sink into his groin. So close. Her hand settled gently against his biceps. It scalded him through layers of wool and linen. Branded him as hers.

"Lucien," she whispered. "Are you ...?"

"Yes," he gritted. "Of course I will accompany you."

One heartbeat. Two.

Her hand fell away. He felt her draw back, heard her footsteps whisper a retreat toward the door. "Thank you," she said, her voice thicker than before, as though she were having trouble forming the words.

She must resent me so, he thought. *And well she should.* Escorting her to the second Gattingford ball of the season was the least he could do, as it would be the final piece in restoring her reputation. He was not the husband she deserved. But he could fulfill at least one promise he'd made to her. It was a risk. She had only married him to resolve the scandal. After tonight, that would no longer be a concern. She would have no more need of him.

Clearing her throat, she drew his attention once again. "We shall dine here, before we leave. Lady Gattingford's offerings are simply ghastly." She paused. "Cook had planned to serve haddock, I believe."

He squeezed his eyes shut. Fish again. Well, on the bright side, he supposed Victoria still cared enough to be angry. It was a hopeful sign.

"However, I have asked her to prepare roasted duck instead. Her brandy sauce is excellent."

The door clicked as she exited the room.

Perhaps "hopeful" had been a bit premature, he thought wryly. She had even given up on her transparent attempts to punish him. He could only conclude one of two things: Either she was beginning to forgive him, or she no longer gave a damn.

His head dropped as despair overwhelmed him. He'd been asking himself for days how it was possible to keep her in his life. He knew she would not divorce him—she would never again invite such scandal—but with the duke's help, she could live separately in ease and comfort. Apart from him. Forever.

He was willing to stand and accept her anger, ready to plead for her forgiveness. But if he had destroyed whatever affections she had for him—if she could not love him—none of that would matter.

He glanced around the room absently. Blue walls. Bare wooden floors. The first time he had entered Victoria's studio, it had stunned him. Nothing of his sister remained here, not the ormolu clock on the mantel or the bureau where she had placed a vase of rosebuds. Not even the stain of her blood on the floor. Now, the room was entirely Victoria's. *That's good,* he thought. *Better to remember Marissa elsewhere—perhaps in the garden back at Thornbridge.*

An unexpected smile tugged. She'd been a wild thing, his sister. Her hem had always been stained by rainwater, grasses, and the dirt of the places she loved to explore. She'd had a habit of traipsing over acres of woods, ambling along the brook that cut through their land. She had said it was the only time she ever felt entirely at peace.

He blinked and felt something trickle down his face.

Are you at peace now, little one?

It was a question he suspected he would ask for the rest of his life. Even if Colin Lacey were punished. Even if Blackmore suffered for killing Gregory. Somehow, he knew none of it would ever be enough, because it could not undo what had been done.

Swiping at his face, he slowly wandered about the room. Yes, it was Victoria's place, now. She had made it her own.

His eyes fell on the chairs near the empty fireplace.

Resentment rising, he recalled walking into the room earlier, seeing her and Tannenbrook together. She had asked James to sit for her. Not Lucien. James. Why? What was so compelling about bloody James Kilbrenner that she simply had to sketch the bloody giant?

Spotting her sketchbook resting on one of the chairs, he snatched it up and flipped open the brown leather cover.

His breath stopped, heart turning over painfully. It was not James. It was ... him. Lucien. He was seated beside a window, his face shuttered and yet sad. Hollow. Lost.

He ran his fingers gently over the sketch, tracing the path her hands had traced. She must have drawn him from memory. The forms were excellent, her strokes bold and confident. And yet, it was not simply technique. The portrait was sensitive and nuanced, her empathy for her subject woven into the shading of dark and light, the lowered tilt of his chin, the vulnerability of his hand, lying open and empty on the arm of the chair. Such a gifted artist, his wife.

He turned to the next page, his eyes flaring in surprise.

It was him again. This time, he was lying in their bed, his mouth curving slightly upward as he slept, the sheet wrapped about his hips. She must have sketched him after they'd made love.

Another page, another portrait of him. And another. And another. Dozens, in fact.

She had drawn him in every conceivable pose—nude and clothed, laughing and brooding, contemplative and impassioned. She made studies of his entire form, detailed sketches of his hands, his eyes, the contours of his chest. She seemed especially fond of the lower half of his face—his lips and jaw.

He felt himself grinning like a fool. A fool besotted with his wife, discovering that perhaps, just perhaps, she felt the same for him. He swallowed, almost afraid to believe it.

Coming to the last page, he saw the portrait she had done today, the one of James. His friend's craggy, blunt features were far from handsome, but Victoria had managed to capture the keen intelligence in the sharpness of his eyes, the stubborn determination in the hardness of his jaw, the secretive darkness in the shadows of his brow. It was a brilliant representation of the man.

But one thing it did not show—the infatuation of the artist with her subject. Every drawing of Lucien was redolent with adoration. If nothing else, the sheer quantity demonstrated that. Feeling more hopeful than he had in weeks, he moved to set Victoria's sketchbook on her work table. That was when he spotted her easel, covered with a large cloth, presumably to protect her painting from dust.

Curious, he lifted the linen, folding it carefully back to reveal ...

Himself.

Or, rather, a more magnificent version of himself.

Heart thumping painfully inside his chest, Lucien stared into his own eyes and suddenly understood.

The woman who painted this saw him. *Knew* him down to his very soul. And she loved him deeply. It could not have been clearer.

Spinning and tilting, his world changed, expanding to include this new knowledge. Joy—precious and fragile—sprang from a part of himself he had thought lost.

She loved him.

But would she forgive him? For the first time, he realized it might be possible. He *could* earn her forgiveness. He *could* regain her trust.

It was far from guaranteed. Unlikely, perhaps. But there was a chance. And nothing mattered more.

Chapter Thirty-Two

*"Lemons are sour. They require an equal amount of sweet
to be palatable. Perhaps you hadn't heard, my dear."*

—The Dowager Marchioness of Wallingham to Lady
Gattingford after unintentionally imbibing said lady's lemonade.

THEY ARRIVED AT THE GATTINGFORD BALL AMIDST AN
explosion of murmurs. Victoria clutched Lucien's arm a bit
harder as they were announced, struggling against a sudden
attack of nerves.

She glanced down at her gown. The peacock-blue silk
shimmered in the candle glow, silver embroidery along the bodice
reflecting light. The neckline was squared and lower than a day
dress's, but perfectly respectable for evening. Nothing marred the

fabric's surface, thank heaven. For a moment, she had wondered if that was the reason so many people were staring.

A portly gentleman bumped her arm, forcing her more tightly against her husband's side. It was an absolute crush, with barely enough room to breathe, and dozens of eyes were upon her.

Lucien scanned the crowd with a commanding glare as though daring the gawkers to offer insult. His arm slid around her waist. "They must have noticed how lovely you are, my dear," he whispered close to her ear. "It does bear commenting upon."

She stared up at him, startled by the intimacy. His eyes glittered in a way she had not seen in over a week. A lock of black fell over his forehead, causing a squeeze of longing to run down her arm and into her fingertips.

Dressed in finely tailored black, relieved only by the stark white of his cravat, he was her dark angel once again. She wanted to kiss him, right there before the eyes of the ton.

Earlier in her studio, she had been almost afraid to hope— too many questions yet remained unanswered. Would Lucien seek retribution upon Colin? Would her love for him survive if he harmed her brother? Did he truly care for her, or had he simply been pleased with her and satisfied with his scheme?

As she had watched him at the window, looking out at the fog, she had known two things: She wanted a real marriage with Lucien. And if he did not love her, could not set aside his animosity toward her family, there was very little chance of it. She had teetered on a thin edge between hope and despair, watching her husband battle his demons.

Now, feeling the connection to him spark again ... It was most encouraging. She sighed and tilted her lips up toward his.

"Why Lady Atherbourne! And Lord Atherbourne." The shrill voice of Lady Gattingford intruded. "Splendid to have you here."

Blast. Honestly, the woman had horrid timing.

She approached them from the left, a tallish, stout figure with a slight stoop about her shoulders, accompanied by Lord Gattingford. He was equal in height, but considerably leaner, pale and hawk-nosed, wearing an unfortunately vibrant yellow waistcoat.

Victoria managed to work up a smile. "Lady Gattingford, thank you for the invitation. I must say, the ball appears a smashing success."

The graying brunette scrunched her nose in an oddly girlish gesture. "A mad crush, I daresay."

As Lord Gattingford and Lucien engaged in a gentlemanly discussion about the benefits of a well-sprung carriage, Victoria allowed herself to be pulled away by Lady Gattingford. "Now then," the older woman said, her voice low and confiding, as though they were long friends. "Lady Berne informs me you have introduced her to a new modiste. Mrs. Bowman. You must tell me about her."

Victoria's brows rose and her eyes widened in surprise—not because Lady Berne had shared such a tidbit, but because Lady Gattingford was being quite friendly. Considering the last time she had seen her, the matron was regaling a crowd with Victoria's moral shortcomings, this was nothing less than miraculous.

"I—well, yes. Certainly." For several minutes, they discussed the remarkable talents of a certain Italian seamstress. Victoria remained nonplussed at the woman's convivial demeanor. Upon being invited to the Gattingford rout, she had expected politeness, perhaps. Instead, it was as though the scandal had never occurred.

Most strange.

"My lady, I was delighted to receive your invitation, though I must tell you, it was a bit of a surprise."

The woman's brows arched. "Oh, you mean because of ..." She gestured toward the terrace doors, then tsked and swept her hand back and forth dismissively. "Pish posh. My dear Lady Atherbourne, I regret that I misunderstood the events that occurred when last you were here, but thankfully I have since learned the truth of your situation."

"You—you have?"

She nodded, gazing out over the crowd as a queen would survey her subjects. "Indeed. Lady Wallingham has been most informative." Lady Gattingford opened her lace fan with a flick of her wrist and gave Victoria a sideways smile. "I must say, Stickley did seem a robust sort. One would never suspect his little problem, but thank heavens your dear Atherbourne was so persistent."

"Er—problem?"

An eyebrow arched and the lady's gaze drifted to her smallest finger, extending straight outward from the lace fan. Slowly, the finger curled downward. "A most unfortunate malady, to be sure," she whispered.

Realizing suddenly to what the matron was referring, Victoria blushed furiously. "Lady Wallingham told you *that?* About Lord Stickley?"

The fan worked vigorously. "Oh, not to worry. I am the soul of discretion. Besides, this has all worked out rather well for you, has it not?" She pointed her fan in Lucien's direction. "Such a dashing young man. And to think he loved you so dearly, he could not bear to be parted from you. Why, it fair stirs my heart. Of course, there are those who will never understand the siren call of great love. Lady Rumstoke and Lady Colchester have not experienced it, so how could they possibly do so? *I*, on the other hand, have been blessed to have made its acquaintance. Just as you have, my dear." Sniffing with emotion, she pressed her fan over her heart as she gazed in the direction of a certain bright-yellow waistcoat. "Is he not the handsomest man you have ever seen?"

Victoria turned and saw Lord Gattingford standing next to Lucien. Even now, her eyes found him as though magnetized. "Yes," she said softly. "He is."

Their conversation ended as they were joined by Lady Wallingham and Lady Berne, both dressed in jewel-toned silk. Lady Wallingham did not wait long to send Lady Gattingford scurrying. "Who would suspect so many would still be in town to attend, eh? I am certain you would have arranged for additional seating had you but known." The arch tone and lofty tilt to the dragon's chin caused the hostess to excuse herself and hurry through the crowd, presumably in pursuit of more chairs.

With a flick, Lady Wallingham deployed the silk fan dangling from her wrist, examining Victoria through crafty eyes. "I believe victory is ours, my dear. And a satisfying one it is."

Lady Berne smiled brightly and nodded in agreement. "Everyone is saying what a handsome couple you and Lord Atherbourne make. How it is easy to see it was love that brought you together."

Victoria pressed a hand to her chest, realizing they were right—the scandal was over. Certainly, there would still be those who remembered, and whispered about it. And Lord Stickley might never forgive her—especially given the new rumors the dragon had spread about him. But she and Lucien had been accepted back into the fold. And she had Lady Wallingham and Lady Berne to thank.

She began with Lady Wallingham. "My lady, I do not know how to express the depth of my gratitude," she began, impulsively reaching out to take the dragon's hands in her own. She was mildly shocked at how fragile and small they felt. "Without your support and wise counsel, this surely would not have been possible."

Momentarily surprised, Lady Wallingham froze and stared back at Victoria. Lady Berne nudged her friend's shoulder. "Perhaps a simple, 'You are welcome,' would suffice, Dorothea."

Realizing Lady Wallingham was disconcerted by the overture, Victoria loosened her hands immediately. But the old woman clung and squeezed her fingers gently before releasing her. "You will come and visit me at Grimsgate Castle," she declared superciliously. "It is the least you can do. Bring that scoundrel you married."

Victoria grinned and nodded. "It would be our pleasure, my lady."

She turned and hugged Lady Berne, whispering, "I could not have asked for a better friend than you have been."

The diminutive, rounded woman sniffed and then pulled back to beam a watery smile at Victoria. "I am dreadfully happy for you, dear girl."

For the next half hour, their triumph was confirmed as Victoria was greeted warmly by several patronesses of Almack's, pulled aside for friendly conversation with a group of debutantes—including the Aldridge twins—and complimented on her gown seven times.

She had not been this popular *before* the scandal. Lady Wallingham's influence was powerful, indeed.

Reaching the refreshment table, she sighed in relief. The heat and closeness of the ball was positively stifling. Even Lady Gattingford's dreadful lemonade seemed tempting. She poured herself a cup and sipped it, wishing she had thought to bring a fan.

"I would offer to take you out to the terrace," a dark voice whispered in her ear, "but we would not want to set tongues wagging again, would we?"

Her stomach gave a tiny flip of excitement. Tingles ran up her arms and into her neck. Slowly, Victoria set her cup on the table and turned. "Lucien," she murmured softly.

His eyes—those beautiful, storm-cloud eyes—sparkled and crinkled at the corners as he gave her a wicked half-grin. Almost immediately, however, Lucien's smile disappeared and his gaze jerked away when they heard an announcement at the entrance to the ballroom.

Her heart dropped, chest tightening painfully as she swung around to see the man she had never expected to come here, of all places.

What is he doing? Please, God. Please. Let this night not turn into a disaster.

She felt Lucien move away, and after a moment's hesitation, followed him. By the time she reached his side, he was already standing before her brother.

Looking cold, composed, and handsome in his dark coat and breeches, Harrison greeted Lucien with a simple, if terse, "Atherbourne."

The crowd around them stared in silent anticipation. Would they attack one another? Would one of the men issue a challenge that would end in violence? Even Victoria did not know. Long seconds passed in which she tried to think how to prevent the coming confrontation. She could leap between them, but that might make things worse. She could pull Lucien away, perhaps. Or greet Harrison as though nothing was amiss. At best, it might delay the inevitable, but at least it would save them all a painfully public row. Deciding she must take action, she looped her arm through her husband's and said his name under her breath.

His other arm stretched forward without warning, causing Harrison to frown and glance down—at the handshake awaiting him.

"Your grace," Lucien said, his voice strong, his jaw determined.

Harrison grasped the offered hand, accepting the truce with a polite nod. The handshake did not last long, but it didn't have to. The gasps of the crowd echoed her own astonishment.

Consciously closing her mouth, she swung her gaze rapidly between the duke and her husband. Two of the men she loved most in the world.

Her brother bowed to her and reached for her hands. "Victoria, you look lovely this evening. I trust you are ... well?"

Tears springing unexpectedly to her eyes, she smiled up at Harrison and nodded. "I am ..." She glanced to her right where her husband still stood, his expression unreadable. "I am better than I have been in a long while."

Behind them, the first notes of a quadrille began. Harrison asked Victoria if she would care to dance, and she searched immediately for Lucien's reaction. He gave her a half smile and said, "Go and dance, love."

She took her brother's arm. As they made their way through

a press of bodies to the dance floor, Harrison quietly asked, "You are truly happy, then?"

She considered the question. Was she happy? After all that had occurred, all Lucien had done to damage her reputation, and then her relationship with her family?

"Yes," she answered finally. And it was true. "Our marriage is far from perfect. *He* is far from perfect, as am I. But we are connected—bound to one another in a way I cannot explain. I love him. It gives me great hope for the future."

Harrison nodded and paused at the edge of the dance floor, staring straight ahead at the dancers as they gathered into the proper formation for the group dance. "He asked me to come tonight, you know."

"He did?"

He nodded. "Surprised me, as well. But as long as his sole aim is to ensure your contentment, then we will have few disagreements." When he spoke again, his voice was unusually thready. "That is all I ever wanted for you, Tori. To be cared for as you deserve." He cleared his throat before continuing. "If you ever have need of me, you have only to say so. I shall always be at your disposal."

Oh, now he was truly going to turn her into a watering pot.

"I know," she said. "I love you too, Harrison."

Thankfully, their dance gave them an opportunity to recover, and she was smiling from ear to ear by the time they finished. Just then, Lucien arrived to claim her for a waltz. He and Harrison acknowledged each other again, their exchange polite, if a bit stiff and guarded.

"You have never looked more beautiful, angel," Lucien remarked as he swept her into his arms. "Or happier."

Her skin, her stomach, her heart—every part of her sang and lit from within, overjoyed to be in his embrace once more, even if it was only for a dance. "Thank you for what you did, Lucien. Your cordiality toward Harrison was—Well, it meant a great deal to me. If I seem happier, that is why."

As they made a graceful turn, his eyes captured hers. She was shocked by what she saw. It was as though a veil had been stripped away, as though she were seeing Lucien for the first time. Longing, regret, adoration. All were there, exposed and offered without hesitation.

He loved her.

Her breath halted in her lungs.

"I would do anything for you, Victoria," he rasped. "For your happiness. Anything. I would swim until I drown. Walk until no ground remained. You asked once if you mattered to me at all. The answer is this—you are the *only* thing that matters."

Blinded by tears, she stumbled through another turn. Lucien's strong arms steadied her, then quickly swept her off the dance floor, guided her through the doors and out to the terrace.

The din of voices and music receded. Cool air whispered across her skin, but she barely noticed. She covered her face with her hands, tears leaking from her eyes and into her gloves. Tears of relief, of joy.

He *loved* her. It was like a dream.

His arms wrapped around her and a hand stroked her hair. "I am ashamed of the way I treated you, love. I will understand if you cannot forgive me. I do not deserve it. But I pray you will."

She sobbed and grabbed his face in her hands. Her mouth met his in a fiery charge, her tongue seeking his, her hands clutching the sides of his head. Initially, he was too stunned to react. But within seconds, he pulled her fiercely against his body and took control of the kiss, pressing her aching breasts flat against his chest, cupping her nape with one large hand.

Pulling back to catch her breath, she braced her hands on his chest and sobbed, "I love you so, Lucien. I might burst with it."

He chuckled and stroked the tears from her cheeks, his forehead meeting hers. "I love you too, angel. Do you know you have been that for me? My angel. You rescued me from a very dark place."

"I don't know how you survived at all, Lucien. Losing your family that way, and after Waterloo," she whispered. "I understand why you hated Harrison, why you felt it necessary to try to gain justice." A thought occurred to her, and she groaned, shaking her head. "Colin behaved abominably toward Marissa. Is it possible, do you think, for you to somehow forgive him?"

"I—I honestly don't know. His actions resulted in my sister's death. Forgiveness may not be possible." He paused. "But if realizing my mistakes has taught me anything, it is this: The choice between your happiness and making Colin pay for his sins is an easy one. I will always choose your happiness. I will choose *you* above all else."

She met his eyes, seeing the remorse swimming there.

"If I could go back to the night when we first met on this terrace, I would not have involved you—"

"If you hadn't," she said softly, "I might be the Marchioness of Stickley at this very moment. And, believe me, I much prefer being your viscountess." Grinning, she gave him a gentle kiss.

"I do not deserve you," he said, his voice raw, his eyes naked.

"Perhaps not. But you have me, just the same." She smiled up at him as a cool night breeze surrounded them. It was a bit damp and smelled of coal smoke, but at least it was not the stifling heat of the ballroom. She glanced reluctantly toward the doors. "Do you suppose we must return to the ball? Oh, Lucien, I cannot wait to depart for Thornbridge so we can truly begin our life together. London is necessary, but I prefer the country. Much better light. That reminds me, will there be a room I can use as a studio? It needn't be a bedchamber—"

"Victoria."

"Yes?"

"Hush, so I may kiss you."

Gazing up at her husband, Victoria sighed. She reached up to cup his jaw, drew his head down to hers, and whispered against his beautiful lips, "Oh, very well."

Epilogue

*"The greater one's pride, the more disastrous the fall.
I shudder to imagine the catastrophe awaiting Blackmore,
should he ever meet his match. Do you suppose there is
any way to hasten such a thing?"*

—THE DOWAGER MARCHIONESS OF WALLINGHAM to Lady Berne
upon news that the Duke of Blackmore successfully persuaded
Lord Wallingham to part with one of his prized hunters.

"A MR. DRAYTON FOR YOU, YOUR GRACE."

Harrison glanced up at where Digby stood between the
library doors. The butler wore a forbearing expression.

"Send him in."

Digby plainly did not care for the runner, whom he considered lowly, furtive, and coarse. But Harrison admired the man's perseverance and discretion. He was effective and could be intimidated into action, which was all that was required.

"Your grace." The runner was disheveled as usual, his dark hair tousled by the wind, his caped great coat making his shoulders appear broader than normal. "You asked to see me?"

"Mmm. Sit, Drayton. I have rather a strong curiosity about something and thought you might provide answers."

Wariness stilled the man's features, but he slowly approached the chair Harrison indicated and sat.

"Excellent. Now then, previously you reported my brother had traveled to Brighton, is that right?"

Cautiously, Drayton nodded.

Harrison held up a stack of papers, frowned at them as though perplexed, then leveled a flat stare at the runner. "Most peculiar. I have here no fewer than twelve markers, all demanding payment for recent losses at gaming establishments here in London."

The runner's eyebrows shot up, then lowered in a glare at the papers.

"Now, unless Digby has been trotting off to Boodle's in his off hours, I suspect Colin is not, in fact, in Brighton."

Drayton shifted in his seat. "No, your grace. He must have returned without my men discovering it."

"That would be logical." Harrison's reply was clipped and dry as he returned the markers to his desk.

"I will locate him, your grace."

He pinned Drayton with a hard stare. "By noon tomorrow. I want details, Mr. Drayton. I trust I am clear."

The runner nodded vigorously, jumped up from his seat, and gave a quick bow before departing. He brushed past Digby, who stood just beyond the doors. The butler moved silently to Harrison's desk and presented a salver with several envelopes.

"Your correspondence, your grace. I believe there is a letter from Lady Atherbourne."

Immediately, Harrison's heart lightened. He reached for the stack and thanked Digby, who bowed and left. Harrison noted the butler had placed Victoria's letter on top. He stroked the fine paper with his fingers, seeing her graceful, looping script on its surface.

After everything that had happened—the revelations about Colin's horrid behavior toward Marissa Wyatt, the girl's death, the duel, and then Atherbourne's attempts to seek vengeance—Harrison was grateful his connection to Victoria remained intact. He had been so disgusted by Colin of late that a true rift had formed between him and his brother. He kept watch on him through Drayton, but they hadn't spoken in over two months. With Tori now ensconced happily with her husband in Derbyshire, Clyde-Lacey House felt rather empty. He knew he should return to Blackmore Hall—there were matters to attend that could not be entrusted to his steward. And he would. But not just yet.

Shaking off the annoying melancholy that had settled over him, Harrison neatly sliced open the letter from Victoria and glanced through it, his eyes widening in genuine surprise, a slow smile spreading across his face. That smile disappeared as he reached the end of her missive, a vague sense of alarm ascending his spine. *Love,* he thought in disgust, releasing a quiet snort. *What a damned nuisance.*

Dearest Harrison,

I was delighted to receive your letter, and it will please you to know Mama's necklace arrived safely, as well. When I wear it, I am reminded of the day Papa gave it to her, of the affection they must have had for one another, though it was not always plain to those of us looking on.

To answer your query, yes, I remain happier than I could have imagined. In fact, I am positively over the moon, and I suspect you will be as well, when I tell you our news. In a few short months, you will be an uncle. The physician confirmed the babe shall likely arrive in the spring. You simply must come for a visit and meet your new niece or nephew. I have spoken to Lucien about it, and he agrees, so do not frown at me. If only Colin were not in such a poor way, I would gladly share the joyful news with him, as well. I worry for him, pray for him.

Speaking of worry, I recently received a letter from Lady Jane Huxley. You remember her, don't you? The second daughter of Lord and Lady Berne. She has become a dear, dear friend, and her letter sounded—how shall I say it?—lonely. A bit despairing. I must ask a favor of you, Harrison. During the coming season, whenever possible, please ensure she dances at least one dance, even if you must partner her yourself. The marriage mart is harrowing for a young woman, and I wish for her to find the same happiness I now enjoy.

I wish the same for you, as well. You have often said, "Everything in its own good time." Well, I say, there is no time like the present. Lucien has warned me against matchmaking. Frankly, I do not share his caution. But then, perhaps your true love will appear before I find it necessary to intervene. One can hope.

Your loving sister,
Victoria

What happens next? Read on for an **excerpt** from Book Two in the Rescued from Ruin series.

Now available!

The Truth About
Cads and Dukes

ELISA BRADEN

The Truth About Cads and Dukes

FROM THE OPPOSITE SIDE OF THE CARRIAGE CAME A TART admonishment. "You did not bring a book along, did you, Jane?"

Jane felt her mouth tighten. "No, Mama."

"How do you expect to acquire a proper suitor in the pages of a novel? I daresay it is impossible."

"Yes, Mama."

"I should not need to remind you this is your *third* season."

"No, Mama."

"You must seize upon every opportunity. Goodness knows how much longer these occasions shall present themselves."

"Yes, Mama."

Their father, kindly man that he was, took Mama's hand in his own and squeezed. "Let her be, Meredith. She agreed to come along, did she not?" He gave Jane a wink.

In truth, Jane had not precisely *agreed* to attend Lady Gilforth's ball. Instead, she had been informed it was occurring, that she was expected to accompany her parents and Maureen, and that she was forbidden to bring the novel she'd been reading when Mama had entered the library. Before a protest had reached her lips, her mother had held up a hand and said, "I trust you understand fully," with brows arched expectantly over wide brown eyes.

What else could Jane say, other than, "Yes, Mama"? For the last two seasons, she had disappointed her sweet, good-humored mother to the brink of desperation. The specter of spinsterhood for her second-oldest daughter had added more than a few strands of white to Meredith Huxley's brunette coiffure.

Briefly, Jane had contemplated telling Mama about Colin Lacey, if only to ease concerns that she was incapable of cordial interaction with a gentleman. She had rejected that catastrophically bad idea an instant after it had occurred. Lord Colin's behavior, while charming, was not that of a suitor. He was kind and amusing but often distracted, as if his mind was preoccupied with other matters.

Having witnessed a number of love matches play out before her eyes, including those of her best friend and her sister, she understood the difference. She refused to raise her mother's hopes when he obviously intended friendship, rather than romantic attachment. Fortunately, Genie had proven a rather clever ally in disguising the purpose of their outings. It had cost Jane nearly her entire allowance, of course, but she was learning much about her sister's hidden talent for subterfuge.

She sighed and resumed staring out the carriage window at the bustling lane. Lady Gilforth lived across Mayfair from their London residence on Grosvenor Street. It was a tolerably brief carriage ride, she supposed, providing one was not required to listen to one's mother worry aloud about otherwise sensible girls who chose "storybooks and poetry over securing a sound match."

Jane did not fault her for her consternation. In looks, she and Mama were much the same: more plump than was permissible; a short, round nose most would describe as a pug; and coloring that blended nicely into wood paneling. But in every other way, Jane and her mother were a study in contrasts:

Lady Berne was effusive, gracious, warm. Since her youth, Mama's humor and kindness had shone from her, attracting numerous friendships and the eye of Jane's father, the future Earl of Berne, in her first season. Annabelle, the oldest of the five girls, shared this disposition, as did Maureen and Genie and even young Kate, albeit to lesser degrees.

Jane, to put it simply, did not.

Little wonder Mama was confounded by Jane's inability to attract even one suitor. *She* had never been consigned to dwell on the fringes of ballrooms with the old flowers and the wallflowers—or, as Jane had privately dubbed them, the Oddflowers.

She sniffed and shifted subtly in her seat, feeling the carriage slow as they approached Lady Gilforth's town house. How was she to endure an entire ball without a book to keep her company? Was she expected to gaze out at the crowd, marveling at Sir Barnabus Malby's ability to recall the steps of a dance while mesmerized by a passing bodice? Or perhaps she should admire Penelope Darling's braying chortle at every tedious quip from Lord Mochrie.

Truthfully, it was enough to make any "otherwise sensible" girl dash out to the nearest terrace. Of course, Victoria had tried that, and she had been quite thoroughly ruined. So, perhaps not the best idea.

"Jane, are you coming?"

Her head swiveled back toward the open door of the carriage, through which she could see her mother, father, and sister staring at her expectantly.

"Of course," she murmured, scrambling down from the carriage. Adjusting her Kashmiri shawl across her shoulders, she could not suppress a shiver of dread.

Maureen looped an arm through hers. "Imagine. This may be a night we remember for the rest of our lives."

Casting her sister a sideways glance, Jane lifted a skeptical brow.

"I saw that," came Mama's customary reprimand, followed by

a hushed warning. "Kindly demonstrate you are capable of being pleasant and agreeable, Jane. I will not have it said my daughter is a churl. Lady Gilforth's influence is swiftly growing, and Lord Gilforth is much admired within the House of Lords. All of the finest gentlemen shall be in attendance." The martial gleam in her eye was alarming, for Mama was typically a jolly sort. Soon, however, the reason behind her fervor was revealed: "I have it on good authority *his grace* is expected."

Maureen's gasp was echoed in Jane's heart, though likely for different reasons.

"Wellington? I thought he was still in Paris," their father interjected.

Mama's fan tapped Papa's arm as she tsked. "Not Wellington. Blackmore."

The dawning realization on Papa's face was followed swiftly by an amused twinkle. "In that case, you girls should be on your best behavior."

"Precisely." Mama directed her emphatic affirmation at Jane, who clutched her shawl a bit tighter as they waited for the other guests crowding Lady Gilforth's door to move forward. This was shaping up to be a crush.

Sighing prettily, Maureen remarked, "He is very handsome. And distinguished."

And insufferable, Jane added silently. *A judgmental, pompous ice king who needs nothing so much as a sharp blow across his ... pride.*

"The fortune and title add a certain appeal as well, I daresay."

Jane frowned at Papa, who grinned at her as if they shared a private joke, then held his arm out for Mama so they could enter Lady Gilforth's foyer. Sometimes, she did not understand her father's jests. To her mind, the Duke of Blackmore was the least amusing topic imaginable, unless one pictured him receiving a well-deserved comeuppance.

Last season, Blackmore had even dared reprimand Jane directly—in her own home, no less. It was only the second time they'd had occasion to speak. Granted, she and Genie had been squabbling, as sisters tended to do, but how was she to know the blasted eighth Duke of Blackmore would be lurking in the shadows of her family's drawing room, awaiting a visit with Lord and Lady Berne? Only after she'd threatened to throw Genie bodily into the fireplace had he revealed himself, hands clasped behind a rigid back, jaw locked tight against possible cracking— wouldn't want a shred of emotion to escape, after all. Had he been anyone else, she would have described him as bristling with disapproval. But Blackmore did not bristle. He was like a blade— merciless and precise. It had taken mere seconds for him to reduce Jane to feeling all of ten years old, caught nipping Papa's cognac or stashing a toad in Mama's silver teapot.

Taking a deep breath, Jane reminded herself that, even if he deigned to attend Lady Gilforth's ball, he would be too busy fending off marriage-minded young ladies and their voracious mothers to take any notice of her. Certainly, for politeness' sake, he would greet Mama and Papa, probably even bow to her and Maureen, but that was likely to be the extent of their interaction.

She sniffed and adjusted her spectacles, then lightly smoothed the yellow primrose silk of her gown along one hip. *You need only curtsy, Jane. Give him a "your grace," and nothing more.* Feeling the tightness in her belly ease, she waited for Lady Gilforth's butler to announce them, her eyes quickly examining the edges of the long, spacious drawing room. Along one pale-blue wall sat a row of cream-colored settees and dark-blue velvet chairs, already half-populated by familiar figures: Sallow, thin Miss Sutherland, now in her fifth (and probably last) season. The aged Lady Darnham, whose face appeared to be formed entirely of smile-shaped creases. The alarmingly tall, redheaded Miss Lancaster, with her unfortunate tendency to crush gentlemen's feet while dancing ... and walking ... and, oddly enough, while dining.

Ah, yes. A wry grin tugged. *The Oddflowers are well represented this evening.* Her eyes drifted to a pair of open doors on the far wall, through which lay the dining room where Lady Gilforth had set up the refreshments. *Hmm.* If she were to sit at the near end of the Oddflower wall, she could occupy herself with an occasional trip to the refreshment tables. Hardly a thrilling journey, but an acceptable way to distract oneself and help time pass more quickly. *Yes, indeed. A sound plan.*

A sharp nudge in her ribs brought Jane's eyes around to Maureen.

"Mama was right," her sister whispered theatrically behind her fan. "He is here. Do you suppose he is seeking a wife?"

Jane followed Maureen's gaze. He was not difficult to spot—taller than John, their brother, who was an even six feet, Blackmore stood half a head above most other gentlemen. She also had to admit—grudgingly—that Maureen had not exaggerated when she'd called him handsome.

He was. Quite so.

The jaw that favored a locked position was strong and square and lean. A straight, refined nose acted as a symmetrical anchor between lofty cheekbones, which sat beneath a piercing pair of blue-gray eyes. On the whole, if she was bound by honesty, his blond male beauty was undeniable, in much the same way as the Elgin marbles were objectively masterful. Jane imagined if the English nobility possessed a pantheon of gods like that of the ancient Greeks, he might be considered their Apollo, except Apollo had never been as powerful as the Duke of Blackmore, nor as intimidating.

"Well, whether he is here to find a duchess or not," Jane finally answered, "I recommend keeping your distance. I understand frostbite is rather painful."

An hour later, Jane was thankful for her strategy of making occasional trips to the refreshment tables. Lady Gilforth had outdone herself. To quench revelers' appetites until supper, two long sideboards were strewn with a wide variety of tidbits, from tiny cheesecakes to flaky biscuits. Anyone who had attended a ton ball knew how it felt to be famished by the time supper was announced. Such interim offerings were most welcome. Additionally, at the center of each sideboard sat a silver bowl of delicious punch—sweet, tangy, and a bit spicy.

Jane poured her fourth cup, wondering if this time, she might place that elusive spice. Cinnamon? She shook her head. No. Not cinnamon. But perhaps it was a blend of orange and mulled wine. That made more sense. Clove, cinnamon, and nutmeg might together produce the heady flavor. Perhaps even with a dash of peppercorn.

Peering through the doors into the drawing room, she watched dancers swirl around the center of the floor in a quadrille. How many quadrilles had she witnessed over the past three seasons? Too many. Waltzes? Too many. The motions of every season were the same, and Jane had grown deeply weary of each and every one.

Sighing, she took another sip and longed for a nice, distracting novel.

Being an Oddflower gave one a unique perspective on the spectacle of the standard ton event, as she was able to observe the motions and repetitions without direct participation. Her brother, who was on his grand tour of the continent, had recently sent a crate full of treasures to Berne House, including a fascinating clock that, when striking the hour, extended a tiny bird on a branch from a crevice above the clock face. The bird, having no will of its own, was controlled solely by the regular movement of the clockwork mechanism.

That was how she regarded the motions of the London season: rote gestures orchestrated by an apparatus immune to its objects. Curtsy, whirl, bow, titter, fan, smile, tilt, and again. And again. The same motions. The same routine. She supposed there was a point to it all. Ladies must find husbands and gentlemen must find wives. But, being all but locked outside the process, she could not help noting its monotony.

Inside her mind, she began a letter to Annabelle, who was now blessedly free of such obligations, having married last

August. Of course, Annabelle had adored the season with all its
trappings, insisting on enjoying two of her own before marrying
Lord Robert Conrad, whom she had loved devotedly since
childhood.

Dearest Annabelle, Jane would write. *Lady Gilforth's
refreshments are magnificent. For nearly two minutes in every
twenty, I cease pining for a novel that will allow me to forget my
misery, and simply relish her ingeniously spiced punch. I suspect it
contains more than a minor quantity of wine.*

She glanced down, seeing the remnants of her fourth cup.
Feeling pleasantly warm, she placed it on a tray and braced
herself for the long journey back to her seat along the
Oddflower wall. As she entered the drawing room, a masculine
shout of pain arose from the center of the quadrille dancers,
drawing her attention.

"Oh, dear, Sir Barnabus, was that your nose?" Charlotte
Lancaster's flame-red hair was visible above most of the other
ladies' heads, and even those of many gentlemen. "I do beg your
forgiveness. I fear my elbow has a mind of its own. Are you quite
all right?" Jane had heard her apologize for habitual clumsiness
before, but Miss Lancaster ordinarily sounded more sincere. Sir
Barnabus Malby's misplaced nose was probably less to blame
than his wandering eyes. Miss Lancaster had rather modern
notions about such things. Come to that, so did Jane. But even
the portly, malodorous Sir Barnabus did not ask Plain Jane
Huxley to dance. *Well,* she decided, *there are benefits to being
ignored, after all.*

Tucking her lip between her teeth, she rose up on her toes
to see if she could get a glimpse of the man's face. Perhaps Miss
Lancaster had bloodied his nose. *Now, that would be interesting.*
A black lapel appeared in front of her. She moved to her left,
but so did the masculine wall wearing the black coat and white
cravat. And now it was closer, so it obscured even more of her
line of sight. She scooted to her right. Again, the gentleman
glided in the same direction. Huffing in exasperation, she

looked up to see who was so blasted determined to place himself between her and the commotion.

"One might have hoped for improved comportment in a lady entering her third season," the precise, clipped, unmistakable voice of her nemesis intoned from his lofty height. "Perhaps I expect too much."

Eyes widening, heart thudding hard against bone, Jane felt the hated heat of embarrassment burn through her in a wave. Blackmore. The great, golden god of ton propriety was reprimanding her for having simple, natural curiosity. The last time he had done something similar, they had been standing in her family's drawing room. She and Genie had been arguing over a book Genie had stolen. Jane had made an empty threat about throwing her sister into the fireplace.

"What book is so precious, I wonder, that it draws threats of burning one's sibling?" She remembered his voice, slicing flinty and cold across the room. *"Nothing to say for yourself, then?"* And she had been struck dumb, frozen by the shame of the accusation, never mind how unfair it might be.

It was the same now, as if an entire year had not passed, as if, instead, her only task had been to continuously stand before him, awaiting his harsh assessment. How dared he? Not even her father or brother, either of whom would be within his rights, would castigate her so. Who was the bloody Duke of Blackmore to her? No one. He was Victoria's brother, not hers. *Therefore, he is Victoria's problem. Not mine.*

Backing away one step, she cleared her throat, gathering herself to deliver an equally icy greeting before escaping back to her Oddflower seat. But the "your grace" that she intended refused to emerge. Her mouth worked, but her voice did not. She swallowed, feeling the crimson fire beneath her skin intrude like another presence.

She felt his blue-gray eyes travel over her gown, then back up, pausing at the modest neckline and returning to her face. Cool and remote, they seemed to be cataloging her features as a stable master might note the condition of a mare. "Have you danced yet this evening?"

Blinking slowly, she wondered at the question, which had sounded grudging, like he did not wish to be there at all. What in heaven's name was he doing? Why was he continuing to speak with her? This was the sort of thing a gentleman might say if he was trying to persuade a lady to ... no. It was impossible. She needed to provide him an acceptable opportunity to withdraw. That was all.

She shook her head and swallowed, eyes darting between him and the doorway to the dining room. "I—I'm afraid the heat has caused a frightful thirst. I was just going to retrieve another cup of punch when you arrived."

A single aristocratic brow elevated. "Again? Is this not the fifth such venture?"

For the second time that evening, Jane was struck straight down to her slippers by a statement from the Duke of Blackmore. Had he been *watching* her? A strange shiver burned over her skin, different than the flush that had engulfed her earlier, but just as heated.

"No one should require so much refreshing," he stated assuredly. "Perhaps if you were to dance, you would not be inclined to consume in such quantity."

And the Ice King returns, she thought. *Well, at least he is predictable.*

Blackmore's shoulders straightened further, his jaw tilting to an arrogant angle. "A waltz shall begin soon. Will you consent to dance it with me?"

Upon further consideration, perhaps not so predictable.

She would have gasped, but she couldn't seem to find her breath. Or the ability to move. He had just asked her to dance. *He,* the unanimously agreed-upon Catch of the Season—every season—had asked *her,* the quintessential Oddflower, to dance a waltz.

Growing visibly disgruntled by her silence, the tall, blond Apollo of the aristocracy, bit out, "When a lady is asked to dance, it is customary to answer."

He was right. She must answer him. And she would. Clenching her teeth, Jane marshaled every scintilla of courage to be found inside her plain, round, Oddflower body, and gave him the answer he richly deserved.

"No." It emerged as a whisper. Swallowing past all trepidation, she repeated the word in her normal voice, pinched though it might be. "No. I don't believe I shall dance with you, your grace."

WANT MORE OF JANE'S STORY?
THE TRUTH ABOUT CADS AND DUKES IS AVAILABLE NOW!
FIND IT AT WWW.ELISABRADEN.COM

More from Elisa Braden

*Be first to hear about new releases, price specials,
and more—sign up for Elisa's free email newsletter at
www.elisabraden.com so you don't miss a thing!*

Midnight in Scotland Series
*In the enchanting new Midnight in Scotland series,
the unlikeliest matches generate the greatest heat.
All it takes is a spark of Highland magic.*

THE MAKING OF A HIGHLANDER (BOOK ONE)
Handsome adventurer John Huxley is locked in a land dispute in the
Scottish Highlands with one way out: Win the Highland Games.
When the local hoyden Mad Annie Tulloch offers to train him in
exchange for "Lady Lessons," he agrees. But teaching the fiery, foul-
mouthed, breeches-wearing lass how to land a lord seems impossible—
especially when he starts dreaming of winning her for himself.

THE TAMING OF A HIGHLANDER (BOOK TWO)
Wrongfully imprisoned and tortured, Broderick MacPherson lives for
one purpose—punishing the man responsible. When a wayward lass
witnesses his revenge, he risks returning to the prison that nearly killed
him. Kate Huxley has no wish to testify against a man who's already
suffered too much. But the only remedy is to become his wife. And she
can't possibly marry such a surly, damaged man...can she?

Rescued from Ruin Series
Discover the scandalous predicaments, emotional redemptions,
and gripping love stories (with a dash of Lady Wallingham)
in the scorching series that started it all!

EVER YOURS, ANNABELLE (PREQUEL)
As a girl, Annabelle Huxley chased Robert Conrad with reckless abandon, and he always rescued her when she pushed too far—until the accident that cost him everything. Seven years later, Robert discovers the girl with the habit of chasing trouble is now a siren he can't resist. But when a scandalous secret threatens her life, how far will he go to rescue her one last time?

THE MADNESS OF VISCOUNT ATHERBOURNE (BOOK ONE)
Victoria Lacey's life is perfect—perfectly boring. Agree to marry a lord who has yet to inspire a single, solitary tingle? It's all in a day's work for the oh-so-proper sister of the Duke of Blackmore. Surely no one suspects her secret longing for head-spinning passion. Except a dark stranger, on a terrace, at a ball where she should not be kissing a man she has just met. Especially one bent on revenge.

THE TRUTH ABOUT CADS AND DUKES (BOOK TWO)
Painfully shy Jane Huxley is in a most precarious position, thanks to dissolute charmer Colin Lacey's deceitful wager. Now, his brother, the icy Duke of Blackmore, must make it right, even if it means marrying her himself. Will their union end in frostbite? Perhaps. But after lingering glances and devastating kisses, Jane begins to suspect the truth: Her duke may not be as cold as he appears.

DESPERATELY SEEKING A SCOUNDREL (BOOK THREE)
Where Lord Colin Lacey goes, trouble follows. Tortured and hunted by a brutal criminal, he is rescued from death's door by the stubborn, fetching Sarah Battersby. In return, she asks one small favor: Pretend

to be her fiancé. Temporarily, of course. With danger nipping his heels, he knows it is wrong to want her, wrong to agree to her terms. But when has Colin Lacey ever done the sensible thing?

THE DEVIL IS A MARQUESS (BOOK FOUR)
A walking scandal surviving on wits, whisky, and wicked skills in the bedchamber, Benedict Chatham must marry a fortune or risk ruin. Tall, redheaded disaster Charlotte Lancaster possesses such a fortune. The price? One year of fidelity and sobriety. Forced to end his libertine ways, Chatham proves he is more than the scandalous charmer she married, but will it be enough to keep his unwanted wife?

WHEN A GIRL LOVES AN EARL (BOOK FIVE)
Miss Viola Darling always gets what she wants, and what she wants most is to marry Lord Tannenbrook. James knows how determined the tiny beauty can be—she mangled his cravat at a perfectly respectable dinner before he escaped. But he has no desire to marry, less desire to be pursued, and will certainly not kiss her kissable lips until they are both breathless, no matter how tempted he may be.

TWELVE NIGHTS AS HIS MISTRESS (NOVELLA – BOOK SIX)
Charles Bainbridge, Lord Wallingham, spent two years wooing Julia Willoughby, yet she insists they are a dreadful match destined for misery. Now, rather than lose her, he makes a final offer: Spend twelve nights in his bed, and if she can deny they are perfect for each other, he will let her go. But not before tempting tidy, sensible Julia to trade predictability for the sweet chaos of true love.

CONFESSIONS OF A DANGEROUS LORD (BOOK SEVEN)
Known for flashy waistcoats and rapier wit, Henry Thorpe, the Earl of Dunston, is deadlier than he appears. For years, his sole focus has been hunting a ruthless killer through London's dark underworld. Then Maureen Huxley came along. To keep her safe, he must keep her

at arm's length. But as she contemplates marrying another man, Henry's caught in the crossfire between his mission and his heart.

ANYTHING BUT A GENTLEMAN (BOOK EIGHT)

Augusta Widmore must force her sister's ne'er-do-well betrothed to the altar, or her sister will bear the consequences. She needs leverage only one man can provide—Sebastian Reaver. When she invades his office demanding a fortune in markers, he exacts a price a spinster will never pay—become the notorious club owner's mistress. And when she calls his bluff, a fiery battle for surrender begins.

A MARRIAGE MADE IN SCANDAL (BOOK NINE)

As the most feared lord in London, the Earl of Holstoke is having a devil of a time landing a wife. When a series of vicious murders brings suspicion to his door, only one woman is bold enough to defend him— Eugenia Huxley. Her offer to be his alibi risks scandal, and marriage is the remedy. But as a poisonous enemy coils closer, Holstoke finds his love for her might be the greatest danger of all.

A KISS FROM A ROGUE (BOOK TEN)

A cruel past left Hannah Gray with one simple longing—a normal life with a safe, normal husband. Finding one would be easy if she weren't distracted by wolf-in-rogue's-clothing Jonas Hawthorn. He's tried to forget the haughty Miss Gray. But once he tastes the heat and longing hidden beneath her icy mask, the only mystery this Bow Street man burns to solve is how a rogue might make Hannah his own.

About the Author

Reading romance novels came easily to Elisa Braden. Writing them? That took a little longer. After graduating with degrees in creative writing and history, Elisa spent entirely too many years in "real" jobs writing T-shirt copy ... and other people's resumes ... and articles about gift-ware displays. But that was before she woke up and started dreaming about the very *unreal* job of being a romance novelist. Better late than never.

Elisa lives in the gorgeous Pacific Northwest, where you're constitutionally required to like the colors green and gray. Good thing she does. Other items on the "like" list include cute dogs, strong coffee, and epic movies. Of course, her favorite thing of all is hearing from readers who love her characters as much as she does. If you're one of those, get in touch on Facebook and Twitter or visit **www.elisabraden.com**.